Jill Mansell lives with her family in Bristo[...] field of Clinical Neurophysiology but now [...] far too much TV and would love to be one of those super-sporty types but basically can't be bothered. Nor can she cook — having once attempted to bake a cake for the hospital's Christmas Fair, she was forced to watch while her co-workers played frisbee with it.

But she's good at Twitter!

Just *Heavenly*. Just *Jill*.

No one can resist a Jill Mansell novel . . .

'Bursting with humour, brimming with intrigue and full of characters you'll adore — we can't think of a better literary remedy' ★★★★★
Heat

'To read it is to devour it' *Company*

'A warm, witty and romantic read that you won't be able to put down' *Daily Mail*

'Slick, sexy, funny' *Daily Telegraph*

'Mansell's fiction is a happy leap away from the troubles of today' *Sunday Express*

'A sure-fire bestseller' *Heat*

'Jill Mansell is in a different league' *Sun*

'Delightful' *Daily Express*

'Utter indulgence' *News of the World*

But don't say we didn't warn you . . .

'Pick this up at your peril: you won't get a thing done till it's finished' *Heat*

P.S. 'Your beach bag will be empty without it' *Heat*

By Jill Mansell

Jill Mansell

PERFECT TIMING

headline
review

First published in 1997
by HEADLINE PUBLISHING GROUP

First published in paperback in 1997
by HEADLINE PUBLISHING GROUP

This edition published in paperback in 2014
by HEADLINE REVIEW
An imprint of the HEADLINE PUBLISHING GROUP

12

Cataloguing in Publication Data is available from the British Library

ISBN 978 0 7553 3166 6

Printed and bound by CPI Group (UK) Ltd, Croydon CR0 4YY

Headline's policy is to use papers that are natural, renewable and
recyclable products and made from wood grown in sustainable forests.
The logging and manufacturing processes are expected to conform
to the environmental regulations of the country of origin.

HEADLINE PUBLISHING GROUP
An Hachette UK Company
338 Euston Road
London NW1 3BH

www.headline.co.uk
www.hachette.co.uk

For Lydia and Cory, with my love.
Special thanks as well to Postman Pat and Sooty,
without whose videos this book would have
taken twice as long to write.
Thanks also to Abby, my favourite step-daughter, for all
her help.

Chapter 1

The thing about going out on your hen night, Poppy Dunbar couldn't help noticing, was that nobody – but nobody – bothered to chat you up.

It possibly had something to do with the three inflated condoms tethered to the top of her hat and the L-plate hung around her neck, sending out the signal: 'Don't bother, boys.' She was about as off-limits as it was possible to get. All of a sudden – as far as men were concerned – she had become invisible. It felt weird, after years of nightclubbing and being chatted up. She'd never actually been unfaithful to Rob, of course, but it was still nice to be noticed.

'Tell me about it.' Dina, when Poppy had passed this observation on earlier, was able to sympathise. 'I'm in the same boat, aren't I?' She pulled a gloomy face. 'Nobody makes a pass at you when you're nine months pregnant. It's like being a nun.'

Not that Dina was in too much danger of being mistaken for a nun right now, not while she was smack in the middle of the dance floor giving it all she'd got. At her request the club DJ was playing the old Madonna song, 'Like a Virgin'. Dina's white Lycra skirt was edging its way up to mid-thigh and her black patent high heels reflected the fluorescent lights zapping and crisscrossing overhead.

For a pregnant nun she was doing pretty well, thought Poppy. If her husband Ben could see her now he'd have a fit. Dina's dance style bordered on the frenzied; much more of it and she would go into labour. If that happened she would

1

miss both the wedding and her chance to wear her new pink straw hat. Oh dear, Poppy thought with amusement, what a wicked waste of twenty-two pounds ninety-nine that would be. Ben would be furious.

Poppy left her three fellow hens to it and made her way to the loo. Determined not to be hungover at her own wedding she had spent the night on 7-Up, which was going through her like Niagara Falls.

'Don't do it, pet,' said one girl, eyeing the hat and L-plate and rolling her eyes in mock-horror as she squeezed past Poppy.

'Getting married and not even pregnant,' teased another, 'there's posh.'

Studying her reflection in the mirror as she washed her hands, Poppy thought: Damn, I look a prat in this hat.

It would be more than her life was worth, though, to take it off. This was the ritual, the way things were done. Out on your hen night you were supposed to look daft and anyone who didn't was a complete killjoy. The girls would never forgive her.

Silly hat intact, Poppy emerged from the loos and began making her way back through the heaving masses. The dance floor, over to the left, was by this time as jam-packed as those Japanese commuter trains where everyone got levered in by merciless guards.

The air was stifling, smoky and multi-perfumed. Poppy turned right instead and threaded her way between tables. Double doors at the back of the club led down a flight of stone steps and out into a walled garden.

It was a heavenly summer evening. The sky was bright with stars. What she needed, Poppy decided, was five minutes outside before Dina and the girls realised she was missing out on all the fun.

Halfway down the broad stone staircase she passed a couple, arm in arm, heading back inside. With his free hand the boy was lighting a Silk Cut. Just for fun, once the cigarette was lit, he brushed it against Poppy's hat. One after

2

the other, like gunfire, two of the condoms exploded. Poppy, taken by surprise, promptly lost her balance and tumbled down the last few steps. With a squeal she landed in a heap on the grass at the bottom.

It was all highly undignified. Her skirt flew up and her L-plate ricocheted off her chin. The big toe on her left foot hurt like anything. Only her stupid hat remained intact.

People were staring. At the top of the steps the boy with the cigarette looked aggrieved. 'That's not my fault,' he told his girlfriend. 'I mean, it's not as if I *pushed* her.'

'Silly sod,' his girlfriend replied in loving tones. 'Come on, your round. I'll have a double rum-and-black.'

'It's okay, I've got you,' said a male voice. Poppy, who was busy cursing under her breath and tugging her skirt down, felt a supporting arm go around her waist. The voice went on, 'I don't think anything's broken. Can you make it over to that bench?'

She found herself being helped to her feet and led across the lawn by someone whose rumpled dark curls gave him the look of a wayward cherub. A cherub with cheekbones. His eyes, so dark they seemed black, were in marked contrast with his white shirt. He was tall, Poppy registered, and thin, and extremely brown. As he lowered her onto the wooden bench she also noticed very white teeth, two of them endearingly crooked, and a quirky infectious smile.

'Thanks.' Grateful to have her dignity at least semi-restored, Poppy straightened her L-plate. 'As if I wasn't already feeling daft enough.'

'I'm afraid your accessories have had it.' He indicated the burst condoms now dangling limply from the brim of her hat. 'I hope you weren't saving them for a special occasion.' He paused for a second, his dark eyes searching Poppy's face. 'When is it? The wedding?'

It was the weirdest sensation ever. Quite suddenly Poppy felt as if she'd known him all her life. Her breath caught in her throat.

3

'Tomorrow.' This was ridiculous; her heart was doing some kind of frantic can-can in her chest. In an effort to distract herself from the strangeness of what seemed to be going on, she bent down and pulled off one shoe. 'Looks like I'll be hopping down the aisle. I must have landed on my big toe. If it swells up I'm sunk.'

'My name's Tom, by the way.'

'Right. Tom. I'm—'

'Poppy. I know. I heard your pregnant friend say it earlier.'

Poppy, seldom at a loss for words, could only sit and watch as he reached for her foot, held it in the palm of his hand and carefully inspected her poor bruised toe.

'You'll live,' he finally pronounced.

'Ah, but will I limp?'

He smiled and Poppy's stomach turned over. Ye gods, she thought helplessly, what's *happening* here?

'It isn't swollen enough to be broken. We could put a cold compress on it if you like. Either that or cancel the wedding.'

'And give my future mother-in-law a nervous breakdown,' Poppy joked feebly, wondering when she was going to start feeling normal again. 'Please. Five hundred sausage rolls are baking as we speak.'

Several feet from where they sat was a lily pond with a small fountain. Tom took a dark blue handkerchief from his pocket and held it in the stream of water splashing down from the stone statue of a frog. Returning to the bench he rested Poppy's bare foot across his knee and wrapped the handkerchief around the injured toe. Without even thinking Poppy took off her hat and L-plate.

He glanced sideways at her. 'Won't your friends be wondering where you are?'

'Probably.' Poppy no longer cared. 'Won't yours?'

'Mine have left. I came down from London for the weekend,' Tom explained, 'to stay with my brother and his girlfriend. About an hour ago they launched into the most tremendous argument. The thing is with their fights, they're

4

great ones for throwing plates at each other. So when they rushed off home,' he concluded with amusement, 'I thought I'd better stay put for a while. Leave them to it.'

He's from London and I've definitely never seen him before, thought Poppy in a daze. How, when I know absolutely nothing about this man, can I feel as if I've known him for years?

Tom slowly massaged her instep as he spoke. 'Of course, now I'm glad I stayed.'

'You are? You mean you have a thing about feet?'

He laughed. 'Maybe that too. Damn. Is this seriously bad timing or what?'

Poppy's heart did another ungainly flip-flop. If he meant what she thought he meant it was exactly what had been going through her mind too. Except that this whole thing was ridiculously far-fetched. A spot of instant mutual attraction was one thing, but actually falling in love – really in love – with a total stranger couldn't possibly exist. Could it?

It's a nervous reaction, she told herself, a subconscious last-minute panic. I'm just grateful someone's paying me a bit of attention at last, even if I did have to mangle my toe to get it.

'I wish you weren't getting married tomorrow,' said Tom.

'Coo-eee! There you are.'

Yelling over the heads of the dozen or so people separating them, Dina clattered down the flight of steps in her ludicrous high heels. Poppy whipped her foot off Tom's lap.

'Hiding away,' Dina chided, inspecting Tom with interest. 'Whatever are you doing out here? And who are you?'

'Your friend fell down the steps. She thought she might have broken her ankle,' said Tom. 'I'm a doctor.'

Poppy stared at him. 'You are?'

He grinned.

'Poppy, you're hopeless.' Dina turned once more to Tom. 'Well, *is* it broken?'

'No.'

'Good. So I can drag her back onto the dance floor.'

Dismayed, Poppy said, 'Oh but—'

'Come on now, no excuses.' Dina had her by the arm. She smirked. 'You don't have a leg to stand on.'

'But my toe,' wailed Poppy, who more than anything else in the world wanted to stay outside. 'It *hurts*.'

Dina rolled her eyes. 'If you think that hurts, try having a baby.'

'Maybe you should,' Tom said quietly. He was no longer smiling. 'Go back inside, I mean. I'm sorry about . . . you know, just now. I shouldn't have said it.'

'Said what?' Dina demanded.

'He told me I looked a prat in a hat,' lied Poppy, standing up at last and realising he was right. She had to go inside and pretend this encounter had never taken place. She had to look as if she was having heaps of fun. And tomorrow she had to marry Rob McBride.

'Go on.' Tom's coal-black eyes hadn't left her face. His smile was bleak. 'Happy wedding and all that.'

''Bye.' Poppy bit her lip.

'Quick!' screeched Dina, almost yanking her arm out of its socket as a change of music filtered out through the double doors. 'Gary Glitter, my *favourite*.'

Her big toe still hurt like crazy but Poppy no longer cared. She had danced non-stop for the past hour, forcing herself not to think of Tom. He had gone, anyway. She had seen him leave. It had just been one of those mad moments and now it was over. She was going to concentrate on real life instead.

By ten to two the DJ was winding up for the night. The last three or four records were always slow ones. Susie and Jen were dancing with two brothers who claimed, somewhat dodgily, to be airline pilots. Dina was massaging her aching ankles under cover of their table. She gave Poppy a hefty nudge. Poppy, who was hunting in the bottom of her bag for money for the taxi, didn't look up.

'Oh doctor I'm in trouble,' sang Dina. She didn't sound a bit like Sophia Loren.

'What?'

'That chap who couldn't keep his hands off your foot.' Triumphantly, she watched Poppy's head jerk up. 'Hmm. Looks like he can't keep away either.'

'You're having me on.'

'If you want to dance, dance.' Dina looked smug. 'Don't mind me.'

The last record of the night was 'Lady in Red'.

'Thank God you aren't wearing something red,' said Tom. 'That really would have been too kitsch for words.'

Poppy, whose heart was going nineteen to the dozen, didn't tell him she had red knickers on.

She said, 'I thought you'd left.'

'I did. Then I came back. I had to.' Tilting his head he murmured into her ear, 'I want you to know I don't make a habit of this. It isn't some kind of bizarre hobby of mine, in case you were wondering.'

Over his shoulder Poppy saw Jen and one of the airline pilots cruising at low altitude towards them. Jen winked.

'Watch what you're doing with my future cousin-in-law,' she instructed Tom. 'By this time tomorrow she'll be an old married woman. We're under instruction to keep our eye on her tonight.'

This is awful, thought Poppy, beginning to panic as the song moved into its final chorus. Any minute now the night will be over, it'll be time to leave. How can this be happening to me? I need more *time*—

In a low voice Tom said, 'Will your friends miss you if we sneak out now?'

'Of *course* they will.' Close to despair Poppy felt her fingers dig helplessly into his arms. 'Dina's already phoned for a cab to take us home.'

'Okay, I'll leave it up to you.' He shook back a lock of curling dark hair, studying her face intently for a second.

7

'Delgado's, that all-night café on Milton Street. You know the one, directly opposite the university?'

Poppy nodded, unable to speak.

'I'll wait there. Until three o'clock. If you want to see me, that's where I'll be. If you don't . . . well, you won't turn up.'

'This isn't funny.' Poppy realised she was trembling. 'I'm not enjoying this. I'm hating it.'

'You mean you wish you hadn't met me?' Just for a second Tom traced a finger lightly down the side of her quivering face. 'Fine, if that's how you feel. If it's how you *really* feel. Go home. Get a good night's sleep. Carry on as if tonight never happened. Get married—'

'Our taxi,' Susie declared with a melodramatic flourish, 'is waiting.' She passed Poppy her handbag and began to steer her in the direction of the door. Glancing from Poppy to Tom and back again she chanted, 'Ladies and gentlemen, your time is up. No more flirting, no more smoochy dances with handsome strangers, no more scribbling your phone number in Biro on the back of his hand and praying it doesn't rain on the way home. The girl is no longer available. Tomorrow, she gets hitched.'

Chapter 2

The journey from the centre of Bristol back to Henbury at two in the morning normally took ten minutes. This time the trip was punctuated with a whole series of stops and starts.

It's worse than musical bloody chairs, thought Poppy, willing herself not to scream as Jen, spotting a still-open burger bar, begged the driver to pull up outside. Susie had already sent him on a convoluted tour of local cash dispensers in search of one that worked. If Dina announced that she needed to find yet another public loo, Poppy knew she would have a complete nervous breakdown. At this rate it would be four o'clock before they even arrived home.

But they made it, finally. Dina, with her stressed bladder, was dropped off first. Then Susie, then Jen. Kissing each of them goodbye in turn, Poppy wondered how they would react if they knew what was racing through her mind. Jen was Rob's cousin, Dina his sister-in-law. Only an hour or so ago Susie had confided tipsily, 'If I could meet and marry someone even half as nice as your Rob I'd be *so happy*.'

'Edgerton Close is it, love?' asked the taxi driver over his shoulder when only Poppy was left in the car.

Poppy looked at her watch for the fiftieth time. Quarter to three. She took a deep breath.

'Delgado's, Milton Street. Opposite the university. Hurry, please.'

Delgado's was a trendy post-nightclub hangout popular with students and diehard clubbers alike. Poppy, who had visited it a few times in the past, knew its atmosphere to be far more of a draw than the food.

But with its white painted exterior and glossy dark blue shutters it certainly looked the part. On a night like tonight Poppy knew it would be even busier than usual, packed with people showing off their tans, making the most of the perfect weather while it lasted and pretending they weren't in Bristol but in the south of France.

As her taxi drew up outside Poppy wondered just how stupid she would feel if she went inside and he wasn't there. She looked again at her watch. One minute to three.

Then she saw him, sitting alone at one of the sought-after tables in the window. He was lounging back on his chair idly stirring sugar into an espresso and smoking a cigarette.

Poppy's pulse began to race. Twelve hours from now she was due to walk down the aisle of St Mary's church on her father's arm. Twelve and a bit hours from now she would become Poppy McBride, wife of Robert and mother – in due course – to three, maybe four little McBrides. It was all planned, right down to the middle names and the colour of the wallpaper in the nursery. Rob was a great one for thinking ahead.

'Here, love?' The taxi driver was showing signs of restlessness. When Poppy still didn't move he lit up a cigar and exhaled heavily, making smoke ricochet off the windscreen and into the back of the cab. This usually did the trick.

Poppy didn't even notice. She saw Tom look at his own watch then gaze out of the window. She knew, without a shadow of a doubt, that if she stepped out of the taxi now her life would be changed drastically and forever.

The taxi driver shifted round in his seat to look at her. 'Don't tell me you're dozing off back there.'

Hardly. Poppy, awash with adrenalin, wondered if she would ever sleep again. Her fingers crept towards the door handle.

'Look, love,' began the driver, 'we can't—'

'Edgerton Close.' Poppy blurted the words out, clenching her fists at her side and willing herself not to leap out of the cab. 'Please.'

'You mean back to Henbury?' The driver stared at her in disbelief. 'Are you sure about this?'

'No, but do it anyway.' She turned her face away from Delgado's and held her breath until the taxi reached the far end of Milton Street. It was no good, she couldn't go through with it.

The bad news was, she didn't think she could go through with the wedding either.

Since sleep was out of the question Poppy didn't even bother climbing into bed. Instead, making herself cup after cup of tea and pacing the moonlit back garden as she drank them, she went over in her mind what had happened so far. And, nerve-rackingly, what had to be done next.

By six o'clock the sun was blazing down out of a flawless duck-egg blue sky and upstairs Poppy heard her father begin to stir. She showered, pulled a comb ruthlessly through her tangled hair, cleaned her teeth and threw on a white tee-shirt and jeans. Then she tapped on his bedroom door.

'Dad? I've made you a cup of tea.'

Since the death of Laura Dunbar ten years ago there had been no other woman in her father's life. Poppy had missed her mother desperately following the nightmarish accident when an out-of-control lorry had careered down Henbury Hill smashing into Laura and killing her outright. Her mother had been fun-loving, vivacious and openly affectionate. She had also doted on Poppy, her much-loved only child.

In the first unbearable months following the accident Poppy had secretly wondered why the lorry couldn't have suffered brake failure in front of her father instead. It was shameful to even think it, but at twelve years old you couldn't always control your thoughts. And it would have been so much easier to lose the withdrawn, humourless, silent parent who didn't even seem to like her that much anyway.

But it hadn't happened that way. Laura had been the one to die and Mervyn Dunbar had never made any attempts to replace her. Gradually Poppy had grown used to the fact that from now on there would be just the two of them. Poppy had made heroic attempts to learn to cook. A cleaning woman came in twice a week to keep the place hygienic.

Despite Poppy's best efforts her father had continued to treat her as more of a stranger in the house than a daughter. In turn she had taken to going out a great deal. He was her father but Poppy wasn't sure she loved him. It was hard to love someone who so plainly didn't love you back.

Now, having knocked on his bedroom door, she waited downstairs in the kitchen. Ten minutes later he appeared, fully dressed, in the doorway.

'Dad, I can't do it. I'm going to have to call the wedding off.'

Poppy watched him heave a sigh before reaching slowly for his cup of tea. When he had taken the first sip he would pull a face. She knew this because it was what he always did when she had made the tea.

'Why?' her father said at last when he had swallowed and grimaced. 'What's he done wrong?'

'Nothing. Rob hasn't done anything wrong.' Poppy pushed her fingers through her wet hair, wincing as a strand of it caught up in her engagement ring. The small diamond twinkled in the sunlight. She would have to give it back. 'It's me. I just can't go through with it.'

'And it's taken you until now to realise this?'

'I know, I know.'

'Do you enjoy it?' her father said bitterly. 'Causing trouble?'

She stared at him, appalled. 'Of course I don't!'

'You've always caused trouble.'

'I have *not*,' Poppy almost shouted, outraged by the lie. If there was one thing she'd never been, it was a troublemaker.

'You're like your mother.' Mervyn Dunbar's voice dropped

to a hoarse undertone. With her red-gold hair pushed away from her forehead like that, Poppy so resembled her mother it was unnerving. And she was twenty-two now; the same age Laura had been when he had first met her.

How he had loved Laura, he thought wearily. And how she had hurt him in return.

'What do you mean?' Poppy began to feel sick. She had never heard him say anything like this before. Her mother wasn't a subject he had ever seemed to want to discuss.

Mervyn Dunbar finished drinking his tea. 'Nothing. I'm just saying you like a bit of drama, that's all. So what happens after you've called the wedding off? Have you thought about that?'

'Not really—'

'And where will you live? Or,' said Mervyn heavily, 'does this mean you'll be staying on here?'

It was ironic, thought Poppy, that she should ever have worried about having to leave her father to fend for himself. Not normally slow, it had taken her until now to realise he would actually prefer her out of his way.

'It's all right, I'll move out.' She spoke jerkily, not having had time yet to think things through. 'I don't know where. Maybe out of Bristol. At least that way I won't keep bumping into Rob and his family. And all his friends—'

Poppy jumped as out in the hall the newspaper clattered through the letter box. She looked up at the clock on the kitchen wall. Ten to seven. Oh dear, she'd better get a move on. Poor Rob. He wasn't going to be very pleased.

Chapter 3

This was pretty much the understatement of the year. Having walked the half-mile or so to the semi-detached house where Rob lived with his parents and younger brothers, Poppy and her aching toe arrived at seven o'clock to find the McBrides already up and rushing about. Margaret McBride, who had insisted on doing all the food for the reception, was cling-filming everything in sight and ferrying trays of hors d'oeuvres out to the cars standing in the driveway. The younger boys were stuffing themselves with Scotch eggs while their mother's back was turned. Their father, sitting straight-backed on the kitchen doorstep like the army man he had once been, was vigorously spit-and-polishing a long line of shoes.

'You what?' said Rob, when Poppy told him in the privacy of the ultra-tidy sitting room.

'I'm sorry, I'm so sorry. I can't marry you.' She winced inwardly at the sound of her own voice saying the words. Poor Rob, he really didn't deserve this.

Poppy wished she didn't have to be here doing it, inflicting all this pain. The temptation to forget the whole thing – to just go ahead, what the hell, and marry the man – was huge. She could understand why not many people called off their wedding on the day it was due to take place.

What was really awful, she realised when she looked up moments later, was that Rob was smiling.

'Poppy. Come on now, love, calm down. It's *normal* to have last-minute jitters, you know it is. Don't you remember, there was a piece about it in that magazine of Mum's last week? She read it out to you.'

Poppy went rigid as, still smiling, he pulled her into his arms for a reassuring hug. Horrors, he didn't believe her . . .

'This isn't a last-minute jitter.' She lifted her chin, realising she had to make certain this time she was getting through. 'I mean it, Rob. I'm sorry, I know you're going to hate me for doing this but we have to cancel the wedding. We really *have* to.'

As Susie had observed last night, it would be hard to find a better husband than Rob McBride. He was charming, he was honest, he was generous to a fault. With his solid physique, his unflashy good looks, his heroic job as a fireman and his kindness to old dears and small children alike, he was everything a girl could want. He didn't drink, gamble or womanise. He knew how to put up shelves. He didn't even mind that Poppy couldn't cook.

Staring at her now, Rob said, 'Is this a joke?'

'No.'

'Poppy, you can't just cancel a *wedding*—'

'Yes we can.'

'But why would you want to?' Rob was no longer smiling. His complexion had turned three shades paler. His dark eyebrows drew together as he tried to make sense of what was going on. 'This isn't very bloody funny, you know. Come on, tell me what's happened. Why don't you want to get married?'

His body was well-muscled, honed to perfection with regular sport and weight-training exercises. Poppy could see that every one of those muscles was in a state of rigidly controlled tension. At least she didn't have to worry that he might hit her. Wife-battering wasn't something Rob would ever go in for. Except, Poppy realised belatedly, she wasn't going to be his wife. She was the bitch jilting him practically at the altar. He might not be able to resist giving her a quick slap across the face.

'I said,' Rob repeated stonily, 'why don't you want to get married?'

'Look, it's not you, it's me,' Poppy rushed to explain. 'You haven't done anything wrong. This is all my own fault. The thing is, it wouldn't be fair to marry you. Not fair to you or me. Oh Rob, I know I keep saying I'm sorry, but I *am*. You see, I don't love you enough—'

'Someone else.' The words came out through gritted teeth. Rob's light grey eyes were like ice-chips. 'Is this what you're trying to tell me? You've met someone else?'

It was no good. Poppy realised she might as well be honest. He deserved that much.

'In a way, I suppose. But—'

'In a way?' shouted Rob. 'In a *way*? And just what the fuck is *that* supposed to mean?'

Poppy tried to imagine what was going on at this moment on the other side of the sitting-room door. Rob's family must by this time be listening to every word. Their ears would be suction-cupped to the freshly glossed wood.

'I'm not leaving you for another man, Rob.'

The look of absolute horror on his face said it all.

'Not another woman either,' Poppy went on hastily. 'Please, try and understand. I'm not leaving you *for* another man but it is because of another man. He's someone I met, briefly. Very briefly. And I'm never going to see him again. But he made me realise I couldn't marry you,' she said with a helpless shrug. 'He made me realise I don't love you as much as I should. All I ever really wanted, you see, was an excuse to leave home and become part of a . . . a *happy* family.'

'So all the time I've been putting in extra hours, getting a bit more money together for the house,' said Rob slowly, 'you've been screwing some other bloke behind my back.'

'No. I wasn't. I didn't sleep with him,' Poppy explained. 'I didn't even kiss him. I know it sounds bizarre—'

'Bizarre's hardly the word I'd have called it. Will you look at the time?' He thrust his watch under her nose. 'Half past fucking seven. We're supposed to be getting married in six hours. What are you, some kind of sadist? If you had to call the thing off, couldn't you at least have done it before now?'

'No—'

'Who is this lover boy anyway?' Rob demanded furiously. 'For his sake it had better not be anyone I know. *And* you can tell me how long it's been going on.'

'It's no one you know,' said Poppy. 'It's no one *I* know, come to that. And it hasn't been going on any time at all,' she added wearily. 'I only met him last night.'

The next hour was so horrible it seemed to drag on for weeks. Poppy, effectively cornered by Rob's unhappy family, began to wonder if she would ever be allowed to leave. Most alarming of all was their absolute refusal to accept her decision. Margaret McBride carried on grimly clingfilming sausage rolls and plates of cheese-and-asparagus quiche.

'You don't mean it,' Rob's father said for the tenth time. He gestured towards the kitchen table, heaped with prawn vol-au-vents and tubs of Twiglets. 'You can't let good food like this go to waste.'

'I'll pay for the food,' Poppy said in desperation. 'I'll pay for everything. *Please* can't we phone the vicar—?'

'Never mind the cost,' shouted Margaret McBride. 'What about the humiliation? How's our son supposed to live this down? You're not even being logical, Poppy! If you were running off with another man I could understand it, but this ... this is just a whim, a stupid idea you've got into your head. And it's selfish. *Selfish*,' she raged on, tears welling in her eyes, 'because you will destroy my son if you go through with this. How will he ever live down the shame?'

'What shame?' Rob demanded hotly. He had had enough of this. It was plain to him that Poppy had no intention of changing her mind. Sod it, why should he have to stand here listening to his own mother fighting his battles for him? She was making him sound a complete wimp.

He turned to face Poppy. 'You're the one who should be ashamed of yourself.'

'I *know*,' Poppy pleaded. She didn't care how angry he got – it would almost be a relief if he did punch her on the nose – she just wanted the showdown over with. 'I know and it's *all* my fault—'

'Damn right it is.' Rob's muscles were still bunched up, but he didn't hit girls. Never had, never would. That didn't matter though; there were other ways of getting back at Poppy Dunbar, better ways of hitting her where it hurt. Silkily he said, 'So what does your dear old Dad make of all this? You have mentioned it to him, I suppose?'

'He's not thrilled.' Poppy began to relax slightly. Rob sounded as if he were starting to accept the situation at last. 'He said I was causing trouble again—'

'You did enough of that, didn't you, when you were born?'

'Rob.' His mother spoke in warning tones.

Puzzled, Poppy echoed, 'When I was born?'

'Why should he give a toss, anyway, whether you get married or not? Mervyn Dunbar isn't your father.' Rob revelled in the moment. His mouth curled with pleasure. 'Dear me, so surprised,' he drawled triumphantly. 'I thought everyone around here knew that.'

Chapter 4

At twenty-two Claudia Slade-Welch had a great deal going for her. She knew this because people were always telling her so. She was lucky to have thick blonde hair, lucky to have splendid breasts – no need for a Wonderbra there – and lucky to have legs long enough to counterbalance what might otherwise have seemed a rather large bottom.

The luck didn't end there. As if all this wasn't enough for one girl, Claudia had also been blessed with an endlessly glamorous mother, and a father who wasn't only charming but famous to boot. Only when she was asked where she lived were people able – for a few fleeting seconds – to feel sympathetic towards her rather than envious. Renting a room in a friend's house didn't have much of a glamorous ring to it, they thought. It sounded mundane, if not downright dull. Until someone else happened to mention in passing that the friend in question was Caspar French. Then everyone, especially the women, changed their minds in an instant and gasped, 'My God, how fantastic! You lucky, *lucky* thing . . .'

The trouble was, as Claudia had come to realise over the years, she never actually felt as lucky as everyone else thought she should feel. As a child, reading endless Enid Blyton books, she had first suspected that her mother wasn't a normal Enid Blyton-type mother. Normal Enid Blyton-type mothers were never called Angie for a start. Nor did they wriggle into glitzy mini dresses and flirt with almost everyone in trousers, from her husband's celebrated circle of fellow actors to Claudia's own beloved form teacher at school, Mr Elliott.

Time hadn't improved matters. Normal mothers were supposed to be looked up to. Claudia, growing and growing like an over-watered sunflower, had overtaken tiny five-foot-tall Angie by the time she was eleven. Being ten inches taller than your own mother, she discovered, wasn't a comfortable sensation. Nor was it helped by Angie's habit of pointing it out at every opportunity, of faxing diet sheets to the matron at her daughter's school and of wailing loudly at parties: '... and I thought the whole *point* of having girls was so one could borrow their clothes! I mean, tell me, where did I go wrong?'

It wasn't the kind of remark an Enid Blyton mother would make. For a time Claudia's father had remonstrated with his wife, in that famously sexy, laid-back manner of his. But Angie, who had never taken any notice of anyone, least of all her husband, had carried on regardless. Then the divorce had happened and Claudia had seen little of her father for the next few years. On his infrequent trips back from Hollywood she hadn't dared to whinge. Instead she had stoically endured her mother's careless insults, pretending instead to be as happy as anything. As she grew older, she took care never to introduce Angie to any boyfriends she particularly liked.

One week after her eighteenth birthday Claudia had moved out of the family home and into the first of several chaotically shared flats.

But there was never any real getting away from Angie, short of upping sticks and emigrating to Siberia. For the past two years she had been passionately involved with an already married hotel owner on the Costa Smeralda and Claudia had enjoyed the break. Now that affair was over. The hotel owner, possibly fearing for his health, had decided to stay with his rich wife. And Angie Slade-Welch – together with her sickening twenty-one-inch waist and size-three satin stilettos – was back.

She hadn't been invited to tonight's party but had, predictably, turned up anyway. Watching from a safe distance as her mother approached a well-built sculptor friend of Caspar's and swung into action, Claudia absently helped herself to three prawn and cucumber canapés from the tray of a passing waitress.

'If you want to do something useful,' said a voice at her shoulder, 'you could always introduce me to that hunky chap talking to your mother. When she's finished with him of course.'

Claudia turned to Josie, an ex-flatmate from last year.

'By the time my mother's finished with him there might not be much left to introduce.'

Josie giggled. 'Well, if there is.'

'And I don't know who he is anyway.' Claudia tried not to sound annoyed, but it was a bit much. It was her birthday, supposed to be *her* party and she had forked out a fortune on caterers, yet Caspar had done his usual trick and casually suggested he might invite a few of his friends along too. 'Just to make up the numbers,' he'd said with a grin before she'd had a chance to object. 'No need to look so alarmed, Claudie, only half a dozen or so. No undesirables, I promise.'

It was her own fault, Claudia decided with a sigh, for having been stupid enough to believe him. But it was still irritating, having her own party invaded by so many of Caspar's friends that there were more strangers in the house than people she actually knew. They ate like gannets too. The expensive caterer, thin-lipped because she had only been asked to supply food for forty guests, had just warned her they were about to run out.

What annoyed Claudia most of all was the fact that – having successfully hijacked her birthday party – Caspar hadn't even had the common courtesy to show up. And everyone thinks I'm so lucky to be living in this house, thought Claudia, her expression mutinous. Huh.

'Where is Caspar anyway?' asked Josie, her appreciative eye still lingering on the broad shoulders of the sculptor.

Claudia pulled a face. 'Congratulations. You're the fiftieth person to ask me that question tonight.'

'Come on, cheer up.'

Claudia tried. 'Okay. Sorry. He's just impossible, that's all.' Flipping back her heavy blonde hair she shook her head in exasperation. 'D'you know, it's not as if he's even gone out anywhere. He's upstairs in his studio, bloody *painting*. I went up and banged on the door at nine o'clock. He wouldn't come out. He said he was on a roll and didn't dare stop.' Claudia, whose knowledge of art was pretty much limited to the water-lily print on her duvet cover, glanced up in disgust at one of Caspar's paintings hung above the mantelpiece. 'I mean, it isn't as if there's any hurry. His stuff sells really well now. He's hardly short of cash.'

Josie was slightly more knowledgeable. 'Money means nothing to these artistic types.'

'Evidently not.' Claudia spoke with feeling. 'Particularly when it comes to offering to go halves on the food.'

'Stop moaning. You don't know how lucky you are.' The waitress was back with her tray. Josie chose the canapé with the biggest prawn on top. Through a mouthful of puff pastry she said, 'I'd love to live here.'

'That could be arranged. Oliver's moving out at the end of the week. He's going back to New York.' Claudia's mind was on other things. This was the third time the red-haired waitress had circulated with the same tray. She touched the girl's arm. 'Excuse me. We'd like to try the blinis.'

'Sorry, they've gone,' said the girl with the red-gold hair. 'These cucumber thingies are all that's left.'

The mini blinis stuffed with Sevruga caviar, a speciality of Kenda's Kitchen, were what Claudia had been looking forward to all evening. Instead they'd been guzzled by a bunch of gastronomic philistines who would no doubt have been just as happy with sardines on toast. This really was the living end.

Bloody *bloody* hell, Claudia seethed inwardly, not trusting herself to speak.

'Um, if there's a room going free in this house,' said the waitress, 'I'd be interested.'

Claudia couldn't have looked more startled if one of the prawns had opened its mouth and asked the time.

Josie burst out laughing. 'Talk about seizing the moment.'

'Sorry,' said the waitress, registering the expression on Claudia's face, 'but if you don't ask you don't get. And I am desperate.'

Poppy wasn't exaggerating. Cancelling her wedding three months earlier had been the easy bit. Becoming known – practically throughout north Bristol – as The Girl Who Jilted Rob McBride, had been much more of an ordeal. An old lady whose ginger cat Rob had once rescued from a tree had shouted abuse through the letter box of Poppy's home. She had received horrible phone calls. One of Rob's ex-girlfriends from years ago, passing her in the street, had called her a bitch. And Poppy's father – except he was no longer her father – had said coldly, 'I think you'd better go.'

Which was why, just four days after her non-existent wedding, she had found herself on a coach bound for London. Poppy had chosen this city for three and a half simple reasons. Firstly, more coaches travelled more often to London than to anywhere else. She had also, on a school day trip years ago, fallen in love with the Portobello Road and Petticoat Lane antiques markets.

The third reason, so flimsy it only just qualified as one, had to do with her real father. Poppy needed time to make up her mind about this. Even if she wanted to try and find him, she realised her chances of doing so weren't great. All she did know was the name of the man who had had a brief but passionate affair with her mother, and that he had once – twenty-two years ago, for heaven's sake – lived in London.

But if this was flimsy it was nothing compared with the fact that London was also home to Tom, which was why she had only allowed it to count as half a reason. Poppy knew, with the benefit of hindsight, that she had been spectacularly stupid, but at the time she had made a conscious decision not to ask. And now it was too late, she thought ruefully. When you weren't even in possession of something as basic as a person's surname . . . well, then you *really* didn't have a hope in hell of finding them again.

Still, she had at least had one thing going for her on arriving in London. She hadn't expected too much of the place, hadn't imagined the streets to be paved with gold.

And she had been right, they weren't, but Poppy had taken the grim reality in her stride, refusing to be appalled by the low standard of rented accommodation available within her price range. She also refused to be offended by the amount of unfriendliness she encountered, which some people appeared to have elevated to an art form.

Mentioning no names, thought Poppy now. Manfully keeping her opinions on the subject to herself, she directed a guileless smile at the tall, blonde, stroppy-looking girl whose party – and home – this evidently was.

'The room,' Claudia said at last, 'isn't going . . . free. This isn't the Salvation Army.'

No, thought Poppy, they're far more welcoming.

'I didn't mean free-free,' she explained patiently. 'I meant available. Look,' she went on, 'this chap Caspar I keep hearing about, maybe I could have a word with him, see if he'd be willing to let me take the room.'

'Why are you desperate?' said Josie, who was incurably nosy.

'You should see the place I'm in at the moment.' Goodness, a friendly voice. Poppy turned to her with relief. 'Purple wallpaper with yellow lupins all over it. Holes in the carpet, missing floorboards, groping old landlord, incontinent cat – you name it. There's a heavy metal freak upstairs and a Glaswegian bloke with a beard who steams his own haggises. Or haggi. Anyway, the smell is terrible. The flat's a dump. But this,' Poppy concluded with an appreciative sweep of her arm, '*this* is a fabulous house. I mean it, I would be so happy to move in here! This place is a palace—'

'The trouble with palaces,' Claudia cut in, 'is they cost more to live in than dumps. I don't want to sound funny—'

Of course you do, Poppy thought.

'– but I doubt very much if you could afford the rent.'

'I might be able to,' Poppy said mildly. 'I only do this in the evenings. I do have a proper job.'

'Oh.'

'What is it?' Josie asked, warming to the girl who was standing up so well to Claudia at her huffiest.

'I'm a stripper,' said Poppy simply. 'It's great, and it pays well. I recommend it. If you ever want to earn good money, just become a stripper in a pub.'

Chapter 5

Poppy paused for breath at the top of the third flight of stairs then knocked on the dark green door as Claudia had instructed. Several seconds passed before an abstracted male voice said, 'Yes?'

'Um, hi. My name's Poppy Dunbar. I wondered if I could see you.'

'Let me guess,' said the voice through the door, 'you're a friend of Claudia's and she's sent you up here to act as bait. Your job is to lure me down to her party.'

'Not exactly.'

'Bullshit.' He sounded amused. 'I know the way her mind works. Don't tell me, you're a ravishingly beautiful blonde.'

'Nope.' Poppy smiled. 'A ravishingly beautiful redhead.'

'Hmm, shock tactics.'

'I'm not one of Claudia's friends either. She only sent me up here because she couldn't think how else to get rid of me.' Poppy thought for a moment then added, 'And maybe to punish you for not putting in an appearance downstairs.'

'Punish me? What are you, a tax inspector? A ravishingly beautiful redheaded tax inspector,' Caspar mused. 'Surely there's no such thing.'

'Open the door,' said Poppy, 'and find out.'

The attic studio was large, taking up the entire top floor of the house. There were canvases everywhere, propped against the white painted walls, stacked untidily on chairs and littering the polished wooden floor. Also occupying space were three sofas – one dark blue, one black velvet, one tartan. There was also, Poppy couldn't help noticing, an unmade king-sized bed.

'Good heavens, a choice of casting couches.'

Caspar French, who was tall and tanned and very blond, broke into a broad grin.

'We aim to please. I'm puzzled though.'

'Oh?'

'Well, I'm fairly sure we haven't met before. And you say you aren't a friend of Claudia's.' He paused, picked up an already opened Beaujolais bottle, held it up to the light and discovered it was empty. Reaching for a Kit-Kat instead, he dropped the wrapper on the floor, broke the bar in two and offered half to Poppy. 'So what I don't understand is how you came to be at the party. Unless we've been gate-crashed. Are you sure you aren't an undercover tax inspector?'

'I work for Kenda's Kitchen,' said Poppy, 'the caterers.'

'Ah.' Caspar nodded. 'And how's it going? Is Claudia happy with the food?'

'She might have been if your friends hadn't eaten it all. I'm afraid Claudia isn't very pleased with you.'

'I'll survive. I'm used to it.'

The area over by the window appeared to do duty as Caspar's idea of a kitchen. As well as chocolate to sustain him there were cans of Coke, a few half-full coffee cups littering the floor, an empty pizza box and several more wine bottles. Picking his way barefoot through the chaos Caspar discovered one that hadn't been opened. 'Hooray. White all right with you? Looks like something Australian.'

'Thanks but I can't. Much longer up here and I'll get the sack.' Poppy, suddenly nervous, wiped her damp palms on the back of her skirt. 'The thing is, I overheard your friend Claudia saying you had a room to rent. So, I'd like to volunteer myself for it.'

Unable to find a corkscrew Caspar had given up on the wine. Instead he began cleaning brushes, carefully soaking each one in turn in a jug of white spirit before going to work on them with a rag which had evidently once been an evening shirt. He was wearing a pale yellow cotton sweater with the sleeves pushed up, and extremely paint-spattered white denims. The smell of the oils he had been using still permeated the air. On the easel in the centre of the room stood the current work-in-progress, two almost completed figures sprawling comfortably together on a sun-drenched lawn, their heads bent as though they were sharing a secret.

'Gosh, you're good,' exclaimed Poppy. Realising she sounded surprised she added hastily, 'I mean, I'm no expert—'

'That's okay. You're right anyway. I am good.' Caspar turned and winked at her. 'I'm up-and-coming. According to the dealers, at least.'

'You're certainly good at changing the subject.' Poppy was bursting with impatience. 'Go on, give it a whirl,' she begged. 'Say I can move in. I am house-trained. I pay my rent on the dot. I even Hoover occasionally.'

'You haven't seen the room yet. Are you an undercover journalist?'

'I'm not an undercover anything.' Poppy glanced at her watch. 'But I'll definitely get the sack if I don't shoot back downstairs. Look, will you at least think about it and let me know?' Seizing a nearby pencil – a sooty 6B with meltingly soft lead – she scribbled her address and phone number across the back page of an old *Daily Mail* and underlined it twice for good measure. Never again was she going to make *that* mistake.

'I'm trying to decide what it is you have,' said Caspar. 'Nerve or style.'

Poppy handed him the newspaper. 'Can't I have both?'

Back downstairs she found herself cornered almost at once by Claudia.

'Well, what did he say?'

'That I had a nerve,' Poppy dutifully replied.

'Just what I thought he'd say.' Looking immensely pleased with herself, Claudia smoothed back her blonde hair and waved hello to someone behind Poppy. When she chose to use it, Poppy thought, she actually had a nice smile. 'You see,' Claudia went on, 'maybe it's different where you come from but around here introducing yourself to total strangers and asking if you can come and live with them isn't really done.'

'No. Sorry.' Poppy hung her head. 'Sorry.'

'Well then, that's that sorted out.' Having won, Claudia was prepared to be magnanimous. 'I'm sure you'll find somewhere else to live soon enough,' she said kindly. 'By the way, did Caspar mention anything about coming down to the party?'

The words Caspar had affectionately employed were; 'Silly old bag, let her sweat.' But Claudia wasn't the only one who could be gracious in victory.

Poppy said, 'I'm sure he'll be here soon.'

'I say,' purred Angie Slade-Welch twenty minutes later. 'You have to admit there's something awfully attractive about a man who just doesn't give a damn.'

'Mother, Clark Gable's dead.'

'Never mind Clark Gable.' Angie was beaming away like a lighthouse. 'Your landlord's turned up at last. Does he cultivate that just-got-out-of-bed look or is it natural?'

'It's accurate,' said Claudia in pointed tones. 'He spends his life just getting out of bed. Beds, rather. Oh for heaven's sake,' she sighed, catching a glimpse of the paint-spattered white jeans. 'He could have changed into something decent before he came down. He's not even wearing *shoes*.'

'Nice feet,' Angie observed with a nod of approval. 'Anyway, why should he wear shoes? This is his house. He can walk round stark naked if he likes.'

Claudia cringed. 'Don't tell him that. You'll only put ideas into his head.'

'Or yours.' Angie loved to embarrass her daughter. 'Come on, you can tell me. What really goes on in this house when there are just the two of you here? Is anything likely to develop, do you think—?'

'Mother!'

Angie shrugged. 'Only asking, my darling. You never tell me anything so how else can I find out? And he *is* irresistible, isn't he? Go on, whisper it.' She lifted herself playfully on tiptoe, tilting her head. 'You can't tell me you don't fancy him rotten. And living together like this . . . well, he must have made a pass at you at some stage.'

A glass bowl of cornflowers stood on the marble mantel-piece. Claudia, in front of it, realised she had been abstractedly de-petalling the blue flowers. This was the effect her mother always managed to have on her. What Angie actually meant was that Caspar must have made a pass, *even* at her, at some stage.

He hadn't though. In all the time she'd known him, thought Claudia, there hadn't been the least bit of a pass made. Not even the teeniest hint of one.

As for the other less than delicately worded enquiry . . . of *course* she fancied Caspar rotten. She did feel, however, that she was hiding it well. To look at her nobody would ever guess. And, Claudia thought with feeling, just because she did fancy him didn't mean he wasn't also wildly infuriating to live with. Caspar might be irresistible but he was irres-ponsible too.

'No,' she told her mother, quelling the urge to seize the front of Angie's bronze satin bustier and haul it upwards. Over the past hour it had slithered lower and lower, revealing a perilous amount of pert bosom. Her mother had no doubt arranged for this to happen. She was proud of her small but perfectly formed breasts.

'No pass? Oh bad luck.' Angie's blue eyes gleamed like sapphires. 'Never mind, you can always live in hope.' The toe of her tiny shoe nudged a pile of shredded petals into the fireplace. 'Poor flowers, whatever did they do to deserve this?'

'Claudie, you look gorgeous. Happy birthday,' said Caspar, coming over at last and kissing her warmly on both cheeks.

It was the type of gesture that could never be mistaken for a pass. It was also, thought Claudia, the first time she had seen him all day. Having crawled home at dawn and slept until mid-afternoon Caspar had been closeted ever since in his studio, supposedly working.

He smelled of toothpaste and turpentine. He had also been using her Nicky Clarke shampoo again. As she breathed it in Claudia wondered how someone could be so incapable of remembering to buy his own shampoo, yet never *ever* run out of oil paints.

'You're late. Your friends have eaten all the food.' She turned and pointed to the guilty-looking lurcher brought along by Caspar's sculptor friend. 'And that hideous mongrel has slobbered his way through a whole basket of chocolates. Charbonnel et Walker champagne truffles,' Claudia added, though why she bothered she didn't know since Caspar was a stranger to remorse. 'They were a present from the girls in the office.'

'Dear old Hoover, such a connoisseur,' Caspar said fondly. 'He's always appreciated a decent class of chocolate.'

'And thanks for the birthday card.'

'Oh dear, you are cross with me.' He grinned. 'I know, why don't I paint you one?'

Claudia wasn't going to be won over that easily. 'Most people grow out of giving home-made cards by the time they're ten.'

'You'll have to excuse my daughter,' sighed Angie, 'it's so long since she last got laid.'

'Mother—'

'Only teasing, sweetheart.'

Realising she wasn't having the best of evenings, Caspar put one arm around Claudia's brown shoulders. 'I'm sorry I didn't buy you a card. I thought maybe we could go some-where nice for lunch tomorrow . . . as a kind of belated present.' His mouth twitched. 'Or do you hate me too much?'

'That depends.' Claudia's resolve began to weaken, as Caspar had no doubt known it would. 'Somewhere how nice?'

'The Marigold.' He knew it was one of her favourite places to go. Luckily it was one of his too. 'Come on, cheer up. We can go berserk on oysters and champagne. You know you want to.'

'I know *I'd* want to.' Angie's smile was catlike. 'Sounds heavenly. Is there room for one more?'

Caspar looked at Claudia.

Angie pouted. 'Just a little one. Oh please, couldn't I come too?'

'Um . . .' said Caspar.

The last person on earth Claudia wanted muscling in on their cosy lunch à deux was her man-eating mother.

'No,' she said before Caspar was obliged to be polite. 'You could not.'

Chapter 6

Becoming successful and earning serious money for the first time in his life hadn't changed Caspar one bit; he was as careless with it now as he'd ever been, only these days he had more to be careless with. Five years ago, as a poverty-stricken student, he would have spent his last tenner in the world on fish and chips and a bottle of Bardolino to cheer up a miserable flatmate. Now it was lunch at The Marigold and a bill that would run into hundreds of pounds. Caspar wasn't bothered; as long as everyone had a good time he was more than happy to sign the cheque.

When he looked back over the past decade Caspar marvelled at the way his life had changed. A much-loved only child, he had astonished his un-artistic parents from an early age with his passion for painting. Once over their surprise, they had supported him wholeheartedly. Money they might not have, but belief in their son's talent and their endless encouragement meant more to Caspar than all the financial help in the world. He would get by; he was used to being poor. Besides, poor was what art students were supposed to be. Leaving home, moving to London and struggling to survive on a grant the size of a peanut was what being a student was all about.

Henrietta Malone had lived at 15, Cornwallis Crescent for forty-eight years. A genteel, four-storey Georgian terraced house in East Kensington, it was the home to which her husband Edmund had brought her as a young bride almost half a century earlier, a house large enough to accommodate any number of offspring and with a well-tended garden to match.

Sadly, Henrietta had been unable to bear children but by the time she and Edmund discovered this they had grown to love the house anyway. Only when her beloved Edmund died in his sleep – at the age of seventy-four and after forty-four years of quietly happy marriage – did the house seem too big to carry on living in alone.

Henrietta yearned for company, and not the kind you were apt to find in some depressing old folks' home. Instead, much to the horror of her more strait-laced friends, she pinned an advertisement to the notice board in the entrance hall of St Martin's School of Art.

Within a fortnight she had what she had always wanted, a house that shook with music, clattering footsteps and laughter, a house full of surrogate children who teased her unmercifully, shocked the neighbours and called her Hen. Broke but cheerful, they kept the most extraordinary hours and wore even more extraordinary clothes.

Henrietta adored them all but she especially adored Caspar, who had fallen instantly in love with the airy, skylighted studio on the top floor and who had moved in within hours of setting eyes on it. Over the course of the next two years other students came and went but Caspar stayed firmly put.

Henrietta never failed to be entertained by Caspar – her golden boy, as she secretly thought of him. Not only good-looking but charming too, he was a joy to have around. And he was talented. She was particularly touched, with Christmas approaching, when she discovered by chance that in order to pay his rent on time he was going without food.

In an effort to help out, Henrietta had visited Caspar in his studio, admired a recently completed painting and offered to accept it in lieu of money. But Caspar, politely refusing her offer, had by the skin of his teeth managed to scrape together just enough cash.

Two weeks later on Christmas Eve he had given Henrietta the painting she had liked so much.

Henrietta knew how much of a struggle it was for Caspar to find the rent each month, yet not once did he let her down. He was also unfailingly cheerful and willing to help out around the house if jobs needed doing which were beyond Henrietta's capabilities. She didn't care how untidy he was, how many girlfriends he brought back to his rooms or how many she had to fib to on the phone when Caspar absentmindedly double-booked himself. He might be feckless but he made her laugh and she loved him to bits. He truly was the son Henrietta had never had.

Shortly after her seventy-fifth birthday Henrietta suffered a mild heart attack. 'Oh Hen,' Caspar chided when he had arrived at the hospital that evening armed with masses of yellow tulips, half a dozen Agatha Christies and a big bottle of her favourite scent, 'are we going to spoil you rotten when you come home.'

But Henrietta hadn't come home. A second heart attack three days later proved fatal. Caspar and the other tenants attended the funeral and simply assumed they would have to start searching for somewhere else to live.

Nobody was more astounded than Caspar when Henrietta Malone's lawyer informed him that 15, Cornwallis Crescent was now his. Henrietta, it transpired, had had no living relatives. With characteristic panache she had bequeathed hefty sums of money to Dr Barnardos, a donkey sanctuary in Sussex and the Chelsea Pensioners. Nobody who had known Henrietta had had any idea she was worth so much.

As far as Caspar was concerned this was the turning point of his life. Within the space of a few months he had acquired – thanks to Henrietta's amazing generosity – a house that was covetable by any standards. He had also graduated with honours from St Martin's and been showcased and favourably received in several prestigious Cork Street galleries. There was now a growing waiting list of customers eager to sit for Caspar French, the rising young star of the art world. They wanted their portraits painted while they could still afford him.

The Marigold, in Covent Garden, was all oranges and greens with a tropical air to it and exotic waitresses in Carmen Miranda hats. It was popular with celebrity types, which meant everyone was always looking at everyone else.

This was why Claudia so loved the idea of coming here and being seen with Caspar French. It did her ego the world of good to see people clocking them together, assuming they were a couple. Besides, for all his faults Caspar was great fun to have lunch with. When he turned on the charm he could make a sack of potatoes feel chic.

As they walked in together and heads began to swivel, Claudia experienced that familiar surge of pride. Caspar, in a pale pink jacket and baggy cream trousers, was looking so effortlessly elegant and Brideshead-ish it quite hid the fact that in reality he couldn't give a monkey's what he wore. When he was this blond and tanned – and in such a good mood – he was just about irresistible.

Glad she had worn her most slimming black linen dress, Claudia held in her stomach and slithered gracefully between tables which at other times might have seemed too close together. She felt terrific. Caspar was treating her to a belated birthday lunch, she had successfully fobbed off her attention-seeking mother and grilled oysters were the dish of the day. What more could any girl want?

'You've got blue on the sleeve of your jacket.' Reaching across the table to touch the smudge of oil paint she found it was still wet.

'I was working before we came out.'

'Hiding, you mean,' said Claudia, 'in case I dragooned you into helping clear up the mess.'

'I'm no good at that kind of thing,' Caspar protested. 'Anyway, it was your party.'

'It was your friends who played skittles with beer cans in the drawing room. You should have seen the state of the place this morning. *And* all the flower vases were full of beer—'

'I thought we were here to celebrate. You aren't allowed to nag me to death,' Caspar argued good-naturedly. 'Not at these prices.' Turning to the wine waiter he pointed to one of the bottles on the list. 'A couple of these, I think, to start with.'

'And this can be cleared.' Claudia pointed to the third place-setting, taking up unnecessary space on the table. 'We're just two.'

The wine waiter, who knew better, hesitated.

'Oh, didn't I mention it?' Caspar looked amused. 'We're three.'

'Not my mother.' Claudia felt the hairs rise at the back of her neck. She was so outraged she could barely speak. 'Please, *not* my mother.' She did a double-take as a figure behind the wine waiter stepped to one side. Recognising with mounting horror that distinctive riot of red-gold hair and unable to help herself, Claudia wailed, 'Oh no, not *you*.'

'Oh dear, better break it to me gently.' Glancing at Caspar, Poppy started to laugh. 'Which am I then? The devil or the deep blue sea?'

'Come on now, you're over-reacting,' said Caspar when Poppy had beaten a diplomatic retreat to the loo. 'Oliver's moving out. We'll have an empty room. I don't see why you're so against her moving in.'

Claudia wasn't entirely sure herself, she just knew that if Oliver had to be replaced by a female she would much prefer a plain one.

'That girl eavesdropped on a private conversation,' she said crossly. 'Then she butted in. How pushy can you get?'

'She saw an opportunity and grabbed it.' Caspar shrugged. 'Makes sense to me.'

'You don't need to replace Oliver anyway,' Claudia

pleaded. 'You don't need the money any more.'

This was true, but tenants weren't only about money. Just as Henrietta had rented out her rooms for the company, so Caspar chose to do it for the simple reason that it made life so much easier for him. If he lived alone he knew full well he would never be able to fathom out the central heating system. He would leave gas rings burning and there would be no one else around to turn them off. He would be forever locking himself out of the house and there would be nobody else there to let him in, just as there would be no one else to wash up, maintain a modicum of order, remind him to pay bills and remember to buy all those boring but necessary items such as toothpaste, chocolate Hob Nobs and fresh milk.

'That's a selfish attitude,' said Caspar. 'Think of the housing shortage. All the homeless on the streets.'

'Bull.' Claudia wasn't falling for that. 'And she isn't homeless. She's a stripper in a pub.'

Caspar raised his eyebrows. Poppy, back from the loo, slid into her seat and wondered if Claudia would ever forgive her.

'I strip furniture.' She tried to sound apologetic. 'I work for a chap who runs a stall in Markham Antiques Market. He loaned me out to a friend of his who needed help renovating fixtures in a pub off the Portobello Road. I'm sorry,' she said to Claudia as the waiter refilled their glasses. 'I don't know why I made it sound the way I did. Sometimes I speak without thinking.'

'And sometimes you just lie,' Claudia replied stiffly. 'I asked you what Caspar said when you went up to see him. You told me he said you had a nerve.'

'Actually that's true.' Caspar was grinning. 'I did. But I also said she could move in.'

She had been made fun of, Claudia realised. For their own amusement. The fact that she hadn't approved of Poppy Dunbar was more than likely what had prompted Caspar to say yes. And now here they were, ganging up on her already . . .

'I'm really not as awful as you think I am.' Poppy was trying to be helpful. 'We just got off to a dodgy start.'

You're telling me, thought Claudia as Poppy offered up her glass for a clink. So much for her happy birthday lunch.

'Are you after Caspar?' she asked later, when he had disappeared up to the bar in search of cigarettes.

'Is that what you thought?' The look Poppy gave her was sympathetic. 'Not at all, and that's the honest truth. I'm a bit immune to men at the moment, if you must know. Had a traumatic time, not long ago, so I'm steering clear for the time being.'

From the way Poppy spoke Claudia knew she meant it. Reassured, she said, 'Oh.'

'Why, are you?'

'After Caspar, you mean?' Claudia blinked rapidly. 'Of course not.'

'Lucky old us then.' Smiling, Poppy acknowledged Caspar's imminent return to the table. 'From what I gather he has more than his share of a reputation.'

'Claudia once told me I was lucky to be male,' said Caspar, sitting back down, 'because if I were a girl I'd be a tart.'

'I like the word strumpet,' Poppy said dreamily.

Claudia was addicted to problem pages. Bursting to know, she leaned forward. 'So what was this trauma?' she said, her imagination working overtime. 'Was it something awful? What *happened* to make you immune to men?'

Chapter 7

Poppy couldn't wait to pack her bags and escape the gloomy confines of her Balham bedsitter. Moving into Caspar French's million-times nicer house was a dream come true, even if it did have Claudia in it.

Jake Landers, Poppy's boss at the antiques market, offered her the loan of one of his vans.

'Thanks – ' Poppy was touched by his kindness – 'but there's no need. All my stuff fits into suitcases.' At the expression on Jake's face she added lightly, 'I went minimalist when I left home.'

So minimalist that she no longer possessed so much as a living relative. Not one who would speak to her anyway. The truly ironic thing was, the shock discovery that her father wasn't actually her father hadn't come as that much of a shock at all. Not an awful one at least.

Surprise had swiftly given way to relief. Not being liked by your own father was unnatural and Poppy had always wondered what she'd done to deserve it. Now she knew the truth she could stop worrying. Not being liked by a man whose wife had made you the laughing stock of Henbury twenty-two years earlier was far more understandable. Only Mervyn Dunbar's determination to maintain outward appearances had kept the marriage going. The affair, once over, was evidently never mentioned again and Poppy, born nine months later and fooling no one, had been formally passed off as his own.

Dozens of people, including the McBrides, had known

about it. Poppy continued to be amazed by the fact that she had never learned the truth before now. All in all, she felt it was a shame it had remained a secret for so long.

'Well, if you need any help,' said Jake, 'you know you only have to ask.'

Poppy knew. She also knew how lucky she was to have landed a boss as brilliant as Jake. He was quiet, maybe even a bit on the shy side, but he had a dry sense of humour and the patience he exercised with Poppy – who was forever bombarding him with questions about antiques – was phenomenal. At twenty-eight he lived alone but Poppy knew nothing beyond that. Unlike her, Jake kept his private life pretty much to himself.

Another endearing quality about Jake was the way he genuinely didn't realise how good-looking he was. His own appearance clearly wasn't something with which he ever concerned himself. His dark hair was cut for him in a little shop three doors up from the antiques market, by a barber who might be unfashionable but who was at least fast. Jake's long-lashed dark brown eyes were hidden behind spectacles that looked like something his grandfather might have passed down to him. His body seemed all right – as far as Poppy was able to tell – but his dress sense was frightful. All she could say about Jake's clothes was that they were clean.

Poppy had fantasised once or twice that beneath the Clark Kent exterior was a Superman waiting to burst out, but she knew deep down there wasn't. From time to time Jake would find himself being chatted up on the stall, usually by women a few years older than himself in search of someone to mother. It was so sweet watching him because he obviously didn't have the least idea what to do with them. Eventually Poppy would take pity on him and intervene, allowing Jake to melt gratefully into the background.

He had never said as much but Poppy assumed he was gay.

'Thanks.' Poppy reached up to take the steaming mug of

tea Jake had brought down from the café on the top floor of the antiques market. She had enjoyed her week stripping in the pub in Portobello but it was nice being back here on the stall.

For a Friday afternoon the market was quiet. In between customers, most of them browsers who preferred to be left alone, Poppy had been reading up on Georgian teapots. Jake, just back from the monthly sale at Lassiter's Auction Rooms in Bermondsey, began unpacking a box of assorted silver photograph frames.

'Look at that.' Balancing her tea on the flat, glass-fronted jewellery cabinet, Poppy picked out one of the larger frames with its photograph still in place. The sepia-tinted print, dated 1925, was of a stiffly posed family. Mother, father and assorted children stared unsmilingly up at her. 'They all look like their father. Minus the moustache.'

'You could polish up these frames if you like,' offered Jake. He pointed to the hallmark on another frame. 'Date?'

'George the something.' Poppy wasn't in the mood for hallmarks. She looked again at the sepia print. A small knot began to tighten in the pit of her stomach.

'Fifth,' said Jake. 'George V.' He frowned. 'You seem a bit . . . are you all right?'

'Hmmm?'

'You don't look quite with it.'

Poppy broke into a grin. In his dark green cardigan full of holes, his blue and white striped shirt and brown houndstooth check trousers, if anyone was looking not quite with it, it was Jake.

'Sorry, I was thinking.'

Jake, who had heard about little else for the past week, said, 'About the move I suppose.'

'Actually no. I was wondering if I look anything like my father.'

'Ah.' He had heard about this too, over the course of the last three months. 'Well, I can't help you there.'

'I want to find him,' said Poppy, the words coming out in a rush. Quite suddenly it mattered more than anything else in the world. She felt like an alcoholic begging for a drink. 'I know I probably won't be able to but I have to at least give it a try. I *have* to—'

'Are you sure?'

Poppy had been um-ing and ah-ing about this for weeks. Jake's only experience in the matter was of an adopted schoolfriend who had managed to trace his natural mother then been traumatised by her refusal to meet him. Some things, Jake felt, were best left unmeddled with.

But Poppy had made up her mind. 'I must. It might be impossible. But it might not. He could be living just round the corner from me. Imagine if he was and I didn't *know* . . .'

'How are you going to do it?'

She nodded in the direction of the phone books stacked up beneath his cluttered desk.

'There are seventeen A. Fitzpatricks listed in the London area. I'll start by phoning them.'

'Try and be a bit discreet,' said Jake. He wouldn't put anything past Poppy. She was liable to turn up on their doorsteps armed with a do-it-yourself DNA testing kit.

The few details Poppy had been able to glean about her father had come from Dina, who had in turn learned them from her mother-in-law Margaret McBride. According to this third-hand information her mother had met Alex Fitzpatrick at a country club on the outskirts of Bristol. She was working there behind the bar and he had played the trumpet in the resident jazz band.

Alex had moved down from London to take the job, because even if the pay was peanuts it was better than nothing at all. He might have been poor but jazz was his great love; it was what he lived for.

Laura Dunbar, so legend had it, was finding married life less enthralling than she had been led to expect. Meeting

Alex Fitzpatrick, who kept nightclub hours, drank Jack Daniels on the rocks and laughed at the deeply suburban lifestyles of the members of Ash Hill Country Club, had knocked her for six.

Alex had a gravelly Cockney drawl, a quick wit and a career in what could just about be called show business. He also made Laura laugh, which mattered more than anything. She fell in love with Alex Fitzpatrick, ignored the fact that he had a wife waiting for him back in London and threw herself headlong into a recklessly indiscreet affair. It became the talk of the country club. It wasn't long before everyone knew, including Mervyn Dunbar.

But Mervyn, who loved his wife, sensed that if he kicked up a fuss he would only lose her. Electing to sit it out and pray that nature would run its course, he grimly feigned ignorance instead.

Six weeks later, as the summer season was drawing to a close, Alex Fitzpatrick's wife was watering a hanging basket when she fell off a stepladder and broke her leg in three places.

Alex explained to a devastated Laura that he had to go back to London. His contract at Ash Hill was pretty much up anyway, and now his old lady needed him. They'd had a laugh, hadn't they? They'd had a great summer together but now it was time to move on. She had a husband, he had a wife. Of course he'd loved Laura, but this was how things were. No need to get all dramatic over a bit of harmless fun.

Laura was devastated but she had her pride. To be fair to Alex, he had never talked about leaving his wife; she had just hoped he might.

Hiding her true feelings, refusing to cry in front of him, Laura kissed Alex goodbye. When she discovered three weeks later that she was pregnant she knew at once who was the father. She had been far too busy making love with Alex to have any energy left for Mervyn.

Mervyn, who wasn't stupid, was equally aware of whose

44

baby it was. When he'd wanted nature to take its course he hadn't meant in this fashion.

But at least he had his wife back, which was what Mervyn wanted most of all. He also privately suspected that he might not be able to father children of his own as a result of a nasty attack of teenage mumps. Maybe in time, he decided, he would be able to forget who the biological father of this child really was. Maybe he would learn to love it as if it were his own.

Poppy knew all this because her mother had confided as much in her small circle of friends, one of whom had been Margaret McBride. Pride had prevented Laura from ever contacting Alex Fitzpatrick to let him know she was carrying his baby. Instead she had immersed herself in the business of becoming a born-again good wife.

When Poppy had been born Mervyn had, in turn, tried his hardest to experience true fatherly feelings. The trouble was, they hadn't been there. And he had been unable to summon up any.

But the secret of Poppy's parentage had been kept, from herself if from no one else, and her mother's tragic death had only compounded people's determination to preserve it. To lose one parent was terrible enough, they whispered to each other. Imagine the effect it could have on a vulnerable twelve-year-old to discover that the one you had left wasn't a real parent at all.

If only they'd known, Poppy thought ruefully, how glad I would have been to find out.

But it was time now to go into action. She had waited long enough. Since she'd moved to London, wondering who her real father might be had knocked everything else out of her mind – even Tom. The sooner the noisy Australian from the basement flat stopped yakking to every friend he'd ever had and got off the communal payphone, the sooner she could make a start.

When he had at last finished Poppy ran downstairs and bagged the phone, kneeling on the dusty floor with her list of A. Fitzpatricks in one hand and a pile of twenty-pence coins in the other. Her heart pounded against her ribs as she began to dial. Imagine, within seconds she could actually be speaking to her father . . .

Each time the phone was picked up at the other end, Poppy asked in a businesslike voice to speak to Alex Fitzpatrick. Ten minutes later she was three-quarters of the way through her list, having got through to an assortment of Alans, Alistairs, Alisons and Andrews . . . even an Ahmed.

Then she struck lucky.

'Alex?' said a middle-aged sounding woman. 'I'm sorry, you've just missed him. May I take a message?'

Poppy gulped. This really could be it.

'Um . . . maybe I'll try again later. What time do you expect him home?'

'Well, nine-ish. He's gone to cubs.' The woman began to sound nervous. 'Is this about Ben's birthday party last week? Oh dear, you aren't Lucy-Anne's mother are you?'

Another ten minutes and she was finished. Not only a crushing disappointment, Poppy thought mournfully, but a waste of an awful lot of twenty pences.

How stupid to think finding her father would be that simple.

The next morning, bright and early, Poppy arrived on the doorstep of 15, Cornwallis Crescent.

'Please, it's only ten o'clock,' groaned Claudia, opening the door in her blue and white towelling dressing gown.

Poppy looked hurt. 'Caspar said any time I liked.'

'Caspar would.' Claudia was gazing askance at the two modest suitcases on the top step. 'He doesn't even hear door bells before noon. That can't really be all you've got.'

'I do what the glossy magazines say to do,' said Poppy. 'I may not have many clothes but I always buy the best.'

They both knew this was a big lie. For lunch at The Marigold, Poppy had turned up in cut-off black jeans and a Rocky Horror tee-shirt.

Claudia said gloomily, 'God, I hope Caspar knows what he's doing.'

'Oh look, I'm here now.' Poppy picked up her suitcases. 'And whether you like it or not I'm moving in. We may as well be friends.'

'Real friends,' Claudia pointed out, 'don't wake you up at ten o'clock on a Saturday morning.'

'I'm sorry, I won't do it again.' Carrying her cases through to the kitchen, Poppy heaved the smaller of the two up onto the fridge and began unzipping it.

Next moment a multi-coloured explosion of tights and tee-shirts hurtled out. It was like one of those trick cans full of snakes.

'What—' began Claudia.

'Come on, cheer up and grab a couple of bowls.' Having at last found what she was searching for, Poppy held them up. 'This one's to celebrate me moving in and this one's your belated birthday present.'

Claudia gazed at the two tubs of rapidly melting Ben and Jerry's. Other people celebrated with champagne, she thought. Poppy Dunbar had to do it with Chunky Monkey ice cream.

Chapter 8

Three weeks later, on a wet Wednesday afternoon, the weather was so depressing that Caspar decided he couldn't possibly work. This was the trouble with skylights and broad attic windows. When the rain came down, you knew about it.

To cheer himself up – and take his mind off the fact that the painting he was supposed to be working on should have been finished a week ago – Caspar watched a bit of lunchtime *Coronation Street* and polished off the bowl of cherry tomatoes he'd spotted earlier in the fridge. Then he helped himself to a cappuccino mousse with whipped cream on top.

By now *Coronation Street* had finished and been replaced by one of those audience participation talk shows. This one was about shoplifting. A skinny woman in an orange wig stood up to announce that she was a professional shoplifter. Another boasted about having once shoplifted a three-piece suite. The talk show host said this almost deserved a round of applause and the audience, unsure whether or not they were supposed to clap, looked nervous and fidgeted in their seats. The host then introduced this week's expert, a woman psychiatrist with a face like a bulldog, and Caspar fell asleep.

He was woken up an hour or so later by the door bell. Opening the front door he found Claudia's mother shivering on the top step. It was still pouring with rain.

'Come in, you're drenched.' Caspar pulled her inside and ushered her into the sitting room. 'Sorry, I was asleep.' He switched off the television and made a token effort to plump up the squashed sofa cushions. 'Claudia isn't home from work yet. She'll be back around five. Can I get you a drink?'

Angie Slade-Welch smiled at the sight of Caspar, so streaky-blond and deliciously tanned, in his turquoise tee-shirt and white shorts. He looked like a beach bum, and not a day over twenty-two.

'I knew Claudia wouldn't be here.'

She also knew that so long as you were prepared for it, a bit of rain didn't go amiss. The damp, dishevelled look suited her down to the ground. It was why, having been dropped off by her driver right outside the house, she had waited half a minute before ringing the bell. Plenty of Audrey Hepburn eye make-up and a fragile smile, and Angie could take on the world.

As long as the mascara was run-proof.

'You knew Claudia wouldn't be home yet? Oh dear,' said Caspar. 'In that case I hope you haven't come here to ask embarrassing questions behind her back. My mother did that once when I was in the fourth form. She cornered the French mistress, convinced that I was being led astray—'

'And were you?'

'Of course.' He grinned. 'But it improved my French no end. So, is that really why you're here? You want me to dish the dirt on your daughter's love life?'

'Not at all.' The only love life Angie was interested in was her own.

'You want to find out if she's happy here?'

Angie shrugged and shook her head. 'No, but you can tell me if you like. She's had a couple of moans about the new girl . . . what's her name? Poppy.'

Never one to boil a kettle when he could open a bottle instead, Caspar was relieved to discover an unopened bottle of Pouilly Fumée hidden behind the mineral water at the back of the fridge.

'Ah yes, Poppy and Claudia.' He filled two glasses and passed one to Angie. 'The harem, as some of my not very

49

witty friends have taken to calling them.'

'And are they?' Angie raised an interested eyebrow. 'Your harem?'

Caspar pulled a face. 'They bear a passing resemblance. Claudia doesn't trust Poppy an inch. Now I know what it would be like, keeping a wife and mistress together under one roof. Except,' he added with a grin, 'I'm not sleeping with either of them.'

'How quaint.' Angie could imagine how desperately Claudia would have liked to. She would leap at the chance. Caspar evidently wasn't interested. Good.

'In fact neither of them are to my knowledge sleeping with anyone,' he went on, 'which means there isn't really any dirt to dish.'

'Some harem.'

'So if it isn't a rude question,' said Caspar, 'why are you here?'

'I'd like you to paint me.'

Angie crossed one slender charcoal-stockinged leg over the other. She was wearing an efficient-looking grey pin-striped suit today, tightly belted to show off her tiny waist. Unfastening her bag she took out a calfskin-bound diary.

'Um . . . no offence, but I'm pretty expensive,' said Caspar. It was always better to come out and say it straight away, particularly when the potential client was someone you knew. Even friends-of-friends had an embarrassing habit of expecting you to do it for free.

'That's all right, so am I.' Leaning closer, Angie gave him a conspiratorial look. 'The thing is, I want the painting for Hugo. It's his fiftieth birthday in December—'

'If you want it finished by December I'm going to have to charge more,' Caspar interrupted. 'Look, it's going to be six grand. I'm sorry, but my manager would shoot me if I said anything less.'

Privately he was marvelling at the choice of gift. How many men would want to so much as glance at a portrait of their ex-wife, let alone be given one for their birthday? What if he threw darts at it?

'Six grand, no problem.' Angie Slade-Welch was unperturbed. 'He'll be paying for it anyway.' She smiled. 'One thing I will say for Hugo, he's a perfect gentleman when it comes to alimony.'

Poor Hugo, thought Caspar. With four ex-wives to support no wonder he kept having to fly over to Hollywood to star in the kind of mega-budget movies he despised so much. Small wonder too that none of the ex-wives had ever bothered to remarry. When the payoffs were that generous, where was the incentive?

Caspar, who didn't have anything as efficient as a diary, led Angie Slade-Welch upstairs to his studio. The back of the door was covered with pinned-up business cards and scraps of paper with names and phone numbers scrawled across them. Some had dates and times added in brackets. This was Caspar's filing system. It was a miracle he ever got anything done.

'Mondays are good for me.' Angie was flipping through pages with beige, French-manicured nails. 'Wednesdays . . . no, that's aromatherapy. Um, Thursday afternoons could be arranged. Or maybe Friday mornings . . .'

They haggled amicably for a few minutes. Caspar never felt like doing much at all on Mondays. Finally they settled on three preliminary sittings to be going on with.

'This Friday then.' Caspar prepared to show her out. 'No need to worry about getting your hair done, not at this stage. But bring a couple of outfits so we can decide what'll look best. Nothing too fussy—'

'Nothing fussy at all,' Angie promised, her mouth registering amusement. 'Did I not mention it earlier? I want this to be a nude portrait.' She paused, waiting for his reaction. 'That's not a problem for you, is it?'

'Not exactly a problem for *me* . . .' Caspar was looking doubtful.

'Well then, that's fine. If you're worried about my daughter,' said Angie with a careless shrug, 'don't tell her. This is a private business transaction between consenting adults. Claudia doesn't need to know.'

After a rotten day at work and a rain-drenched dash from the tube Claudia wasn't thrilled to come home and find Caspar and Poppy gossiping together in the sitting room, cosily sharing a packet of Jaffa Cakes and showing no sign whatsoever of doing anything about the mountain of washing-up in the sink.

She was even less enchanted when she spotted the empty bottle of Pouilly Fumée up on the mantelpiece. Two glasses stood side by side on the low coffee table next to the carton that had earlier contained her favourite cappuccino mousse.

Next moment her attention was distracted by something more awful still –

'Ugh – UGH!' screamed Claudia, shuddering with fear and revulsion. She pointed at the carpet beneath the table. 'SPIDERS!'

Caspar craned his neck to see. He grinned, leaned over the edge of the sofa, scooped them up and lobbed them at Claudia.

'Don't get in a flap, they're only tomato stalks.'

'*Oh.*' Claudia was still trembling. 'You really are the living end . . .'

'Sweetheart, I wouldn't have thrown them at you if they'd been spiders.'

'Not that,' Claudia wailed, glaring at him. 'They were *my* tomatoes. This,' she jabbed a finger at the empty carton, 'was my cappuccino mousse. And I was saving that wine for a special occasion!'

'This afternoon was a special occasion.' Caspar thought of the six thousand pounds. 'That's why I opened it.' Then, since Claudia was looking very cross indeed, he added, 'I'll buy you another one.'

'That's not the point.' Claudia hadn't inherited her mother's gift for looking good when wet. Her hair was a mess and her navy mascara had run dramatically down her face. Turning to include Poppy in the diatribe she went on, 'You didn't even leave enough for me to have a glass. You had to jolly well drink it all.'

Poppy had only arrived home from work ten minutes earlier herself. She looked indignant. 'It wasn't me, it was—'

'Anton. From the gallery.' Caspar indulged in a bit of improv, sensing that now was not the time to tell Claudia her mother had been round. 'He dropped by to show me the brochure for next month's exhibition.' Ad-libbing shamelessly he went on, 'It looks completely brilliant. Anton says it's already attracting interest from dealers in Japan—'

The phone rang. Claudia picked it up.

'For you.' Tight-lipped, she handed the phone to Caspar. 'It's Anton. Calling from New York.'

Caspar, well and truly caught out, grinned. 'Told you Concorde was fast.'

'I'm not one of your girlfriends,' Claudia said bitterly. 'You don't have to lie to me.'

53

Chapter 9

'Didn't I tell you Angie Slade-Welch was trouble?' said Caspar when Claudia had disappeared upstairs to have a long hot sulk in the bath.

'You could have turned her down,' Poppy protested. 'You could have said no.'

He pulled a face. 'I'm not famed for my ability to say no.'

'Well, I just hope she's worth it. You haven't even seen her with her kit off yet.'

'I don't think there's any danger she'll fail the audition.' Caspar was doodling in the margins of the *Radio Times*. Glancing up, catching the expression on Poppy's face, he began to laugh. 'Well I'm sorry. I'm just being honest. You were the one who asked how my day had been. If you're going to disapprove, I won't tell you anything in future.'

'I'm not disapproving. I'm interested. It's the big difference between men and women, isn't it? You don't have to love someone, or even like them very much, but if you're a man you'll still sleep with them.' Poppy tore open a packet of crisps with her teeth. 'It's a bit of entertainment, a nice way of passing the time. Like doing card tricks or playing Trivial Pursuit.'

'I'm not completely indiscriminate,' Caspar protested. 'And okay, I might not be in love with these women but I do like them. Claudia's mother knows the score. She doesn't expect anything more than a fling. She certainly doesn't *love* me.'

'I suppose.' Poppy shrugged. 'It just seems weird.'

'You've had a sheltered upbringing.' Caspar drew a caricature of one of the ITN reporters, naked at his newsdesk.

'I have not!'

'What I'm saying is, you met this boyfriend of yours when you were seventeen. You went steady for a few years, got engaged, planned to get married . . . he's probably the only bloke you've ever slept with.'

'So?' Poppy demanded hotly.

'I just think you should get out and about a bit more,' Caspar explained. 'Live a little. Go to parties, meet new people.'

'Sleep with new men.'

'Yes.'

'Why?'

'Because,' Caspar sounded exasperated, 'you're twenty-two years old and you're single. It's what twenty-two-year-old single girls *do*.'

Poppy sighed. She only wished she could. It was over six months now since she had left Bristol and she was still unable to summon up so much as a flicker of interest in a member – any member – of the opposite sex.

She didn't even know if it had happened as a result of meeting Tom or as a side effect of calling off the wedding to Rob, but happen it had. The way things were going Poppy was beginning to wonder if, libido-wise, she would ever feel normal again. It wasn't as if she was unhappy or depressed either, because she wasn't. She just felt as if her heart had been snipped out and swapped for a block of ice.

And like the Cointreau lady, it was taking a hell of a time for the ice to melt.

Caspar was still watching her.

'Well I'm sorry,' said Poppy, 'but I don't want to run round London waving my knickers in the air. I told you before, I'm not interested in sex. I'm immune.'

'I just hope it isn't catching.' He grinned and held up the magazine so she could see his latest effort. A caricature of her with manic ringlets, a halo and a Just Say No tee-shirt stood alongside a wicked one of Claudia, looking hopeful, with Just Say Yes Please emblazoned across her vast bosom.

'Poor Claudia. Be nice to her.' Poppy, who had to be at work by seven, forced herself to her feet.

'What are you doing?'

'You told me I should go to parties and meet more people.'

'I'm talking about places where you aren't the one passing round the vol-au-vents,' said Caspar.

'Yes, well. I have an exorbitant rent to pay. And a pig of a landlord.' Hearing footsteps on the stairs, Poppy grabbed the *Radio Times* and tore out the page he'd doodled on. Claudia wasn't likely to appreciate the joke. She crumpled the unflattering caricature into a ball and threw it just in time into the bin.

'Right,' Claudia announced, smiling at them both. 'I feel better now. Sorry I lost my temper before.. Who'd like a cup of tea?'

Amazed, Caspar and Poppy both put their hands up.

'I'll make a big pot.' Claudia beamed again, to prove they were forgiven. 'And I bought some Hob Nobs on the way home. Oh great, my *Radio Times*. Let's have a look at what's on tonight . . .'

'Well?' Returning at midnight Poppy poked her head round the sitting-room door. 'At least you're still alive. But will she ever speak to either of us again?'

'I'm exhausted. I've spent the whole evening being nice,' said Caspar. 'Not that kind of nice,' he added as Poppy's eyebrows rose.

'All that fuss over one lousy missing page.' Working in the evenings meant Poppy barely got to watch any TV nowadays. She glanced across at it as the film Caspar had been watching drew to an end. The credits began to roll. The name Fitzpatrick made her heart leap for a moment but it was only someone called Shona Fitzpatrick, one of the supporting actresses in the cast.

Sensing something was up, Caspar followed her gaze. He caught the name just before it slid off the screen.

Then he had a brainwave.

'Why don't you advertise on television for your father?'

Poppy looked at him. 'Now that is a terrific idea. Why didn't I think of it months ago? Hang on a sec,' she patted her jeans pockets, 'where's my purse? I know I've got sixty or seventy grand here somewhere.'

'Okay, okay. There is such a thing as free advertising,' Caspar reminded her. 'You could wait until the next big rugby international at Twickenham, make up a banner with Desperately Seeking Alex Fitzpatrick plastered across it, and streak across the pitch at half-time.'

'Desperately Seeking Attention, more like. Not to mention a chilly night in the cells.' Poppy conjured up a mental image of herself without any clothes on, being chased around the rugby field by a lot of smirking policemen. 'Anyway, I don't have the chest for it.'

'I'm trying to help,' said Caspar, 'and all you're doing is making feeble excuses. How about advertising in the newspapers then? That needn't cost much.'

'I know, but it's not very subtle either.' Poppy had already considered this idea. 'The thing is, I'm not looking for a missing person. I'm looking for someone who had – and probably still does have – a wife. The chances are that he has kids of his own. How are they likely to feel, discovering that he had an affair with my mother all those years ago? I don't want to hurt anyone,' said Poppy, 'or be the cause of some awful showdown. Any way of tracking him down would have to be discreet.'

'But you still want to try.'

Poppy was leaning against the sitting-room door restlessly turning the handle this way and that. She nodded.

'More than anything. I want to meet him, even if he

doesn't know who I am. I just need to know what he's like.' She took a deep breath, frustrated by her own helplessness. 'I might love him to bits, he might be perfect. On the other hand he could be awful.'

'Then again,' said Caspar, 'why should you be the only one around here with a parent who's awful?'

Poppy looked shocked. 'Your parents aren't, they're brilliant.'

'I didn't mean me. I'm talking about Angie Slade-Welch.'

'Goodness,' Poppy mocked. 'So does that mean you won't be sleeping with her after all?'

'I said she was an awful parent.' Caspar grinned. 'I daresay she's better in bed.'

Poppy went upstairs to catch a few hours' sleep. She was running the stall single-handed tomorrow while Jake toured the auction rooms. Ever since she had shooed away a wasp with her rolled-up programme and found herself the new owner of a twenty-foot refectory table riddled with wood-worm Jake hadn't let her within screaming distance of a gavel.

Caspar, who wasn't tired, spent the night working in his studio. He made great progress with the painting Angie Slade-Welch had admired earlier.

He wondered as he worked how long it would be before Angie made her move. That she would make a play for him wasn't in doubt; it was more a question of when. Caspar squeezed the dregs of a tube of cobalt blue onto his palette, chucked the empty tube in the direction of the bin and began blending the blue with viridian. Some women, enjoying the sense of anticipation, confined themselves to gentle flirting for the first three or four sittings. Others, eager not to waste a moment, made their intentions obvious straight away. Caspar had a bet with himself that Angie Slade-Welch would make her move at the end of the first sitting. She didn't seem the type to hang around.

He then surprised himself by wondering whether or not he should go along with it. This was startling because it had never before occurred to him not to.

Caspar put down his brush. Reaching absently for a can of Coke he drank from it, his gaze fixed on the ink-black sky through the uncurtained windows, his thoughts elsewhere.

This was all Poppy's fault. It was thanks to her that he was actually thinking of not sleeping with someone. Not because he had been lectured to, either, by some born-again do-gooder droning on about the evils of promiscuity. That was always guaranteed to backfire. It was, thought Caspar, enough to send anyone hurtling into the nearest bed.

But Poppy hadn't done that. Nor was she a droning do-gooder. She had simply wondered what the purpose of it was, when there was no love involved.

And now, for the first time in his life, Caspar found himself wondering if maybe she didn't have a point.

The rain had by this time stopped. There still wasn't a star in sight. Caspar wiped his paint-stained hands on his trousers and resumed painting, his brush moving more or less automatically over the canvas as he thought some more about Poppy Dunbar and the things she had said to him tonight.

The perfect solution, of course, would be to sleep with her.

Caspar grinned to himself and loaded a clean sable brush with cadmium yellow. He liked Poppy, had liked her from the first moment he'd met her. She had spirit and energy and she made him laugh.

She also had amazing hair and a flawless creamy complexion which was certainly undeserved considering the rubbish she ate. These plus points, combined with yellow-green eyes and a curvy mouth that always seemed on the verge of a smile, meant she looked every bit as good as the models who were forever throwing themselves at him.

But Poppy wasn't throwing herself at anyone. She had erected an invisible barrier around herself, a kind of aura that sent out the signal: Definitely Not Interested. This was a natural enough reaction, considering what she'd gone through earlier in the year. Caspar had never experienced it himself because he'd never had to endure any form of emotional trauma, but he was perfectly prepared to believe it existed. He'd heard about all that stuff on Richard and Judy.

The thing was, it was beginning to intrigue him now. He couldn't help wondering if he could *make* Poppy be interested in him.

What a brilliant challenge that would be. He needn't bother with a pushover like Angie Slade-Welch, he could concentrate all his attentions instead on Poppy, who would be so much more fun to sleep with.

Caspar was painting faster and faster. The more he thought about it the more the idea appealed. He would be helping Poppy over her ice-block, as she called it. Mentally they were well matched. Physically – he just knew – they would be perfect. Damn, they'd be great together . . .

Watery sunlight streamed through the windows of the studio as Caspar put the finishing touches to the painting on the easel before him. He stretched, glanced at his watch – eight thirty – and wandered downstairs.

There was a plate of toast, thickly buttered just the way he liked it, on the kitchen table. Exerting tremendous self-control Caspar left it there and began breaking eggs into a frying pan instead. Moments later Poppy shot into the kitchen half-dressed to fill up the kettle and wrench the lid off the biscuit tin.

She looked stunned when she saw him.

'What are you doing?'

Caspar, who would have thought it was obvious, said, 'Cooking.' Proudly, he added, 'Eggs.'

'I mean what are you doing up? It isn't even nine o'clock.'

'I haven't been to bed. Damn—' Showing off with the fish slice he managed to break two yolks.

Poppy looked puzzled. 'Why on earth not?'

'I've been working.' He paused, meaningfully. 'And thinking . . .'

But Poppy was late for work. The kettle hadn't boiled because Claudia had unplugged it to make way for the iron. The iron was still there. With a mouth full of chocolate biscuit and her back to Caspar so he wouldn't see her knickers, Poppy seized the opportunity to get the worst of the creases out of her skirt.

'Most people take their clothes off before they iron them.' She turned and grinned at him.

'Most people take their clothes off the minute they walk into your studio, but it doesn't mean I have to. It isn't compulsory.'

The skirt, being only small, didn't take long. When Poppy had dragged a pair of tangled black tights out of the tumble drier, helped herself to another handful of Bourbons and located her black suede shoes under the kitchen table she blew a kiss in Caspar's direction and made a dash for the front door.

'Hell,' Caspar sighed, staring down at the eggs in the pan. Poppy had distracted him. They were hopelessly overdone.

'Yuk,' said Claudia, coming into the kitchen with her coat on.

She wrinkled her nose. 'How on earth did you manage to *burn* them?'

Caspar was starving and there weren't any eggs left. Nor, he discovered as Claudia finished her mug of tea, were there any more teabags.

'You haven't eaten your toast,' he said before she left.

'Oh . . . I wasn't hungry . . .'

When the front door had banged shut behind her, Caspar snatched up the toast he had so heroically resisted earlier. But it was too late, the butter had begun to congeal. The toast was soggy and stone cold. So much, thought Caspar, for being considerate and exerting self-control.

It didn't take much longer for his second good resolution

to bite the dust. What had seemed such a great idea last night was – in the cold light of day – becoming an altogether dicier prospect. As he went through the plan again and realised just how fraught with pitfalls it was, Caspar felt his resolve begin to drain away. By the time he'd finished the last piece of horrid toast he knew for certain he couldn't go through with it. There were heaps of reasons why not.

Poppy was a friend, for a start, a cheerful tenant he'd be sorry to lose should the plan backfire. Also, any kind of goings-on between the two of them would be bound to upset Claudia. She would *hate* it.

The major stumbling block, though, was Poppy herself. *She* might not be interested. She might not want to be won over, either. She might say no and mean it, and he would *really* hate that.

He would hate it even more if she laughed.

Damn, thought Caspar, why take the risk? Knowing Poppy she'd laugh her socks off. And even if she didn't, what could ever come of it anyway? He didn't exactly have the greatest track record in the world.

No, Caspar decided, the smart thing to do was to forget all about seducing Poppy, to put the idea completely out of his mind and simply think of her as one of the lads instead.

Far better to stick with the devil you knew.

Caspar sighed. It was seriously unlike him to change his mind like this; in fact, it had to be a first. But some weird inner instinct told him he was right to do so.

Bugger it, he might as well sleep with Angie Slade-Welch after all.

Chapter 10

Poppy couldn't help feeling sorry for the women in Caspar's life.

Not Angie, who was quite old enough to take care of herself. But Poppy certainly felt for the girlfriends who so patently adored him and whom he treated so casually in return. Fibbing over the phone to them on Caspar's behalf was one thing; Poppy had had plenty of practice doing that.

But when the girls were nice and you had to deal with them in person – actually face to face, with that awful trusting look in their eyes – it was hard, sometimes, not to interfere.

If you had an ounce of compassion in your soul, it could be downright impossible.

Jake was out on a buying expedition when Kate Mitchell came into the antiques market. She waited patiently for Poppy to finish selling a Staffordshire stirrup cup to a middle-aged Swedish woman in a purple mac.

Poppy liked Kate, who was sweet-natured, friendly and fragile-looking. When she discovered the purpose of Kate's visit she knew the time had come to start interfering like mad.

'I know it's only October but I always buy my Christmas presents early,' Kate explained with an apologetic smile. 'The thing is, I'm a bit scared of antique shops but I knew if I came here you wouldn't let me be ripped off.'

''Course I wouldn't.' Poppy thought what a shame it was that Jake couldn't be here to eavesdrop on such a compliment. 'And we've got some terrific presenty-type things. Who are you buying for, family?'

63

'Caspar actually.' Kate's cheeks went a fetching shade of pink. 'I don't have much money but I really want to get him something nice. In fact I spotted something a moment ago while you were with the lady in the mac . . .'

Poppy's heart sank. Kate was leaning over the glass-topped jewellery cabinet pointing an almost translucent index finger in the direction of a diamond tiepin. The ticket price was four hundred pounds, which she knew perfectly well Kate couldn't afford.

Poppy also knew it didn't matter how nice a person *she* thought Kate was; Caspar was beginning to tire of her puppy-like devotion. A turkey had more chance than this relationship did of lasting until Christmas.

'A . . . tiepin?' Poppy hesitated, stalling for time. 'Um, does Caspar *own* any ties?'

'It's all right,' Kate blushed again. 'I know he doesn't. It's kind of a private joke between us. You see, I was teasing Caspar, telling him he'd have to wear a tie one day when he got married.' Throwing caution to the wind she added in a rush, 'So I thought what a brilliant present it would be . . . and who knows, it might even prompt him to . . . well, think weddingy thoughts . . .'

Poppy felt numb. How embarrassing, and she wasn't even the one saying it.

'Couldn't you just buy him a tie?'

'Come on, unlock the cabinet,' pleaded Kate. 'It's okay, I know how much it costs. That doesn't matter.' Shyly she added, 'Caspar's worth it.'

He's NOT, Poppy wanted to shout, but all she could do was unlock the cabinet and hand over the tiepin. She could hardly cram it into her mouth secret-agent style and swallow it.

'Four hundred pounds,' Kate murmured, gazing at the centre diamond and turning it this way and that to catch the light. 'Four hundred pounds . . .'

This was what people did when they were too nervous to

haggle. Normally, to put them out of their misery, Poppy would have said, 'Well, for you, three fifty.'

'I know, and I'm afraid I can't drop the price.' She rolled her eyes. 'Jake can be so *mean* sometimes. If you ask me he's gone way over the top with this one. I doubt if it's worth two hundred, let alone four.'

'Oh, but it's so beautiful—'

'In fact,' Poppy had an inspired thought, 'I'm not even sure Caspar likes diamonds. I've got a feeling he thinks they're naff. What I know he *really* likes is topaz.'

Kate looked startled. 'Topaz?'

'Topaz and silver. He was talking about it just the other night. According to Caspar it's a classic combination, like Laurel and Hardy . . . caviar and vodka . . . Pearl and Dean . . .' Poppy waved frantically across to Marlene, whose stock of jewellery was more extensive than Jake's. 'Hey, Marlene! D'you still have that tiepin, the topaz and silver one I saw yesterday?'

Marlene nodded. Poppy turned triumphantly back to Kate.

'Take my advice, get him that one. It's a dream, Caspar will love it.'

'But—'

'And don't be afraid of Marlene. The ticket says eighty,' Poppy beamed. 'Be firm. Tell her you won't go a penny over forty-five.'

'G-goodness,' stammered Kate, backing away in the direction of Marlene's stall. 'Thanks, Poppy.'

'Thanks Poppy,' said another quiet voice behind her.

Brimming with guilt she spun round. Jake was back from trawling the auction rooms and had – quite unfairly, she thought – sneaked in the back way rather than through the glass double doors of the main entrance where she could have spotted him at once.

Poppy squirmed and wondered how long he'd been listening.

'Long enough,' said Jake, since the unspoken question was

fairly obvious. He took off his glasses and rubbed them on the elbow of his threadbare black cardigan. It was a habit he resorted to when his patience was tried, usually by Poppy. That and the sorrowful look he gave her – minus the terrible glasses – always made Poppy feel ashamed. It would be so much easier to bear if he'd only yell at her, call her an imbecile, give her a Chinese burn . . .

'Jake, I'm sorry, but I *couldn't* sell her the tiepin.' In the nick of time Poppy remembered to lower her voice. 'The poor thing's crazy about Caspar . . . she doesn't know he's about to dump her! And she's only an apprentice textile designer so she earns peanuts. Think about it, Jake, you *can't* stand by and let someone spend that much money when you know they're about to be ditched.'

Slowly Jake shook his head. He knew Poppy's intentions were good. He just wished they didn't have to cost him so much.

'Okay, I see your point. But Poppy, please. I have rent to pay, bills to settle –' he paused for added gravitas – 'your wages to find each week.'

Poppy looked miserable. 'I really am sorry.'

'Just remember, we're here to try and make a living. Caspar French's love life isn't my concern—'

He broke off as Kate returned. She was clutching the tiepin, now gift-wrapped.

'You were right,' she told Poppy happily, 'this one's perfect, much more Caspar's style.'

Poppy still thought it was like buying a CD for someone who didn't have a CD player, but that was up to Kate.

'Right, well, I'll see you on Thursday,' Kate went on, 'for Caspar's preview night. You're going, aren't you?'

Poppy nodded. The Denver Parrish Gallery on Cork Street was showcasing the work of three artists, one of whom was Caspar. The exhibition was attracting a huge amount of interest and the preview night promised to be a glitzy affair.

'And you too?' Kate turned and smiled at Jake, who looked uncomfortable.

'Oh no, I haven't been—'

'Yes!' exclaimed Poppy, seizing the opportunity to make things up to him. 'Of course you must come! You can be my partner. It'll be great, free champagne and all the pistachios you can peel—'

'I can't.' Jake cut across her frenzied babbling. 'I'm meeting someone on Thursday night.'

'He wasn't happy with me,' Poppy confided later on that afternoon. Jake had popped out to the bank and Marlene had wandered over for a gossip. They were sharing a bag of sherbet lemons. 'Poor old Kate, she doesn't have much luck with men. I even caught her discreetly giving Jake the once-over. Didn't have the heart to tell her he was gay.'

'Probably gay,' Marlene corrected. 'We don't know for sure.'

'Bet you fifty pence he is. Damn –' Poppy looked dismayed – 'is that the last one? We'll have to break it in half.'

The phone rang while Marlene was sawing energetically at the last sherbet lemon with an Edwardian letter opener.

'Hello?' said Poppy, picking it up.

'Oh, hi,' a male voice sounded surprised. 'Um . . . Jake not there?'

'I'm afraid he's popped out. Can I help you?'

'Okey-doke. If you could just pass a message on to him.' It was, Poppy realised, an extremely camp male voice. Like Julian Clary on helium. 'Tell him Ellis called and I'm ever so sorry but I can't make it on Thursday night after all. Something's come up –' he tittered – 'so we're going to have to get together some other time.'

'Gosh, this is a terrible line,' said Poppy, before pressing the phone triumphantly against Marlene's ear, 'could you say that last bit again?'

'Okay, okay,' Marlene grumbled two minutes later, 'you

were right and I was wrong, Jake's gay and I owe you fifty pence.'

'Not to mention half a lemon sherbet.'

'Consolation prize.' Marlene popped both halves into her own mouth.

'Poor Jake, stood up by Ellis. Never mind,' Poppy brightened. 'Now he can come along to Caspar's opening night after all.'

Chapter 11

Thursday evening hadn't got off to the greatest of starts as far as Claudia was concerned. Her period was due, which always made her puff up like an adder. This meant the dazzling new black dress she'd bought three days earlier – before PMT had struck – was showing the strain.

She began to feel better once she'd organised the narrow crisscross strapping across the back and trained herself not to breathe. Maybe she looked pretty good after all. The dress, from one of the new young designers at Hyper Hyper, had cost a bomb. Claudia gave herself an extra morale-boosting squirt of Arpège, checked her hair and make-up for the fifth time and sashayed downstairs to the sitting room where Caspar, Poppy and Kate were having a celebratory first drink.

'Oh,' said Claudia, coming to an abrupt halt in the doorway.

'Oops,' said Poppy, looking up.

'Snap,' said Caspar with a grin.

Claudia didn't know whether to stamp her foot or burst into tears. There was only one thing more galling than someone else wearing a dress almost exactly the same as yours, and that was discovering how much better they looked in it than you did. Damn, *damn* . . .

'When did you buy that?' Claudia blurted out, her tone accusing. More to the point, how could Poppy-the-pauper possibly have been able to afford it?

'Oh dear.' Kate was looking worried. 'I'm sorry, I lent it to her.'

Kate was even harder up than Poppy. Unable to help herself, Claudia declared, 'My dress cost three hundred and seventy-five pounds from Cher Balakiel at Hyper Hyper.'

'Blimey,' said Poppy. She looked at Kate in amazement.

'Mine was twenty-four ninety-nine,' Kate confessed nervously. 'From George at Asda.'

Claudia was unable to join in the cheerful banter in the taxi taking them from Kensington to Cork Street. She wished she hadn't been so stubborn now. All she would have had to do was run back upstairs and change into something else. It would have taken two minutes and then she could have put the incident out of her mind.

Instead here she was, looking like half a book-end – the *big* half – at the beginning of an evening that was bound to end in tears.

'Come on, cheer up,' said Caspar as he helped her out of the cab. 'It doesn't matter, really it doesn't.' He gave her a squeeze. 'Imagine what it's like for men. Is their day ruined if someone else turns up at the office in a grey suit?'

It was Caspar's big night. Claudia didn't want to be a party pooper. She watched Poppy and Kate walk into the lit-up gallery ahead of them.

'I'm sorry, I just . . .' She pointed helplessly at Poppy, with her red-gold hair swept up in a dashing topknot. Who needed a tan when you had skin like double cream? Poppy's colouring was the perfect foil for the intricately crisscrossed back and shoulder straps. Her figure was perfect. She was even wearing sheer stockings and black high heels.

'Don't be daft, you both look great,' said Caspar.

Claudia had spent years feeling inferior to her mother. Now it was happening all over again. She felt her lower lip begin to tremble.

'Poppy looks better.'

'Only because we've never seen her tarted up before.' Caspar had been pretty startled himself by the transformation. 'Whereas you always look smart. Let's face it, the way Poppy normally goes around she's hardly likely to be mistaken for Ivana Trump. I really thought she'd turn up tonight in jeans and Doc Martens.'

Claudia pulled herself together. She forced a watery smile. 'I wish she had.'

By nine o'clock the gallery was heaving. Among the guests were buyers, dealers, journalists and a sprinkling of rent-a-celebs, the kind who would jet in from Surbiton for the opening of a jam jar.

Claudia was putting a brave face on things but the fact that she didn't actually know anyone else there meant she was forced to stick with Poppy and Kate. Extra annoying was the way flashbulbs kept going off but every time she turned to see if she was included in the picture, the photographer seemed to have been aiming at Poppy instead.

Caspar had been commandeered by the owner of the gallery who was busily introducing him to all the most influential journalists and buyers. Kate, happy to watch from a distance as her future husband was fêted by a Greek billionaire, was dreamily imagining the blissful life she and Caspar would lead when they were married.

Poppy was determined to enjoy herself. Taking an evening off from Kenda's Kitchen made it doubly important that she should – if you were losing a night's wages you *had* to have a good time. She just wished Claudia would lighten up, start smiling a bit. And where was Jake anyway? He'd promised to be here by nine.

Claudia saw Jake first, threading his way quietly towards them through the squashed-together crowds.

'Good grief, train-spotter alert,' she crowed. 'How on earth did *he* get in?'

Then she cringed, realising who this must be, as the train-spotter touched Poppy's bare arm.

It was at moments like these that Poppy felt most

protective towards Jake. This must be what it was like for mothers when their child was pushed off the swing by a bully. Dying to punch Claudia on the nose she said brightly, 'Hooray, you're here at last. Jake, you've met Kate already. This is Claudia, who's in a stinking mood, so don't bother speaking to her.' She beamed up at him. 'And I'm Poppy, remember me?'

'Just about.' Jake smiled slightly. 'You've got make-up on. And you've grown a few inches since five o'clock.'

'Caspar said I had to look smart. These heels are murder. You don't know how lucky you are . . .'

Poppy's voice trailed off. She was somewhat hazy on the subject of gay men. Were they more likely to dress up in women's clothes than straight men? Was Jake a bit of a closet Lily Savage? Poppy's mind boggled at the thought. You never knew, maybe he had a suitcase hidden under his bed crammed with suspender belts and stilettos. It would certainly explain his absolute lack of interest in boring old men's clothes.

'Yes, I'm glad I'm not wearing high heels,' Jake said drily.

Kate was peering at her. 'Poppy, are you all right?'

Poppy was envisaging Jake in a figure-skimming Shirley Bassey number. She pulled herself together. So what if he was a transvestite in his spare time? He could wear whatever he jolly well liked.

Jake had in fact done that anyway, turning up in threadbare beige cords, his favourite green sweater with the holes in the elbows and an equally ancient dark blue shirt.

Claudia, clocking each sorry item in turn, marvelled at Jake's nerve. He certainly stood out among the expensive designer suits and arty-farty, natty-cravatty outfits favoured by the other men in the gallery.

Nobody else was wearing an anorak.

Chapter 12

But as the evening wore on Claudia began to regret calling Jake a train-spotter. Granted, at first glance he looked terrible – and he especially didn't fit in with her mental image of how someone called Jake *should* look – but in a weird way he was beginning to grow on her. Claudia was used to noisy, flashy wine-bar types who drove fast cars and always did their chatting up with one eye on the door in case someone better walked in. Their interests in life were making money, getting legless and getting laid and they liked to do all these things as quickly as possible because – as they were so fond of saying – time was money.

Jake was unlike anyone Claudia had ever met before and she was confused. So confused that she couldn't even make out whether or not he was chatting her up.

Having excused herself earlier to visit the loo, Claudia now made her way back to the section of the gallery where the others were. There hadn't been any recognisable chat-up lines, that was for sure, but once or twice the look in Jake's eyes and the tone of his voice had made her think yes, he *was* flirting with her. It was subtle stuff, all very low-key, but she was almost certain it was there. And the more she thought it might be, the more attractive Jake became – in a subtle, bubbling-beneath-the-surface kind of way.

Something else that drew Claudia to him was the easy way he dealt with Poppy. When Poppy did something annoying at home, Claudia went ballistic. Jake's laid-back attitude was a revelation. It was also a bond, something they shared in common.

'It must be dreadful,' Jake had said earlier in his gentle, not-quite-serious fashion. 'She's bad enough to work with. Actually living in the same house must be hell.'

Now, returning from the loo, she saw that one of Caspar's friends had joined their party.

'. . . and don't expect any sympathy from Claudia,' Jake was saying, 'she's on my side.'

This time the look he gave her was almost proprietorial. Claudia experienced a warm glow in her stomach. She liked being on the same side as Jake.

'This is terrible,' complained Poppy, 'I'm being ganged up on. Thanks, Jake, I wish I'd never invited you now.'

Claudia was glad she had. In her excitement she downed her drink in one go. Goodness, it was warm in here. If she pretended to sway a bit in the heat she could brush her bare arm against Jake's woolly-jumpered one. Juvenile but exciting. Thank heavens he'd taken off his anorak.

'More drinks?' Jake said hurriedly. 'Same again all round? And, er, maybe we should take a look at the pictures. It's why we're here, after all.'

Kate was hailed by someone she knew. Poppy and Claudia trooped obediently across to the nearest wall to inspect a garish yellow and pink abstract by one of the other showcased artists. It was eight feet square and eye-bogglingly intricate. The title was 'Knitting; the dropped stitch'.

'Good job my granny's dead,' said Poppy, 'she'd have had something to say about that.' She peered over the shoulder of the Japanese man in front of her, studying the price list on his brochure. 'Fourteen thousand pounds, good grief.'

'Don't,' Claudia hissed. 'It's embarrassing.'

'Damn right it's embarrassing. Fourteen grand for that! I'd far rather have a Caspar French,' Poppy went on, 'in fact I'm going to ask Harry to buy me two. I overheard one of the

New York dealers just now saying they're the hottest investment since De Kooning.'

The Japanese buyer's ears twitched. Seconds later he
moved off.

'You don't for one moment think he believed you,' sneered
Claudia. 'Honestly, that is *so* juvenile.'

Poppy was stung. She'd thought it was a a brilliant ploy.

'It might work. If I heard someone saying something like
that, I'd believe them.'

'Yes, well. You're gullible. Most people have more sense.'

'Thanks.'

Poppy gritted her teeth. If Claudia was going to start
harping on about being gullible she might be forced to
remind her who had just forked out three hundred and something pounds for a copy of a chainstore dress.

But this time, for once, Claudia backed down.

'Okay, I'm sorry.' She shook her head to show Poppy she
meant it. This was Caspar's exhibition and it mustn't be
spoiled. Besides, she was bursting to bombard Poppy with a
million questions about Jake.

The apology had made Poppy instantly suspicious. She
moved along and began studying another of the bizarre
abstracts. This one, turquoise and grey, bore the title 'A Kiss
in a Tree'.

'Anyway, you were right,' Claudia ventured, eager to clear
the air. 'Caspar's stuff is tons better than this rubbish.'

A very tall, bearded man with hooded grey eyes gave her
an angry stare.

'That's the artist,' murmured Poppy.

'Shit.'

'Only joking.'

Poppy grinned. Claudia suppressed the urge to throttle her.
Instead, in casual tones she said, 'Jake's quite nice, isn't he?'

'Who, you mean Jake my boss? *Train-spotter* Jake?'

Claudia look flustered. 'It was only the anorak. Well,
and the trousers. What I mean is, he's better than you expect

75

'. . . once you actually get to know him.'

Poppy looked amused.

'I'm sure he'll be flattered to hear it.'

'I can't remember,' Claudia blurted out in desperation, 'if you said he was married or living with someone.'

'Now this,' said Poppy, 'is what I call interesting. Don't tell me you're keen on Jake.'

Why did she have to look so . . . so *gleeful*? Affronted, Claudia lifted her chin.

'I'm only asking. Why shouldn't I? He's obviously keen on me.'

Poppy grinned. 'No he isn't.'

'Yes he is.'

'Claudia, I promise you. He isn't.'

'You don't know that.' God, Poppy could be a cow sometimes. 'What are you, some kind of world authority on The Kind of Girls Men Go For?'

'Calm down, calm down.' Poppy made soothing gestures with her hands. 'You've got hold of the wrong end of the stick.'

If I could get hold of the right end, Claudia thought vengefully, I'd hit you with it.

'Look,' Poppy continued, 'what I meant was, Jake doesn't go for *any* kind of girl. He's gay.'

Claudia was stunned. 'Gay? Are you sure?'

'Sure I'm sure. He keeps pretty quiet about it, but he definitely is,' Poppy explained in businesslike fashion. 'That's why there's no point trying to chat him up. So you see, I wasn't being bitchy when I said he wouldn't be interested in you, I was just being honest.' Unaware that Jake was back from the bar and standing right behind her, she went on: 'I know it's sad but what can you do? Jake's as bent as a nine bob note. Actually I think he may be a transvestite too—'

'RIGHT,' Jake hissed into her ear, 'that is ENOUGH. What in heaven's name do you think you are PLAYING AT?'

Poppy jumped a mile. The voice was so filled with fury

she barely recognised it. When she turned and saw the look in Jake's eyes she felt herself go white. She had never seen him so mad before. She wouldn't have believed him capable of such blood-curdling fury.

'Oh Jake, I'm sorry . . . I know it isn't something you make a song and dance about –' help, more visions of Shirley Bassey – 'but I just thought it would be easier to explain to Claudia why she shouldn't . . . um, why you . . . er, wouldn't . . .'

Jake looked ready to explode. Poppy gave up trying to explain. Cringing, she edged a few inches backwards. What a good job they were surrounded by people so Jake couldn't bellow at her.

'I-do-not-believe-this.' He wasn't bellowing. The words were spat out through gritted teeth, which was bad enough. 'Let's get one thing settled right now. I am not gay. I never have been gay and I never will be gay.' His dark eyes, like twin coals, bored through his spectacles and directly into Poppy's brain. 'And I'm sorry to disappoint you but I don't wear women's clothes either.'

'Oh,' said Poppy in a small voice. 'Jake, I'm sorry. My mistake.'

'You see, this is *exactly* what she's like,' Claudia told Jake with an air of triumph. 'She says things without thinking, just comes out with these ridiculous statements—'

'I didn't say it without thinking – ' Poppy was indignant – 'I just thought the wrong thing in the first place.'

Jake had begun to calm down. At least, steam was no longer billowing out of his ears. He frowned. 'But why, what made you think it? I never gave you any reason to believe I was gay.'

Poppy squirmed. Why *had* she thought it?

'I suppose because you don't have a girlfriend.' Oh dear, that sounded pitiful. 'And you never say much about your social life. Um . . .' Yes, that was it! '. . . and then there was that phone call from Ellis!' She seized gratefully upon it, like a lifebelt. 'You were supposed to be meeting him tonight, remember? But he had to cancel—'

'Ellis Featherstone,' said Jake with a sigh, 'lives three doors away from me. He's the local co-ordinator for Neighbourhood Watch. Yes, Ellis is gay,' he concluded evenly, 'but I'm fairly sure it's not catching.'

'Okay, so I made a mistake.' Poppy still couldn't get over the change in Jake. Talk about the worm turning, she marvelled. Jake had turned into a full-grown leopard.

Poppy wasn't the only one impressed by the transformation. Claudia couldn't stop gazing at Jake. The news that he wasn't gay after all had cheered her right up. Emboldened by all the adrenalin whooshing through her veins she seized one of the drinks Jake had carried back from the bar and glugged down another glass of slightly warm champagne.

'What made you say it tonight, anyway?' Jake persisted. In his other hand was Poppy's drink. Before he could pass it to her, Claudia whisked it from his grasp.

Poppy opened her mouth to explain.

'Well—'

'The truth is, she couldn't believe you were chatting me up,' Claudia blithely cut in, her tongue by this time thoroughly loosened. 'I told her you were, she said you weren't.' Breathing in, so her chest swelled out like a pouter pigeon, Claudia gave Jake the benefit of her perfect cleavage. 'Poppy can't believe any man would want to chat me up.'

It was like a mating dance, thought Poppy, struggling to keep a straight face as Jake's eyes inadvertently dipped into the cleavage then slid nervously away. It was like one of those displays of plumage you saw birds doing on David Attenborough programmes. Claudia was silently commanding Jake to respond and chat her up some more. Poor Jake, over his passionate outburst now, was looking downright scared.

Several minutes of awkward small talk later, Jake made his excuses and left.

'Well, thanks,' snapped Claudia when he had gone.

'Oh come on,' Poppy sighed. She had had more than enough of Claudia for one night.

'He would have asked me out, you know. You frightened him off.' Claudia glared at her. 'And don't tell me you didn't do it on purpose.'

By midnight the last guests were drifting away into the night. Only when Caspar had flagged down a cab and piled his own small party inside did he realise why Poppy and Claudia had spent the last couple of hours at different ends of the room.

'Come on, no need for this.' Buoyed up by the success of the exhibition, Caspar attempted a reconciliation.

'I'm all right,' sniffed Claudia. 'It's her. Jake would have asked me out if she hadn't stuck her oar in. If you ask me, she's jealous.'

'Jealous?' shrieked Poppy. 'You were the one who called him a train-spotter! Then you started flaunting your chest at him. He only left early because he was too embarrassed to look at you.'

'Girls, girls,' said Caspar. By the sound of her, Claudia had been drinking for England. He watched her struggling to light the tipped end of her cigarette. Luckily the lighter was upside-down too.

'*And* you're jealous because my dress cost more than yours did,' Claudia declared, giving up on the cigarette and chucking it out of the cab window.

'Oh yes, of course I am.' Poppy lifted her eyebrows in a what-can-you-do-with-a-mad-woman? kind of way.

'Don't do that with your eyebrows,' howled Claudia.

'I'll do whatever I like with my eyebrows. I paid three hundred and seventy-five pounds for them at Hyper Hyper.'

Claudia wondered if she'd ever wanted to strangle anyone this much before in her life. There was that hateful, barely-visible grin again, the one Poppy used when she was making fun of her.

'You're going to regret this.' Realising she didn't have the strength for anything more physical, Claudia waggled an index finger at Poppy instead. 'I was going to tell you something. Something important. You should, you know . . . you should be *nice* to me . . .'

Poppy thought she'd been an awful lot nicer than Claudia deserved. Exerting superhuman control, she said, 'Go on then, what is this oh-so-important thing I need to know?'

'I'm not sure I want to tell you.' The pointed finger jabbed like a conductor's baton. 'I don't think you deserve to know. You shouldn't—'

'Oh for God's sake,' yelped Poppy, throwing herself back in her seat, 'will someone please shut this girl up? What have I done to deserve *her*?'

'Claudia,' said Caspar not unkindly, 'shut up.'

'But—'

'No, I mean it. You've drunk enough to float the QE2.'

'Oh well,' Claudia looked affronted, 'in that case I won't breathe another word.' She shook back her heavy blonde hair. 'Not one single word about the pianist at the Cavendish jazz club . . . the pianist whose name happens to be Alex Fitzpatrick . . .'

Chapter 13

Claudia woke up next morning with a cracking headache. When she rolled over and realised her alarm clock hadn't gone off, and that it was now nine thirty, she groaned aloud.

'It's okay,' said Poppy, nudging open the bedroom door with her elbow and plonking a tray on the end of Claudia's bed. 'I turned off the alarm. And I've phoned your office. I said there'd been a car crash outside the house and you'd rescued a little old lady from the wreckage. You had to wrap her severed finger in frozen peas and take it along to the hospital but you'd be back at work this afternoon.'

Claudia nodded, winced and clutched the side of her head. Getting into a sitting position was worse than climbing Everest. One thing about Poppy, she certainly came up with some inventive reasons for being late for work.

'Here, drink this.' Poppy passed her a cup of tea. She dropped three paracetamols into Claudia's trembling outstretched hand. 'And I've made you some toast if you think you can keep it down.' She hesitated, then went on, 'And I'm sorry if I was horrible last night.'

'I'm sorry too.' Claudia looked shamefaced. It had all come hurtling back to her. 'I didn't behave very well either. I can't believe I threatened not to tell you about the Alex Fitzpatrick thing.' She gulped down the last few mouthfuls of too-hot tea. It singed her tonsils but quenched her raging thirst. 'I would have told you, of course I would.'

'I know.'

Poppy had barely slept. She still hadn't been able to get

over the hand fate had played in Claudia's revelation. To think, if Ellis Featherstone hadn't phoned up last week she would never have come to the inescapable conclusion that Jake was gay. She wouldn't have told Claudia, Jake wouldn't have overheard and the ensuing furious row would never have taken place. And if it hadn't, Claudia wouldn't have stropped off to the far end of the gallery and happened to overhear a couple of jazz-buff art dealers chatting amicably about the blues style of the resident pianist at a tucked-away little place called the Cavendish Club.

It was mind-boggling. As far as Poppy was able to work out, she owed it all to Neighbourhood Watch. Either that or to the entire criminal fraternity, because if it weren't for them the Neighbourhood Watch scheme would never have been invented.

'So d'you think he's the one?' ventured Claudia. 'Could he really be your dad?'

Poppy was sitting on the bed hugging her knees to her chest. No longer tarted up, as Caspar so romantically called it, she looked about sixteen with her red-gold hair flopping into her eyes and the remains of last night's hard-to-get-off mascara clinging to her lashes. She was wearing a yellow sweatshirt and polka-dot leggings, and her feet were bare.

'I think he really could be.' She nodded, resting her chin on one knee. 'But there's only one way to find out. I'm going along to the Cavendish Club tonight.'

Hopefully, Claudia thought, she would be over her hangover by then. 'Would you like me to come with you?'

'Would you?' The look Poppy gave her was one of amazement mixed with relief. 'I'd love you to. That'd be such a help.'

Heavens, thought Claudia, startled that she had even suggested it. Looks like we might be going to get along after all.

She glanced at her watch. It was now quarter to ten.

'Shouldn't you be at work too?'

82

'I phoned Jake.' Poppy helped herself to the toast Claudia was too hungover to eat. 'Said I'd be late.'

'Did you use the severed finger?'

'No. He never believes my excuses.' Poppy looked gloomy. 'It's a waste of time thinking them up.'

'But he's speaking to you, that's something.' Claudia felt her heart do a small practise flutter. 'Did he . . . um, mention me at all?'

'Actually he did,' said Poppy with a grin. Good old Jake, at least he hadn't borne a grudge. 'He said he had a hot date for tomorrow night and please could he borrow your little black dress.'

The Cavendish Club, in Covent Garden, was reached by teetering down a flight of steep, ankle-ricking steps. Converted from an old wine cellar with arched brick ceilings and uneven flagstone floors, it had a smell all its own – a sweet, pervasive mixture of damp, drink and nicotine. The regulars were the genuine jazz buffs, but the Cavendish was well-known enough to attract a wide mix of visitors ranging from students to tourists.

Luckily there were no dress rules.

'We look like The Odd Couple,' Claudia complained as they made their way there. She was wearing a charcoal grey polo-neck cashmere jersey, expensive black trousers and a discreet amount of gold, very chic if she did say so herself. Poppy had turned out in a miles-too-big white tee-shirt that kept slipping off her shoulders, and ancient jeans.

'You didn't like it when we wore the same thing.'

'I know. I just thought you might want to look smart . . . to meet your father . . .' Claudia began to wish she hadn't raised the issue '. . . that is, if it *is* him.'

Poppy wasn't going to admit she'd tried on practically every outfit in her meagre wardrobe before coming out. She glanced across at Claudia as they approached the Cavendish, already belting out music at only eight o'clock.

'What's he going to say, "Oh no, sorry, you aren't wearing top-to-toe Armani, I can't possibly acknowledge you as my daughter"? Please,' said Poppy defiantly. 'If he *is* my father, whatever he's wearing isn't going to make an ounce of difference to me. I daresay he'll forgive me if my tee-shirt isn't haute couture.'

The stage upon which the band played was situated at the far end of the largest of three interconnecting cellars. Their instruments were there, and a lanky youth was setting up mikes, but the music they had heard outside came from a tape deck at the back of the stage. The members of the band were, by the look of it, over at the bar getting a few quick drinks down them in order to sustain them through their set.

'Is that them?' whispered Claudia as they approached the bar.

Poppy was staring at the backs of their heads. Since the posters outside the club advertised Alex Fitzpatrick and the Cavendish Four, and there were five men talking music at the other end of the bar, it seemed more than likely.

'Well?' Claudia hissed excitedly, 'is one of them your dad? Can you tell just by looking? Is it the bald one, d'you think?'

Poppy's heart was flapping like a mad parrot in a cage. Which one of these middle-aged men was Alex Fitzpatrick?

This is crazy, she thought, sinking onto a high stool for support. How *can* I tell if one of these total strangers is my father? How can I possibly know?

Seconds later, she knew.

It happened so fast Poppy was glad she was sitting down. One of the men, the one on the far right with the dark red waistcoat and the hair just below collar-length, turned to speak to the barman. As she caught that first glimpse of his face Poppy felt as if all the air was being vacuumed from her lungs. The thud of recognition was so powerful it could have knocked her off her feet.

This is him, she thought dazedly. It *is* him. I know it, I

don't know how I know it, I just do . . .

'That one?' squeaked Claudia, intercepting the look on her face. She did a quick double-take, her own eyes registering doubt. 'You think so? He doesn't look a bit like you. I can't see any resemblance.'

The man they were both studying so intently wasn't particularly tall. He was solidly built with a well-developed paunch. His wavy hair, dark flecked with grey, was swept up at the sides and long at the back – this was clearly no bank manager they were looking at. His eyes were dark brown, his face generously lined. The nose was big, the chin a double. When he laughed a gold tooth glinted, matching the glittering chains around his neck and wrists, and the matchbox-sized rings on several fingers.

Poppy smiled to herself. Oh dear, Claudia must be horrified. She had been and gone and got herself a father with No Taste.

'Are you absolutely sure?' Claudia murmured at her side.

Poppy nodded.

'But I don't . . . you aren't anything like him.' Claudia was floundering. 'Maybe it's one of the others . . .'

He was wearing a white shirt with diamanté buttons and a red velvet waistcoat. His dark green trousers were on the tight side. One of the other members of the band was telling a joke. When he reached the punchline Poppy saw her father throw back his head and roar with laughter. He had a loud, uninhibited gravelly laugh that made her tingle all over. She loved it. She had always adored men who laughed like that.

'It could be the one on the left,' Claudia suggested hopefully. 'His hair's kind of reddish. What about him, Poppy? He looks quite nice, don't you think?'

A woman had emerged from the cloakroom. Poppy and Claudia watched her clatter across the flagstones in her high heels and join the group at the bar. She kissed each of them in turn, saving the one in the red waistcoat for last. He got a noisy, enthusiastic, lipstick-loaded kiss on the mouth.

'Come on then, help me up!' The woman grinned broadly, holding out her arms so he could lift her onto the high stool at his side. When she was in position she leaned forward and kissed him again. 'Thanks love, and I'll have a gin and orange.' She turned and beamed at the rest of the band. 'Come on lads, time for one more before you go on. These are on Alex.'

Unable to handle anything stronger, Claudia ordered a bottle of Beck's for Poppy and a Perrier for herself. The band were up on the stage now, playing some clumpy-sounding jazz. The club was packed and everyone else seemed to think it was terrific. As far as Claudia was concerned, it sounded a lot like tuning up.

As for poor Poppy, how on earth was she feeling? She wasn't saying much, that was for sure. And no wonder, thought Claudia, who had every sympathy. As if Alex Fitzpatrick wasn't bad enough, there was that dreadful woman with him . . . wife, lady friend, whatever she was. Either way, Claudia decided, she made Bet Lynch look demure. She sounded like something out of *EastEnders*. And she was downing gin and orange like it was going out of fashion.

Claudia flushed, remembering why she was on Perrier tonight. The difference was, this woman looked as if she drank gin for breakfast.

'So what happens next?' she said, because the appalling music was showing no sign of grinding to a halt. The band looked as if they could happily play on all night. How was Poppy planning to introduce herself to her father anyway? By leaping up onto the stage, grabbing a mike and doing an impromptu *This Is Your Life*?

Chapter 14

'Excuse me,' said Poppy, 'but is Alex Fitzpatrick the one at the piano?'

The woman, who was wearing Day-Glo pink nail polish, drew on her Rothman's and nodded.

'Yes love, that's him.'

'Um . . . right. He's good, isn't he?'

Brilliant, just brilliant, thought Poppy, realising that her wits had inconveniently upped sticks and deserted her. Oh, but trying to strike up a conversation with a complete stranger *was* hard when your heart was doing a triathlon in your chest.

'One of the best,' said the woman, blowing a flawless smoke ring.

Her hair was very blonde and fastened into a plait coiled like a snake on top of her head. Long twiddly bits curled in front of her ears, lacquered into place so they couldn't get tangled up with pink earrings the size of Jaffa Cakes. At a guess, she was in her mid-forties. The heavy make-up was very sixties, very Carnaby Street. She was wearing a tight turquoise blouse, a pink skirt and a pair of turquoise stilettos with stupendous heels. She also wore an amazing amount of jewellery, among it an ornate gold wedding ring, an eternity band and an engagement ring so colossal it couldn't be real.

'Um, could I borrow your lighter?' said Poppy, realising too late that she didn't have a cigarette. Didn't even know how to smoke, come to that.

The blonde woman passed across a heavy enamelled lighter. Claudia stared at Poppy. Poppy tugged at a loose thread on the side seam of her Levi's and burned it off.

'There, thank goodness that's done. It's been annoying me all evening.'

The woman smiled slightly. 'So long as you don't set light to yourself.'

Encouraged by the smile Poppy said, 'Look, sorry if I'm being rude, but are you Alex Fitzpatrick's wife?'

'I am, love, for my sins.' The woman began to take notice. Bright blue eyes studied Poppy's face. 'What's this then, twenty questions? Don't tell me you're his new bit on the side.'

'Oh no, *no*—'

'Joke, love. My Alex don't have bits on the side.' She laughed huskily then coughed and lit another cigarette. 'He wouldn't dare, he knows I'd kill him.'

'I'm not one, anyway,' said Poppy. 'I'm just a terrific fan of your husband's. You must be so proud of him . . . to have a talent like that.'

' 'Course I'm proud of the old bugger. What I don't understand – ' his wife gestured in the direction of the stage – 'is how you can be such a fan of his when you didn't even know which one he was.'

Poppy's mind raced.

'Well, you see, I'd never liked jazzy stuff before. But my boyfriend – ex-boyfriend – had a tape of this completely brilliant music, and I fell in love with it. He told me it was Alex Fitzpatrick,' she said brightly, praying that Alex had brought out a tape at some stage in his career, 'and I just thought he was the best jazz . . . um . . . player I'd ever heard. So that's why I had to come here. I'm sorry, this must be a complete pain for you, I'm sure you must be forever getting hassled by fans.'

'Not so you'd notice,' the woman said good-naturedly. 'Well well, so your ex bought a copy of Alex's tape. We always wondered where the other one went.'

'Mrs Fitzpatrick, could I buy you a drink?'

'Rita, love. Call me Rita.'

'And my name's Poppy Dun—' Poppy's mouth screeched to a halt; saying Dunbar could be risky. 'Er . . . Dunn. Poppy Dunn.' She swivelled round and tapped Claudia on the arm. 'This is my friend, Claudia Slade-Welch.'

Claudia had been trying to melt into the background. She managed a faint smile and a nod.

'Not enjoying yourself, love?' Rita evidently thought it was funny. 'This place not your cup of tea?'

Claudia sounded pained. 'Oh no, it's fine. Really—'

'I dragged her along,' said Poppy. 'That's the trouble with being a girl. Going out to clubs and things isn't something you can do on your own. I mean, I'd love to come here every week but I'd be dead embarrassed, sitting by myself—'

'No need for that.' Rita Fitzpatrick wiggled an over-here finger at one of the girls behind the bar. 'I'm always around, you can sit with me. I'm not wild about the music myself, mind, but we can keep each other company.'

'That's so nice of you,' Poppy said happily.

'I know.' Rita winked at the barmaid. 'I'm just an all-round terrific broad. Stand by, Effie. This young lady's about to buy me a drink.'

'Alex, you've got yourself a fan at last,' crowed Rita. She waved away the pea-soup fog of cigarette smoke swirling around her head and pulled Poppy forward. 'Meet Poppy Dunn.' Stifling yet another burst of husky laughter she added, "The other one's Claudia, but she ain't a fan. She reckons your music's the pits.'

'Oh but—'

'Never mind, at least one of them's got taste.' Alex Fitzpatrick grinned, mopping his forehead with a black silk handkerchief and glugging thirstily at the pint of lager Rita had just ordered for him. 'Poppy. Good to meet you.' He put his drink down and shook her hand, because Poppy had hers determinedly outstretched. 'So, not seen you before. First time, is it, here at the club?'

Poppy's shock of recognition earlier had been so vivid she hadn't been able to help wondering if he would feel it too. Of course, he hadn't. Trying not to feel let down, Poppy concentrated instead on his hand which was actually quite difficult to shake, what with all those thumping great rings in the way.

'First time.' She nodded in agreement, hoping she didn't look like one of those dogs in the back window of a car. Alex Fitzpatrick's hand was warm, squarish, capable-looking. The handshake was firm and perfectly ordinary. There were no special effects, no thunderbolts or lightning flashes, to startle him into realising who she really was.

'Effie, before I forget,' said Rita. She began rummaging through her handbag, a vast pink leather affair with gold elephants appliquéd around the base. 'Friday the fourth, make sure you get the night off.' She found a wad of invitations, flipped through them and handed Effie hers. 'Our silver wedding, we're having a bit of a bash,' Rita explained for Poppy's benefit. Gazing proudly across at Alex she went on, 'Twenty-five years, can you believe it? And we're as happy now as we ever was. I tell you, I wouldn't be without this gorgeous man, not for the world . . .'

'She adores him,' Poppy said gloomily.

It was midnight, they had caught a taxi home and met up with Caspar on the doorstep. Caspar had been out to dinner with a leathery Australian heiress called Darlene; since she had bought five of his paintings last night he had felt duty-bound to accept her invitation. The one for dinner, anyway.

'Darlene the Dingo?' Realising he'd come out without his key, Caspar waited for Claudia to unlock the front door. 'I know she adores me. I just don't want to sleep with someone who looks as if she might howl—'

'Not Darlene,' said Claudia. 'This woman we met tonight. Her name's Rita.' She paused for effect. 'She's Alex Fitzpatrick's wife.'

'Oh dear,' said Caspar when Poppy had run briefly through the events of the evening. 'I see why you didn't blurt it out. How to wreck twenty-five years of happy marriage in one minute flat.'

'Can you imagine?' Poppy sighed. 'The stupid thing is, they're such a . . . a *couple*, I don't think I could tell just him. They don't seem the type to keep secrets from each other. It wouldn't be fair.'

'If he's your father,' Caspar pointed out, 'he kept quiet enough about what he got up to with your mother.'

'I know, I know. But that was over twenty years ago.' Poppy realised she was instinctively defending Alex Fitzpatrick. 'Maybe he and Rita were going through a rocky patch. The thing is, they're happy now.'

'So what are they like?' asked Caspar as the living-room door opened and Claudia came in with a tray of coffee.

Poppy looked at Claudia.

'Go on. You tell him what they're like.'

'Oh . . . nice.'

Claudia did her best to sound as if she meant it. Personally she would have run a mile, if not several thousand, had Alex and Rita Fitzpatrick turned out to be related to her. But she was damned if she was going to give Poppy the chance to call her a snob.

'Is that it?' Caspar was waiting for more. 'Just . . . nice?'

'Well, charming,' Claudia floundered. 'And friendly . . . yes, friendly. Um . . .'

'Common as muck,' Poppy added, to be helpful. 'It's okay, you can say it. Dripping with the kind of jewellery you buy on market stalls. Loud. Liberace meets *EastEnders*, you know the kind of thing. And they know how to drink. He doesn't look like me but he definitely is the one. When he laughs – no, just *before* he laughs, he reminds me of me.' She swallowed, looking away as her eyes welled with unexpected tears. 'It feels so strange. He's my dad. I really have found him at last.'

91

'The thing is,' said Caspar, 'is he going to find you?'

'Bleeding caterers,' Rita grumbled the following Monday. 'Been and had a bust-up, haven't we? I told 'em last week I wanted one of them hollow cakes with a girl jumping out the top and they said no problem, they was all "Yes modom, no modom". Then this afternoon this poncy woman phones up and tells me they can't do it after all.' She lit a cigarette and heaved a sigh. 'So I told them to stuff their vol-au-vents, we'd get another firm to do the job. Boy, was Alex mad with me. He says serve me right if I end up having to do the bleeding lot meself.'

'It's short notice.' Poppy's brain was working overtime. This knees-up of Alex and Rita's was being held at their home in the East End of London. Poppy had a vivid mental image of the house, a modest two-up, two-down bulging with sixties' memorabilia to match Rita's clothes. Nothing exotic, that was for sure. Rita didn't go out to work and Alex played at the Cavendish because he loved it, not for the money it brought him. It was a standing joke in the club that the bar staff earned more than the band.

Poppy didn't care about that but she was burning with curiosity to see her father's home for herself. This could be my big chance, she thought. So long as Kenda's Kitchen didn't turn its delicate nose up at the idea of bridge rolls and bits-on-sticks for fifty in not-very-glamorous Bethnal Green.

'I work for a firm of caterers.' Poppy searched her jacket pockets and by some miracle came across one of Kenda's elegant dark blue and gold business cards. They were forever being urged to press them upon likely customers. Well, now she was. 'I know it sounds a bit posh but they're all right really. And there's a chance they may be able to fit you in. Shall I give them a quick ring and ask?'

Kenda answered the phone herself. She had a fluty, up-market voice that sounded like panpipes. Poppy asked if they could take on a booking for this Friday, raising her own voice to make herself heard above the music in the club.

'You'll have to speak up,' twittered Kenda, 'goodness, what a racket. But yes, we can manage Friday . . . there's been a cancellation. What would the client's requirements be?'

'She can do it.' Poppy turned with relief to Rita. 'She wants to know the kind of food you need.'

'Here, let me have a word.' Rita took over the phone and began to bellow down it. Poppy imagined Kenda cringing genteelly at the other end. 'Okay love? Top of the range we're after. Best you've got. Forty quid a head? Yeah, sounds about right. And numbers . . . ooh, to be on the safe side, make it two hundred and fifty.'

Caspar arrived at the club at eleven o'clock to give Poppy a lift home. He found her still shell-shocked.

'Two hundred and fifty times forty,' Poppy said numbly before Rita teetered back from the loo in her fake leopardskin high heels. 'I keep getting my noughts crossed. Is it . . .?'

'Ten grand.'

'Ten grand,' echoed Poppy. 'Hell's bells.'

'Why?' He looked amused. 'Have you been betting on the horses? Is this money you've lost or won? Careful how you answer that – I may have to ask you to marry me.'

'Sshh, can't tell you now.' Poppy elbowed him in the ribs. Rita was heading towards them. 'Here she is. And Alex is over there . . . up on the stage, purple waistcoat . . .'

'Honestly, Poppy,' Caspar chided as he drove her home, 'you are hopeless. You *and* Claudia. Couldn't you tell those diamonds were real?'

'Just don't tell Jake.' Poppy pulled a face. Jake had spent countless hours patiently teaching her the difference between clever imitations and the real McCoy. How stupid of her to assume that such vast chunks of gold and such super-sparkly stones had to be fakes.

Caspar grinned. 'You know what this means, don't you? All the evidence points to it.'

As far as Claudia was concerned it was the greatest sin of all. Her lip invariably curled in disdain whenever she uttered the dreaded words.

'Aaargh,' gasped Poppy, clutching her mouth in horror, '*nouveau riche.*'

Chapter 15

Caspar wondered idly if it had ever occurred to Claudia that she might be the product of *nouveau riche*-ness herself. After all, Hugo Slade-Welch had struggled as an actor for years before hitting the serious big-time. Thanks to intensive voice training and rather distinguished good looks he had cornered the market in David Niven-ish roles but he made no secret of having worked during those tough early years as a coal miner, a debt collector and a bricklayer's mate. Even Angie, before Claudia had been born, was rumoured to have been pressed briefly into service as a waitress in a transport café in order to make ends meet.

The difference, Caspar supposed, was that Hugo and Angie both looked and sounded as if they had been born into privileged lifestyles. They had good taste, they always knew which knife and fork to use and they wore exquisite clothes.

Well, most of the time.

Angie was draped across the bed, her golden body bathed in sunlight. She lay in a semi-reclining position with one arm flung above her head and the other resting on the pile of tasselled pillows beside her. One foot dangled lazily over the side of the bed. As middle-aged bodies went, hers was pretty much flawless. And Angie knew it.

'What are you thinking?' she purred.

'I hate that question.'

This was an understatement; it was one of Caspar's least favourite questions in the world. It was what girlfriends always seemed to start saying when they sensed they were on the way out. It was a bad sign and Kate had been asking it for the past fortnight. She had begun complaining wistfully that his mind always seemed to be elsewhere then looking terrified in case she was right. The trouble was, the more she said it, the more Caspar knew she would have to go.

Angie, who didn't fall into the category of about-to-be-discarded girlfriend, simply grinned.

'In that case,' she said unperturbed, 'why don't I tell you what I'm thinking instead?'

'Go on.' Caspar tried to look as if he didn't know what was coming next.

'I think we've waited long enough.' Mindful of the fact that he was putting the finishing touches to her upper half, Angie didn't move a muscle. All she did was smile. 'I think it's about time we got to know each other better. I think,' she added with a delicately raised eyebrow, 'it's time you joined me on this bed.'

To be fair, she had exceeded his expectations. Caspar had expected her to make her move much earlier than this, but here they were, five sittings down and only one to go. He was impressed.

'Look, thanks, but I can't.'

It was a toss-up which of them looked more surprised. Caspar even had the grace to blush. The dreaded N-word wasn't something that featured too strongly in his vocabulary.

As if realising that he might have a bit of trouble with it, Angie said, 'You mean you're turning me down? You're saying *no*?'

'Mmm.' Caspar frowned and pretended to concentrate on the canvas. Good grief, no wonder he'd never tried it before. Saying no was awful. It was embarrassing.

It was the last time he listened to Poppy too. This was what happened when you listened to a girl whose favourite film was *The Sound of Music*.

'Why don't you want to?' Angie sounded annoyed. 'What's wrong, am I the problem? Or is it you?' Her eyes narrowed, her tone grew scathing. 'What exactly do you mean by can't?'

Caspar gritted his teeth. Having aspersions cast on one's ability to perform was something else new to him.

'I'm not impotent if that's what you're getting at.'

Angie was really offended now. Rejection was bad enough on its own. To be buck-naked *and* rejected was the complete pits.

'So it's me,' she said flatly, although she still didn't see how it could be. Not with a body this perfect.

'Of course it's not you.' Caspar glanced at his paint-splattered watch. 'It's somebody else.'

'Not that clingy girlfriend of yours, the one who always looks as if she's just seen a ghost.'

'Not Kate.' He was damned if he was going to tell her it was Poppy.

'Who then?'

Thank goodness time was up. Caspar stepped away from the easel and began cleaning his brushes even more thoroughly than usual.

'Who?' persisted Angie, climbing irritably off the bed and into her discarded clothes. '*Who*?'

It was funny how fast you could go off people. In the space of a few minutes any lingering desire he might have felt for her had simply evaporated.

'What a coincidence,' said Caspar, wishing she would hurry up and leave, 'I hate that question too.'

Poppy hadn't spoken to anyone from Bristol for months. Finally, testing the water, she posted a birthday card off to Dina with her new phone number written inside. If she didn't hear anything back she would know she was still persona non grata and about as popular as bubonic plague.

The moment the card dropped through the letter box Dina was on the phone.

'You didn't even tell me you were leaving!' she screeched. 'I thought we were friends and all you did was bugger off

97

without a word. Poppy, how *could* you? Did you seriously think I wouldn't be on your side?'

In a word, yes. Poppy looked out of the window at a young girl pushing a pram across the road. She and Dina had got on well enough together but this was largely because of the McBride connection. It wasn't as if they'd been best friends since school or anything dramatic like that.

'Sorry,' said Poppy. 'I suppose I didn't imagine anyone would be on my side.'

'Thanks a lot!' Dina raised her voice to be heard above an infant wail. 'Shows how much you know. If I hadn't been stuck in that sodding hospital with me legs up in stirrups I'd have been round like a shot.'

Since Margaret McBride was an intimidating mother-in-law, this sounded a lot like bravado to Poppy.

'You'd have *been* shot, that's for sure.' She didn't bear any grudges. If she'd been Dina she'd have taken the easy option and gone into labour too. 'So, catch me up on all the gossip. How is everyone? How's that noisy baby of yours?'

'Oh, *he's* all right. I'm the one tearing my hair out.'

Poppy was sympathetic. 'Is he terribly hard work?'

'No. I just think I'm going to have to kill Margaret. Margaret-I-know-best-McBride.' Dina heaved a sigh that sounded as if it had been held in for weeks. 'Poppy, I mean it. You have no idea how lucky you are. You got out in the nick of time. She is the mother-in-law from hell, and if she tells me one more time how I *should* be burping, feeding, changing, washing and kissing my own child –' Dina's voice rose to a frenzied wail – 'I swear I'll boil the interfering old battle-axe in baby oil.'

Phew. Poppy, sitting in the window seat, hugged her legs and decided she had indeed had a lucky escape.

'Anyway,' Dina went on, apparently recovered, 'everyone else is fine. Rob's going steady with a nurse. Her name's Alison. Fat ankles, but she's okay. Ben's all right but he's working all the time so I hardly see him. Susie and Jen are the same as ever. I'm a bit bored with them, actually. Um, that's about it, there isn't really much else to tell you.'

Poor Dina. Not having a thrilling time, all in all. Poppy wondered idly what Alison looked like apart from the ankles and whether she and Rob would get married. She wondered if he would risk a second attempt and hoped he would.

'Oh, Mum said she saw your father in Debenhams the other day, arm in arm with Beryl Bridges. They were looking at duvet covers,' Dina related with glee, 'and they looked dead embarrassed when Mum said hello.'

Beryl had been widowed two years ago. She did tons of voluntary work and was an enthusiastic churchgoer. Maybe, thought Poppy, her father would marry again too, now he had the house to himself.

Except he wasn't her father.

Poppy debated telling Dina that she had tracked down the real one and decided against it. Dina was such a blabbermouth. Besides, it hardly seemed fair when Alex Fitzgerald wasn't even aware of it himself.

'You know what I need?' Dina declared with an air of recklessness. 'I need to get away from here. I need a break, even if it's just a few days.'

Poppy realised where this was leading. Subtlety had never been Dina's strong point.

'How about that cousin of yours, the one in Blackpool?' she suggested. 'You and Ben and the baby could have a long weekend up there.'

'Oh, thanks a bunch,' Dina groaned, 'why don't I invite Margaret and all the rest of the sodding McBrides along while I'm at it? Poppy, they're the ones I need a break *from*. Ben included! All this happy families stuff is suffocating me. I've got to get out of Bristol . . .' This was it; this was what she'd been building up to. '. . . pleeease, Poppy, I'm desperate! And we're friends, aren't we? Be a doll. Say I can come and stay with you.'

'Dina, I would if I could. But I can't,' said Poppy. 'This

isn't my house. I can hardly ask Caspar to put up a friend and a baby—'

'No baby,' Dina responded like a shot, 'just me. Margaret'll be in seventh heaven,' she added caustically, 'having Daniel all to herself for a few days. Bloody old witch.'

She really was hell-bent on escape.

'The thing is,' Poppy prevaricated, 'my room's only tiny.'

'And who am I, two-ton Tess? All I'm asking for is a bit of floor space.' Dina was wheedling now. 'I'll sleep under the bed if it makes you happier. In the bath, even.'

'Well . . . I'll have to ask Caspar first.'

'Ask Caspar what?' said Caspar, pushing open the sitting-room door with his knee. His arms were full of canvases as yet unprimed. 'If it's "I'll have to ask Caspar if he'd like a cup of tea and a Marmite sandwich", the answer's yes.'

'Who's that?' Dina was all ears at the other end of the phone. 'Your landlord? Ask him now. Go on.'

Poppy was torn. Sorry though she felt for Dina, she didn't really want to be the one held responsible for whatever she might get up to. Dina's wild streak, tempered recently by marriage and motherhood, was clearly wrestling its way back to the surface. Poppy dreaded to think what the McBride mafia would have to say if they knew who was putting Dina up.

'Ask me what?' repeated Caspar, dumping the blank canvases on the sofa.

Dither, dither . . .

'I know what I forgot to tell you,' Dina cried, playing her triumphant ace. 'Guess who I bumped into at the club the other week? That chap of yours, the one with the dark curly hair.'

Saliva turned to sawdust in Poppy's mouth. She stared at her bare toes, pressed against the sash window frame. She wished Caspar wasn't there, shamelessly eavesdropping. She couldn't believe Dina had waited until now to mention it.

'Which chap?'

'You know, the dishy doctor who couldn't keep his hands off you.' Dina gurgled raucously down the phone. 'Well, your foot anyway. Come on, you remember! Couple of dances, couple of snogs and the next day you cancelled your wedding. *That* chap with the dark curly hair—'

'I did *not* snog him,' Poppy blurted the words out without thinking.

Caspar looked up in amazement.

Dina sounded gleeful. 'So you do know who I mean.'

'Did you . . . um, did you speak to him?'

'Hang on a sec, how completely weird, I can't remember.'

Dina was smirking, Poppy just knew it.

'Of course you remember.'

'Nope, it's gone.' Brightly, Dina said, 'Mind's a blank, a complete blank . . .'

Blackmail, how outrageous. Poppy sighed and turned to Caspar.

'Is it okay if a friend comes to stay for a couple of days?'

'A few days,' Dina corrected. 'Make it a few.' She giggled. 'I'll need time to get over the jet lag.'

'Of course.' Caspar was still stunned by the earlier mention of snogging. 'Of course it's okay.'

'So what's she like?' he asked when Poppy had hung up the phone. 'My type?'

Poppy wished Dina could have said something a bit more informative than a cheery 'I'll tell you when I see you.' She wanted to know *now* what Tom had said.

'Well,' demanded Caspar, '*is* she my type?'

Men. Poppy gave him a look. 'She's got a husband and a baby.'

Privately she thought that in her present mood Dina would be anybody's type.

'Talking of babies, I'll tell you what's really amazing,' said Caspar. 'Angie Slade-Welch. That woman actually gave birth to Claudia . . . and I swear she has no stretch marks at all.'

101

'Well, you'd know.'

Honestly, Poppy thought, how come everyone else seems to be so much more brazen than me? Am I abnormally repressed?

'It's my job to know.'

'And is she as great in bed as you expected her to be?' The words slipped out. She hadn't meant to ask. She didn't even *want* to know, for heaven's sake.

'No idea.' Caspar looked innocent. Then he grinned. 'Our relationship is purely professional.'

'And if you believe that,' said Poppy, 'you'll believe anything.'

Chapter 16

Poppy had braced herself beforehand but Alex and Rita's home still came as a shock when she saw it for the first time. In the dank back streets of Bethnal Green it stood out like a wolfhound among terriers, a wolfhound with a diamond-studded collar at that.

This was Southfork with sequins, Poppy realised. The house was immense. There was a chandelier the size of a hot-air balloon in the downstairs loo.

She couldn't help wondering where the money for all this had come from. Was her father a member of the infamous East End underworld? Was he a drugs baron? A porn king? Oh help, Poppy thought nervously, I hope it isn't anything too sordid—

'Chop-chop,' said Kenda, in her element as she bustled past. 'No daydreaming. Poppy, back onto this planet please. Stop wishing your rich friends could adopt you and get on with folding those napkins. Janet, straighten your apron. And Claire, get those ice buckets filled. I said stop daydreaming, Poppy—'

'Sorry.' Poppy bent her head and set to work but there were so many thoughts whizzing around her brain it was hard to concentrate on napkins. Apart from anything else, Kenda had just hit a particularly pointed nail on the head.

Poppy began to wish she hadn't come here. Seeing for herself just how rich Alex Fitzpatrick really was only made matters more complicated than they were already.

Until today her reason for not telling him who she really was had been Rita.

Now, Poppy knew she definitely couldn't say anything. If she did she would look like a fortune-hunter, desperate to cash in on the fact that the father she had never known had somehow managed to end up rolling in it. Alex would think she had only turned up to demand her rightful share.

If it was rightful. But . . . how *had* he made so much?

Behind her, Janet and Claire were discussing British Rail sandwiches. Poppy hoped her father wasn't one of the Great Train Robbers.

'There's a swimming pool outside you wouldn't believe,' said one of the other waitresses on her way back from unloading the second van. 'It's big enough to float a yacht on.'

Poppy hoped her father wasn't anything to do with Robert Maxwell. She hoped he wasn't Robert Maxwell reincarnated.

'Right now everyone, let's start carrying the food through to the dining room,' instructed Kenda. 'Smoothly and efficiently please, before the guests begin to arrive. And I know I don't need to remind you of this,' she added with a steely glimmer in her eyes, 'but I trust everyone will behave in a professional manner.'

Poppy flushed on Alex's behalf. What Kenda meant was no behind-the-back smirking at either the decor, the guests or Alex and Rita themselves. They might not live in Belgravia but they were paying an arm and a leg for the services of Kenda's Kitchen tonight. Kenda, who had been battling the recession along with everyone else, could do with a few more like them on her client list. She wasn't going to risk offending the Fitzpatricks or any one of their less than salubrious guests.

'Got you slaving, has she?'

Poppy grinned as Rita whispered the words not very subtly into her ear. 'What's she like then, this Kenda with the posh voice? Bit of a bossyboots, am I right?'

'Well, strict,' said Poppy, 'but fair.' Struggling to be loyal, she added, 'These things need a lot of organising. Someone has to be in control.'

'In control.' Rita rolled her eyes. 'Yeah, I can just see her in a leather basque and high heels, going, "You do as I say, you naughty boy", and beating her hubby with a bloody great whip.'

So much for everyone being on their best behaviour and not smirking at the Fitzpatricks, thought Poppy. Poor Kenda, if she knew she was being made fun of by Rita she would be appalled.

For tonight's party Rita was wearing a violet lamé dress with a seriously plunging neckline and high-heeled gold sandals. A couple of extra blasts on the high-velocity sunbed had deepened her tan and yesterday's trip to the hairdresser had resulted in a baby-pink tint on top of the blondeness. Her eye make-up, a symphony of pinks and mauves, matched her nail polish. Around her brown neck hung a new necklace studded with sapphires.

'Like it?' Rita saw Poppy's gaze linger on the necklace. Proudly she ran her fingers over the raised stones. 'Twenty-five sapphires, one for each year we been married. Alex designed it himself, got a jeweller mate of his to make the necklace up.'

Maybe Alex was a diamond smuggler. This possibility rather appealed to Poppy; it had a romantic ring to it. She knew she should be circulating with trays of food but her curiosity was threatening to get the better of her. She had spent the last two hours eavesdropping as frantically as she could, to no avail. The guests, a wide mix of down-to-earth Cockneys and members of the Cavendish jazz crowd, weren't telling her what she wanted to know.

Poppy had only the haziest of ideas when it came to property valuation but the house alone must have cost a million. Then there was the bright red Rolls Royce with the personalised plates out on the drive . . . goodness, you'd have to smuggle an awful lot of diamonds to support a lifestyle like this.

It was no good, she had to ask.

'Rita . . . I hope this isn't an incredibly rude question . . .'

'Mmm?' Rita's attention was being drawn elsewhere. At the other end of the room Alex and his band had launched into a rousing, jazzed-up version of 'Knees Up Mother Brown'. Suddenly everyone was dancing. Rita was clearly dying to rush over and join in.

'It's just, this house.' Having started, Poppy felt compelled to finish. 'Um . . . I couldn't help wondering where the money . . . I mean, it must have cost a fortune . . .'

Alex was belting out the chorus on his Bechstein. Everyone sang along. Rita, gazing in adoration at him, said, 'Sorry, what?'

'You and Alex,' Poppy shouted above the noise of the music. 'How did you GET SO RICH?'

'Mrs Fitzpatrick, I'm so sorry,' murmured Kenda, gripping Poppy's elbow with such force she felt her funny bone start to go. Smiling fixedly at Rita, Kenda wheeled Poppy round and propelled her in the direction of the kitchen.

'What in heaven's name do you think you're playing at?' She hissed the words, bullet-like, into Poppy's ear, as shocked as if Poppy had been asking how they'd caught syphilis. 'What did I say earlier about professional behaviour? I warn you, Poppy, you're treading a very fine line. Any more of this nonsense and you are *out*.'

Poppy did as she was told. She returned to the kitchen, armed herself with two fresh trays of devils on horseback and spent the next twenty minutes dutifully offering them around.

Then she watched one of the other musicians take over at the piano. Alex, kissing Rita's hand, led her into the centre of the room. Cheered on by the noisier guests he made a short speech thanking everyone for being with them tonight and Rita in particular for marrying him in the first place. Then they danced together to 'If You Were The Only Girl In The World'. Everyone whistled and applauded before piling back onto the dance floor themselves.

'What did you *do*?' whispered Janet as she passed Poppy going in the other direction. 'Kenda's blowing a gasket. She asked me if you were on drugs.'

'Honestly.' Poppy sighed. 'From the way she's going on, you'd think I'd been spitting in the soup.'

Janet said, 'If you had, you wouldn't be the first.'

Poppy carried on serving. Physically she was doing her job but mentally she was checking out every detail of the house. As much as she dared, anyway; she was going to get some pretty funny looks if she started rummaging through the cupboards under the stairs.

Still, she was seeing enough to get the idea. At a guess, a team of top-class interior designers had been called in. They had organised, amongst other things, the elegant pleated curtains, the concealed lighting, the dado rails and the white Italian marble kitchen. Rita and Alex had said how lovely, so as not to hurt the design team's fragile feelings. Then the moment they'd left, they had set to work putting their own personal stamp on the place.

Brightly patterned rugs were strewn around, probably to cheer up the tasteful taupe carpet. Even brighter lampshades, frilled and fringed to distraction, were perched on imitation Oscar lampstands. Ornaments thronged every available surface. There was enough Capo di Monte to stock a factory. Huge gilt-framed photographs of Alex and Rita hung on every wall.

One of the doors off the wood-panelled hall led into a library with no books but plenty of videos in imitation leather covers. There was also a cinema-sized television screen. The black leather sofa in front of it was piled high with fluffy toys. An oil painting of a liquid-eyed spaniel hung over the fireplace. Another, of Elvis, adorned the opposite wall.

Goodness, Claudia would sneer if she could see this. Poppy glanced down at the shag pile carpet, deep enough to need mowing. It wasn't her own taste but she felt oddly comfortable in the room. Alex and Rita had furnished it to suit no one but themselves. Which was, really, how homes should be furnished.

The door swung open behind her and Poppy jumped, guiltily aware that she had no business being in here.

'Aha,' purred a male voice, 'caught you.'

A stray remote control had been buried in the depths of the shag pile at Poppy's feet. When she jumped, she unwittingly turned the video recorder on. A naked couple romping together in bed appeared up on the giant television screen. Poppy went scarlet, dumped her tray of canapés on the gilt-embossed coffee table and grabbed the remote control. A million buttons later she managed to find Off.

'No need to look so shocked.' Her male intruder was grinning from ear to ear. 'Nothing wrong with a bit of nookie between consenting adults. All in favour of it, myself.'

Poppy remembered serving him earlier when she had been passing round the smoked salmon parcels. He was in his thirties, she guessed, with gelled-back hair, a reddish complexion and confident, wide-boy smile. He was wearing a well-cut grey suit, the jacket lined with bright blue silk. A mobile phone stuck out of his pocket. He was well-built but not particularly tall and spoke rapidly, like a stock market trader, with a slight London accent.

'Hey, hey, not so fast,' he said as Poppy seized her tray and attempted to breeze past him. He put out an arm to stop her. 'We can carry on watching together. Come on, sit down, take the weight off your feet. Let me have that remote control . . . hey, *relax*, I said . . .'

Poppy gave up on breezing. Breezing wasn't going to do the trick. This chap was one of those take-what-you-want types and his arm was tightening around her waist like a boa constrictor. Now she remembered he was the one who'd been drinking champagne out of a half-pint glass. He was drunker than he looked. Grinning triumphantly he flipped Poppy's silver tray over, catapulting two dozen angels on horseback in all directions. She felt his hot breath on her face as he yanked her towards him. There were bits of spit at the corners of his mouth. At such close quarters the smell of hair gel was overpowering.

'Let go of me,' said Poppy. Feeling wimpish, she added, 'Please.'

'Whoa, no need to panic! Nobody else is coming in here. I noticed you earlier, y'know. I like redheads. Sweetheart, sweetheart, stop fighting it! I fancy you, you fancy me. How about a little kiss to get us warmed up?'

'No.' Poppy hesitated. What would Kenda want her to say? 'No . . . thank you very much.'

He grew more insistent. The grip around her waist tightened another couple of notches. 'Just a little kiss. Don't be a spoilsport. This is what parties are all about, a bit of fun—'

Breezing was by this time out of the question. Poppy was hemmed in, pinned firmly against a black and gold lacquered sideboard with a heavy crystal whisky decanter on it, together with six matching tumblers. She felt behind her, located the neck of the decanter and picked it up. Heavens, it was even heavier than she'd thought.

'Please let me go.'

'Are you kidding?' He laughed, his mouth approaching hers, his left hand zooming in on her right breast. 'Just as we're getting to know each other at last? Baby, don't you know how to *have* fun—?'

It seemed an awful waste of whisky. It was bound to be a blended malt. Still, Poppy decided, better this way than a whack over the head with several hundred quid's worth of lead crystal. Less brain-damaging at least.

She tipped the contents of the decanter over his ultra-gelled hair. Glug, glug, glug . . . within seconds he was drenched from head to foot.

'Sorry,' said Poppy as he let out a bellow of rage. Next moment the library door was pushed open and Alex appeared.

He stared at Poppy with the empty decanter still in her hand. He looked at his whisky-soaked guest. Then he examined the sole of his left shoe and discovered one of the scattered angels on horseback clinging to his heel.

'Hmm.' Alex glanced with regret at the puddle of whisky sinking into the carpet around the other man's feet.

'Sorry.' This time Poppy meant it.

'No need. I can guess what happened. Derek been up to his usual tricks, has he?'

'She was begging for it,' Derek said irritably. 'I'm telling you, begging for it.'

'You always say that. You always *think* that.' Alex sounded resigned. He turned to Poppy. 'He's just a lech. Predictable too. As soon as I heard the racket I guessed he'd done it again. Are you all right, pet?'

Poppy nodded. Moments later she stopped being all right. Like a traffic warden turning up just when you'd parked somewhere clampable, Kenda loomed in the doorway.

'Right,' she said, taking in the scene far more swiftly than Alex had done and drawing her own tight-lipped conclusions, 'that is IT, Poppy. You have brought disgrace upon Kenda's Kitchen. I warned you earlier. I gave you every chance.' She paused. The performance was as much for Alex's sake as Poppy's. Clients who spent, spent, spent like the Fitzpatricks deserved nothing but the best. 'Your behaviour tonight has been abysmal,' she concluded rigidly. 'You are fired.'

Bugger, thought Poppy.

'Don't look at me,' said Derek, even though nobody was. 'It ain't my fault. She asked for it. Look at the state of my flamin' suit.'

'Please,' Alex said reasonably, turning to Kenda, 'there's no need to sack anyone. Derek's pretty tanked. He got carried away, that's all. Polly had to defend herself. She couldn't let herself be slobbered over, could she, without putting up a bit of a fight?'

'Poppy,' said Poppy, feeling hurt that he hadn't even

remembered her name. 'Not Polly. It's Poppy.'

'Sorry love.' Alex winked, then returned his attention to Kenda. 'Come on, give the girl a break. You don't really want to kick her out into the snow.'

'I'm afraid I have no other choice,' Kenda replied with an air of finality. She looked at Poppy. 'And before you leave you can clear up this appalling mess.'

There were angels on horseback everywhere. Bits of oysters and strips of smoked bacon were strewn across the shag pile. One oyster had landed on top of the framed painting of Elvis.

It *was* an appalling mess. Poppy prayed the carpet wasn't ruined beyond repair. She picked up the silver tray, bent down and began picking the oysters out of the carpet.

'Stop it.' Alex reached down, seizing her by the elbow. He pulled Poppy to her feet and gave her arm a reassuring squeeze. 'You don't have to do that. If you ask me, this woman here's been bloody rude to you. Well out of order.'

'I . . . I . . .' stammered Poppy.

'And if she's giving you the boot anyway, I reckon you ought to let her pick up her own sodding oysters. Why should you do it,' Alex demanded, 'if she's already sacked you? Tell the old cow to get stuffed.'

Poppy hadn't cried when she'd cancelled her wedding. She hadn't cried when she'd made the discovery that her father wasn't her father. She hadn't even cried the other night when Caspar had raided the freezer and pinched her last Magnum.

'There. *Now* see what you've done.' Alex pointed an accusing finger at Kenda. His identity bracelet glittered in the light. 'And you wouldn't even listen to her side of the story.'

Poppy wasn't crying because she'd lost her job. She was crying because her father had his arm around her. He was comforting her, defending her, just as a real father should. It was a feeling Poppy had never experienced before and she'd never realised until now how much she had been missing out on.

Since she didn't have a cold, Poppy didn't have a hanky. Alex whisked a red and white spotted one out of his waistcoat pocket and shoved it into her hand.

Derek, still dripping whisky, grunted something about a change of clothes and disappeared.

'Good riddance to him,' said Alex. 'Silly sod. His old lady'll give him what for when she sees the state of him.'

'I'll send one of the other girls in,' Kenda announced coldly. 'To clear up.'

'It's all right.' Poppy sniffed loudly and wiped her eyes with the spotted hanky. 'I'll do it.'

'Are you going to give this girl her job back?' demanded Alex.

'No, I am not.'

'Right then,' Alex said as he turned Poppy in the direction of the door, 'you're coming with me. What you need is a drink.'

Chapter 17

'I was going to ask if you're feeling better now, but I don't think there's much point,' said Alex.

Poppy was panting for breath, having danced non-stop for the past twenty minutes with a beaming barrel of a clarinet player called Buzz.

'Now I know how to jive,' she gasped. Buzz had to be in his early fifties. Who would have thought someone so old would be so amazingly mobile? Even now he hadn't stopped but had deposited Poppy on the arm of a chair and begun twirling Rita around the floor instead.

'Look at my girl,' said Alex, watching the pair of them with pride.

For someone who must get through forty fags a day Rita was doing pretty well herself. Her cocktail dress flared alarmingly out at the waist as Buzz launched her into a spin.

'Come on, have another drink.' Alex waved a bottle over Poppy's nearly-empty glass.

She let him pour.

'Thanks for sticking up for me earlier,' said Poppy. 'And for letting me stay on.' It was almost midnight. Kenda and the others had done their duty and left in the vans. Relations between Kenda and Alex had been frosty to say the least.

'Hang on, before I forget.' Alex dug in his pocket and pulled out a handful of crumpled notes. He passed Poppy a couple of tenners. 'For your cab home, seeing as you've missed your lift. We're carrying on for a few hours yet, mind. Not planning on having an early night, were you?

Not about to go and do a Cinderella on us?'

'What, and risk losing one of these elegant glass slippers?' Poppy waggled her black shoes, which were flat and sensible to match the plain white shirt and black skirt worn by all Kenda's employees. The female ones, anyway.

Alex looked appalled. 'You poor kid, I didn't think! How can you relax and enjoy yourself like that, stuck in that stupid uniform when everyone else is dinked up? Here –' he grabbed her arm and pulled her towards the door – 'come on, the least we can do is lend you something decent. Rita won't mind. Just have a rummage and pick out whatever you want.'

They were up the winding staircase, along the endless landing and into the master bedroom before Poppy could even think of a tactful reply. The bedroom, which had to be forty feet square, was lined with mirror-fronted walk-in wardrobes. The carpet was fluffier, thicker and whiter than Pekinese fur. Arranged along every window sill were yet more soft toys.

'Go on, help yourself,' Alex urged, plonking himself down on the rippling water bed as Poppy gazed helplessly at row upon row of Rita's clothes. 'Anything you like. Don't worry, it's good stuff. And it's all clean.'

Poppy pulled out the plainest dress she could see, of royal blue taffeta with long sleeves, an over-sized Peter Pan collar and a scalloped hem. It was a couple of sizes too big but the style of the dress meant it wouldn't matter too much. And unlike all the pinks, oranges and reds Rita favoured, it wasn't going to clash alarmingly with her hair.

'Good choice,' Alex nodded his approval. 'Know what colour that is, Poppy? Bristol Blue. Like the glass. I've got a few pieces in one of the cabinets downstairs. Beautiful stuff, it is, Bristol Blue glass.'

'I know it,' said Poppy. 'I'm from Bristol. I was born there.'

'Yeah? Great place.' Alex was still lounging on the bed, propped comfortably on one elbow. His dark eyes lit up at the memory. 'I worked there once, years ago. In some poncy country club, playing in the resident band. I had a terrific time there.'

I know you did, thought Poppy. Her heart was hammering. It was now or never. She hadn't planned to say it, but how could she pass up an opportunity like this?

'What a summer that was.' Alex was half-smiling to himself. 'I'll never forget it.'

What do I say? Poppy's brain went into frantic overdrive. How do I say it? What if the shock's too much for him and he has a heart attack on the spot?

'Um . . . was that the Ash Hill Country Club?' Poppy ventured. She was trembling, she realised. Even her voice sounded shaky. At this rate she was the one heading for the heart attack.

'Ash Hill, that's the one!' Alex beamed. 'You know it?'

How about: No, but my mother was once on intimate terms with their pianist.

Or: Yes, Dad, actually I do.

Poppy practised the words in her head and chickened out. Her cowardly tongue had superglued itself to her teeth. How about if she could think of a less corny way of doing it? What if she just went for total simplicity and said, 'Look, Laura Dunbar was my mother.'

'L-look,' Poppy stammered, struggling frantically to free her tongue from her teeth. 'L-L-L—'

'There you are!' cried Rita, materialising in the doorway. Still barefoot, neither of them had heard her approach. 'Buzz said he saw the two of you disappearing upstairs.'

'It was Alex's idea. To stop me looking like a waitress.' Awash with guilt and praying Rita wouldn't leap to the wrong conclusions, Poppy held up the blue dress.

'I said you wouldn't mind,' Alex put in equably.

' 'Course I don't mind.' Rita sounded outraged by the suggestion. 'But that dull old thing? Are you sure?'

The dull old thing had the kind of designer label Poppy

had only read about in magazines. Her fingers curled around the padded silk hanger. 'Oh, it's great.'

'Well, I'll leave you girls to it.' Alex ambled out, patting Rita's generous backside as he went.

Poppy slithered gratefully out of her uniform. Rita sat at her Hollywood-style dressing table and primped. She glanced at Poppy's reflection in the mirror.

'I'm worried about you.'

'Me? Why?' Poppy was wearing a pale blue cotton bra and orange pants. She put the expensive dress on quickly, before Rita could change her mind about lending it to someone with such deeply unworthy underwear.

'Losing your job. I feel responsible.'

'Don't be! I'll be fine, really—'

'Bloody Derek, he's such a prat.' Rita whisked an extra layer of blusher onto her cheeks with a huge brush. Indulgently she said, 'I don't know, suppose it runs in the family.'

Eek! Poppy's blood ran cold. She hoped she hadn't just been snogged by her uncle.

'You mean he's related to Alex?'

Rita had begun vigorously Ultraglowing her neck and cleavage. She let out a bellow of laughter.

'Good job he didn't hear you say that! I meant *my* family, love. Derek's a cousin of mine. Been a prat all his life, too. Ow, I knew I should've given that jiving a miss.'

Poppy watched Rita flex her left knee as if it hurt.

'You were dancing like a pro. I was impressed.'

'Yeah, and it'll give me gyp tomorrow.' Rita carried on massaging the area below her knee. 'I broke my leg a long time ago. In three places. Nasty business it was.'

Of course, the fateful break. Poppy wondered what would have happened if Rita hadn't had her accident. Alex wouldn't have needed to rush back to London, her mother would have told him she was pregnant . . . who knows? He might have decided to stay with Laura after all. He might have divorced

Rita and married her mother instead. And I, thought Poppy, would have had a whole different life, an unimaginably different life . . .

'You're miles away, love.'

'I was. Sorry.' Poppy shook her head and grinned. What had Rita been talking about? Oh yes, the leg. 'I bet it put you off hanging baskets for life.'

Rita looked at her strangely.

'How on earth did you know that?'

Hell's bells, this was what happened when you didn't pay attention.

'You told me,' said Poppy.

'I don't remember.'

'A couple of weeks ago, at the Cavendish Club.' She improvised wildly, banking on Rita's fondness for a drink to get her out of this mess. 'I told you about Claudia setting her heart on a couple of hanging flower baskets and Caspar offering to kidnap next door's, and you said, "Bloody hanging baskets, I was nearly killed once, by a hanging basket". And then you told me about falling off the ladder and breaking your leg.'

'Blimey,' said Rita.

'It was the night you were drinking tequila slammers with Harry Osborne. You must remember that!'

'I remember the headache the next morning.' Rita pulled a face, gave her hair a one-for-the-road burst of hairspray, and stood up. 'Oh well, I'll blame Harry for that. Ready to go back down, love? The dress looks terrific.'

'This house is terrific.' Poppy seized her chance as they headed for the stairs. 'Have you lived here long?'

'Couple of years.'

It was no good, she had to ask.

'So does Alex have . . . um . . . another job?'

Rita glanced at her. 'You mean how come we're living in a place like this, Bethnal Green's answer to Buck House?'

'I know I'm being rude.' Poppy tried to look ashamed.

'I'm sorry, I'm the nosiest person I know.'

'That's all right, petal. Only natural to be curious. No mystery to it anyway,' Rita continued smoothly. 'Alex was just in the right place at the right time during the property boom.'

'Property? Buying and selling houses?'

'Yeah, that's it. Then he invested in a high-risk land deal in Spain. Three years ago the deal came off. And we woke up one morning a few million quid richer than we'd been the night before.'

The words sounded well-rehearsed, as if they'd been trotted out a few million times themselves. One thing was for sure, thought Poppy: Rita wasn't telling her the truth.

'Here we are.' Proudly, Alex steered Poppy into the drawing room where an illuminated cabinet contained his small collection of Bristol Blue glass. One shelf was occupied by a set of four goblets, three lozenge-stoppered decanters and a single spirit bottle.

Poppy recognised the spirit bottle at once. There was another one, just like it, in the house where she had grown up.

'Two hundred years old,' said Alex, 'can you credit it?'

'Cheeky bugger,' Rita retorted over his shoulder. 'I am not.' She winked at Poppy and said to Alex, 'Have you told her yet?'

'Told me what?'

'Me and Rita, we've had an idea.' He grinned. 'To make up for you losing your job.'

Poppy's heart began to race. She struggled to contain her excitement. This is it, she thought, hardly able to believe her luck, they're going to offer me work! They want to employ me as a . . . as a . . .

Poppy wasn't quite sure what, but she didn't care. She would clean, do odd jobs, mow the lawn, anything. Dammit, she'd even cook.

'Go on love, you tell her.' Rita gave Alex a nudge.

'The dress,' said Alex kindly. 'It suits you, love. We want you to have it. And no arguments; it's yours.'

Chapter 18

The last time Dina had visited London had been on a school trip to the Science Museum which had bored her stupid. The highlight of that outing had involved eyeing up another coachload of schoolboys from Birmingham, one of whom had thrown a doughnut at her in the Museum coffee shop. The lowlight had been getting a love bite on her neck from spotty Stuart Anderson on the journey home.

But that had been yonks ago, when she was just a kid. This is far more like it, Dina thought gleefully. No more stupid school uniform. No bossy Miss Wildbore, head of physics, barking at her to pay attention. No Mr Killjoy-Carter telling her to wipe off that lipstick or else.

Best of all, no baby.

'You jammy thing, have you fallen on your feet here or what?' Dina crowed with delight. She threw herself down on the sofa and gazed rapturously around the room.

Poppy knew she had to find herself another job fast if she wanted to stay here. At this rate she was going to end up a pub stripper after all.

'Never mind my feet.' She'd turn her attention to the job dilemma later. 'What did Tom say to you when you saw him?'

'Talk about uncool,' mocked Dina. 'Anyway, who said he said anything?'

'But he did.' Poppy knew Dina too well. She wouldn't have been able to resist talking to him.

'We-ell maybe. Good-looking, isn't he? All that curly hair. And those *brilliant* eyes . . .'

'I could always pull out your toenails one by one.'

Poppy was too shattered to play games. She had only managed three hours' sleep. She'd been hokey-cokeying and singing bawdy songs until five in the morning, in an haute couture dress.

Dina gave in. 'Okay. Well, I was there with Maggie and I spotted him right away. He was wearing a red and white striped shirt and white jeans. Brilliant bum, too. Well, I said "Hi" when we went past him to get to the bar and he didn't twig at first, what with me being a bit of a different shape.' Smugly, Dina patted her flat-as-a-pancake stomach. 'So I reminded him who I was and he kind of lit up and got interested. Asked me what I'd had and how the baby was getting on. Then he kind of took a deep breath and asked how you were.'

'*And*?'

'I told him nobody had heard from you for yonks. I said you'd called off the wedding and done a bunk. I'm telling you, you should have seen the look on his face . . .'

'What kind of look?' Poppy tried not to shriek. Dina was spinning this out on purpose.

'Oh, kind of . . .' Dina mimed it. 'No, hang on, maybe a bit more like . . .' She tried again, then shrugged. 'Well, pretty much gobsmacked. So I told him, then, all about you turning up at Rob's house the next morning, and how Rob wouldn't believe you when you said it was all off, and how Margaret was doing her nut and trying everything to make you change your mind because she'd never be able to live down the shame.'

'What did he say when you'd finished telling him all that? Or,' said Poppy evenly, 'was it kicking-out time by then?'

Dina looked offended. 'He said if I ever heard from you, to give you his phone number and address.'

'He *gave* them to you?'

Yes, yes! This was better than Poppy had even dared to expect. She had to control herself, sit on her hands. The temptation to frisk Dina, to rifle through her pockets for the precious information, was strong.

'He gave them to me.' Dina blinked. Nobody, thought Poppy, wore quite as much navy-blue eyeshadow as Dina.

'Well? You're here now, you can give them to *me*.'

'Except I kind of lost the piece of paper. Well, the beer mat,' gabbled Dina. 'You see, he wrote it down on the back of a beer mat and I put it in the side bit of my white handbag, the one with the chain strap. So it wasn't my fault,' she went on defensively. 'It's not as if I chucked it in a bin or something, like on purpose. It just . . . fell out of its own accord.'

'You've lost it,' Poppy echoed. Trust Dina to raise her hopes and then dash them. Anyone with a grain of compassion would never have done it like that. Anyone with an ounce of common sense, for heaven's sake, would have left out the whole bit about the beer mat.

Poppy wasn't yelling at her but Dina could tell she was upset.

'I'm sorry,' she said, looking perplexed. 'I didn't think it was that important. I mean, it wasn't as if you called off the wedding so you could run away with this chap instead, was it? You said you were never going to see him again. I didn't realise getting his number was such a big deal. You should have said.'

I hadn't realised it either, Poppy thought glumly. Until now.

When she had said goodbye to Tom that night she had still been intending to marry Rob the next day. The subject of phone numbers had deliberately not been raised because that would definitely have been tempting fate. When you felt that strongly about someone and you were marrying someone else, their phone number was a dangerous thing to know.

But she hadn't married Rob. She hadn't been able to stop thinking about Tom either.

'It's okay,' said Poppy wearily. 'You're right, it wasn't your fault. I should have said.' She heaved a sigh. 'Just, if you ever bump into him again, could you take his number and not lose it?'

'Oh, I won't,' Dina shook her head vigorously. 'Bump into him again, I mean. He told me the brother he was staying with in Bristol was on the verge of emigrating to Australia.'

'Terrific.'

'I did kind of glance at the beer mat,' Dina was trying to be helpful, 'before I put it in my bag.'

'And?' Poppy hardly dared to hope.

'It said Notty something. Maybe Nottingham. Or Notting Hill.'

'In other words,' said Poppy, 'not a clue.'

A hyperactive six-year-old would have been easier to handle than Dina. By Sunday afternoon Poppy was on her last legs and down to her last fiver in the world. On Saturday they had shopped. On Saturday night they had visited more bars and clubs than she had known existed. On Sunday morning Dina had dragged her out again, to Camden Lock market. From there they had moved on to Covent Garden. At four o'clock they arrived back at Cornwallis Crescent. Dina had to leave at six to catch the coach home.

The trouble with Dina, Poppy decided, was she looked as if she were giving every man she met a lascivious once-over. She *was* giving every man she met a lascivious once-over. The drawback was letting them know it.

But Dina was unstoppable. She had been let off her leash for the weekend and was making the most of it. London was terrific, London was glamorous. It was also teeming with men.

And she hadn't had to change a nappy once.

'That girl is so brazen,' Claudia said scornfully when Poppy had dragged Dina downstairs to pack.

'I know, isn't it great?'

Caspar loved it, of course.

123

'It is not. She hasn't stopped flirting with you since she got here. And all you're doing is encouraging her.'

He grinned. 'Is that against the law?'

'She's married,' Claudia reminded him. 'And she's got a baby.' Acidly she added, 'Somewhere.'

'So, okay, chances are she isn't a virgin.' Caspar loved teasing Claudia. It was the perfect pastime for a Sunday afternoon. Well, maybe the second most perfect.

'All this promiscuity. Don't you get tired of it?'

'I'm getting tired of being lectured to about it.' First Poppy, now Claudia. Caspar was tempted to boast about turning Angie down, but sensed her daughter might not appreciate it, seeing as she didn't know about Angie's clandestine visits to the house in the first place.

Claudia was jealous. She knew this was because she'd been going through a bit of an arid patch recently, man-wise, but it only made Caspar's lack of interest in her more hurtful. Not to mention the shaming débâcle with Jake . . .

Things just weren't going her way right now. Claudia wished she knew what she was doing wrong. She flipped shut the copy of *Cosmopolitan* on her lap and gazed moodily at the model on the cover.

'So who's your ideal woman?'

'Someone who doesn't lecture me, who doesn't go on and on and on about boring morals—'

'Seriously.'

'Someone who doesn't take me seriously.' Caspar stretched. 'Oh, I don't know. Maybe I haven't met her yet.'

'But what's your ideal *type*?' Claudia was frustrated; she wasn't going to give in. 'I mean, short or tall, blonde or dark?'

No mention, Caspar couldn't help noticing, of medium-sized redheads.

'I like all kinds,' he said with unaccustomed tact. 'Anyway, personality's more important than looks.'

'Oh sure, as if you'd ever go out with some old boiler just because she told great jokes.'

Claudia abandoned *Cosmo* and started giving her nails their second coat of plum polish. Caspar couldn't figure out for the life of him why women wore the stuff.

'Depends how great the jokes are,' he said, 'and whether she laughs. Laughter's sexy. Men like girls who laugh.'

Right on cue, the sound of Dina gurgling like a drain drifted up the stairs.

'Okay,' Caspar amended, 'men like most girls who laugh.'

'Are you trying to tell me I've been a miserable old cow lately?'

'Well, the odd smile now and again might help.'

Claudia looked doubtful. She tried one.

'You mean like this?'

'Ravishing.'

She broke into a grin, blew on her wet nails and chucked over a pen.

'Go on then, get some paper. Write down all your best jokes.'

Chapter 19

Poppy gazed at the emerald earrings, pear-shaped and lavishly set in twenty-two carat gold. Jake was out at an auction and she wasn't – strictly speaking – allowed to do any buying herself. But even she could see these earrings were special; if she turned them down she could be missing out on a terrific deal. And where would be the sense in that?

The woman selling the earrings was middle-aged and frail, with a genteel manner and a high-pitched quavery voice.

'They were my grandmother's,' she explained to Poppy, 'but the time has come to sell. I don't want to, of course. Grandmother would be *so* disappointed . . . oh dear, but Christmas is coming and since my husband died it's become harder and harder to manage.'

'The thing is,' said Poppy, 'my boss isn't here at the moment. If you could come back tomorrow—'

'I'm sorry, my dear. I really wanted to get it over and done with today. I'm afraid I find this whole business rather distressing.'

'How much were you hoping to get for them?'

The woman, close to tears, dabbed at her eyes with a pink hanky and shook her head. 'I don't know – whatever you think is fair. Maybe . . . two hundred?'

Poppy reached beneath the counter and took out the cash box. The earrings were easily worth that. She smiled conspiratorially at the poor grief-stricken woman.

'I tell you what. Let's make it two hundred and fifty.'

Jake was right beside Poppy the next day when the policeman approached the stall. He didn't say anything, just held up a photograph.

'Nope,' said Poppy, having studied intently the face of a buxom girl in a dark green ballgown. 'Sorry, never seen her before in my life.'

Next to her, Jake groaned.

'Not the face, madam,' said the policeman with the merest hint of a sneer. 'The earrings.'

'Oh bugger,' wailed Poppy.

'We caught her this morning, trying to off-load more stolen goods.'

Poppy didn't dare look at Jake.

The policeman bent over to study the contents of the jewellery cabinet. Within seconds he spotted the earrings, marked at four hundred and fifty pounds.

'I'm afraid we'll need to take these from you, sir.'

Poppy stared at the policeman. Anyone could hire an outfit like that from a fancy-dress shop . . .

'Wait!' she yelled. 'You can't expect to waltz off, just like that, with a pair of valuable earrings! We'll see some identification,' she demanded hotly, 'if you don't mind.'

'Oh Poppy,' Jake sighed.

The policeman flashed his card at her. He smirked.

'What a shame you didn't think about that before.'

Jake was still speaking to her, but only just. The policeman, quite unfairly Poppy felt, had delivered a depressing lecture, warning her of the dangers of handling stolen goods. To listen to him, you'd have thought she was the mastermind behind Brink's-Mat.

The sight of Claudia colliding in the doorway with an impressively endowed woman in a fedora brought much-needed light relief to the afternoon. Their bosoms clashed. They ricocheted off each other like Sumo wrestlers. The woman in the hat glared at Claudia. Claudia, who felt she had right of way, glared back.

Poppy collapsed in giggles, which didn't help. Claudia had spent the last two hours planning her entrance and it hadn't included this. Trust it to happen when she was seeing Jake again for the first time in weeks. Just when she wanted to look cool.

Not to mention cheerful.

'Shame you weren't wearing a double-breasted jacket,' said Poppy, who was being a damn sight too cheerful. 'Then you might have won.'

Claudia tried to appear unconcerned. She smiled, as Caspar had advised her to do. It was a weird sensation, thinking about your smile while you were actually doing it. Claudia hoped it looked more natural than it felt.

She swung the smile from Poppy to Jake and quickly back again. Jake was wearing a beige and brown checked shirt and crumpled black trousers, and his dark hair was sticking up at odd angles at the back. Really, thought Claudia, if it weren't for those dark eyes of his, nobody would look at him twice. And even they were hidden behind Sellotaped-together spectacles . . .

Not that she was even interested, anyway, Claudia hastily reminded herself. An impoverished antique dealer in an anorak wasn't her idea of happy-ever-after. Jake was only someone she had decided she could practise on in the meantime. She could use him to try out her new smile.

'Well, this is an honour,' Poppy prattled on, since Claudia's collision appeared to have robbed her of the power of speech. 'Your first visit to our humble stall. You haven't come all this way, have you, to tell me off for leaving the butter out of the fridge?'

'Actually, I came to pass on a message. You had a phone call earlier, from some chap called Matthew Ferguson.' It was hard going, smiling and talking at the same time. Claudia's cheek muscles were starting to ache. 'He said to let you know the job was yours and he'd see you tomorrow night.'

'I've got the job,' squealed Poppy. 'Brilliant!'

'I didn't know you'd applied for one.' Claudia was curious.

'It was Caspar's idea. He had a word with a friend of his. I went to see him last night.'

Caspar's idea. Claudia experienced a spasm of jealousy. It sometimes seemed that all Poppy needed to do when she wanted something was ask Caspar. Place to live? No problem. New job? Here you are, take your pick! Like some fairy godmother he would wave his magic wand and effortlessly grant yet another wish.

'What is it, more waitressing?'

Several of Caspar's friends owned restaurants.

Poppy looked smug. 'Modelling.'

Oh, now this was too much.

'You can't be a model,' Claudia replied crushingly. 'You're too short.'

'Not a model-model. Not catwalks and *Vogue* covers,' explained Poppy. Her mouth twitched. 'What I'll be doing involves fewer clothes.'

'You mean topless? Oh my God!' Claudia gasped, no longer envious. How disgusting. How *degrading*. Furthermore, it wasn't even as if Poppy had an impressive pair of boobs.

Filled with indignation – not that she would do it for the world – Claudia thought: *I'm* the one with the boobs.

'Actually,' said Poppy, 'fewer clothes than that.'

'Nude?' Claudia gasped. 'You're going to be *nude*? What, like in . . . *Playboy*?'

By this time even Jake was beginning to look alarmed.

'It's for life drawing classes at St Clare's College of Art.' Poppy broke into a grin. 'There, you see? Nothing disreputable after all! I'll be doing four nights a week, for the students taking evening classes. All I have to do is lie back and think of . . . well, whatever I want to think of, and let everyone else do the work.' She beamed. 'Good, eh?'

'You're serious?' Claudia couldn't believe it. How could Poppy possibly think that what she'd be doing was respectable? 'You'd really parade around naked for a bunch of dirty leering old men?'

'I won't be parading around. And they aren't dirty old men. It's an art college,' said Poppy patiently, 'not a strip club in Soho.'

'Ugh. It's repugnant.' Claudia had forgotten she was supposed to be smiling. She shuddered in disgust. 'They'll see . . . *all* of you.'

'So? I'll be able to pay *all* my rent.'

'Well, you wouldn't catch me doing anything like that. I *couldn't*.' Claudia looked across at Jake for support. 'Could you?'

'Um . . . well, no, I suppose not.' Jake tried to bury himself in a brochure for Lassiter's next furniture auction.

'Look, it pays as much as Kenda's Kitchen and it's a damn sight easier on the feet. I'm doing it and that's that,' said Poppy. 'Now, is there anything else anyone would like to lecture me about or can I take my tea break?'

Claudia remembered her other reason for coming here and seized her chance. She turned to Jake.

'Well now, seeing as I've found you, I may as well spend some money. Perhaps you could help me choose a present for my mother. Something classy, elegant . . .'

I might not be classy and elegant like Angie Slade-Welch, thought Poppy resentfully, but at least I'm getting paid for being painted in the nude. I'm not the muggins who had to pay Caspar six thousand pounds.

'Actually,' said Jake, 'Poppy could be the one to help you there.' Claudia was smiling – no, baring her teeth – at him as if her life depended on it and it was making him nervous. 'I need to talk to Terry about picking up that set of rattan chairs,' he went on hurriedly, turning to Poppy for help. 'Is that okay? Can you take your tea break later? I really must speak to him now.'

'What's the matter with him?' asked Claudia, disappointed, when Jake had rushed off.

130

'I don't know. What's the matter with your face?'

Claudia looked alarmed. Her hands flew up. Was her foundation streaky, her mascara smudged?

'No, your mouth.' Poppy was genuinely trying to help. She did a fair imitation of the smile Claudia had practised for so long in front of the mirror. 'It's your wisdom teeth, isn't it? They're playing up again. You really should see the dentist and have them out.'

Upstairs in the coffee shop Jake sat alone. He was pretending to read the paper and thinking about Claudia. More to the point, he was telling himself what a hopeless coward he was when it came to socialising with the opposite sex.

The fact that he was even thinking about it was all Poppy's fault. For years he had led the kind of life that suited him most. Basically this involved steering clear of the opposite sex.

He had been comfortable doing this because the odd bit of loneliness was so much easier to cope with than the traumatic process of meeting girls, deciding which ones you liked, figuring out if they liked you back, plucking up the courage to ask them out . . .

As far as Jake could see, the whole tortuous dating business was a nightmare, an endless procession of trial and error that seemed far, far more trouble than it was worth. How many relationships lasted the course these days anyway? Look at the way his parents had fought before splitting up. No, those kind of complications he was better off doing without.

It was only since Poppy had come to work for him that Jake had begun to wonder if maybe there was something missing from his life. Not that he was secretly lusting after Poppy, because he knew he wasn't. It was more to do with the way she had taken control of her own future. She had seized it, given it a damn good shake and forced new things to happen. Poppy was fearless, impulsive and determined to make the most of every moment. She seldom bothered to worry about what might happen if she got something wrong.

This wasn't necessarily a plus, Jake thought with a wry smile. Especially when you were her employer. But at least Poppy had a go at whatever she set out to do.

He knew she must think his lack of a social life downright weird.

And now here I am, thought Jake, beginning to wonder if maybe she wasn't right.

He looked at his watch. Half an hour had passed. It should be safe by now to venture back downstairs.

It wasn't as if Claudia wasn't nice, because she was. It wasn't as if he didn't find her attractive, either, because he did. Perhaps if I take it slowly, one step at a time, Jake told himself, I could mentally gear myself up towards asking her out. In a couple of years time.

When he hit the bottom step he saw that half an hour hadn't been long enough. Claudia was still there, evidently torn between a pair of rococo candlesticks and a blue and white Florianware pottery vase.

'. . . are you serious? You've really never been to a car boot sale?' Poppy was saying as Jake approached. 'You don't know what you're missing – they're brilliant fun! If you want to give them a whirl, Jake can tell you the best ones to visit. He goes every Sunday, don't you, Jake?'

This was it, this was his big chance. Taking a leaf out of Poppy's book, Jake plunged in.

'There's a good one out at Henley this Sunday. I could pick you up if you like, we can go together . . . it's best to be there early, I'd have to be at your house by eight . . . and there's a pub overlooking the river, which does terrific food. We could have some lunch there afterwards . . .'

Jake ran out of words. Luckily he'd said all he needed to say. There, he'd done it. The last time he'd asked a girl out he'd been nine years old.

Golly, thought Poppy, astonished and impressed. She

turned expectantly. All Claudia had to do now was say yes.

'Oh, I would have loved to.' Claudia was stricken by the bad timing. If it had been anything else she would have cancelled like a shot. 'But I have to go to a christening on Sunday. My cousin's little girl. They're doing it in Brighton. What a *shame* . . .'

Poppy looked at Jake. It was like prodding a snail and watching the head shrink back beneath the shell.

'No problem. Just a thought. It really doesn't matter. Is this what you've chosen for your mother?' Jake held up the blue and white vase, his hands trembling slightly. 'Did Poppy tell you it's Florianware? Eighteen-nineties, and signed by Moorcroft—'

'How about the following Sunday?' Poppy couldn't bear it. She couldn't let him change the subject. 'You could go then instead. How about it, Jake? The Sunday after next?'

'I'm away that weekend,' said Claudia unhappily. 'Staying with Harriet and Tim in Wales.' Even to her own ears it sounded feeble, and she knew it was the truth. Heaven knows how it must sound to Jake.

'I'm busy as well.' Jake wished the ground would swallow him up. He wished he'd stayed put in the coffee shop for another thirty minutes. He definitely wished he hadn't made a complete dick of himself. How *could* he have been stupid enough to think Claudia would want to go to a car boot sale with him? I mean for God's sake, thought Jake despairingly; of all the glamour spots of the world, a *car boot* sale.

Chapter 20

Caspar was on his way out to a party in Belsize Park the following evening. He offered to drop Poppy off at St Clare's en route.

'Nervous?'

'What, of your driving?' Poppy grinned and shoved a jelly baby into his mouth. 'I'm used to it by now.'

'Nervous about the class. Getting your kit off.'

'Yes.' She could admit as much to Caspar. 'But that won't last, will it? The first five minutes will be the worst.'

'Sure you don't want me to come in for a bit, keep an eye on you?' He winked. 'Make sure they don't laugh? *Ouch*—'

Poppy whacked him on the arm.

'Thanks, but no thanks. I'll be okay. I just hope the heating's on.'

Caspar's petrol light flashed with renewed urgency. Spotting an Esso garage up ahead, he pulled onto the forecourt.

'Won't be a minute. Give me one more jelly baby . . . not another green one,' he protested, because Poppy always fobbed him off with those. His eyes lit up as he glimpsed a coveted red jelly baby in the bottom of the bag.

Poppy had seen it too.

'Here, have a lovely yellow one – no, no!' She let out a yelp as Caspar made a grab for the bag. They wrestled over it for several seconds. Then the bag split. Jelly babies catapulted in all directions.

Grinning, Caspar picked the red one off the dashboard and popped it into his mouth.

'You should know better than to fight with me. Don't I always win?'

'Petrol,' Poppy reminded him, because if he didn't get a move on she was going to be late.

While Caspar was filling up she slid off the passenger seat and began collecting the scattered jelly babies. By the time she scrambled upright he had disappeared into the shop to pay.

If she hadn't been so busy chasing jelly babies, Poppy realised afterwards, she would have seen Tom sooner.

If she'd stayed down on the floor a few seconds longer she would have missed him altogether.

But there he was, clearly visible under the bright fluorescent garage lighting, making his way back from the shop with a packet of Benson & Hedges and a can of Coke in one hand, a copy of the *Evening Standard* in the other. The tangled curls and glittering dark eyes were just as Poppy remembered them. He was wearing jeans – maybe the same pair he had worn last time she'd seen him – and a dark grey polo-necked sweater beneath a black leather jacket. The way he walked was the same. Nothing about him had changed. If she touched him, Poppy realised, she knew exactly how he would feel.

She sat frozen in the passenger seat, too shocked at first to react. It felt like hours but was probably no more than a couple of seconds. I've got to move, thought Poppy, dazed. I've got to attract his attention.

Tom's car was obscured from view by an RAC van. All she could see was the bumper. But he was heading for it, and if she didn't do something sharpish he was going to climb in, start the engine and disappear.

Galvanised into action, Poppy launched herself at the door handle. As she did so, the car Tom was about to get into started up. Someone else was driving. Poppy panicked and tugged again, frantically, at the handle. Slippery with sweat, her hand slid off. The car with Tom inside began to move

135

and thanks to the angle of the RAC van and the petrol pumps she still couldn't get a good look at it.

'Stop . . . help . . . WAIT . . . STOP!!' screamed Poppy, realising too late that she was the helpless victim of a child lock. Any second now the car would pull out into the road. This had been her chance in a million and she'd almost blown it. Her heart racing, Poppy threw herself across to the driver's side and leaned as hard as she knew how on the horn.

'Here. Don't say I never buy you anything.'

An unopened bag of jelly babies landed with a crackly thud in Poppy's lap. Caspar climbed back into the car.

'What's the matter with you?'

'Nothing.' Poppy was too shell-shocked to explain. She felt sick. She couldn't eat a jelly baby now to save her life.

'Last-minute panic?'

'No.'

'Well, something's happened.'

'Your car horn doesn't work.'

Caspar waved his keys at her. 'Not without these in the ignition.'

Hell.

'And there's a child lock on this door. You don't *have* children,' said Poppy.

'The chap I bought the car from had them fitted. Kate was showing me yesterday how to work them. Sorry, couldn't you open the door?' said Caspar. 'I didn't realise they were still switched on.'

Around Poppy, at varying distances, sixteen pupils stood before their easels observing, drawing, re-drawing and shading the contours of her body. Every detail mattered. Their concentration was total. When they spoke they did it in whispers.

The group comprised seven women and nine men, ranging in age from eighteen to eighty. The only disparaging remark about their new model had come from a tall older woman in a hand-crocheted tunic, complaining about Poppy's lack of saggy bits and wrinkles. Nobody had ogled her, either. They were too busy drawing to leer.

Poppy gazed at a peeling patch of wall. Her mind was elsewhere – back on a chilly garage forecourt on the Marylebone Road – but her body was right here doing its job.

At least seeing Tom again had given her something else to think about other than the fact that she was sitting here minus her clothes.

Money had been tight for the last few weeks and Poppy had been forced to give the Cavendish Club a miss. When she visited it the Friday before Christmas she heard the jaunty, bluesy sound of Alex on the piano as she reached the stone steps leading down to the entrance of the club.

Inside, half the office parties in London appeared to have crammed themselves willy-nilly into the three interlinked cellars. The place was heaving with tipsy secretaries and excitable clerical types with their shirtsleeves rolled up and their ties skew-whiff. Everyone was celebrating their last day at work. Ugly men waving scrawny bits of mistletoe were looking hopeful. There was a lot of smudged lipstick about. Poppy found herself fending off the enthusiastic attentions of a burly lad in a reindeer suit.

'If you don't give me a Christmas kiss, you'll hurt my feelings,' he pleaded.

'If you don't take your hands off my bottom,' said Poppy with a grin, 'I'll rip your antlers off.'

She found Rita in her usual corner of the bar, looking festive in a bright red dress and snowman earrings. The first thing she did was buy Poppy a drink.

'Still speaking to us then? I thought you might have decided you'd had enough of these jazz types.' She watched Poppy take a thrifty sip of her lager and downed her own drink in one. 'Come on love, get it down your neck. Don't worry, I'm buying.'

Was Rita looking older? Were there shadows under her eyes, carefully but not totally masked by concealer? Poppy watched her stub out one cigarette and straight away light up another. There was an air of recklessness about her tonight, a definite I-could-do-with-a-Valium look in her eyes. The smile was put on. And she kept glancing across in the direction of the stage, as if compulsively checking that Alex was still there.

Maybe they've had a fight, thought Poppy. Maybe Rita had been a bit free and easy with her own Christmas kisses and Alex had got jealous. Or vice versa.

Or there was more to it than that and she had discovered he was having an affair—

Poppy stopped herself before she got carried away. This was her trouble, she was always imagining things and leaping to conclusions. There were, after all, any number of reasons why Rita might be on edge.

Poppy glanced over her shoulder and saw a pregnant girl standing over by the fire exit. Rita had mentioned ages ago that she hadn't been able to have children. Briefly, almost casually, she had said, 'No, no kids. It just didn't happen. Still, never mind.' But behind the brave, don't-care façade Poppy had glimpsed the pain, and the number of soft toys in Rita's house had been another giveaway. The sight of a pregnant woman must remind her every time of what she had missed.

As for her and Alex having an argument . . . so what? It was what married couples did, and for the most mundane reasons. Alex had probably left his socks on the bathroom floor . . . squeezed the toothpaste in the middle . . . spent too long with his mates in the pub.

'Let's hear what you've been up to then.' Rita finished the second cigarette in a series of fast, jerky drags. 'Managed to get yourself another job?'

Poppy told her about St Clare's, which had now broken up for Christmas. Then she went on to tell her about the end-ofterm party in a pub around the corner from the college, where during the course of the evening each student in turn had come up to her and said, side-splittingly, 'Gosh, I didn't recognise you with your clothes on.'

'They're a nice enough crowd,' Poppy sighed, 'but their idea of humour is to say, "What's this, cellulite?" And you should see some of the finished drawings. One old dear had me looking like Joyce Grenfell on speed. She's seventy-three and thinks she's Picasso, except she wears a black wig. Rita, are you okay?'

'Hmm? Sorry, I missed the last bit. Something about cellulite.'

'What's wrong?' asked Poppy.

She watched in horror as Rita's heavily mascaraed eyes brimmed with tears.

'Damn, this is doing my image no good at all.' Rita's voice cracked. She fumbled uselessly in her bag for tissues.

People were beginning to notice and Rita's make-up was woefully un-waterproof. Poppy led her through the crowded cellar to the exit.

'I hate these sodding steps,' mumbled Rita. 'Oh God, we're going to freeze to death. What do I look like? I *swore* I wouldn't let this happen . . .'

Poppy had brought her outside because she knew the ladies' loo would be packed. Now they'd reached the top of the steps she wondered what to do next.

'Where's your car?'

'Parked round the back.' Rita sniffed. 'I haven't got the keys. They're with Alex.'

A black cab turned the corner. Poppy flagged it down.

'Where to, love?'

'I don't know.' Poppy looked at Rita. 'Home?'

'Not without Alex. Oh, I get it.' Rita shook her head. 'You think we've fallen out. It's not that.' Wearily she added, 'I only wish it was.'

The streets were icy. Poppy's feet were numb. She started

to shiver. The cab driver was beginning to look fed up.

'We don't want to go anywhere,' she told him, pulling open the door and jumping inside. 'Just keep the engine ticking over. And the heater on.'

Rita sobbed noisily. The cab driver provided a box of Kleenex. Poppy had to wait several minutes before she heard what had happened.

'. . . you know what men are like, all this macho "I'm okay" stuff, when really all they are is scared out of their wits.' Rita sighed and blinked back more tears. 'Well anyway, Alex wasn't feeling so clever so in the end I made the appointment for him. We went together and the woman checked him out. Dead nice, she was. Kept saying she was sure it wasn't anything to worry about, but to be on the safe side he'd better go and have a few tests. So we went along for those this morning. We've got to see the specialist tomorrow for the results. Oh Poppy, I know what they're going to tell us.'

Rita's voice began to break again. The floor of the cab was covered with bits of damp shredded tissue. With practically no make-up left she looked quite different. Poppy held her hand.

Reassurance wasn't what Rita wanted. Cheer-up-it-might-never-happen speeches would do no good because as far as Rita was concerned, it already had.

'He's being so brave,' she told Poppy. 'Just carrying on as if nothing's changed. I'm the one showing myself up, bawling like a baby. It's just, I feel so helpless . . . and so bloody *angry* . . . Christ, I'm the one who drinks too much and smokes too much. If something like this has to happen, why can't it flaming well happen to me?'

All Poppy could do was sit there and listen while Rita ranted on. By the time the meter had clocked up eight pounds fifty, the tears had pretty much dried up. By ten pounds fifty Rita had renewed most of her make-up. Poppy paid the cab driver while Rita did her lipstick, and realised that she would have to go home now. All she had left was enough money for the bus.

'You're a good girl.' Rita gave her an awkward hug. 'And thanks for putting up with me. What a way to spend an evening, eh? You must've been bored stupid, having to listen to me droning on and on. God, I'm a selfish cow.'

'You aren't.' Poppy hugged her back. 'Look, I have to go now. Give my love to Alex.'

At home in bed, Poppy couldn't sleep. She lay staring up at the ceiling thinking about Alex and going over in her mind everything Rita had said.

I've only just found him, Poppy thought with trepidation. This can't happen. I can't lose him again. Not yet.

Chapter 21

Poppy caught the coach to Bristol on Christmas Eve. She hadn't told Dina she was coming down; she wasn't staying long. This was purely a duty visit.

When she arrived she felt even more of a stranger than she had imagined. Beryl Bridges was there, in a pale blue hand-knitted twinset, putting the finishing touches to plates of sandwiches and home-made cakes. There were doilies on the plates. The tea service was one Poppy hadn't seen before. When Beryl reached for the teapot and said coyly, 'Shall I be mother?' Poppy felt a twinge of alarm. Beryl was nudging sixty; surely she hadn't gone and got herself knocked up?

'We're getting married,' Mervyn Dunbar announced when the tea had been poured. He no longer took sugar, Poppy noticed. Beryl was probably behind that too.

'Oh . . . well, that's good news.' Poppy smiled at them both. 'Congratulations.'

'Next week,' said Mervyn. 'Down at the Register Office. Nothing fancy. No big party or anything.'

Of course not, Poppy thought. Wouldn't want to break the habit of a lifetime.

'Just a couple of my friends as witnesses,' Beryl put in hurriedly. 'And a spot of lunch afterwards.'

'So don't worry about having to trek down here from London all over again.' Mervyn blinked. Poppy turning up like this out of the blue had unsettled him. He had his own life now, and Beryl to share it with him. Knowing that Beryl would never sneak off behind his back with another man gave him indescribable peace of mind, whereas seeing Poppy again only served to remind him of all the misery and humiliation his first wife had put him through. 'There's no need,' he went on brusquely. 'We understand. It's a long way.'

It certainly was, Poppy mused. Even longer when you weren't wanted at the wedding.

'Still, you've got your own life to lead, haven't you?' Beryl said brightly. 'Up in the big city! Must be lots going on there, eh love?'

'Oh, lots.' Poppy nodded in agreement. She had no intention of telling them she had met her real father. She finished her tea and reached down to the raffia bag at her feet, pulling out Mervyn's wrapped Christmas present. Luckily, gardening books were his passion so he was easy to buy for.

Lucky too, thought Poppy, that I'm pretty passionate about washing. She thanked Mervyn for her own present, which she knew was Yardley soap. It was wrapped in last year's paper, which had been kept and recycled.

'Actually,' said Poppy, 'I was going to ask a favour.'

Mervyn looked wary. 'Oh yes?'

'You know that blue spirit bottle, the one on the shelf out in the hall. Was it my mother's?'

Bits of old glass were of no interest to Mervyn Dunbar. He nodded.

'She came home with it one day, before you were born. Bought it in Clifton. Waste of money, I told her.' His eyes flickered. 'Why? Valuable, is it?'

'Not really,' Poppy fibbed, because Bristol Blue glass of that age could fetch hundreds of pounds at auction. 'It's the same colour as the curtains in my bedroom, that's all. I wondered if I could have it.'

Claudia always enjoyed the *idea* of going along to her mother's drinks parties. Angie invited so many men you never knew who you might meet. It was only when she was there she started wishing she hadn't come.

The trouble was, having spent ages looking forward to it, the event itself was bound to be a let-down. As in childbirth, Claudia conveniently forgot the bad bits – like the fact that her mother spent the whole time shamelessly hogging the limelight and always bagged the best men for herself.

'You look gorgeous, like an ice cream,' one of them told Claudia now. He was spectacularly drunk but so good-looking he could get away with it. 'Can I lick your shoulder? Do you taste as good as you look?'

Claudia began to perk up. How lucky she'd chosen to wear the ivory satin dress and not the blue wool one, and how right she'd been to keep up those sessions on the sunbed. She preened a bit, then squirmed with pleasure as the man began to drop nibbling little kisses along her collarbone.

With a whoosh of Chanel Number 5, Angie materialised beside them like an unwanted genie out of a lamp.

Her smile was provocative.

'Why bother with Walls economy-sized vanilla,' she purred, 'when you could be enjoying Häagen-Dazs?'

She slipped out of her jacket and offered the man her own bare shoulder. 'Go on, try me. And be honest, which would you prefer? A dollop of plain old vanilla or a little taste of heavenly Caramel Cone Explosion?'

'Honestly darling, I don't know why you have to be so touchy.' Mindful of the perils of dehydration, Angie poured herself another glass of mineral water and yawned. 'It was just a bit of fun. You're lucky Carlo only nibbled your shoulder.'

Claudia had managed to contain herself until the party was over. By the time the last of the guests had drifted off into the frosty night she'd had a good three hours in which to seethe.

'I'm not talking about my shoulder being nibbled,' Claudia howled. 'Having my shoulder nibbled doesn't *shock* me . . . what I can't bear is the way you always have to barge your way in and start showing off.'

144

Angie began to laugh.

'Oh dear, you mean the bit about economy blocks of ice cream? Sweetheart, you are so sensitive about your size! It was a joke, that's all.'

'You couldn't bear to think that someone like Carlo might have been more interested in me than in you.' Claudia glared at her accusingly. 'You had to shimmy up and start diverting his attention.'

'Fairly easily accomplished,' Angie retaliated. 'I mean, he hardly had to be prised off you, did he?'

'Now you're being spiteful.'

All the pent-up resentment of the past months was on the brink of spilling out. Having Angie back on the scene must have been more of a strain than she'd realised. Claudia gave her mother a measured look. 'And you're showing yourself up,' she said coldly. 'Has it ever occurred to you that some people might be watching the way you carry on and laughing at you behind your back? Not everyone thinks you're completely irresistible, you know. You aren't that perfect.'

Angie was no longer looking amused. If there was one thing she really couldn't bear it was the thought that she was being laughed at. It was only a cheap jibe of course – nobody *was* laughing – but the fact that Claudia could even make such a snide remark . . . well, it really pissed her off.

'I didn't say I was perfect,' she bristled. 'Or irresistible. Not that I can recall any complaints—'

'For God's sake, *there* you go again.'

'Oh please, can I help it if men find me attractive?'

'Not all men,' Claudia repeated through gritted teeth. This evening's episode had really bugged her. This time her mother wasn't going to get away with it. 'Not all men. Not Carlo, And,' she added for good measure, 'not Caspar either.'

Right. That was it. Mockingly Angie said, 'Caspar? Oh, you mean the Caspar *you've* had such spectacular success with? Dear me, so what you're saying is, if I were to make

145

myself available to Caspar French, he wouldn't be the teeniest bit interested. Is that it?'

'That's it.' Claudia looked triumphant. Inwardly she thought: If I have to bribe him with every last penny I own, Caspar is never going to sleep with you.

Angie uncurled herself and rose from the sofa. She crossed the room to where the Christmas tree stood. It was an impressive ten-footer smothered in Victorian lace and beeswax candles. A mountain of exquisitely wrapped gifts was piled around the base. Angie reached for a large flat rectangular package done up in tartan paper. She handed it to Claudia with a tight little smile.

'Go on, open it.'

'Why? It's not mine.' Claudia looked at the label, which bore her father's name. Hugo was flying over from Los Angeles on Boxing Day.

'Just open it.'

The crimson ribbons unravelled, the paper fell open and the layers of tissue paper seemed to peel back of their own accord. Claudia sat gazing down at the picture on her lap. Her mother, naked and golden, sleepy-eyed and smiling, gazed back up at her. As if the carved wooden headboard of the rumpled bed on which she lay wasn't enough, there was the signature in the bottom right-hand corner to dispel any last lingering doubts.

'What a talented boy he is.' Smiling at the look on Claudia's face, Angie heaved a pleasurable sigh. 'And what fun we had! No wonder you're so keen to get to know him better,' she added in a taunting whisper. 'He even exceeded my expectations! Darling, you simply must give Caspar a try. I do recommend him. You're missing out on a treat.'

146

Chapter 22

With the proceeds of the Angie Slade-Welch portrait Caspar had sent his parents on a Mediterranean cruise. On Christmas night his mother, overwhelmed by the sheer opulence of the ship and two unaccustomed glasses of Amontillado, phoned to tell him there had been a choice of seventeen different vegetables served with lunch. There was also a waterfall – yes, an actual *waterfall* – inside – yes, actually inside – the boat.

'I've never seen anything like it before in my life,' she gasped happily. 'Talk about grand! Caspar, you should see it . . . this whole trip's like a dream come true. Oh, I do wish you could've come with us. You'd have had such fun—'

'I'm just glad you and Dad are enjoying yourselves.' Much as he loved his parents, the prospect of going away on holiday with them filled Caspar with alarm. 'And we're having fun here. We cooked a pretty mean lunch between us.'

'Not with seventeen different kinds of vegetables.'

'Maybe not.'

'And I'm not doing the washing-up,' his mother boasted.

'Neither am I.'

'Oh Caspar! You haven't left the girls to do it all.'

'Would I?' He grinned.

'You are naughty.'

'I am not. We used paper plates.'

People had been dropping in and out all day. Friends not caught up in the family-visiting routine had called by, staying for lunch or for a few drinks, enjoying the relaxed atmosphere and informal hospitality. At six o'clock Kate left to spend the evening with her parents. Claudia disappeared into the kitchen to deal with the washing-up.

'What washing-up?' Caspar protested.

'We didn't cook with paper saucepans, stupid.'

'Come on, leave all that. We'll do it tomorrow.'

'You mean I'll do it tomorrow.'

Caspar leaned against the kitchen door. He watched Claudia push up her sleeves in businesslike fashion and run a torrent of hot water into the bowl. He wondered if she'd had some kind of upset with her mother. She hadn't been in a bad mood today, but there had been a definite edge about her. He sensed something wasn't right.

Caspar wondered if it was him.

'Claudie, have I done something wrong?'

'Wrong? You?' Claudia was whipping up a mountain of bubbles. She shook her head. 'No. I don't suppose you have.'

'What's that supposed to mean?'

'It means you're the same now as you've always been. And I don't suppose you'll ever change.' She plunged her hands into the soapy water and began trawling for cutlery. 'After all, why should you?'

Claudia knew she shouldn't snipe, but she *was* fed up. It just seemed so unfair, Caspar and his endless capacity for sex, her with no sex life at all . . .

Caspar looked closely at her, but Claudia was busy looking closely at the washing-up. He assumed this was some veiled reference to the fact that he never did any.

It was Christmas. He experienced a pang of guilt.

'Okay, point taken. We'll go shopping next week. Get a machine to do the dirty work for us.' He gave her an encouraging nod. 'How about it, would that cheer you up?'

Claudia turned and stared. Surely he wasn't offering to buy her a vibrator! She went bright pink.

'Caspar, are you drunk?'

'No.' Well, not plastered.

'So what in heaven's name are you talking about?'

He looked perplexed. 'A dishwasher.'

Despite herself, Claudia began to giggle. This was why she could never stay angry with Caspar for long. Okay, so he had slept with her mother. But Angie was the one she was unable to forgive.

'Are you okay?' asked Caspar.

Claudia had no intention of bringing up the subject of his fling with Angie.

'I'm okay,' she said.

She was damned if she'd let Caspar think she cared.

The door bell rang. They heard the clatter of footsteps as Poppy raced across the hall.

'Who's that?' said Claudia.

'Could be Jake. She mentioned he might drop by.'

Claudia flushed again. Maybe she should nip upstairs quickly and re-do her make-up. She was sure her T-zone was shiny; a dab of powder wouldn't go amiss.

Poppy yelled to Caspar that *The Sound of Music* was on and Julie Andrews was going mad with a machete. Caspar took another bottle of wine from the fridge and made his way back to the sitting room. Claudia scrubbed away at a roasting tin and told herself that all she had to do when she joined the rest of them was act naturally, treat Jake as if he were any other casual dropper-in . . . and not make a prat of herself.

'Hello,' said Jake.

Claudia jumped, the sponge in her hand skidded up the roasting tin and a wave of greasy water shot over her white shirt.

'Sorry, I didn't mean to scare you.' Jake passed her a tea towel and watched as she mopped her wet front. 'Caspar forgot the corkscrew.' He paused. 'Merry Christmas, by the way.'

Act normal, act casual, thought Claudia frenziedly. She

wondered if a festive kiss on the cheek might be on the cards then realised at once she didn't have the nerve to try.

'Um . . . Merry Christmas. The corkscrew's over there. On the . . . um . . . fridge.'

And why do I get myself into this ridiculous state anyway, she thought crossly. I mean, look at him, look at that grey sweater . . . and those terrible trousers . . . how *can* I be nervous around someone who wears what looks like a school uniform left over from the last war?

He really really isn't my type, Claudia reminded herself. Apart from anything else he isn't even rich.

Moments later it struck her that she didn't need to be nervous anyway. Jake had invited her to visit those car boot sales the other week, hadn't he? And she hadn't been able to go. Maybe, thought Claudia, I could make up for it now. In, of course, a casual and natural manner.

'Will you be finished soon,' said Jake, 'or shall I bring a glass of wine through for you?'

'Don't worry.' Claudia smiled over her shoulder at him in Lauren Bacall-ish fashion . . . well, apart from the shiny nose. 'Almost done. Actually, I've been invited to a small party at a friend's house over in Baltic Wharf. If you'd like to come along you'd be welcome . . . I mean, we could go together. They're . . . um . . . nice people,' she added hurriedly, 'and very casual. Not a bit smart.'

Claudia winced; she hadn't meant to put it quite that baldly.

'Thanks, but I promised I'd call in on a friend of mine.'

For a second Jake looked amused. As well he might, thought Claudia. Here he was, getting his own back, turning *her* down for a change.

'Truly, or is that a bit of a flimsy excuse?' She tried to sound playful – like Lauren Bacall huskily asking Bogart if he knew how to whistle.

Jake reached for the corkscrew and moved towards the door.

'Truly. I'm expected for drinks at nine. At a friend's house.' Again that glimmer of a smile. 'You may remember me mentioning him once before. Ellis Featherstone. He runs our Neighbourhood Watch.'

By eight o'clock Poppy and Caspar were alone, sprawled in front of the television with a whole evening's uninterrupted supply of chocolate. *The Sound of Music* was over, Poppy had already eaten eleven feet of orange Matchmakers and neither of them could understand the rules of What's Your Fetish?, a board game given to Caspar by the hopeful blonde receptionist at the Denver Parrish Gallery.

'Maybe it's just as well.' Caspar abandoned the box of cards that went with it. The top card had begun, somewhat dubiously, 'Take two cans of whipping cream and a tin of pineapple rings . . .'

'We could watch my Gary Glitter video.' Poppy looked hopeful.

Caspar pulled a face. 'I bought the thing for you. Wasn't that enough?'

'You'd love it.'

'I wouldn't, I promise.'

'You are such a disappointment to me,' Poppy said sorrowfully. 'We like nearly all the same things. I don't understand how you can not love Gary Glitter.'

It was true, Caspar realised. They did like a lot of the same things. Well, as far as films and food and jokes were concerned anyway. Caspar smiled to himself. Morally, of course, they had their small differences.

'Now that we're on our own,' said Poppy, 'I have a bit of a confession to make.'

'Brilliant. Something sordid, I hope.'

'It's about that tiepin Kate gave you.'

When she had finished, Caspar grinned.

'Makes no difference to me. Diamonds or no diamonds. When am I ever going to wear a tie?'

'On your wedding day, according to Kate.'

'But I'm not going to be marrying Kate.'

'You see, that's why I made her buy the cheaper tiepin,' Poppy explained. 'I didn't even think you'd last this long. I was sure you'd have dumped her by now.'

'I tried, believe me.' Caspar shuddered at the memory. 'She got herself . . . well, into a bit of a state. She kept crying "Not before Christmas, not before Christmas", so in the end I gave up.' He shrugged and leaned over the edge of the sofa, delving into the box of Liquorice Allsorts Poppy had just opened. 'I'll do it properly next week.'

'Poor Kate.'

'Poor me.' Caspar looked indignant. 'It isn't fun, you know. Finishing with people who don't want to be finished with.'

'My heart bleeds.'

They watched a bit of the Bond film in companionable silence, Caspar stretched out across the sofa and Poppy sitting on the floor propped up against it.

She was right in front of him, hugging her knees and idly twiddling a purple sweet wrapper between her fingers, oblivious to the fact that Caspar's gaze had shifted from the television to the back of her neck.

He looked at Poppy, jolted to realise how much he still wanted her. She had tied her hair up with a black ribbon and loose red-gold tendrils curled around her ears. She was wearing the white stretchy top thing that Claudia had given her for Christmas and which, confusingly, appeared to be called a body. Caspar didn't care what it was called, he just liked the way the wide neckline curved, ballerina-style, around Poppy's slender shoulders, leaving the back of her neck bare.

Caspar realised he was fed up with trying to think of Poppy as just one of the lads. It wasn't working and it was as frustrating as hell.

It wasn't a sudden decision. He'd been exerting heroic self-control for weeks. Well, now it was Christmas night and what better time could there be to make his long-awaited move?

Reaching out, Caspar briefly touched the nape of Poppy's neck. His fingers rested against the sensitive ridge of bone where her spine began.

'Ooh, lovely,' Poppy squirmed with delight. 'Scratch my back.'

It wasn't quite the promising start he'd hoped to make. Every time Caspar tried to slow down to sensual-massage speed, Poppy shouted unromantically, 'Up a bit, left a bit – no, no, *much* harder than that!'

'Isn't it amazing,' she puffed minutes later, 'how just when you think you've got one itch sorted out, another three pop up out of nowhere. They must breed like rabbits.'

Lucky old itches. Caspar, unused to having to plan his next move – or, worse still, wondering if it would actually work – shifted a few inches further along the sofa. Now he was in line with Poppy's head. Surely, if he kissed the back of her neck, she'd begin to get the message?

Or would he be better turning her slowly round to face him? Then he could lean forward and kiss her on the mouth?

Damn, some things simply weren't meant to be plotted in advance . . . and seduction strategy was one of them.

'Poppy.'

'No I won't.'

Talk about flat-out rejection. Startled, Caspar said, 'Won't what?'

'Make the tea. It isn't my turn.'

'Oh.' He took a deep breath. As well as the white stretchy top thing, she was wearing the perfume Dina had given her for Christmas, an amazingly restrained scent considering who had chosen it.

'Yes, thanks, great,' prompted Poppy when he didn't move. 'I'd love a cup.'

Caspar breathed in again, inhaling the delicate peppery-flowery scent.

'I don't want any tea.'

Poppy, enjoying herself, twisted round and grinned up at him.

'I didn't ask you if you wanted any. I said I did.'

Right, thought Caspar, as nervous as any adolescent. *Now.* Go go go—

The phone rang, out in the hall.

'Three to one it's Claudia reminding me to switch her electric blanket on,' said Poppy, leaping to her feet. 'Evens it's one of your devoted girlies. Are you in or out?'

Caspar rolled onto his back and closed his eyes.

'Definitely out.'

Chapter 23

She came back looking sombre.

'It was Rita. I left a message on their machine yesterday. She's just got back from the hospital.'

'Bad news?'

'They don't know yet. Not for sure, anyway.' Poppy sighed and sank down onto the sofa, absently pushing Caspar's legs out of the way. 'They get the results of the exploratory op tomorrow. But the surgeon's already warned them not to get their hopes up.'

'Poor you.' Caspar gave her knee a comforting pat. It was surprisingly easy, now seduction was off the agenda.

Poppy sighed. There was no point feeling sorry for herself.

'Poor Rita.'

'At least you found him. That's why you came to London, isn't it?'

'Oh yes.' She nodded, then hesitated. 'Well, that was the main reason . . .'

'There was something else?' To cheer her up, Caspar gave her a nudge. 'What, you really came here because you'd read that piece about me in the *Sunday Times* and you thought here was a man you had to get to know?'

A flicker of a smile. 'Um . . .'

'Go on, you can admit it. You saw the photos of me and went "Cor!". You knew you had to leave Bristol and come in search of Caspar Fr—'

'I had to leave Bristol to escape the McBride lynch mob.' Poppy started to laugh. Since there was nothing she could do about Alex she was grateful for the distraction. Especially today.

Maybe making her laugh was the answer.

Caspar said, 'No, no, that wasn't it. You realised life would have no meaning until you met me. Don't you see?' He looked triumphant. 'This explains why you've never been able to summon up any interest in anyone else. It explains your ice-block. You've been crazy about me all along.'

Poppy blew him a kiss.

'I'd be even crazier about you if you made me that cup of tea.'

'There.' Back from the kitchen several minutes later, Caspar handed Poppy her mug. 'Talk about a one-track mind. There is more to life, you know, than tea tea tea.'

'Okay, if it'll stop you making fun of me, I'll tell you the whole story,' said Poppy. 'The real reason why I have such an abnormal lack of interest in men.' She gave him a warning look. 'And don't you dare laugh.'

'Me? Laugh? Why would I laugh?'

'Because it sounds too dopey for words,' said Poppy. She clutched her mug of tea in both hands and began to explain about Tom.

'Good grief,' said Caspar when she had finished. 'I thought it was just a case of cold feet. Why did you never tell us before?'

'Like I said, it sounds stupid.' Poppy bit one of her finger-nails. 'And I thought it would have worn off by now. The thing is, it hasn't. I only have to accidentally *think* about Tom and my stomach goes all squirmy. I can't help it, I've never felt like this about anyone before. It's starting to make me nervous. I mean, what if this feeling never goes away?'

'Would it help,' said Caspar, 'if I told you he was probably married with three kids and a Volvo?'

'He isn't. I just know he isn't.'

They were employing different tenses, Caspar noticed.

'Was he good-looking?'

'Of course.'

Caspar experienced a stab of jealousy. 'What, better than me?'

Poppy smiled. He sounded so shocked.

'Oh, heaps better,' she teased.

'In that case he's bound to be a shit.'

'Oh well, you'd know.'

'The thing is,' Caspar said vigorously, 'you have to be practical about this. How long *can* you go on pining for this Mr Wonderful? I mean, let's face it. This is London. You're not going to bump into him walking down the street.'

Caspar stayed up long after Poppy had gone to bed. One way and another it had been an eventful evening. He understood a lot more now. The bad news was, it had made him want Poppy more than ever. Finding himself in competition with the absent Tom had only increased his interest. And to think that Poppy should have seen him in the petrol station only the other week . . .

I must have been standing right next to him, thought Caspar, trying to imagine what might have happened if Poppy had been able to get out of the car. No wonder she hadn't said much afterwards, as he had driven her to St Clare's.

But if she *had* told him then, he might have been able to help. Poppy had forgotten that all garages employ surveillance cameras. Caspar couldn't help thinking that a small bribe might have secured them a re-run of the video tape. Then all he would have needed to do was persuade a policeman friend of his to check out the car's registration number.

It was too late now. The video tape would be wiped over.

Caspar tried to decide if this was good news as far as he was concerned, or bad.

Poppy called round to see Alex when he had been out of hospital for a week. She was alarmed by how much older he

157

looked – and he wasn't the only one. It was the first time she had seen Rita in daylight and without make-up.

Now the initial shock was over they were being determinedly cheerful.

'Look at the state of us,' Alex mocked, squeezing Rita's hand as she bent over him to straighten his pillows. 'Couple of leftovers from Halloween. Can't see anyone wanting to paint us in the altogether, eh love?'

'You'd be surprised.' With a start of recognition, Poppy realised for the first time that one side of his mouth curled differently from the other. Hers did that sometimes, too. 'They like old models, they're partial to a few lines and wrinkles.'

Rita groaned. 'Blimey, you know how to cheer a girl up.'

'I do my best,' said Poppy. She looked at Alex. 'So what's happening? How do you really feel?'

'Like I've been kicked down the Mile End Road and back.' He managed a dry smile. 'But this is nothing, apparently. Once I get started on the chemo I'll really know the meaning of hell on wheels.'

'We're bracing ourselves for the worst,' Rita put in. 'That way, anything half bearable's a bonus. So people keep telling us, anyway.'

I'm not going to cry, Poppy told herself. She turned and stared very hard out of the bedroom window. The sun was shining, the sky was an optimistic shade of blue. Frost gleamed on the broad stretch of lawn below. She still didn't know how Alex and Rita had come by such a home, but what did that matter now? What good was all their dubiously-acquired money when all Alex wanted was a body not riddled with cancer?

She didn't stay long. Alex was clearly worn out.

'Thanks, love, for coming.' He nodded to show he meant it. 'A lot of people have steered well clear. It's all right turning up for the parties drinking my drink and having a knees-up, but when it comes to something like this you don't see 'em for dust.' He coughed and laughed. 'Too scared we might start talking funerals.'

'They're afraid of saying the wrong thing,' said Poppy.

'Like mentioning the d-word. In case it hasn't occurred to us that I might kick the bucket.' Alex patted her hand. 'Anyway, you came. Bless you for that. And it's nice for Rita . . . does her good to see someone she can have a bit of a chat with.'

Not wanting to tire him too much, Poppy rose to leave. She pulled a newspaper-wrapped parcel out of the Sainsbury's carrier bag at her feet.

'I brought you something. I spotted it in an auction the other day. Thought you might like it to keep the other one company.'

Alex unwrapped the spirit bottle and gazed at it in silence for several seconds. Wintry sunlight reflected off the royal blue glass as he turned it slowly in his hands.

'Blimey, talk about coincidence,' Rita exclaimed. 'You always said it was one of a pair, didn't you, love?'

'Which auction room?' asked Alex.

'Oh . . . um . . . Lassiter's.' Poppy began to feel frightened. Had she gone too far this time? 'They do look like a pair, I know, but I expect there were hundreds made. Thousands, even. I mean,' she added hastily, 'it'd be a bit daft, wouldn't it, to only make two?'

'Oh well, never mind.' Alex shrugged; he was no expert. He smoothed the curved side of the bottle with an unsteady forefinger. 'I reckon they belong together now. If you ask me they make a pretty good pair.'

159

Chapter 24

The cold snap ended in the second week of January. Poppy, who'd complained bitterly about never being able to feel her toes, decided that rain was worse. One of her shoes had a hole in it. Her hair went completely mental in the wet. Her Shetland wool sweater smelled of damp sheep.

'And this is supposed to be a treat,' Poppy sighed as they trudged through a churned-up field. Her top half was splattered with rain, her bottom half with mud. She had, brainily, chosen today of all days to wear white jeans and a dry-clean only shirt. The shirt, a market stall bargain, was shrinking faster than you could say cheap import.

'It is a treat.' Jake was brisk. 'Honestly, all this fuss over a bit of rain.'

'A bit! A few dozen reservoirs-full.'

'Your first country house auction,' he protested, gesturing to the imposing building looming out of the semi-darkness ahead, 'and all you can do is whinge.'

Poppy wondered why the field-cum-car park had to be so damn far away from the house. She thought dark thoughts about the people who had organised today's shindig. She wished her shoes didn't squelch.

Jake grinned at the look on her face. 'Okay, okay. You can do some bidding.'

'Really?' Poppy perked up at once. She hadn't been allowed to bid for months, not since the wasp-swatting incident last summer. Still, no danger of any wasps today.

'We'll call it a trial run,' said Jake. 'I have to disappear at lunchtime to see a buyer in Windsor. You can take over while I'm away.'

Chartwell-Lacey Manor heaved with potential buyers. Dealers mingled with members of the public. An awful lot of mud was being trailed through the house.

Poppy envied the sensible people in warm coats and wellies. She queued up for plastic cups of coffee in the east-facing scullery, blowing on her icy fingers and eavesdropping on the gossip of two local women behind her. Jake had briefly outlined the story of Dorothea de Lacey, the recently deceased owner of Chartwell, but he was a typical man, hopeless in the gossip stakes. What these women had to say was far more revealing.

'. . . and what about them daughters of hers?' tutted the one in the purple tea-cosy hat, 'all but tearin' each other's hair out to get their hands on the best bits of jewellery. It's a disgrace, that's what it is. Shame on them, after the way they treated the poor old duck.'

'Except she was 'ardly what you'd call poor,' cackled the other one, pointing to the rolled-up catalogue she hadn't been able to resist buying, even though she had only come along for a nose. 'What about them chandeliers in the ballroom, eh? Imagine 'avin' to get up a ladder and dust all them bits o' glass every week! And did you spot that portrait of Mrs de Lacey when she was young? Up for sale, along with the bleedin' furniture.' She shook her head in vigorous disap-proval. 'Those two money-grubbing bitches didn't even have the decency to keep a painting of their own mother. All they care about is gettin' their greedy 'ands on the cash. I tell you, Mabel, if I thought for one minute our Teresa'd play that kind of dirty trick on me, I'd turf 'er out o' the 'ouse so fast 'er 'eels wouldn't touch the ground.'

'Poor Mrs de Lacey, God rest her soul. Nice old duck, she was,' muttered purple hat. 'What she ever did to deserve daughters like that is beyond me.'

'What the daughters did to deserve all *this* is beyond me,' the other one snorted. 'Eh? Millions, that's what they'll get when this lot's been sold off.'

'Should've left it to a cats' home,' growled purple hat.

The other one chuckled. 'Should've left it to me.'

By the time Poppy found Jake again his coffee was half-drunk and half-cold. He was studying dinner services, making careful notes in the margins of his sale catalogue and keeping a discreet eye on the other potential buyers swarming through the crowded rooms.

'Sorry, I kept getting my elbows bashed.' Poppy handed him his plastic cup with a grimace. 'I had to drink some to stop it being spilt.'

'What's the time?' asked Jake. Viewing went on until eleven thirty when the auction began.

'Only ten. How's it going? Any hot-lots?'

Hot-lots were those attracting a noticeable amount of interest from the dealers. Poppy loved to sound like a pro. When she'd first heard the expression she'd thought it meant stolen goods.

'We aren't interested in hot-lots,' Jake said mildly. He showed her the notes he'd been making, and the prices he'd scribbled next to the items he was interested in. 'Now, I'll be here for the first fifty or so lots. I'll watch you bid, and see how you get on, then head over to Windsor.' He paused and flipped over to the next page of the catalogue. 'Here, you'll be on your own. Carry on bidding and whatever you do, don't exceed the prices I've put down.' He gave Poppy a measured look. 'No getting carried away.'

'What, not even by a knight on a white charger?' Poppy grinned and gave him a nudge. 'You don't trust me an inch, do you? It's okay boss, no need to panic. I'm on my best behaviour. Even better now my feet have begun to dry out. I won't let you down.'

Jake said, 'Hmm,' and drew another Biro from the inside pocket of his ancient Harris tweed jacket. 'Here, you'll want to copy the prices down.'

'No need.' Having swung into super-efficient executive mode, Poppy tapped the catalogue with a forefinger. 'I'll use this.'

By twelve o'clock Poppy had cheered up no end. Chartwell-Lacey Manor was just like something off a film set, the auctioneer was unexpectedly handsome with an almost roguish twinkle in his eye – usually they looked like bank managers about to confiscate your credit card – and the atmosphere was building nicely. It was, Poppy felt, wonderfully dramatic and glamorous. Very Lady Jane and Lovejoy.

She could hardly wait for Jake to leave. She had already bid three times and been successful twice. The adrenalin was swishing through her like nobody's business; and if it was this good bidding with Jake beside her, how much more thrilling was it going to be when she was on her own? It would be like flying solo for the first time, she thought dreamily, without an instructor to stamp on the dual controls . . .

'Okay,' Jake murmured. 'I'm off. I'll be back before three.' He passed the catalogue across to Poppy and pointed to the lot numbers the auctioneer was currently dealing with. 'If you want to grab a sandwich, do it now. You've got twenty minutes before he reaches the Venetian glass.'

Poppy was seriously hard up this week. She batted her eyelashes at Jake.

'Be an angel. Lend us fifty pence for a sandwich.'

'Oh shit, oh help,' Poppy wailed a quarter of an hour later, her blood running cold as she realised what she had done. This was the other kind of adrenalin rush, the nasty kind that seized you when you realised you'd made a balls-up and it wasn't going to go down at all well.

It was the cheap shirt's fault for having shrunk in the rain. As the morning had worn on it had become tighter and tighter. It was like wearing a pantie-girdle over your shoulders.

Worried that at some crucial moment she might not be able to lift her arm to bid, Poppy had nipped into one of the downstairs loos, wriggled out of her sweater and blouse and dumped the blouse in a wastepaper basket. The Shetland wool itched like mad against her bare skin but at least she could breathe again. The sensation of actually being able to inflate her lungs had been positively exhilarating.

So exhilarating, thought Poppy with a sick feeling in her stomach, that she'd danced off to the makeshift canteen for cheese and pickle sandwiches and a Mars bar, quite forgetting to take Jake's copy of the catalogue with her when she went.

Poppy stared wretchedly at the sink where she'd dumped it while she was doing her quick change. That had been twenty minutes ago and the sodding thing had gone, been swiped no doubt by some rotten thieving opportunist too stingy to buy their own.

Stay calm, stay calm, don't panic, Poppy willed herself, before sweat could begin to prickle down her back. She couldn't cope with that *and* the Shetland wool.

Well, it's simple, she decided moments later. I have two choices here. Either I twiddle my thumbs until Jake gets back and tell him I haven't bought anything because I didn't bid for anything because I lost the catalogue with his price list on because I'm a complete wazzock . . . or I have a bash at doing it myself.

With no money left she had to relate her tale of woe to the man selling the catalogues and beg him to let her have one for nothing. Then, curling up on lot hundred and twenty-eight, a Victorian carved walnut balloon back armchair on cabriole legs, Poppy pored over the pages, willing herself to remember which of the items Jake had wanted her to go for. Lots seventy-three and seventy-five, the Venetian glass, she was sure about. And the satin-finished Lalique glass clock, hadn't he scribbled two thou by that? Then there were lot numbers eighty-three and eighty-four, the Ferdinand Preiss figures whose prices she couldn't be certain about. They

164

would probably each fetch around five hundred pounds.

Poppy scribbled her own prices down, keeping her ears pricked to make sure the auctioneer didn't start on the Venetian glass without her. Lot eighty-nine . . . her pencil hovered over the page . . . was a box of assorted paintings. She knew Jake wanted them because when she'd glanced at his list earlier the number had rung a bell; eighty-nine was what she always ordered from their local Chinese takeaway: king prawns with mushrooms and egg fried rice.

'Lot number seventy-three,' announced the auctioneer, making Poppy jump. 'A fine example of Venetian glass, a handmade sweetmeat dish . . .'

Poppy scrawled four hundred next to lot eighty-nine and scrambled to her feet. She wriggled her way into the auctioneer's view and began bidding away. Oh, the giddy adrenalin rush now that she was actually doing it herself . . . no chaperone, no stabilisers!

She didn't get the dish, it went in a frenzy of dealing to a woman in a pink straw hat at the front of the room, but the auctioneer gave Poppy an encouraging wink afterwards. She wondered if it meant 'never mind, better luck next time' or 'hello darling, fancy a drink?' He really was good-looking. Pumped up with adrenalin, Poppy grinned back. Perhaps it meant both.

She didn't get lot seventy-five either, or eighty-three, but she hit paydirt with the second of the Ferdinand Preiss figures, beating off nervous competition from a housewifely-looking woman to clinch the deal for four seven five.

'Sold.' The auctioneer tapped his gavel and nodded at Poppy as if to say 'There, I knew you could do it!' He gave her an encouraging smile. 'Name?'

'Poppy Dunbar.' She had to say it; he looked as if he really wanted to know. Then she remembered who'd be writing out the cheque. 'Um . . . Landers.'

Did he seem disappointed? Did it make her sound married? Poppy ran the fingers of her left hand slowly, front-to-back, through her hair so he would see her ringless state. The exhilaration of bidding – and winning – was still with her. Was this surge of lust real or was she suffering an acute attack of auction-fever?

Poppy didn't know and didn't care. She just wanted to do it again.

And I can, I can, she thought joyfully, studying her catalogue and running her finger down the list. Four more lots, then it was the box of paintings, assorted. She hadn't seen them herself but Jake was always on the lookout for good picture frames.

She'd hazarded a guess and scribbled four hundred in the margin. Poppy bit her lower lip. Maybe, to be on the safe side, she should limit herself to three hundred . . .

' . . . three hundred and fifty, am I bid three hundred and fifty?'

The auctioneer's eyes flickered in Poppy's direction. The corners of his mouth twitched as if he were silently urging her on. She felt hypnotised by the look he was giving her, and by the breathless silence that seemed to have descended on the rest of the room. At this moment she had everyone's rapt attention. So this was how it felt to be the Queen.

Poppy wished she could do one of those slow Lovejoy winks but she knew she'd only look as if a contact lens had popped out. Instead, she nodded, twice, like a chicken.

'Three fifty to the lady on my left. Am I bid four hundred?'

The attention swung to the other side of the room. A male voice – she couldn't see who – said 'Yes.'

Outraged – and not wanting to appear cheap – Poppy shouted 'Four fifty.'

'Five hundred.'

Something weird was happening. Her fingers and toes had gone numb. And she was breathing much too fast. Heavens, never mind looking like a chicken . . . now she sounded like a dog.

Poppy tried to concentrate on the bidding. Even more weirdly, she realised, she no longer knew how much money five hundred and fifty pounds actually was.

'Five fifty? Do I have five hundred and fifty?' The auctioneer was gazing at her once more, lulling her with his voice, coaxing her into saying yes.

'Yes,' Poppy whispered. Then again, more loudly: 'Yes.'

There were no more bids. The gavel went 'tap' on the auctioneer's desk. 'Thank you,' he told Poppy, reaching for his pen. 'Landers. Right, ladies and gentlemen, we now come to lot number ninety . . .'

Chapter 25

'Lot what?' said Jake, his dark eyebrows drawing ominously close together. 'Eighty-nine? I didn't want lot eighty-nine.'

'Yes you did.' Poppy felt the first stirrings of panic. She nodded, to prove herself right. 'King prawns and mushrooms with egg fried rice.'

'*What*?'

'Jake, you definitely marked eighty-nine. I *know* you marked eighty-nine . . .' Her voice began to falter. Numbers were funny things; they played tricks on your brain. She could visualise the menu as plain as day now. King prawns and mushrooms were ninety-eight. Eighty-nine was beef chow mein.

'Poppy, you wrote four hundred pounds next to it.' Jake was sounding less amused by the second. He pointed to her hastily scribbled figures. 'Then you crossed it out and put three hundred pounds for a box of the tattiest and possibly the most terrible paintings I've ever seen in my life.'

'I – I didn't.' Poppy began to stammer. Oh help, now she was feeling really sick. 'Look, I'll p-pay you back . . .'

'You mean you went *over* three hundred? How much,' Jake thundered, 'did you bid?'

It was no good, he was going to find out in a matter of minutes anyway. Poppy braced herself.

'Five fifty.'

The explosion didn't happen. Cautiously she opened her eyes. Maybe he wasn't going to lose his temper with her after all.

'Right, that's it,' hissed Jake. He was white with rage. 'That *is* it. I've had enough. I can't afford you any more, Poppy. You'll have to go.'

Poppy waded through the churned-up field blinking rain out of her eyes. She no longer even cared that she was plastered with mud up to her knees. She was trying to do as Jake had instructed and dump the box of paintings in the back of the van but Jake hadn't told her where he'd parked the van and she couldn't find it.

She barely noticed as a loaded-up lorry trundled past, missing her by inches. All Poppy could think about was Jake, in front of an audience of fifty or so auction-goers, picking through the contents of the box, flaunting her stupidity for all to see. He couldn't have looked more disgusted if they'd been crawling with maggots. Each painting he picked up was worse than the last.

'All I can say about these,' he'd declared icily 'is the best thing about them is the frames.'

The rickety frames were mainly ex-Woolworth, circa thirty years ago. They were made of grimy off-white plastic.

A couple of dealers sniggered.

'I mean, for Christ's sake,' Jake raged, 'how could you even *think* I'd be interested in garbage like this?'

'I didn't see them.' Poppy's voice was small. She felt terrible and Jake wasn't even letting her apologise.

'Then you're even more stupid than I thought.'

'I'll pay for them.'

'Don't make me laugh. Only this morning you had to borrow fifty pence for a sandwich.' He glared at one of the larger pictures, a chocolate-boxy painting of two spaniel puppies peeping out of a flowerpot. Then he dropped it disdainfully back into the box. 'What I don't understand is how you managed to get *up* to five fifty. Was someone else really interested in this rubbish or was the auctioneer bidding off the wall?'

To suggest that she had been bidding against a non-existent buyer was the ultimate insult.

Poppy whispered, 'There *was* someone else.' She saw the auctioneer walking past. No, mincing past. He glanced at Poppy and glanced away again. Up close she saw his eyes were mean and his hair dyed. Bidding-fever had a lot to answer for. She wondered how she could possibly have found him attractive.

Now, out in the rainswept field, Poppy realised she was going round in circles.

The van was nowhere to be seen. She didn't have the nerve to go back inside and tell Jake she couldn't find it. He would only go even more berserk.

She had reached the main gate leading out onto the road. Without stopping to wonder if it was sensible, Poppy hoisted the box of paintings onto her hip and turned left. Left for London. He didn't want to see her again, let alone employ her. Well, Poppy decided, she couldn't face seeing Jake either. She'd been on the receiving end of quite enough fury for one day. All she wanted to do was go home.

'Eeyuch, look at you!'

Claudia, fresh from her bath, looked suitably horrified when she opened the front door.

'Sorry. My key's in my pocket.'

'You're all wet.'

'I'm not, am I?'

Wearily Poppy hauled the box of paintings into the house. What she really longed for was a hot bath but knowing Claudia she'd just emptied the tank.

Claudia, rosy-cheeked and bundled up in a fluffy white robe, padded after her into the sitting room.

'I say, is something wrong?'

'Jake sacked me. I owe him five hundred and fifty pounds.' Poppy collapsed on the floor, pulling off her sodden shoes and socks. 'And I've probably got trench foot. Otherwise everything's fine.'

Poppy was looking sad and bedraggled. To make up for pinching all the hot water Claudia made her a coffee with brandy in it. She listened to Poppy's sorry story while she was doing her make-up. She gave her nails an unnecessary manicure and a final coat of pink polish. She ran upstairs and came down again wearing a new sage green shift dress with expensive looking shoes to match. She squirted herself with heaps of Dior's Eau Svelte.

'Oh,' said Poppy at last. She had been enjoying having someone to moan to. 'Are you going out?'

'Wait until you see him,' Claudia confided gleefully, 'you won't believe it! He's heavenly, completely gorgeous. His name's Will.'

Poppy was astonished. She'd had no idea Claudia could be so enthusiastic.

'When did all this happen?'

'At lunchtime. A few of us from the office went to Rossini's for lunch.' Claudia was practically hugging herself at the blissful memory. 'And he was there with a crowd of friends. The girls kept saying he was looking over but I didn't believe them. Then, just as we were about to leave, he waited until I glanced across . . . and pretended to take one of his eyes out!' Poppy's face was a picture. To show her how he'd done it, Claudia mimed the action. 'He held it in his hand, bent down on one knee and rolled the pretend eyeball across the floor towards me.'

'What did you do?'

Claudia giggled. 'I rolled it back to him.'

'And then he came over,' prompted Poppy.

'And then he came over—'

'And said: "I was hoping you'd catch my eye."'

'Oh bum,' wailed Claudia. 'You've heard it before! I thought it was really original.'

'Sorry.' Poppy felt mean. She began pulling the paintings out of their box. Since she didn't have anything else to do she might as well polish up the few frames that weren't plastic.

'Anyway, his name's Will and he's a broker,' Claudia went on compulsively. 'He lives in Fulham and drives a red Lotus.'

Won't go with your nail polish, thought Poppy.

Claudia smiled a blissful smile. 'And he's taking me to Tatsuso.'

Poppy assumed this was good news. To make up for just now, she said, 'That's terrific.'

The door bell rang. Claudia let out a squeal of excitement. 'That'll be for me! You get it!'

Before Poppy could lever herself to her feet they heard Caspar making his way downstairs and the sound of the front door being opened.

Poppy said, 'It's been got.'

Chapter 26

Caspar had been working up in his studio for ten hours without a break. Coming downstairs in search of banana doughnuts and cadgable cigarettes, he answered the door en route.

'Who is he?' he whispered to Poppy, because Claudia was clearly far too excited to make proper introductions.

'The King of Smooth,' Poppy whispered back. She was marvelling at the sight of Claudia fluttering not just her eyelashes but her whole body at him. She looked at Will Smyth – not Smith – and wondered if he had really been born with that glamorous 'y' or if it was a recent addition, sneaked in there when no one was looking.

Poppy couldn't help comparing him with Caspar. Will's hair was dark and immaculately cut, Caspar's was blond and flopped all over the place. Will was wearing an expensive-looking suede jacket over an expensive-looking golfing sweater over a superbly ironed shirt, superbly pressed trousers and expensive-looking pigskin shoes. Caspar wore no shoes, ancient jeans and a tee-shirt that had been left behind years ago by one of his ex-girlfriends, with 'I love Jason Donovan' on the front.

'What's so funny?' Caspar had intercepted Poppy's side-long glance.

'I'm comparing the two of you. He smells of Givenchy for Gentlemen. You smell of turps.'

'I like the smell of turps.'

'His nails are manicured. Yours are covered in blue paint.'

'Damn, no wonder Claudia prefers him to me.'

'And he drives a Lotus.'

'Oh well, no contest.'

As long as Caspar's battered BMW got him from A to B, he was happy. He couldn't care less about status-symbol cars.

'It's Claudia's lucky day.'

Caspar lifted Poppy's chin. 'Doesn't look like yours.'

'It's been my unlucky day.' Poppy heaved a sigh. 'Claudia got pulled, I got fired.'

'So what else is new?' Caspar grinned. 'Okay, Claudia getting pulled is a bit of a novelty, I'll admit. But you're always getting fired. I thought you'd be used to it by now.'

'Don't make fun.' She prised a hideous old print of Westminster Bridge out of a frame that was at least made of wood, not plastic. If she polished it up it might fetch a fiver. 'I've been a prize prat. This time Jake isn't going to forgive me.'

After much high-pitched laughter and muffled shrieking in the kitchen, Claudia and Will came back. Claudia was holding a bottle of Krug and – precariously – four glasses. Will was holding Claudia around the waist, murmuring something into her ear that was making her blush.

'I thought we could have a drink before we leave.' This was Claudia's way of getting everyone to know each other. She wanted Poppy and Caspar to like Will as much as she did.

'You kept this well hidden,' said Caspar, meaning the Krug. He certainly hadn't spotted it in the fridge.

Claudia looked bashful. 'We only met six and a half hours ago.'

'She's the girl of my dreams,' said Will. He gave her a squeeze and winked at Caspar. 'I like a cosy armful, don't you?'

Claudia mouthed What Do You Think? at Poppy while Will unravelled the wire around the cork. Brightly, Poppy nodded, because if Claudia didn't mind being called a cosy armful who was she to object?

Seconds later the cork flew out of the bottle and bounced off the ceiling. As Poppy held her glass up to be filled, Will deliberately tipped some of the Krug down her front.

'Oops,' he leered, 'now I expect you'll need a hand getting out of those wet clothes.'

'It's a *joke*,' Claudia explained with a girlish giggle. 'He did it at lunchtime, to Daisy from accounts. Everyone thought it was a scream!'

'It's certainly a waste of champagne,' said Caspar.

Will winked again. 'I'd volunteer to lick it off.'

Poppy didn't dare look at Caspar. She took a great swig of her drink instead, so quickly the bubbles went up her nose.

'Well, cheers everyone,' said Claudia happily. Then, as the door bell rang again, 'Whoever's that?'

Will said, 'If it's the wife and kids, don't let 'em in.'

He winked so often, thought Poppy, it was practically a nervous twitch.

Caspar answered the door.

'It's your ex-employer,' he announced, coming back with Jake.

'Oh help,' mumbled Poppy, her gaze flickering nervously to the heap of paintings strewn over the carpet. She couldn't face another shouting match. If Jake accused her of absconding with lot eighty-nine she might have to burst into tears.

'Jake, what a surprise,' exclaimed Claudia. Eager to show off the dazzling new love of her life – ha! this would show Jake the calibre of man she was capable of attracting – she dragged Will towards him. 'You must meet Will . . . we're just off out to dinner . . . Will, this is Jake Landers. Jake, Will Smyth.'

Jake barely glanced at Will as he shook his hand. He muttered, 'Hi,' then turned to Poppy. 'Look, I'm sorry about earlier. I lost my temper and I shouldn't have. You aren't fired.'

'I'm not?'

175

Poppy's eyes swam. She'd been so certain he'd come here to give her another bawling-out.

'I overreacted. I was worried sick when I couldn't find you. How on earth did you get home?'

'A dealer with a van load of Victoriana took pity on me.'

'You accepted a lift from a complete stranger? For heaven's *sake*, Poppy—'

'It was a female dealer. I'm not a complete halfwit.'

'Is that the same as not half a complete-wit?' Caspar wondered aloud.

'Anyway,' Poppy felt honour-bound to tell him, 'she had a quick look at the paintings and said if you wanted to cut your losses she'd take them off your hands for fifty quid.'

'Oh well, I can do a bit better than that,' said Jake. 'After you'd done your vanishing trick I was approached by the chap who'd been bidding against you. His wife had her heart set on the painting of the puppies in the flowerpot – apparently they looked like a pair of spaniels they'd once owned – and he was desperate to get it for her. It's her birthday next week. He's not interested in the other pictures but he offered me three hundred for that one.'

Poppy bit her lip. 'The puppies in the flowerpot?'

'Oh shit.' Jake's face fell. 'Don't tell me. You've already sold it. You threw it in the Thames. You drew moustaches on the dogs.'

'No, it's right here.' Poppy grinned. 'I've even polished the frame.'

'Thank God for that. You had me worried.'

'How do you suppose I've been feeling since lunchtime? So, do I really have my job back?'

Jake nodded. He looked up in surprise as Claudia thrust a full glass into his hand.

'There we are, now we have something else to celebrate,' she said gaily.

'Is it somebody's birthday?' asked Jake.

Will slid his arm around Claudia's hip with a proprietorial air, pulling her against him.

'We're celebrating the fact that I've just walked into this gorgeous girl's life.'

Poppy wasn't the only one who'd been making comparisons. Claudia, revelling in Will's lavish compliments and scarcely able to believe her luck – to think, they'd so *nearly* lunched at Brown's instead – couldn't help comparing Will's suave glamour with Jake's painfully untrendy appearance. He looked dishevelled too, in a Bob Geldof-y kind of way, but you needed to actually *be* Bob Geldof to carry it off.

The thing about Jake, Claudia decided, was he didn't have the first idea about style and grooming and he didn't even have the grace to care. A make-over would do wonders. If he only bothered to smarten himself up he could probably look quite passable, maybe even handsome.

But that was the trouble; he never *would* . . .

'What's the matter,' Poppy teased Caspar, 'jealous?'

He was looking through the untidy pile of paintings, running a finger through the layer of dust covering one of those she hadn't yet blasted with her trusty can of Mr Sheen.

'Mmm?'

He was miles away.

'Bet you wish you were that talented.' Poppy grabbed it from him, held it in front of her, pulled a face and turned it the other way up. 'Now this is what I call a masterpiece. What d'you suppose it is, an aerial view of Dorothea's crazy paving? And this brown splodge at the bottom; that could be a dead hamster . . .'

Caspar ignored Poppy's wittering. He took back the painting and gave it his undivided attention. It was smallish, fourteen inches by ten, and executed in oils. The frame was cheap, obscuring most of the signature. The aggressively abstract nature of the work and the unprepossessing colour scheme – greys and browns with the odd streak of black thrown in for light relief – ensured that neither the auctioneers nor the dealers had paid it more than a moment's attention.

To the casual eye it was a deeply unattractive example of the genre commonly referred to by the public at large as a load of old cobblers.

It had to be a fake, thought Caspar. A copy, an imitation, an 'in-the-style-of' . . .

'What did you say just now?' he demanded suddenly, making Poppy jump. 'Whose crazy paving?'

'Dorothea. Dorothea de Lacey. The woman whose stuff was being auctioned.' There was an odd expression on Caspar's face; Poppy wondered if he had known her. Damn, she hated having to break bad news. 'I'm sorry, she, um, died a few weeks ago. But I'm sure she didn't suffer. It was very peaceful . . . and she'd had a jolly good innings.'

This ludicrous expression always conjured up in Poppy's mind a vision of some tottering old dear in cricket pads and head gear, valiantly defending her wicket. She envisaged Dorothea hitting a nifty six.

Caspar was still studying the painting.

'How old was she?'

'No idea.' Poppy shrugged. So he hadn't known her after all. 'Pretty ancient.'

'Mid-eighties,' volunteered Jake, who had spotted a portrait of Dorothea as a young girl at the sale. It had been painted in 1925. 'Why?'

'Let me take it along to the gallery tomorrow. Show it to someone who knows a bit more about this kind of thing than I do.' Abstract art wasn't his forte. He wasn't going to raise their hopes on such a long shot. But Wilhelm von Kantz had once had a brief affair with an English girl known only as Dorrie. And if this was an undiscovered von Kantz, well . . .

'You mean it could be worth something?' Poppy gazed at the ugly little painting in disbelief.

'Maybe. A couple of hundred or so, anyway.' No one had had more practice at lying to the opposite sex than Caspar.

178

'Who knows? You could even end up in profit.' He gave her a nudge. 'You'll be asking Jake for a pay rise.'

Poppy's eyes lit up. 'Now there's an idea!'

'Thanks a lot,' said Jake.

Will touched Claudia's arm. 'We'd better be making a move.'

Claudia looked around for her jacket, which was draped over the back of the sofa. Spotting it, Caspar passed it across. He said, 'Home by midnight, okay? Don't do anything I wouldn't do.'

Claudia was glad she had at last been cured of her crush on Caspar. There was nothing, after all, more depressing than the prospect of fancying someone rotten for years on end and never being fancied in return.

Thank you, Mother, she thought drily, because the miracle cure was down to Angie. Before, Caspar's astounding success rate with women hadn't bothered Claudia. If anything it had only added to his allure.

Discovering that he had slept with her mother, on the other hand, had had much the same effect as a bucket of bromide. Yuck. Just the thought of them together made Claudia feel sick.

Anyway, she thought smugly, who needs that kind of hassle? I don't *need* to have a stupid crush on Caspar any more.

Nor did she need to worry about those other unfamiliar and even more embarrassing feelings, the ones she'd found herself quietly developing for Jake. Now they *had* been a worry. When you could overlook such diabolical fashion sense, you knew you were in big trouble. Heavens, thought Claudia in alarm, what with his shyness and that haircut and the general lack of interest in the opposite sex, Jake was even more of a no-hoper than Caspar.

But now, thanks to Will, she could put the pair of them out of her mind. He took her hand and gave it a loving squeeze.

I've got someone who thinks I'm the business, thought Claudia, and who isn't afraid to show it. What more could any girl want?

By midnight she knew what Will wanted.

'Oh come on, you know you do too,' he protested, trying to slide his hand for the third time up her leg. 'You invited me in for coffee, didn't you? You can't turn all heartless on me now.'

'I can, I can.' Frantically, Claudia wriggled out of reach. He was right, of course – she *wanted* him to stay the night – but she was even more determined not to be a pushover. She'd read enough women's magazines in her time to know how men operated. They'd take whatever they could get, simply because they were men. But when it came to settling down they wanted a nice girl, one whose bedposts were more or less intact.

Too many notches were a definite no-no, Claudia reminded herself. Okay, it wasn't fair and it wasn't liberated, but that was the way things were. Men respected girls who said no – for a while, at least. If she slept with me on the first date, they'd ask themselves, how many other men has she been with? Oh dear, tut tut, that will never do. Not for the mother of *my* children . . .

'What's the matter? We had a terrific evening, didn't we?' Will was looking hurt. 'I thought you liked me as much as I like you.'

'I do, I do.'

'Hang on, there's an echo in here.'

Claudia began to panic. What if he lost patience with her? What if he took offence at being turned down? What if he decided she'd had her chance and she'd blown it? She might never see him again.

'I just don't want you to think I'm easy, that's all,' she said nervously. 'Because I'm not, but if I let you stay tonight you might think I am.'

'I don't think that.' He gave her a lazy grin. 'I *wouldn't* think it.'

Claudia looked worried. 'The thing is, you *think* you wouldn't think it, but deep down you would. You see, you're only saying this now because—'

'Whoa,' said Will. 'Okay, enough. I give up.'

Claudia bit her lip. Was this the smartest move of her life, or the stupidest?

'I'm going now.' He yawned and rose with reluctance to his feet, avoiding her panicky gaze as he patted his pockets in search of his keys.

Oh God, I *have* blown it, Claudia thought miserably. Before she could stop herself she blurted out, 'Does this mean you don't want to see me again?'

'What? Oh . . . of course not.' He still wasn't looking at her. His manner was vague; he sounded as if he were making polite conversation to a stranger on the train.

'So you *do* want to see me again?'

'Yes, yes.'

'When?' said Claudia.

'What?' He was still hunting for his keys. He shrugged. 'Well, soonish. I'll give you a ring sometime.'

How quickly the best evening of your life could turn into one of the worst. Claudia felt her pride melt away.

'Okay,' she said in a shaky voice, 'you can stop looking for your keys.'

Will glanced at her.

'Why?'

'You can stay.'

He began to smile. The next minute he pulled her into his arms. 'You little beauty! Well, maybe not so little . . .'

Claudia clung to him.

'Just so long as you don't think I'm cheap,' she emphasised. 'I'm not a tart, all right? I don't make a habit of this. In fact, I've never done it before.'

'You mean the poor sods gave in,' Will drawled. He was

grinning broadly. 'When you said no, they thought you meant it. Damn, some men show no initiative.'

He had lifted her into his arms by this time. Claudia felt like a bride being carried over the threshold. As he headed for the staircase she prayed his back wouldn't give out.

She was so happy it took a while for his words to sink in.

'Hang on, you mean you were putting on an act just now? Deliberately making me think I'd never see you again?' She took a playful swipe at his shoulder. 'Oh . . . you!'

'Had to, didn't I?' He paused on the landing to kiss her. 'You were saying no. I had to make you change your mind.' He huffed on his nails and rubbed them with pride against his shirt front. 'Needs must, darling. Where there's a Will there's a way.'

Chapter 27

Poppy had never seen a transformation like it. The effect Will Smyth had had on Claudia was mesmerising. She looked prettier, she was happier, she couldn't stop singing. It went to show, thought Poppy, mystified. There really was no accounting for taste.

'You're home,' Claudia cried when she arrived back from work on Wednesday afternoon. 'Perfect, we can eat right away. I've made a chilli.'

'Made?' Poppy was startled. 'You mean poked holes in the cellophane and put in the microwave?'

'No, *made* made.' Claudia tried to look Delia Smith-ish, as if preparing meals from scratch was something that came perfectly naturally to her. 'Really made. And there's no need to stare at me like that,' she went on defensively. 'It's only chilli.'

'Oh, I get it. Will's coming round to dinner and you want him to see what a perfect wife you'll make.'

'Wrong –' Claudia looked smug – 'so there. I'm meeting him at Johnnie's Bar for a drink.' She beamed. She couldn't *stop* beaming. 'He's going to introduce me to his friends.'

And later, when he brought her home, she would casually ask if he was hungry and they would open the fridge in search of something to eat. Then she would say, even more casually, 'There's some leftover chilli here, we could heat that up. Or I could do cheese and biscuits.'

It was Claudia's subtle approach and she was proud of it. Anyone, after all, could knock themselves out producing a ravishingly formal dinner. Well, she was going to go one better. She was going to really impress Will by being the girl with the ravishing leftovers.

'You keep looking at your watch,' said Poppy, mopping up the last smear of sauce from her plate. She popped the bread into her mouth. 'That was brilliant. Should he have phoned by now?'

'No, no,' Claudia lied brightly.

'Only you seem nervous.'

'Me, nervous? Why would I be nervous? Oh—!'

The phone rang. Claudia leapt on it, her skin prickling all over with relief.

Seconds later she passed it across to Poppy.

'For you.'

Poppy winced. If Will made Claudia happy, she wanted him to phone. If Will made Claudia make stupendous chilli she wanted him to phone almost as much as Claudia did.

'Hi-ya!'

Five minutes later Poppy replaced the receiver.

'That was Dina.'

'I know it was Dina.' Twitchy with nerves, Claudia couldn't help sounding irate. 'I spoke to her first, didn't I?'

'She asked if she could come and stay with us again this weekend.'

'And you said yes. Again.'

'I couldn't really say no.' Poppy shrugged. 'She's hellbent on coming up here. I think she's going through a bad patch at home. Anyway, Caspar doesn't mind.'

Claudia was still fretful. She didn't even dare glance at the phone now. Maybe it was like a watched kettle never boiling . . . if she looked at it, it wouldn't ring.

'Well if you ask me, it's taking advantage. Why can't she book into an hotel?'

Poppy couldn't resist the dig.

'Maybe for the same reason Will didn't book into one the other night. Because it was more convenient to stay here.'

184

Poppy was lying semi-submerged in the bath an hour later when she heard the phone trill again downstairs. Before long Claudia was hammering joyfully on the bathroom door.

'That was Will, ringing to say he's finished work. Just to let you know I'm off out now to meet him.'

Phew, that was a relief. Poppy turned the hot tap on again in celebration, and added another dollop of Body Shop grapefruit shampoo because she'd run out of bubble bath.

'Okay, have a good time.'

'I will, I will!'

'Oh, and I've been thinking about what you said earlier,' Poppy added just for fun. 'The Dina thing. Maybe you're right. I'll tell her to find a B and B somewhere instead.'

Claudia hesitated for less than a second. Will had phoned and all was right with the world.

'Don't be daft, I was only joking,' she cried through the closed door. 'Of course Dina can stay.'

To while away a slow morning, Poppy and Marlene had been giving men marks out of ten for their bums.

'This is sexist,' Jake complained. No matter how hard he concentrated on his accounts he couldn't help but overhear their outrageous remarks.

'You're jealous because Marlene only gave you a seven,' Poppy told him.

'Marlene doesn't recognise quality when she sees it,' said Jake. 'And it's still sexist.'

'It's downright depressing if you ask me.' Marlene pulled a face like Les Dawson. 'I mean it's hardly Bondi Beach around here, is it? Hardly *Baywatch*.' She helped herself to another lemon sherbet, sucking noisily and twiddling the cellophane wrapper around her fat fingers. 'I mean, most of the blokes in here today have *been* bloody antiques.'

Glancing up, Jake spotted Caspar coming in through the double doors.

'How about this one? Is he more your type?'

185

'Average-looking,' said Poppy, sounding bored. She grinned as Marlene's jaw dropped open. 'A five, maybe a six. Not bad.'

'Not bad? Are you *kidding*?' squealed Marlene. 'Look at him, he's gorgeous! Talk about . . . Oh wow, he's winking at me.'

'Actually,' said Poppy, 'he's winking at me.'

It was very quiet on the ground floor. Caspar, whose hearing was excellent, said, 'If you must know, I was winking at Jake.'

'My lucky day,' Jake observed mildly. He gave up on the accounts, which were in a hideous state, and closed the book with a thud. Then he began cleaning the dusty lenses of his spectacles with the sleeve of his plaid shirt.

'It is,' said Caspar. He had come straight from Gillingham's, the prestigious firm of auctioneers in South Kensington whose name was right up there along with Sotheby's and Christie's.

Poppy looked confused. 'Is what?'

Jake, who wasn't so slow, said, 'Really? You mean that little picture's worth a few bob after all? That's great.'

'As a matter of interest,' said Caspar, 'hands up anyone here who knows the name Wilhelm von Kantz.'

Poppy looked blank. Jake looked blank. Marlene, hoping to impress the most heavenly body she'd seen in a long long time, screwed up her eyes and nodded slowly as if the name did mean something to her, she just wasn't sure what.

'Well?' Caspar turned his attention to her.

'Um . . . was he the Red Baron?'

He looked appalled by their stupidity.

'Hopeless, the lot of you. Okay, let me run through this. Von Kantz died two years ago at the age of ninety-three. He was a second-generation American of German-Dutch descent. He was a painter, a womaniser, a serious drinker, and he made a bit of a prat of himself publicly rubbishing the traditionalists and maintaining that his was the only form of art worth the canvas it was painted on.'

'Blimey.' Poppy shook her head in wonder. 'You mean the chap who did "Dead Hamster on a Patio" said that? Some people have a nerve.'

'What?' said Marlene, mystified.

'Go on,' said Jake.

'He came over to England just before the Second World War. He was married – well, married-ish – but he wrote in his diaries about an affair he had here with a woman called Dorrie.'

'Dorothea,' Poppy exclaimed. 'Oh, I love it when things match up! He had an affair with Dorothea de Lacey and he gave her a painting of a dead hamster to remember him by. How romantic can you get?'

'Who did you show it to?' Jake frowned. 'How much does he think it's actually worth?'

'I took it to Gillingham's on Monday. We had to wait until this morning for a couple of their experts to fly back from Boston. I've been with them all morning. They've verified the painting's authenticity. They asked if they could handle the sale.'

Poppy's eyes were by this time like saucers.

'You mean it's worth more than a couple of hundred?'

'Put it this way,' said Caspar. 'When he died, Wilhelm von Kantz was regarded as one of the greatest painters in the world.'

People were staring. The entire antiques market had gone silent. Poppy began to giggle. She punched Caspar on the arm.

'Okay, it's a wind-up,' she told Jake. 'We've been Beadled. Any minute now, the ghost of this loopy artist is going to burst in here and demand his picture back. Wilhelm von Kantz is probably an anagram of gullible nit wits. Watch out for hidden cameras everyone, and stroppy council officials with beards—'

'You really are a bunch of peasants,' said Caspar. 'How

187

can you *not* have heard of von Kantz? You'll be telling me next you've never heard of de Kooning.'

More blank faces. Edward de Kooning, for decades one of Wilhelm's friends and rivals, was possibly the greatest living exponent of this form of art, and nobody here even recognised the name.

'Picasso?' said Caspar. 'Ring any bells?'

'How much is this painting likely to fetch? Jake asked quietly.

Caspar rapped Poppy across the knuckles to regain her attention.

'Will you *stop* looking for hidden cameras? This isn't a joke.' Then he turned to look at Jake. 'Three quarters of a million pounds.'

Chapter 28

'You know what you are, don't you?' Dina said flatly. 'Weird, that's what. Mental. You bid for that picture. That means it's yours. Jake didn't even want the flaming thing. He *sacked* you, for God's sake! I'd tell the stingy bugger to stick his lousy job.'

It was seven thirty on Friday evening and Poppy was ploughing through a bowl of muesli. If she was going to keep pace with Dina in the Malibu and orange department it was best to give her stomach a rock-solid lining before they set out. She looked up at Dina, who was layering bright blue mascara onto her eyelashes.

'Jake isn't a stingy bugger. He's lovely. And I like my job.'

'Yes, but if you had three quarters of a million pounds you'd never need to work again! It'd be permanent holiday time. If I had that kind of dosh,' said Dina vehemently, 'you wouldn't see me for dust.'

Muesli took forever to chew. Gamely Poppy swallowed another mouthful.

'Anyway, it wouldn't be my dosh. It's Jake's picture. He paid for it.'

'He wouldn't *have* it if it wasn't for you.' Dina finished with the mascara and untwirled a bright pink lipstick. 'If you ask me, you should get yourself a bloody good lawyer. You're entitled to at least half.'

'But I didn't ask you.' Poppy wished she had never mentioned the painting now. All she wanted was for Dina to stop going on about it.

189

'Suit yourself.' Dina shrugged, mildly offended by the lack of gratitude. 'I'm on your side, aren't I? I'm your best friend.'

All of a sudden, Poppy thought drily. Money did that to people; it could have the weirdest effects. Like turning casual friends into best ones, as if by magic.

'I can't stay out too late,' she said. 'I've got to be at work by nine tomorrow morning. I'm not going on to any clubs.'

'If I had three quarters of a million pounds,' Dina said dreamily, 'I'd go clubbing it every single night. You wouldn't catch me sloping off early on account of some poxy job.'

Poppy must be going down with something, Dina decided as she let herself into the house much, much later. She hadn't seemed herself at all tonight. She'd been quiet. She'd even snapped once or twice when Dina had brought up the subject of the painting. And when she'd told Poppy about nosy Edna Frost who lived next door to the McBrides and who had last week been diagnosed with lung cancer, the oddest thing had happened.

'Snooping old cow, all she's ever done is make everyone else's lives a misery,' she had told Poppy. 'If you ask me it couldn't happen to a better person. She got what she deserved.'

Okay, Dina acknowledged now with a twinge of guilt, so it wasn't a very nice thing to say, but she had been on her sixth Malibu by then, and Edna Frost had been the neighbour from hell. But what she couldn't get over was the way Poppy's eyes had filled with tears – actual *tears* – as if the news really was upsetting. She hadn't said a word, just sat there with her eyes brimming and her fingers clenching and unclenching in her lap.

Still, never mind. Dina dismissed the bizarre episode with a shrug. Poppy was probably getting her period. And it hadn't mattered a jot that she'd gone home early, as it happened, because by the time the wine bar had called last orders Dina had found herself being chatted up by a couple of guys on a works night out. Once she'd been drawn into conversation with the rest of their party it had seemed only natural that she should go along with them to the Jack of Clubs.

And where's the harm in that, Dina asked herself as she headed through to the kitchen dumping her coat, hat and gloves along the way. What was wrong with a spot of harmless flirting, a bit of smooching to the slow numbers, a quick cuddle in the corner of the club with the less acne-ridden of the two lads who had chatted her up?

Dina wandered around the kitchen. Downstairs in Poppy's tiny room, on the floor beside Poppy's single bed, her sleeping bag beckoned. Except she wasn't in the mood for sleep.

London was for having fun in. Dina's veins were still pulsing with adrenalin. It was only three o'clock; she wasn't even ready to stop dancing yet. And she was so hungry she could eat a – oh wow! a massive helping of home-made lasagne.

How completely brilliant, thought Dina, grabbing the earthenware dish with both hands and knocking the fridge door shut with her hip. Normally when you arrived home starving from a club and looked in the fridge the best you could hope for was half a tin of dried-up baked beans and a bit of green bread.

She zapped the lasagne in the microwave, tuned the transistor radio on the windowsill to an all-night music station and began to sing and dance along to an old Adam Ant hit. She'd had quite a crush on Adam Ant yonks ago, Dina remembered fondly. God, she'd gone to a party once with a white stripe painted across her nose.

'Ant music yo yo yo yo yo,' she warbled, bouncing round the kitchen while the lasagne heated up. 'Ant music yo yo yo yo yo.' Funny lyrics really, when you came to think about it. Still . . . 'Ant music yo yo—'

Dina spun to a halt against the washing machine, clinging on for support. She thought for a moment about climbing inside. She wondered how long he had been standing there watching her. She really wished she hadn't been singing into an imaginary mike.

'Sorry.' He grinned, unrepentant. 'I heard a noise. I thought maybe we had a burglar. Is that what you are, an all-singing, all-dancing burglar?'

'I'm Dina. Poppy's friend.' Behind her, signalling that the lasagne was ready, the microwave went BEE-EEP. Dina jumped again. Heavens, her nerves were shot to pieces. 'Who are you?'

'My name's Will.' His mouth tweaked up at the corners. 'I'm Claudia's friend.'

He was wearing tartan boxer shorts and nothing else. Dina was impressed by his body – he looked as she imagined Will Carling would look in the locker room. He had sleek dark hair like a seal, small dark eyes and just the right amount of designer stubble. He also had excitingly hairy legs – a great weakness of Dina's. Her husband had a good physique but his legs weren't as hairy as these. Besides, when you knew a body as well as she knew Ben's, you were bound to lose interest in the end. As she'd tried explaining to Poppy, you could buy the most brilliant pair of shoes in the world but after a while, they just weren't as brilliant any more. You got bored with them, slung them to the back of the cupboard and bought yourself a thrilling new pair instead.

'Anyway, don't mind me,' Will gestured to the radio, where Adam Ant was still yo-yo-ing away. 'If you want to carry on, feel free.' He winked. 'I like a girl who knows how to have a good time.'

The cheeky bugger was eyeing her up, Dina realised with an involuntary shiver of excitement. She turned to deal with the microwave, standing sideways on so he could see how flat her stomach was. She was immensely proud of her figure and liked to show it off. Not many people could wear cropped tops and skirts this short and get away with it, even if her mother-in-law was forever making snide remarks about catching a chill.

Still, to look at her, Dina thought proudly, you wouldn't think she'd dropped a sprog. This guy Will, for example, would never guess.

'So you're the pushy tart from Bristol who's bored with motherhood and marriage,' Will announced.

Bang went that fantasy. So much for ticking the box if you wanted to remain anonymous. Dina bristled at the slur.

'That's what Claudia said, is it? She's an uptight bitch.'

'Unlike you.' Will looked entertained. 'You're the un-inhibited type. I can tell.'

'I like to have fun,' said Dina, 'if that's what you mean.' Her stomach emitted a terrific rumble. 'Sorry. I'm starving.'

'That smells good.' Will watched as she removed the lasagne from the microwave. Claudia had mentioned something about food earlier but he hadn't been interested then. Now he was quite peckish. He strolled across to the glass-fronted china cabinet and took out two plates.

'Mind if I join you?'

'Get some glasses. There's a bottle of wine in the fridge.' Dina batted her blue eyelashes at him. This was more like it. This was the kind of fun she liked to have. 'We'll have a midnight feast.'

They ate greedily. Dina giggled a great deal at the outrageous remarks Will came out with. He spilled some white wine down her top and told her she should get out of those wet things. He also told her some brilliant jokes. She told him he looked like Will Carling. By the time their plates were empty there were some serious undercurrents going on.

Will pounced as she was carrying the plates to the sink.

'Oooh!' Dina shrieked with laughter and almost dropped the dishes. She pressed her forefinger against her lips. 'Sshh.'

'You're the one making the racket,' Will grinned, 'not me.'

Now she was pinned up against the fridge. Dina could feel the hard ridges of his abdominal muscles pressing into her own bare stomach. She shivered with pleasure. He had a perfect six-pack. When you were married to someone with no visible muscles at all, you appreciated these things.

'What if Claudia wakes up?'

'She won't. She was snoring when I came down.'

'She'll know you've been up to something. You reek of garlic.'

'So do you.' Will's eyes didn't leave hers. His hands roved around her naked midriff. He sighed and his breath warmed her neck. 'You know, you are one hell of a sexy lady . . .'

Claudia had been dreaming about weddings when she was woken by the sound of a shriek followed by a burst of muffled laughter. Caspar and one of his girlfriends, she thought sleepily, or Poppy and Dina arriving back from their night out.

Moments later she woke up properly, her heart racing. Will had gone. And his side of the bed – she patted it frantically – was stone cold. He hadn't just popped to the loo, he had *gone* gone. Home.

Claudia sat up. She felt sick. He'd crept out, making sure not to wake her. She must have said or done something terrible.

Oh God, what if she was hopeless in bed?

She almost wept with relief when she switched on the bedroom light and saw his clothes were still there. No matter how much of a disaster you might be in bed, Claudia reassured herself, people didn't bolt in horror in the middle of the night without stopping to throw their trousers on first.

When she reached the kitchen doorway Claudia wished he had.

What was happening instead was far worse.

'What the fuck is going *on*?' yelled Claudia, and they sprang guiltily apart. Dina, the trollop, pulled down her practically non-existent skirt and combed her fingers hastily through her dishevelled hair. Since it was moussed to the limit, her hand got stuck halfway. Dina wrenched it free, reached for a cigarette instead and with an air of defiance lit it up.

'How could you?' Claudia hissed at her. 'What's the *matter* with you? Don't you care how many people you hurt?'

'Oh I get it,' said Dina, 'this is all *my* fault. I crept upstairs, knocked on your bedroom door and whispered, "Psst, any decent blokes in there? Fancy coming downstairs for a bit of a chat and a snog?" Well, I didn't, so there.' She looked half insolent, half amused. 'For the record, I was minding my own business when Will came down and joined me. We had a laugh, we had something to eat. We got a bit carried away, that's all.' Dina examined her cigarette, took a drag and breathed out a great plume of smoke. 'So don't make out I was the one who made all the running, because I wasn't.'

The little tart didn't even have the grace to apologise. Claudia longed to give her a slap.

'You could have tried saying no.'

'Jesus, will you calm down?' Dina raised her eyebrows in despair. 'It's not as if we were actually at it on the kitchen table. It was only a kiss, okay?'

Will had so far said nothing. Claudia realised she didn't dare look at him. How *could* he, she thought miserably, how could he do this to me? Is getting his end away really all he cares about?

But betrayals weren't only to do with sex. Something else Dina had said clicked into place. Claudia sniffed the air, belatedly recognising the significance of what she could smell.

Garlic, garlic . . .

'You had something to eat,' she said slowly. 'It'd better not have been my lasagne.'

Will spoke up at last.

'Sweetheart, you told me it was left over from lunch. You said it needed to be eaten.' He shrugged good-naturedly.

'Not by her!' howled Claudia.

'Well, how were we to know that? Come on now, no need to get yourself into a silly old state.'

'A silly old state? A silly old state! You were all over her!'

As he turned, Claudia glimpsed his left shoulder. 'You've got scratch marks all over your back! I thought you *loved* me—'

'Excuse me,' said Will stiffly, 'but did I ever say that?'

Dina decided to be helpful.

'Look, if you're one of these hyper-jealous types, maybe it's just as well you found out early on what he's like. You can get treatment for it, you know.'

'For what?' Claudia stared at her.

'Jealousy. They can sort it out these days, you know. On the NHS.'

Claudia spent the rest of the weekend in bed. Alone.

Will had lost patience with her on Saturday morning. He had told her, wearily, to give it a rest, to grow up, to say hello to the real world. Then he had dressed himself, bent over Claudia in bed and given her a perfunctory goodbye kiss.

The garlic fumes had almost knocked her sideways.

'Ciao, sweetheart,' said Will. 'It was fun while it lasted. And don't worry, I'll say hi if we ever bump into each other again.'

Claudia hadn't the heart to argue. She'd been so sure Will Smyth would turn out to be The One. Bloody men, she thought as she huddled miserably under her duvet. First Caspar had to go and sleep with her mother. Now Will had shown his true colours too. Why did they have to be so unfussy, so . . . indiscriminate? Weren't there any men out there for whom one woman was enough?

Poppy, who had slept through the night and missed the whole thing, was amazed by Dina's lack of shame.

'Come on,' Dina shrugged, 'I did the silly bitch a favour. He wasn't her type anyway. She's well shot of him.'

This was undoubtedly true, but there were ways and *ways* of finding these things out.

'You still shouldn't have done it. She was crazy about him.'

196

'All the more reason.'

Exasperated, Poppy said, 'I don't know what you thought you were playing at.'

'Oh, this is good.' Dina grinned, unrepentant. 'Coming from the girl who danced with a stranger on her hen night and ended up cancelling her wedding.'

'Hardly the same thing.'

'Isn't it?' demanded Dina. Her eyes narrowed. 'You *really* want to know what I was playing at? I was playing at having a bit of fun, just like you. I was playing at doing something out of the ordinary. Getting myself a life.'

'You're lucky you didn't get a wallop round the head. Anyway,' said Poppy, 'you've already got a life.'

'I'm bored with that one. I don't want it any more.' Dina had spent ages practising her Paula Yates pout in front of the mirror. She did it now. 'I want one like yours.'

'You've got a baby.'

'I've got a whole family,' Dina wailed, 'not to mention enough in-laws to fill Wembley sodding stadium. That's what's *wrong* with my life!'

'But—'

'Poppy, you don't know how lucky you are, not having any relatives.' She shook her head to show Poppy she couldn't possibly understand. 'I'm telling you, they wear you down.'

Chapter 29

It had only been a fortnight since Poppy's last visit but the change in Alex was shocking. His mind was still clear – he even managed to crack a couple of feeble jokes at Rita's expense – but his body was shrivelling away.

It was a heartbreaking sight.

One of the round-the-clock nurses hired to look after him chivvied Rita and Poppy out of the room after just a few minutes. Alex needed morphine and rest.

'I need a stiff gin,' Rita sighed when they reached the kitchen. She sat down heavily and rubbed her eyes with the heels of her hands. Then she looked up at Poppy. 'The cancer's everywhere. They've given up on the chemo. There's no point. All they can do now is control the pain.'

They drank massive gin and tonics. Rather unsteadily, but feeling that she should, Poppy made a plateful of cheese and tomato rolls.

Rita managed a couple of mouthfuls then gave up and smoked five cigarettes, one after the other, instead.

'Anyway, enough about us,' she said half an hour later. 'Time to change the subject. Come on, Poppy, cheer me up for Gawd's sake. Tell me what you've been getting up to in the last couple of weeks.'

Poppy told her all about the Wilhelm von Kantz painting, which was due to be auctioned at Gillingham's next week. The *Daily Mail* was running a feature on how the lost work of art had been discovered. Dorothea de Lacey's grasping daughters were wild with fury, foaming at the mouth and threatening to sue the auctioneers who had handled the sale at Chartwell-Lacey Manor. Thanks to their incompetence, the sisters had raged at the journalist who had gone to hear their side of the story, they had missed out on a fortune.

'It's quite good, saves us having to feel guilty,' Poppy explained. 'If they'd been nice we would have done. But they sound like complete witches. The journalist told me he'd spoken to practically the whole village. Not one person had a decent word to say about them.'

'So this chap of yours,' said Rita, 'this Jake. Pretty eligible now, is he?'

She was looking more cheerful, Poppy noted with relief.

'Don't start matchmaking. There's nothing like that between me and Jake.'

'All right, what about Caspar?' Rita thought Caspar was wonderful. Stupid name, but that wasn't his fault. Poppy rolled her eyes. 'There's definitely nothing like that between me and Caspar.'

'That's your trouble, there's nothing like that between you and anyone,' Rita pointed out with characteristic bluntness. 'You want to get yourself sorted, girl. Get yourself a decent bloke and settle down. Find one and grab him before someone else does.' She gave Poppy a sly look. 'Are you sure this guy Jake wouldn't fit the bill?'

The auction of the von Kantz at Gillingham's was over in no time flat. Four telephone bidders battled it out and in less than ninety seconds it was all over.

If Poppy had nipped to the loo she would have missed it. She clutched Jake's arm as the auctioneer's gavel fell. Dead Hamster on a Patio had just been bought by a New York collector for seven hundred and seventy thousand pounds.

'How do you feel?' asked Ross Wilder, the journalist from the *Mail* who was sitting next to Poppy.

'I need a pee.'

'Congratulations.' He shook Jake's hand.

'How do you really feel?' Ross murmured in Poppy's ear as they made their way out of the auction rooms.

'Look,' said Poppy, 'since I started working for Jake, all I've ever done is muck things up and lose him money. Now, for once in my life, I've done something right. I couldn't be happier,' she told him firmly. 'Nobody deserves it more than Jake.'

She meant it, she really did. And Ross was almost sure he knew why.

'You and Jake,' he said, nodding encouragement, 'tell me, are you two an item?'

Jake was walking ahead of them. Poppy caught up and tapped him on the shoulder. His green shirt had a nylony slither to it.

'Ross wants to know if you're going to make an honest woman of me.'

'Honest?' Jake looked incredulous. 'Remember a certain cheese and pickle sandwich? You still owe me fifty pence.'

The nurse gave Alex his midday morphine injection. He eased back against the pillows and felt the pain blessedly melt away. With it came the irresistible urge to sleep but he wouldn't. Rita was sending the nurse down for her lunch break, shooing her away so they could have some time alone together. It was like having a bleeding minder, he thought frustratedly. These days they never seemed to get a moment to themselves.

He had to stay awake a while at least . . .

When he woke up, Rita was sitting in the armchair next to the bed reading a newspaper. The play he'd been half-listening to on the radio earlier had finished; a boring lecture about economics burbled on instead.

For several minutes Alex lay there, just watching her. His woman. He loved her so much. They had been such a good team.

God, he hoped she wouldn't drink herself to death when

he'd gone. He hoped she'd meet someone else, in time. He wanted her to be happy again.

Rita looked up. Her face softened.

'You're awake. What are you thinking?'

'That you could do with a visit to the hairdresser. Your roots need doing, girl.'

'You always were a smooth-talking bugger.'

'I mean it. You could give that Nicky Clarke fellow a try. You fancy him, don't you?'

'Not so much as I fancy you.' Rita smoothed his hair away from his forehead. 'How are you feeling? Anything you need?'

Another wave of exhaustion swept over him. Alex squeezed her hand and felt his eyes close.

'You're here, aren't you? You'll do.'

Rita bent over to kiss him. The paper on her lap slithered off her knees and onto the floor.

'Why the *Daily Mail*?' he said as she gathered it up. 'You don't usually read that one.'

'It's got the piece in it about Poppy and that painting she found.' Rita held up the relevant page. 'I was going to show it to you. The reporter reckons there's a bit of a thing going on between her and Jake. Did I tell you how much that painting went for in the end?'

Alex didn't have the energy to study the article himself. His eyelids were closing again.

'Read it out to me.'

He kept his eyes closed while Rita began to read.

' "... and Jake's young assistant, twenty-three-year-old Poppy Dunbar." Talk about not believing what you read in the papers,' crowed Rita, 'they haven't even got her name right. It's Dunn, for Chrissake, not Dunbar. And look, they've done it again – ' she pointed to a section further down the page – 'what's the matter with these people? Why'd they keep putting Dunbar? What a stupid mistake to make.'

Some names you never forgot. Alex was glad his eyes were

closed. His mind flew automatically back to almost a quarter of a century ago. To a country club on the leafy outskirts of Bristol and a beautiful girl called Laura Dunbar.

And then it all clicked into place.

Of course.

It explained everything.

Poppy was Laura's daughter.

Alex frowned slightly. He wondered why Poppy had never told him. Then he remembered something else Rita had just said.

'How old did they say she was?'

Rita double-checked.

'Twenty-three. At least they managed to get that right. It's her birthday in May. Anyway, pay attention. Let me read you the rest.'

She carried on but Alex didn't hear another word.

Poppy Dunbar wasn't only Laura's daughter.

She was his too.

When Rita had finished she looked up. Alex was smiling to himself.

'What?' she demanded.

'Nothing,' said Alex.

Chapter 30

Caspar had spent the afternoon at the Serpentine Gallery supporting an exhibition organised by a friend of his. He had been plied with wine and invited to a party that night by a tall, spikily elegant PR girl called Babs.

He caught the tube back to Kensington. As he made his way out of the station he was spotted by one of the tramps he regularly gave money to.

'Fifty pence for a cup of tea, sir?' The tramp looked hopeful. Caspar normally bunged him a pound.

Caspar hunted in his pockets. Bugger, no coins. Lucky he was in a good mood.

He winked, gave the tramp a fiver and began to move away.

'Hang on a sec,' said the tramp.

When Caspar turned back, four pound coins were pressed into his hand.

The tramp, who had once been a bank teller, said, 'Your change, sir.'

The phone was ringing as Caspar let himself into the house. It was four thirty; Poppy and Claudia were both still at work. Miraculously the ringing didn't stop before he could reach it.

'Hello?' said Caspar.

'Is Poppy there?' said a quiet voice he didn't instantly recognise. 'I'd like to speak to her please. It's Rita.'

Poppy arrived home an hour later. She burst into the untidy

sitting room, hair flying, green eyes alight with happiness.

'Let me tell you, I have had *the* most brilliant day,' she declared with pride. 'Jake let me bid at Lassiter's and I got a Goldscheider face mask for seventy pounds! *And* a Barthelemy bronze for thirteen hundred – is that a bargain or what? Then we went to—'

She stopped abruptly. Caspar's face was sombre. He wasn't interested in her terrific bargains.

'What?' said Poppy, suddenly afraid. Her knees began to tremble of their own accord. 'What?'

'Rita phoned.' Caspar hesitated, then moved towards her. 'I'm sorry, sweetheart. Alex died this afternoon.'

He cradled her in his arms and let her sob.

Poppy got through half a box of tissues. Every time she thought the tears had stopped, they started again.

She was crying, she realised, for all those years she hadn't known her father. All the time she had missed.

Caspar stroked her red-gold hair. He kept his arms around her and couldn't help thinking back to Christmas night when he had so badly wanted to hold her like this.

That feeling hadn't gone away, but now was hardly the moment. All he could do now was comfort Poppy and pray she couldn't read his mind.

He made her a mug of tea, heaping in extra sugar.

'I feel stupid.' Poppy hiccupped, taking the mug and wiping her eyes with another tissue. 'Getting this upset over someone I didn't even know that well.'

'It isn't stupid. He was your father.'

'I got to know Rita better than I got to know him.' Poppy disconsolately blew her nose. 'That's another thing. When I see her at the funeral I can't be this upset. She'll think I'm downright weird.'

'You'll be fine,' said Caspar. 'People do cry at funerals.'

'Yes, but not buckets. Not this many buckets.'

The phone rang. Poppy flinched.

'Oh help, is that her? Did she want me to call her back?'

'No. She just said she'd let you know when the funeral was.'

'Look at me. Listen to me.' Poppy was pale and red-eyed. Her voice was clogged with tears. 'You answer it.'

It was Babs the elegant PR girl. Not thrilled.

'I thought you were going to meet me outside Langan's at seven.'

'Something else came up. Sorry, I won't be able to make it.' Caspar tried not to sound too insincere. He had forgotten all about Babs.

'Go,' sighed Poppy, nudging him. 'Don't stay in just because of me.'

'Oh come on, you said you'd come to the party,' Babs entreated. 'You promised.'

'Sorry, I can't.'

Caspar put the phone down. He turned to Poppy.

'Now you are being stupid. I'm not leaving you on your own.'

'But what about whatsername?' Poppy gestured helplessly at the phone.

'She had legs like Barry Manilow,' said Caspar. 'I'd rather be here with you.'

The phone shrilled again, shortly after Claudia got home.

'It's someone from St Clare's.' She came into the sitting room looking helpless. 'I told him you were ill but he isn't happy. He says he's got a classful of students waiting for a model and if you were ill you should bloody well have let him know.'

'Oh hell,' Poppy mumbled miserably, still on the sofa knee-deep in tissues. 'Look at the state of me. I can't do it.'

'He's not taking no for an answer. He won't get off the phone.'

Caspar looked at Claudia.

'You'll have to do it.'

'What? Are you *mad*?'

'Someone has to.' He shrugged. 'Like you said, they won't take no for an answer. I mean, come on. It's not such a big deal—'

'You bloody go then.' Claudia was staring at him in horror. 'I can't do that! If it's no big deal, you can strip off your clothes for a classful of students.'

Poppy, whose eyes were by this time so puffy she could hardly see, swivelled her head between the two of them. This was like Wimbledon.

'I would. But the class is Study of the Female Form.' Caspar played his trump card. 'And I'm a man.'

'You're a complete bastard,' wailed Claudia. 'No, I'm sorry, Poppy, but you cannot ask me to do this.'

'Please,' Poppy whispered.

'No, absolutely not.'

'Okay. Don't worry. Tell them I'm on my way.'

Claudia watched Poppy sweep a mountain of soggy tissues off her lap. White-faced, frog-eyed and fragile she hauled herself to her feet.

Claudia tried to imagine how she would feel if her father had just died.

Then she tried to imagine how it would feel to be naked in front of a classful of art students, all ogling those bits of her she had spent her entire life trying to keep hidden.

Her most hideous recurring nightmare involved walking into a party and suddenly realising she wasn't wearing any clothes.

'Oh sit down, dammit,' Claudia blurted out. 'You can't go anywhere looking like that. I'll do it,' she announced defiantly and with more than a trace of hysteria. 'Okay? I'll go.'

'Poor Claudia, I feel terrible,' said Poppy when she had left. 'It takes the students six sittings to finish each picture. She's going to be bamboozled into doing it now for the next fortnight.'

'She might enjoy it.'

Caspar had picked up a pencil and notepad. He did a lightning sketch of Claudia, spare tyres atremble, cowering behind a screen in her overcoat, refusing to come out until every student had his blindfold in place.

'She won't enjoy it. She'll hate every second.'

'It'll be character-forming. Anyway,' Caspar spoke with a casual air, 'you mustn't feel terrible. I don't.'

Poppy was instantly suspicious.

'Why should you? What have you done?'

'Nothing much.' Caspar put the finishing touches to his sketch. This time he was unable to hide his amusement. 'Just changed the title of the course from Study of the Human Form.'

'You mean you could have done it? You could have volunteered?' said Poppy accusingly.

'What, get my kit off for a bunch of strangers?' Caspar looked appalled. 'No fear.'

Chapter 31

'You haven't said a word about the money from the painting,' said Jake. Marlene was keeping an eye on the stall while they sat upstairs in a quiet corner of the café. He watched Poppy dunk doughnut number two into her cup of hot chocolate and wondered why she wasn't the size of a sofa.

'What is there to say?' Poppy licked the sugar off her fingers. 'That chap from the paper asked me what I thought you should spend it on and I said a decent haircut.'

'I want you to have half the money.'

Poppy looked shocked.

'I don't want it! It's nothing to do with me. Even if it was, what would I do with it? Seriously, Jake,' she shook her head so hard her spiral earrings almost flew off, 'what on earth would I spend that kind of money on?'

'Buy a house, somewhere of your own.'

The thought of living alone now filled Poppy with horror. As if the Balham bedsitter hadn't been awful enough.

'I don't want a house. I like it where I am.'

'A car, then.'

'I had a car once. All it ever did was break down and run out of petrol. Anyway, the tube's quicker.'

'Jewellery,' hazarded Jake.

'Real jewellery? God, I'd lose it.'

'I don't know.' He looked flummoxed. 'Maybe you could treat yourself to a few things.'

'If you can afford things,' said Poppy flatly, 'they aren't treats.'

'You are weird. Isn't there anything you want? Anything at all?'

I want Tom, thought Poppy. Sadly, he wasn't available in Harrods.

'I know what I'd really like,' she said.

'What?'

'To take you shopping.'

Nervously, Jake said, 'What for?'

'Among other things,' she replied, dunking the last of her doughnut, 'a decent haircut.'

Knowing Jake as well as she did, Poppy realised the key word was speed. No time could afford to be wasted. At the first sign of faffing around, Jake would lose patience and disappear.

They were going to shop SAS-style.

In.

Do the deed.

Out.

'If you make me look stupid,' Jake warned, 'I'll never speak to you again.'

'Don't nag.'

Minutes later he was gazing up in horror at the blue and gold frontage of the hair salon she had brought him to. In Knightsbridge.

'I'm not going in there. That's for girls.'

'It's bi-sexual.'

Poppy pushed him inside.

The male stylist she had booked for the job wore blue leather trousers. His hair was tied back in a blond ponytail.

But he was brilliant at his job.

And he was fast.

'What are we aiming for?' he asked Poppy.

Jake was beyond words. He sat in front of the mirror doing his impression of the incredible shrinking man.

'Think Pierce Brosnan,' said Poppy.

'Mmm, gorgeous.' The stylist ran his fingers experimentally through Jake's wayward hair.

'Is that it?' Jake demanded fifteen minutes later. 'Can I go home now?'

'Contact lenses,' she announced, just to see the expression on his face.

'No way.'

Poppy hadn't expected him to say yes. She took him to an optician and at lightning speed selected a pair of gold-framed, seriously flattering spectacles with amber tinted lenses.

'Don't do that—' Jake tried to stop her snapping his old taped-together horn-rims in half and tossing them into the bin under the optician's desk. 'They can be my spare pair.'

'They can't now.'

Since there was no point choosing clothes Jake would only flatly refuse to wear, Poppy kept it simple. She chose cotton shirts and faded jeans from The Gap, lambswool sweaters in plain colours, brilliantly tailored black trousers, a black leather jacket and three pairs of brogues.

Not a shred of Crimplene, not a pattern in sight.

Poppy surveyed her purchases with satisfaction. If he stuck to these, and only these, not even Jake could make them clash.

Unless . . .

'Socks,' she announced, but Jake had had it up to here with shopping.

'Enough. You can get them another time.' He grabbed the carrier bags from Poppy. 'When am I supposed to wear this stuff, anyway?'

'Every day. All the time.' Kindly, she added, 'You can take them off at night.'

'What about my real clothes?' Jake looked as if he was suffering withdrawal pangs already.

'They aren't real, they're unreal. And if you ever wear any of them again,' she told him, 'I will burn down your house.'

Poppy sat alone at the back of the church and watched her father's coffin slide silently from view. The curtains swished shut. That was it; he was gone.

He never even knew who I was, thought Poppy, biting her lip and willing herself not to cry. If she started again, she might not be able to stop.

The service at the crematorium didn't take long. Stragglers from the last funeral had been there when they arrived and when they emerged afterwards the next lot were already waiting to go in.

It made you think, Poppy reminded herself. All day long, six days a week, people were being brought here to be cremated. And it was happening all over the country . . . all over the world . . .

There was a lot of death about. She wasn't the only person mourning the loss of a parent.

Poppy told herself this, hoping it would help, hoping it might make her feel better.

It didn't.

'You all right, love?' Rita hugged her outside the crematorium while everyone milled around looking at the wreaths on display. 'You're coming back to the house, aren't you? D'you need a lift?'

'I'm okay, Caspar's lent me his car,' said Poppy.

'Sure you wouldn't prefer a lift? We'll be sinking a few.'

Poppy had guessed as much. Knowing she had to drive was her excuse for not getting plastered. Otherwise who knew what indiscretions she might helplessly blurt out.

She squeezed Rita's hands.

'I'll be fine. You're doing brilliantly.'

'Yeah, well. Got to give Alex a decent send-off, haven't we.' Beneath the broad-brimmed black hat and extra make-up Rita was baggy-eyed but determined. 'Flippin' heck, I'd never hear the last of it if I let him down now.'

Alex had his decent send-off. Back at the house it didn't take long for sober commiserations and much eye-dabbing to develop into a rip-roaring wake. Everyone from the Cavendish Club was ·there. Alex's band played all his old favourites. The dancing was uninhibited. At one stage Poppy found herself jitter-bugging with Rita's drunken cousin, who had no memory at all of the last time they had met.

'Come with me a sec,' said Rita, taking Poppy's hand and leading her into the deserted drawing room. 'I've got something for you.'

'What?' Poppy hoped it wasn't another dress.

'A present from Alex.'

Rita took the lid off a Bally shoe box. Poppy half-expected a pair of Day-Glo pink stilettos to wink up at her. She wondered if Alex had really wanted to give her a pair of shoes.

But when Rita peeled away the layers of black tissue, Poppy saw not the dazzle of pink patent leather but the rich gleam of cobalt blue glass.

Rita unwrapped the second spirit bottle, which nestled beside the first. She held them, side by side, up to the light.

'They are alike. I can't tell 'em apart. Anyway, they're yours. Alex wanted you to have them.'

'He did?' Mustn't cry, mustn't cry.

'Said they deserved to stay together.' She clinked the two bottles together and mimed a kiss. 'Reckoned they might miss each other if you split 'em up now.' Fondly, Rita said, 'Silly sod.'

Poppy's stomach did a slow somersault. She wondered if she was reading too much into Rita's recollection of Alex's words.

But could he – *could* he – have realised who she was? Was it possible that he actually could have made that connection, that he might have put one and one together and made three?

Surely not.

But then; maybe . . .

She would never know.

'Did he say anything else?'

Rita thought for a second, shrugged and shook her head. 'No.'

'Oh.'

'Although you can settle a silly argument.' Belatedly Rita remembered. 'Your middle name. It is Teresa, isn't it?'

Poppy looked blank. The subject had come up in conversation the other week. Rita knew it was Teresa.

She nodded.

'See! I told him!' Rita looked triumphant. 'I was right and Alex was wrong. Silly bugger, he was so sure it was Laura.'

It was serious hangover time. Poppy shuddered and gasped as an alarm went off inches from her ear. Now she knew how it felt to be trapped in the bell tower next to Big Ben.

She crawled out of bed, fumbled her way into the shower and clung to the sides while power-assisted needles of boiling water pummelled her brain.

God, that felt awful, worse than when she'd started. Whoever had dared her to down a pint of Malibu and milk deserved to be shot.

When she had finally managed to dry and dress herself, Poppy tottered downstairs.

Rita, in a canary satin robe and matching high-heeled mules, handed her a tumbler of frenziedly fizzing water.

'I know, looks like a volcano about to erupt. I thought four Alka Seltzers,' she said as Poppy peered nervously into the glass. 'Think that'll be enough?'

'I can't even remember setting the alarm clock,' mumbled Poppy. It was unlike her to think of something so sensible.

'You didn't. You just said Jake would swing you round by your earrings if you weren't on the stall by nine. I set it,' said Rita. 'Come along, drink that down. Now, d'you think you could manage a bit of toast?'

Poppy spread the marmalade with a trembling hand. This was kill or cure.

'At least it's shredless,' she said. 'I can't stand marmalade with bits in.'

'Neither can Alex; that's why I buy it.' Rita stopped. She shook her head and corrected herself. 'Neither could Alex.'

There was silence for a fraction of a second.

'Oh buggeration,' sighed Rita, reaching for her Rothmans. She lit one and inhaled down to her toes. 'You'll never guess what else the silly sod wanted me to do. Only give up smoking. Can you imagine?'

'Someone told me once that hangovers are worse when you smoke.' Poppy struggled to keep her toast down as a great waft of eau de fag drifted across the kitchen table. She clutched her head, which was still pounding. 'I can't imagine that.'

'You don't look great,' said Rita, who had probably shipped twice as much but had had far more practice.

'I feel diabolical. I especially borrowed Caspar's car,' Poppy groaned, 'to stop me drinking.'

'Then I went and spoiled it all and begged you to stay. Well, I'm glad you did, even if you aren't.' Rita pushed her fingers through her unbrushed hair. She winced as one of her rings caught in a backcombed bit. 'I didn't want to wake up on my own this morning.'

Poppy couldn't think of anything to say.

Rita twirled the end of her cigarette in an ashtray shaped like an elephant.

'No kids, that's my problem,' she mused. 'Other people have their children to rally round when this happens. Three different people yesterday said wasn't it a shame me and Alex never had any and why didn't I get down to the pet shop?' She said wryly, 'It's a great comfort apparently, when your old man's kicked the bucket. If you don't have kids, get a bleeding dog.'

'Would you?' Poppy looked doubtful.

'Would I heck. Doesn't seem like much of a deal to me. Does a dog argue with you about which channel to watch?

Does he moan about Crystal Palace playing like a wagonload of one-legged monkeys? Can he tell you which shoes look best with your new dress?'

Poppy had finished her toast, which mercifully appeared to be staying down. She knew she wasn't doing a great job conversation-wise but guessed that all Rita needed was someone to talk to.

'There, told you it'd help.' Rita nodded at her empty plate. 'How about a coffee now? I could do you a nice bacon sandwich.'

To Poppy's amazement her stomach gave a greedy rumble of approval. A bacon sandwich would be completely brilliant. She broke into a smile.

Rita jumped up from the table.

'Smoked or unsmoked? And d'you like your rashers crispy or soft? My God, listen to me. Is this what it's like to be a mother?'

'Not at all,' said Poppy. 'If you were my mother you'd be nagging me to tidy my room and telling me to cook my own sodding breakfast.'

'I wouldn't.'

'Oh yes you would. It's what mothers do. And they tell you your fringe needs cutting. Either that or do it themselves,' said Poppy with feeling, 'and never get it straight. In every photograph of me when I was young, my fringe is up to here and crooked.'

Rita laughed. She threw the bacon rashers in the frying pan and leapt back as the too-hot oil began spitting furiously.

'You turned out okay. Your mum would've been proud of you.'

'She wouldn't have thought much of my fringe.'

When the sandwich was made, Rita sat down to watch Poppy eat it.

'If I'd had a daughter I'd have wanted her to be like you.'

'Sure about that? I cheat at Monopoly.'

'Me too.' Rita stirred her lukewarm coffee and fiddled

with an unlit cigarette. 'We wanted children so much, you know. I'd always thought I'd have at least six. As it turned out, we couldn't even manage one.'

'That must have been awful.'

Poppy felt hopelessly inadequate. What else could she say?

'When we found out we couldn't have kids . . .' Rita paused, then shrugged and lit her cigarette '. . . I wondered if Alex would leave me.'

'But he didn't! Of course he wouldn't have,' exclaimed Poppy. 'You two were rock-solid.'

'We weren't always.' With a rueful half-smile Rita glanced up at her. 'We had our share of rough patches, believe me. In those early years.'

'I can't imagine that.'

'Oh yes. He had a bit of a fling once, you know. With some woman in Bristol. Your neck of the woods.'

Poppy's stomach squirmed. Her heart began to race. Thank goodness Rita was now gazing out of the window.

'I never told him I knew,' Rita said absently.

'How . . . how did you?' With difficulty, Poppy swallowed a mouthful of bacon. 'I mean, how did you find out?'

'I got a letter. Anonymous. Telling me my husband was getting up to no good with some married woman.'

'H . . . heavens.'

'I was all set to go down to Bristol and have it out with Alex. Confront her too, if need be. I was . . . *wild*,' declared Rita, her nostrils flaring at the memory. 'A thing possessed.'

Faintly, Poppy said, 'So what happened?'

Rita pulled a face.

'Fell off me bleedin' perch, didn't I? Of all the stupid things to do. There I was, in a right two and eight, about to drive down to Bristol, and I got it into my head that I had to water the hanging baskets before I went. Otherwise they'd have died.'

'Oh—' Poppy realised what was coming next.

'Yeah.' Rita nodded and grinned. 'I came off that step-ladder with a wallop and heard the bones snap in my leg. Crack, crack, crack,' she imitated the sound with relish. 'And that was it. That was me, buggered.'

'So . . . ?'

'So in its own way it did the trick.' Rita shrugged. 'Call it my lucky break. Alex came racing home. He didn't say anything, of course, about whatever he'd been getting up to in Bristol. I didn't mention it either. He was back and that was all I cared about. And from then on I made damn sure he didn't get the chance to do it again. Wherever he went, I went. Wherever he played, I watched. I didn't leave him any spare time for women. Simple as that.'

Poppy was struck by another thought.

'This letter. You never found out who sent it?'

'I had my ideas. Someone took the trouble to find out my address. My guess is the husband of the woman Alex was fooling around with.' Rita shook her head, unconcerned. 'That's something we'll never know.'

Poppy imagined Mervyn Dunbar writing his anonymous letter.

One thing's for sure, she thought: I'm not going to ask.

Chapter 32

Claudia nearly fell over backwards when she walked into the living room and found Jake deep in discussion with Caspar.

He looked so different, not nerdy at all. The haircut, no longer manic Worzel Gummidge, was sleekly dishevelled in a French film-starry way. Gone, too, were the disastrous Jack Duckworth specs. Even the clothes were . . . un-nerdy. Normal.

Jake looked great. Claudia, who hadn't for a moment believed the *Mail* journalist's hints that romance could be brewing between Jake and Poppy, felt jealousy slicing through her like a hot knife. It isn't fair, she thought helplessly, Poppy can't do him up and then decide to fancy him. Not when I've fancied him rotten practically from the word go.

The bad news about the disappearance of the heavy-rimmed Jack Duckworth's was being able to see Jake's long-lashed dark brown eyes that much more clearly. Since they were fantastically sexy eyes this should have been good news but Claudia, trying to smile 'Hi' at Jake without actually meeting his gaze, found it terribly disconcerting. Damn, she wished she'd known he was here. Especially looking like Alain Delon. Now she'd gone all tongue-tied and stupid.

And was it her imagination or had Jake's confidence grown along with the length of his trousers?

'Maybe Claudia can help,' he said, turning to her. 'We were just talking about this chap from Poppy's murky past. Tom. The one she met the night before her wedding.'

'And on that garage forecourt the week before Christmas,' said Caspar. 'Well, not met. Saw.'

'What about him?'

'Jake wants to have a go at tracking him down.' Caspar wasn't wild about the plan. 'He's been watching too much *Columbo* if you ask me. The thing is, even if we could find the bloke, is it a good idea?'

Jake looked at Claudia, willing her to be on his side. He tried not to picture her naked, modelling her glorious body for those lucky, *lucky* art students at St Clare's.

He tried so hard not to picture her naked he forgot why he had been willing her onto his side in the first place.

'Er . . .'

'Um . . .' said Claudia.

For crying out loud, thought Caspar, what is the matter with the pair of them?

'I think if she met him again she'd be disappointed.' Caspar wasn't examining his own motives too closely. All he knew was if Poppy were to fall in love with someone, he wouldn't like it one bit.

'But what if she isn't?' argued Jake. 'It's been almost a year now, and she hasn't been able to get him out of her system. This could be her one chance of happiness.'

'You're beginning to sound like one of Claudia's Mills and Boons,' mocked Caspar.

Claudia flushed angrily. She kept her Mills and Boons well hidden under her bed.

'And you're beginning to sound like a killjoy,' she snapped at Caspar. If it stopped Poppy becoming interested in Jake, she was all in favour. 'I think it's a great idea.'

'She needs cheering up,' Jake said firmly. 'She's been pretty low since the funeral. And since money's no longer a problem, it seems the least I can do.'

'How will you?' Claudia looked interested. Once she got into a conversation with Jake she was okay; the paralysing shyness abated. Those first couple of minutes were the worst.

'We'll take out newspaper ads,' said Jake. With heroic self-control he kept all Claudia's clothes mentally in place. 'The local press as well as the nationals. If that doesn't work we can try radio, maybe even TV. I've made out a couple of drafts, if you'd like to see them.'

'I'd love to see them.' Claudia leaned so far forwards her boobs teetered in their D-cups, on the brink of tumbling out.

Poor Jake's eyes nearly followed suit.

Grinning, Caspar said, 'I'd love to see them too.'

'Will you tell Poppy what you're doing?' Hurriedly Claudia changed the subject.

'Not until we get a result. If we get a result. No point raising her hopes,' said Jake.

Caspar had always run a complicated love-life but now, as spring approached, even he was beginning to get confused.

Kate was still around, chiefly because he hadn't had the heart to get rid of her. Caspar knew he was wasting both his time and hers but what could he do? Every time he tried to ease himself out of the relationship Kate gave him one of those puppy-eyed, please-don't-drown-me-in-a-bucket looks. If he persevered, she dissolved into tears and whispered, 'I don't mind you seeing other women. Really, I don't mind. Just don't finish with me, please . . . I couldn't bear it.'

Feeling trapped and uncomfortable but wondering what else he was supposed to do, Caspar had taken Kate at her word.

He had also got himself slightly more involved than he'd planned with an energetic aerobics instructor. Julia – 'call me Jules' – had a super-honed body, rippling white-blonde hair down to her twenty-two inch waist, and a sunbed tan the colour of Caramac. She also had an insatiable appetite for salad and sex.

Caspar was in favour of the latter but lettuce wasn't his thing at all. Jules had recently begun to take a distressing interest in his diet. 'We only have one body, darling. Think of it as an investment for the future.'

Caspar's idea of investments for the future was buying a scratch card. Twice last week Jules had turned up at Cornwallis Crescent with cellophane-wrapped bowls of lollo rosso, frisée and rocket leaves in a special oil-free dressing, because 'No one can say they don't like salad until they've tried my dressing. I defy anyone to say it isn't out of this world.'

Jules made these pronouncements with missionary zeal. Caspar thought her lovingly prepared salads tasted like grass. He was more interested in her talent for undressing. Jules was wonderfully acrobatic in bed. And he enjoyed driving her to distraction with huge untidy honey and peanut butter sandwiches, currently his favourite après-sex snack.

Then there was Babette – Babs – the elegant PR consultant he had met at the Serpentine Gallery the other week.

Being stood up by Caspar that first night hadn't put Babs off. She had simply phoned him again the next day and asked him when he would be free for dinner. When Babette Lawrenson wanted something, she got it. She had sharpened her skills over the years, starting out as a double glazing doorstepper before moving into PR. Three years ago she had set up her own company. Now she represented a carefully chosen selection of actors, musicians and artists.

She had already offered to add Caspar to her list.

Babette had very short, glossy dark hair, cool blue eyes and a taste for expensive, sharply tailored business suits. She never went anywhere without twin mobile phones – sometimes one at each ear – and her Psion. She was the most organised person Caspar had ever met.

She didn't have time for aerobics classes and she wasn't wild about salad. She was neither thin nor fat, just average. But she knew how to dress to make the most of herself. She always looked, and smelled, stylish. She also had excellent legs.

'We'd make a terrific team,' Babette calmly informed

Caspar on their third date. They were eating roast pigeon with wild mushrooms at Neil's Bistro in Covent Garden. Jules would have shuddered at the sauce and said, 'Not for me, thanks. A minute on the lips and all that.'

'Team?' Caspar watched her neatly spear a mushroom. 'Sounds like a couple of carthorses pulling a plough.'

'That's a typical male ploy,' said Babette.

Caspar grinned. 'I said plough.'

'See, you're doing it again. As soon as a woman mentions emotional commitment, the man panics. He tries to turn it into a joke.'

'What d'you mean, emotional commitment? I thought you were talking about business. Me becoming one of your clients.'

'Oh well,' said Babette, 'that too.'

'Are you serious?' Caspar was enchanted by her upfront attitude. This was the kind of stuff girls kept to themselves. They might think it, but they would die rather than come out and say it.

'Of course I'm serious.' Babette stopped eating. She put down her knife and fork and rested her chin on her hand. Her fingers were strong and capable-looking, French-manicured and ringless. 'I know these things. It's my job to know these things, and I'm good at my job. I'm almost thirty, ready to settle down. So are you.'

'I'm not sure I—'

'Come on,' she chided humorously. 'You've sown enough wild oats to feed Russia. Be honest, aren't you bored with all that? It's time to move on, darling. I'm not saying decide right away, just give it some thought. I'd be perfect for you.' Her cool eyes appraised him for a second. Then she smiled. 'You're certainly perfect for me.'

She had guts, that was for sure. He had to admire her for that.

'Okay, I'll think about it,' Caspar nodded, to humour her. He wasn't entirely certain he knew what he was meant to be thinking about. Had she simply been recommending they carry on seeing each other or was she talking marriage, kids, two point two dogs and a pension plan?

Talk about efficient. Caspar was surprised she hadn't whipped out her Psion and keyed in: Neil's Bistro, 20:25 hrs, proposed to CF. Await decision.

It was an entertaining idea. She was talking about the future and he hadn't even slept with her yet.

Caspar wondered if she would time him in bed with a stopwatch.

'Do you like peanut butter and honey sandwiches?' he asked.

Babette looked amused.

'As a matter of fact, I do.'

Chapter 33

'I've double-booked myself,' Caspar told Poppy when she took a mug of tea up to him in his studio.

He had been on another painting bender, working through the night to finish a huge canvas in oils commissioned by a wealthy Italian banker. Cold sunlight streamed through the skylights, highlighting the thin layer of dust on the room's surfaces. The smell of oil paints, linseed and turps hovered in the air. Caspar took the Batman mug from Poppy, promptly covering it with cadmium yellow paint. His white sweatshirt was streaked with Venetian red.

'You look as if you've been shot.' Poppy unwrapped a Mars bar for him so he wouldn't get paint on that too.

'Probably will be.' He nodded at the door, which served as his diary. The haphazard assortment of scribbled notes pinned to it was escalating out of control. 'I'm supposed to be meeting Babette for lunch. She's introducing me to some journalist who might be interested in doing a piece on me for *GQ*. I'd forgotten I was meant to go with Jules to her best friend's wedding. She's expecting me to pick her up at one o'clock. She'll go ape.'

'Make that triple-booked,' said Poppy. 'Kate rang five minutes ago. She said to remind you about meeting her at one thirty.' Caspar looked blank. 'The preview at the Merrydew Gallery. You promised to take her.'

'Damn.'

'At least she won't go ape,' Poppy reassured him.

'No, just cry.'

'So who'll it be? Who's the lucky winner?'

'I'll think about it.'

Caspar began cleaning the worst of the paint off his hands. Poppy wandered over to the door to take a closer look at the pinned-up notes.

'B. McCloud,' she read, peering at the dreadful writing in green felt tip. 'Is that Bella McCloud the opera singer?'

He pulled a face. 'Ugly old trout wants her portrait done. At least she's keeping her clothes on. First sitting's next week.'

'Not next week. Two o'clock this afternoon.'

'You're having me on.' Caspar looked up. Poppy showed him the note. He winced. 'Bloody hell.'

'What it is to be popular,' she mocked. There was a smudge of blue paint below Caspar's left ear, nestling in the groove between his jawbone and neck. She took the spirit-soaked cloth from him and carefully rubbed it off. Those were the kind of tucked-away smudges Caspar was likely to miss.

He looked down at her, watching the expression of intense concentration on her face. When she had disposed of the smear she spotted another, this time hidden just beneath the hairline behind his ear.

Caspar said, 'It's midday. You aren't supposed to be here either. What happened, did Jake sack you again?'

There. Poppy had finished. Now, whichever of Caspar's girlfriends saw him this afternoon, they could safely nuzzle his neck without risking a mouthful of cobalt blue paint.

'For once, no. I've got a dentist's appointment.'

Poppy tried to sound grown-up and unconcerned. Only wimps were frightened of the dentist.

She just wished she hadn't had that toffee-chewing contest with Marlene last week.

And she wished dental surgeries didn't have to smell so . . . dentisty.

'Scared?'

'Scared? Me? Nooo.'

The trouble with Caspar, Poppy thought with frustration, was nothing got past him. He was brilliant at reading faces.

'So if you aren't scared,' he persisted with evident amusement, 'what are you?'

She may as well admit it.

'Um . . . more like pant-wettingly petrified.'

Downstairs the phone began to ring.

'That'll be for you,' said Poppy. 'One of your dates.'

'In that case, better not answer it.'

'You must. What if it's Bella McCloud?'

'All the more reason.' Just to be on the safe side, Caspar hung onto Poppy's wrist until the ringing had stopped. 'What time's this appointment of yours?'

'One o'clock. Why?'

'Okay. Come on, let's get out of here.'

'Where?' Poppy was confused.

'Don't say I never take you anywhere.' His grey eyes regarded her solemnly. 'We're going to the dentist.'

The surgery was off the Bayswater Road, across the park. Since Caspar's car had been clamped and the sun was shining, they decided to walk.

'You can't come in with me,' Poppy protested. 'I'd really look like a hopeless case.'

'I'm not staying out here,' said Caspar. The waiting room was heaving with kids flinging Liquorice Allsorts at each other. He pointed to a group photograph up on the wall, of the staff at the practice. 'Besides, I wouldn't mind meeting your dentist.'

Poppy's dentist didn't look like a dentist, she looked more like Joanna Lumley. Her tawny-blonde hair was swept back in a severely elegant chignon. Her white coat fell open to reveal a dark blue Lycra dress as tight as a bandage, and the best pair of pale-stockinged knees Caspar had seen in years. She reminded him, he decided happily, of one of those beautiful Russian scientists in *The Man from Uncle*, ice-cool

226

on the outside but when you whipped off their glasses and let down their hair . . .

Poppy's wisdom tooth wasn't only badly cracked, she soon learned, it was growing diagonally and pushing her other teeth out of line. Her heart sinking, she heard the ominous pronouncement: 'You'll be far better off with it out.'

Poppy lay back in the chair, palms sweating, and marvelled at Caspar's idea of keeping her company.

The dentist – 'Please, call me Lisa' – was spending so much time flashing her flawless smile in his direction it was a miracle she hadn't taken out the wrong tooth. Unable to speak, what with the numbness and the mouthful of metal clamps and suction pumps, all Poppy could do was listen to the pair of them chatting each other up. When the thirty minutes of torture were over, the dumpy dental nurse gave Poppy a beaker of pink water and a funnel to spit into. Lisa gave Caspar her business card and scribbled her home number – in case of emergencies – on the back.

Poppy's frozen mouth had turned to rubber. She could no longer spit, only dribble pathetically into the gurgling silver funnel. Ribbons of blood-stained saliva dangled from her chin.

That's it, no toffees ever again, she thought exhaustedly.

It was also definitely the last time she let Caspar come along to give her so-called moral support.

'Don't forget, I'll be expecting to hear from you,' Lisa told Caspar with a dazzling white grin. 'Oh, 'bye,' she added to Poppy as an afterthought.

'Thankth a lot,' mumbled Poppy when they were out of the building.

'No problem.' Caspar was blithely unaware of his crime. 'How d'you feel, still a bit shaky? You've got blood on your shirt,' he pointed out, to be helpful. 'Come on, we'll get a cab home.'

'No, I want to walk,' Poppy said, to punish him. Caspar never walked anywhere if he could help it.

'Are you sure?' A fresh stream of dribble was sliding out of the corner of Poppy's mouth. One side of her jaw had already puffed up. She was beginning to look like a gerbil.

Stubbornly Poppy nodded. They set off up the road.

'Tho? Are you going to thee her?'

Slow to translate, Caspar frowned. 'Who?'

'My dentitht!'

'Oh . . . well, could do. Seems a shame not to.' He shrugged good-naturedly. 'It'd have its advantages, you'd never run short of dental floss.'

'Huh.'

'And she's a dab hand with a drill,' Caspar mused. 'I bet she's brilliant at putting up shelves.'

If not at putting up much of a fight, Poppy thought sourly. Somehow she had expected better of a dentist. It was almost undignified, like witnessing the Queen bopping along to the Spice Girls.

'Come on, cheer up.' Caspar took her arm as they crossed the road, heading for the park. 'It's over now. Look on the bright side; you'll never have to have that tooth out again.'

'Don't you have enough women to worry about already?' Poppy refused to join in. She wasn't in the mood. To punish him some more, she quickened her step. 'I mean, do you *need* to add another one to your litht?'

'Who says I worry about them?' Caspar grinned. 'I'm not worried. The more the merrier.'

'That ith *tho* immature,' snapped Poppy. She dragged another handful of tissues out of her jacket pocket and mopped irritably at her chin. The tissues came away crimson; all this stomping like a squaddie on a route march had brought the bleeding on again. And she might not be able to feel it, but she knew her left cheek was swollen. She must look completely mad.

'I don't know why you're in such a stinking mood,' said Caspar.

Poppy didn't know either. She didn't reply, striding on

across the grass instead. When she tried chewing her lip it felt disgusting, like a car tyre. Behind her she heard Caspar's far more leisurely footsteps, and the brief crackle of a sweet wrapper.

Go on, I hope both your front teeth fall out, thought Poppy vengefully. That would put the frighteners on his precious harem. That should do the trick.

The sun had disappeared behind a bank of ominous grey cloud. A cold wind whistled across the park. As Poppy tugged the flimsy bloodstained collar of her denim shirt up around her ears, fat raindrops began to fall.

To her even greater annoyance, she'd been so set on striding stroppily ahead at a rate of knots that she hadn't thought where she was going. Now, having veered left instead of right, they were closer to the boat houses on the bank of the Serpentine than to the bridge leading across it.

'Where are we going?' protested Caspar. 'This is miles out of our way.'

Poppy hoped he was freezing. She hoped he was hating every minute. It was a comforting thought.

'My feet are starting to ache,' Caspar complained behind her.

Without bothering to look round, Poppy murmured, 'Good.'

Chapter 34

They cleared the trees and approached the water's edge. Poppy, blinking rain out of her eyes, wondered why a dishevelled-looking pensioner would want to wade around in the muddy shallows on such a cold day.

Then she spotted the bottle – whisky-shaped – in the pensioner's hand. Poppy turned and waited for Caspar to catch up.

'He mutht be plathered. Should we try and do thomething?'

'What did that dentist take out, your eyes as well?' said Caspar. 'It's not a he, it's a she.'

Poppy squinted across at the pensioner. In that battered trilby and long flapping raincoat it was hard to tell.

The next moment the pensioner was wading round in a semi-circle, shaking her whisky bottle at them.

'Bugger off!' The throaty, clearly articulated voice that floated across the water towards them was deep-pitched but definitely female. 'Sod off, the pair of you. Nosy bastards, come to gawk. What am I, some kind of peepshow? The latest tourist attraction?' She glared at Caspar and Poppy in disdain, then bellowed 'By God, it comes to something when a soul in torment can't even bloody top herself in peace.'

The voice wasn't only female, it was instantly recognisable.

'Crikey.' Poppy gazed transfixed. 'It'th Eleanor Brent.'

'Whatever you do,' said Caspar, 'don't ask for her autograph.'

Eleanor Brent was one of the darlings of British theatre.

She was practically a national treasure. Never what you could call a stunner, she had made up in talent and character for what she might have lacked in the looks department.

Eleanor's first fifty years had been spent ricocheting from one hopeless marriage to the next. She endeared herself to her public by proving you could be endlessly talented and still spectacularly unlucky in love. She was famous for smiling through her tears and insisting the show must go on.

Now she was in her mid-seventies, still much-loved, still working in the theatre, but no longer a slave to men.

'I've grown up,' she was fond of informing interviewers when they broached the subject. 'Put all that lovey-dovey stuff behind me, thank God. My days of romance are over. Such a relief.'

In which case, thought Poppy, what was Eleanor Brent doing, drunk as a skunk in the Serpentine, hurling insults at strangers and threatening to do herself in?

'I mean it.' The actress stumbled and waved her bottle wildly over her head to balance herself. Her trilby slipped over one eye. 'Get out of here,' she roared, sounding like Margaret Thatcher in need of Strepsils. 'Go on, bloody clear orf.'

To make sure they got the message she stuck two fingers up at them.

'No,' said Caspar.

The deadly glare narrowed.

'Look,' Poppy began to say nervously, 'how can we leave you here? You thouldn't be—'

'Jesus Christ, what are you, a pair of sodding Samaritans? Just turn round and start walking, can't you? I don't *want* to be lectured to about the joys of living by a couple of do-gooders. Apart from anything else, this water is fucking freezing—'

As she bawled out these lines, Eleanor Brent began wading clumsily backwards. Within seconds she was up to her waist.

The rain, pelting down even harder now, pitted the surface of the water like machine-gun fire.

The next moment she lost her balance and toppled over, losing her trilby in the process.

'For heaven's sake,' sighed Caspar, kicking off his shoes. He peeled off his jacket and handed it to Poppy.

'Quick,' Poppy squealed, shoving him forwards and promptly dropping his jacket in a mud slick. 'She'th going to drown!'

The torrential rain had emptied the park as efficiently as Domestos kills germs. There wasn't another soul in sight.

'Damn.' Caspar spoke through gritted teeth. 'She was right about something. It is bloody freezing.'

The trilby was sailing out into the centre of the lake. Eleanor Brent appeared to have sunk. Not without trace, though; a stream of bubbles broke the water's surface ahead of Caspar who was now struggling to keep his own balance.

The bottom of the lake was disgustingly slimy. The thought of what he could be treading in made Caspar wish he hadn't kicked off his shoes. Taking a deep breath he launched himself into a crawl in the direction of Eleanor's bubbles.

This was nothing like *Baywatch*. It didn't bear much relation, either, to the lifesaving techniques he had practised years ago at school, when all you'd had to save was a plastic dummy in a pair of striped pyjamas. Plastic dummies co-operated beautifully. They rolled over onto their backs, let you put one hand under their chins and allowed you to guide them effortlessly back to the side of the pool.

They definitely didn't kick, punch, bite and swear at the top of their voice. Nor did they bash you on the head with a bottle of Scotch.

'Drop it,' Caspar spluttered as Eleanor Brent simultaneously kicked him in the kidneys and lashed out at his face. God, for an old dear she had a grip like superglue. 'Drop that bottle and stop *fighting—*'

'Bog off,' howled Eleanor, her teeth bared with rage. 'Think I want to be rescued by some bloody blond nancy boy who dyes his hair?'

'My hair-is-not-dyed.'

She let out a turkey screech as he managed to prise the bottle from her gnarled fingers. Her nails clawed at his neck, drawing blood. Caspar began to wonder if he was going to have to knock her out cold; at this rate he didn't stand a hope in hell of getting her onto dry land.

The next moment, eel-like, Eleanor slithered from his grasp. She sank again. Caspar dived and dragged her back to the surface. This time she didn't fight back. All her strength had gone, he realised. She had also swallowed a couple of lungfuls of lake.

By the time Caspar managed to tow Eleanor Brent to safety, two cars had stopped. Poppy, who had flagged them down and dialled 999 on the second driver's mobile phone, waded in up to her knees to help Caspar haul the semi-conscious Eleanor out of the water and up onto the grass.

Eleanor promptly threw up. When she had finished she rolled over and aimed a wild punch at Caspar's knees.

'Raving bloody poofter. My second husband was one of 'em. And what the buggering hell have you done with my Scotch?'

'I'm not a poofter.' Caspar rubbed his eyes wearily, then blinked as a flashbulb went off six feet to his left. The driver of the first car was crouching on a muddy patch of grass to get the best camera angle.

'What the bloody hell was that in aid of?' Caspar demanded. Listen to me, he thought. Eleanor Brent's profanity must be catching.

'Come on,' reasoned the man, 'I've got a mate who works in a picture agency. You're Caspar French, aren't you? And that's Eleanor Brent.' As he spoke, he took another shot. 'I can sell these. You'll be a hero.'

'I can hear the ambulanthe,' said Poppy, whose mouth was

hurting horribly. She took off her shoes and emptied them of water.

'Come here.' Caspar patted the ground next to him, thinking that this could give Jake the break he'd been looking for. 'Come and sit down next to me.'

Chapter 35

Poppy spent the next day in bed nursing monumental toothache – or, more accurately, gapache – and gazing morosely at the photographs of Caspar and herself in the papers.

Claudia, who had dumped the whole pile into her lap before rushing off to work, hadn't helped.

'I've heard of bad hair days,' she told Poppy with ill-concealed smugness, 'but this has to be a bad face day. You must be so embarrassed.'

Tactless but true. With her hair plastered down, her white face grotesquely swollen on one side and a dribble of blood smearing her chin Poppy was almost – but sadly not quite – unrecognisable. She looked like a cross between Quasimodo and a vampire left out in the rain.

Caspar, needless to say, looked terrific.

The day worsened as one by one, the women Caspar had stood up yesterday discovered the pictures in their own newspapers.

Caspar made his escape shortly after breakfast, murmuring something vague about having to meet a visiting Hong Kong collector. This meant Poppy was left in the house with only a packet of Nurofen for company.

And a phone that rang every five minutes.

Babette Lawrenson was the first, madder than a wasp because not only had Caspar stood up the journalist from *GQ*, he had made her look a fool into the bargain. It was unforgivable, she raged, not to mention bloody unprofessional. What the hell did Caspar think he was playing at?

Poppy, who hadn't so far met Babette, quailed beneath the onslaught. She wasn't up to this; her jaw felt as if it were being prised apart with the kind of equipment blacksmiths used on horses' hooves. She certainly didn't have the energy to defend Caspar, who might have let Babette down but who had saved someone's life.

As if sensing as much, Babette swapped targets.

'And I'm surprised you haven't seen fit to apologise,' she remarked acidly, 'seeing as you were the one who persuaded him to slope off yesterday afternoon.'

'But I didn't—'

'Funny, Caspar's talked so often about you, I'd imagined someone more attractive. When I saw the photo in the paper I couldn't have been more surprised. I had no idea you were so . . . plain.'

The calculated hesitation indicated that plain was Babette's way of saying she looked a complete fright. Poppy was rendered speechless by the jibe, all the more cruel because it was true.

'Anyway, make sure Caspar rings me the moment he gets in,' Babette concluded briskly. 'Oh, and tell him I spoke to my travel agent last night. If we want to go ahead and book, he needs confirmation by noon tomorrow.'

Wearily Poppy put the phone down. She wished she was one of those people who could leave it off the hook but she wasn't.

Minutes later as she was mournfully examining her reflection in a hand mirror, the phone rang again.

'I've just seen your picture in the paper,' Dina screeched joyfully. 'Not that I recognised you! God, Poppy – what have you been doing to yourself? You look like that chap in *Alien* just before the monster explodes out of his chest. Whatever's happened to your *face*?'

With friends like this, Poppy thought, who needs enemies?

She certainly didn't need Julia's barbed comments. They might not have been as deliberately cruel as Babette

236

Lawrenson's, but the implication was there; Caspar had failed to turn up for Jules' best friend's wedding and it was all Poppy's fault. Somehow she had forced Caspar to go for a walk with her in Hyde Park. He hadn't wanted to, of course; she had dragged him along, subjected him to some insidious emotional blackmail.

Whatever, she was the baddy. She was entirely to blame.

It was almost a relief to field the terse calls from Bella McCloud's manager. At least he didn't sling vile accusations directly at her or tell her she had a face like a monkey's bum.

The next call was from Kate, in tears as usual. She didn't have the nerve to point the finger at Poppy but she undoubtedly thought it. Listening to her being sweet and understanding and asking how she felt made Poppy feel worst of all.

'I'm sorry,' she told Kate hopelessly, 'I didn't ask him to come along with me to the dentist. He just . . . insisted. You know what Caspar's like when he makes up his mind.'

'Of course I know,' Kate sniffed. 'It's not your fault, Poppy. He just decided he'd rather be with you than with me. Oh bugger – ' she blew her nose noisily – 'how can s-someone you love so much make you so mis-mis-miserable?'

The last call came from her dentist, the lovely Lisa, who was too busy inflicting pain of her own to read newspapers. She hadn't heard about the rescue in the park, she was simply phoning to invite Caspar round to her house for dinner that night.

'He's busy,' snapped Poppy.

'Oh, shame. Well, do tell him I called. Maybe another night.'

'Maybe.'

'Is this Poppy?' As if remembering her for the first time, Lisa asked with professional politeness, 'How are you feeling today?'

'Like shit,' said Poppy, and hung up. She had had enough.

When Caspar finally rolled in at six o'clock, she had had time to build up to a simmering state of rage. Misery had given way to irritation. All the blame that had been so unfairly heaped on Poppy by the various women in Caspar's life, she was now ready to off-load onto him.

Her jaw had never hurt more. And the swelling was expanding to unimaginable proportions. The anger inside her grew.

First *Alien*, now *The Elephant Man*, thought Poppy as she caught sight of her reflection in the sitting-room mirror. At this rate I'm going to do John Hurt out of a job.

'You poor thing,' said Caspar, who was in great spirits. 'How about a brandy, would that sort you out?'

'I don't need sorting out,' Poppy snapped, itching to get started. 'You're the one who needs to get yourself sorted out. I'm sick of it, Caspar. Bloody sick of this.' She tried to hurl a piece of paper at him, which didn't really work. She should have written his messages on a brick.

'Ouch.' Caspar pretended to stagger backwards.

'It's not funny. This is the list of everyone who phoned you today. Sorry I didn't have time to type it up – ' Poppy attempted withering sarcasm – 'but I was in bed *trying* to get some sleep.'

'Sweetheart—'

'No! Shut up and let me say this. And don't call me sweetheart,' she yelled, 'because I've had it up to here with your sweethearts. That bitch Babette . . . Kate . . . Julia . . . they all blame me for you standing them up yesterday. It was all my fault, wasn't it, that you let them down! You should have heard the things they said—'

'I'll tell them,' Caspar shrugged. 'No worries. I'm sorry if they gave you a hard time, swee—Poppy, but I'll put them straight. You know I will.'

'That's not the point,' she howled. 'What you need to do is get your act together, stop mucking everyone around and . . . and . . . *grow up.*'

She shivered suddenly, hating the way Caspar was looking at her, half amused and half taken aback. In his eyes she was good old Poppy, someone he could have a bit of a laugh with, someone who would always listen to his mild grumblings when the endless stream of girlfriends made too many demands on his time. Oh, every now and then she might have put up token resistance, Poppy thought with fresh bitterness, but basically, as far as Caspar was concerned, she was on his side.

She was okay. A good sort. A pal.

Every time she had studied the photographs in today's papers Poppy had been struck, painfully, by the differences between the two of them. There was Caspar, blond and godlike, and herself, bedraggled and hoglike. And even though she knew she didn't normally look like that, it still hurt. Like hell.

No wonder Caspar had never made a pass at her.

Shocked that she could even think it – good grief, what was the matter with her today? – Poppy launched into the next wave of attack.

'You know what you are, don't you?' she demanded. 'You are just so damn *selfish*. You don't give a shit about anyone else. As long as you're all right, nothing else matters. What do you care about other people's feelings? Sod all, that's what.'

'You're beginning to sound like Eleanor Brent,' said Caspar. 'Good job we don't have a swear box.'

'Oh ha-bloody-ha.'

The door bell rang. Since Poppy was too busy seething and thinking up fresh home truths, Caspar answered it.

He came back into the sitting room with a cellophane-wrapped bouquet of orange roses and a bottle of Stolychnaya. They weren't for her.

Caspar tore open the envelope and read the accompanying letter aloud.

'Dear boy. Having sobered up, I now have to thank you for coming to my aid yesterday. I did a

239

foolish thing. Mercifully I have lived to regret it. I can assure you I was – headache apart – extremely glad this morning not to wake up dead.

Once more, my heartfelt thanks. Please enjoy the vodka on my behalf, as my doctor informs me I am now on the wagon. He's a bloody old fool – still, this time I can see his point. There shall certainly be no repeat of yesterday's performance. How depressing to think a bellyful of putrid pond water might have been the last drink of my life.

Thank you again. Eleanor.'

'How moving,' Poppy sneered because saying anything nice was by this time completely beyond her. 'What a total hero you are.'

'What a total strop you're in,' countered Caspar. 'Jesus, next time I see some raddled old actress drowning I'll leave her to it.' He frowned. 'Anyway, I still don't understand. Why are you like this?'

'I'm like this because Eleanor Brent thinks you're the bee's knees, and you aren't. You're a complete shit. What's more, I bet you deliberately sloped off this morning,' Poppy accused him, 'just to avoid all the phone calls you knew you'd be getting. You left me to take the flak instead. And some bloody flak it was too. Come on, admit it,' she snarled, 'you weren't really seeing a collector from Hong Kong.'

'Okay, I wasn't. It was someone else. But it was still a meeting I couldn't break.' Caspar looked uncomfortable. He had actually been invited to Kensington Palace to discuss the possibility of a royal commission, but he had been warned not to broadcast this news.

'What kind of meeting? Horizontal, I suppose.'

'Now you're being childish.' He began to lose patience. Poppy was standing with her hands on her hips like a fishwife. 'Look at you—'

'Yes, look at me!' Poppy had spent most of the day peering into a mirror. Every time she did, it seemed she had slid up the ugly-scale another notch. 'Just look at me, fright-night on legs. One more example – as if we bloody needed it – of how self-centred you are.'

'*What?*'

She grabbed one of the newspapers and shoved it at him. Her grotesque, swollen face gazed up from the page.

'How could you have done it? Whatever possessed you?' Poppy demanded furiously. 'You knew how awful I looked, but you had to drag me into the picture anyway – never mind the blood on my chin and my hair being a mess and the fact that I looked as if I'd been chewing a brick. Do you have any idea how humiliating that is? Can you even begin to understand how ashamed I am? No, obviously you can't.' Since all Caspar was doing was looking bemused, she jabbed at the photograph again, so hard her finger went through his face. 'As long as you're looking great, nothing else matters. It doesn't matter how much of a fool you make *me* look. That's why you're selfish.'

So much, thought Caspar, for his spur-of-the-moment plan. If the ploy had worked, if Tom had spotted Poppy's picture in the paper and managed to track her down as a result, presumably Poppy would have been thrilled. As it was, she was all but unrecognisable and even if Tom did recognise her, she looked such a sight he would be more likely to emigrate.

But this was something else he couldn't tell her because as Jake had pointed out, it would be unfair to raise Poppy's hopes until they had a result.

Not that she was being exactly fair, thought Caspar. Talk about ungrateful. It was positively the last time he tried to play Cupid.

In all honesty, he hadn't thought twice about how Poppy was looking when the guy had shown up with the camera.

241

Poppy was Poppy, with her big eyes and her mad hair and the irresistible broad smile that lit up her face.

Not that her face was in much danger of lighting up just now.

'Have you finished?' Beginning to feel hard done by, he wondered briefly if Poppy expected him to apologise. Sod it, why should he? What, after all, had he done that was so wrong?

Poppy glimpsed the flicker of boredom in his eyes. There was resentment there too, resentment no doubt that she had dared to speak her mind. Caspar clearly had no intention of saying sorry.

'Yes,' she snapped. Then, as he turned towards the door, 'No! No I bloody haven't.'

Caspar suppressed a yawn. 'Okay, but try and fit it into the next two hours. I'm supposed to be going out tonight.'

'Don't worry, I won't keep you,' Poppy shot back. 'I'm just saying it's about time you grew up. Sorted yourself out. Why don't you do the decent thing for once, and put your fan club out of their misery? It's not fair on any of them, buggering them around like this. What you need to do is choose one. Go eeny meeny miney mo. Then get married.'

Caspar stared at her. He could still hardly believe they were having this row. He'd had no idea Poppy felt this way about him. She was positively oozing disdain from every pore.

'Right.' His tone was level. 'So. Is that it?'

'That's it,' Poppy's smile was saccharin-sweet. 'There, never mind two hours, I managed to fit it into two minutes. Rather like your sex life.'

Bewilderingly, Poppy realised she was on the verge of tears. She had no idea why, just as she couldn't imagine where all this pent-up fury had come from. God, she thought, appalled, I sound like some screeching fishwife.

But whatever happened, Poppy knew she mustn't let Caspar see her cry.

Chapter 36

Claudia wasn't nearly as sympathetic as Poppy would have liked her to be. Arriving home shortly after Caspar had left the house – without a word to Poppy – she was far more interested in rummaging through her wardrobe and swivelling in front of mirrors to see if last summer's bikinis made her bottom look big. Marilyn, one of the girls from the office, had split up with her boyfriend forty-eight hours before they were due to fly out to the Canaries. Marilyn wasn't heartbroken – 'Ah, he wasn't up to much; what can you say about a man who wears socks in bed?' – and Claudia, desperate for some sun, had offered to take his place.

'By this time tomorrow I'll be stretched out on a beach.' She heaved a blissful sigh and held up a parrot-green swim-suit. 'Does this look as if it's shrunk?'

'You're no help,' Poppy grumbled. 'I've had the biggest fall-out since Chernobyl, Caspar's never going to speak to me again, and you aren't even listening.'

'I am, I am.' There was a hole in the side seam of the green swimsuit. Claudia kicked it under the bed, rummaged in the wardrobe some more and unearthed a burnt orange bikini. 'Now this one's good for sunbathing. But if you try and swim your boobs fall out—'

'We may as well say goodbye now,' said Poppy. 'He's bound to have kicked me out by the time you get back.'

'D'you really think he will?' Claudia let out a shriek of delight as she spotted her favourite white espadrilles. 'You little darlings . . . I've been looking for you everywhere!'

'Not that you care.' Poppy was beginning to feel distinctly unloved. Claudia was hugging her espadrilles like puppies. Any minute now, Poppy thought, she'd give them a couple of biscuits.

'Look,' said Claudia, because Poppy's thunderous expression was putting her off her packing, 'I hate to say I told you so. But be honest, the reason you're upset is because you've only just realised what a shit Caspar is. I mean, isn't it what I've been saying all along?'

Claudia was lying; she *loved* being able to say I told you so. Poppy gritted her teeth and nodded. Under the circumstances she didn't have much choice.

'You always used to think it was funny,' Claudia went on, 'the way he got so muddled up about who he was supposed to be seeing. I felt sorry for them but you just thought it was hysterical.'

'I felt sorry for them too.' Poppy was stung. 'Well, Kate anyway.' She decided she might as well confess. 'I thought you were jealous because you fancied Caspar yourself.'

Claudia didn't howl with laughter; that would have been overdoing it. She just looked suitably amused, as if a small child had told a knock-knock joke.

'I've never fancied Caspar. Oh, I know he has the looks and the charm, but don't forget I've lived here longer than you. I've always known what he's like. Anyway,' she added with a genuine shudder, 'he had an affair with my mother. If that isn't enough to put you off someone, I don't know what is.'

Poppy had forgotten about that. Caspar and Angie Slade-Welch. He had laughingly denied it at the time but of course he had slept with her. As Claudia pointed out, it was pretty yukky. Angie might be glamorous but she was old enough to be Caspar's mother too.

Belatedly Poppy remembered that Claudia wasn't supposed to know about Angie's visits to the house.

'Your mum?' She raised a tentative eyebrow. 'And Caspar?'

Surely Caspar hadn't been indiscreet enough to spill the beans.

Claudia carried on packing. Her expression was matter-of-fact.

'My mother told me. She's on some kind of mission, if you ask me, to prove how attractive she still is to the opposite sex. I think she expected me to be impressed,' Claudia went on drily. 'The trouble is, having your portrait painted and getting slept with by Caspar isn't an achievement. It's par for the course.'

Arriving home from work the next day, Poppy found a note with her name on the front propped up against the biscuit tin.

The house was empty. Poppy's fingers shook as she unfolded the sheet of paper. She hadn't meant all those terrible things she'd said – well, maybe meant them a bit, but that didn't mean she wanted to be banished from Cornwallis Crescent for good.

But all the note said was: Poppy. Have gone away for the week, with Babette. As Claudia is away too, this leaves you in charge of the house (i.e. don't leave front door wide open when you go off to work.) I have bought an answering machine and set it up, so no need for you to take messages. C.

Having vented her spleen yesterday, Poppy had pretty much got her exasperation with Caspar out of her system. Now, re-reading the terse little note, she felt a lump expand in her throat. No Dear Poppy, no jokes, no lighthearted warnings about wild all-night parties. He hadn't even been able to bring himself to sign off with his full name; all she now merited was a chilly initial.

He was still angry with her.

She might not be out on her ear – yet, anyway – but they definitely weren't friends.

TOM: Are you the Tom who visited a Bristol

nightclub last June and met a girl, out on her hen
night, called Poppy?
If you are Tom or you think you may know him,
please phone this number, any evening . . .

Studying the advert in the personal column of the *Evening
Standard*, Jake experienced a rush of something that was a
mixture of excitement and pride. He felt quite private
detectivish, maybe even a bit James Bondy. It had taken him
hours to perfect the wording of the advertisement. He had
been tempted, at first, to put Desperately Seeking Tom. Then
he had toyed – quite daringly for him – with Did You Ever
Meet A Girl Who Wore Durex On Her Head?

In the end he kept it simple. He had bought a mobile phone
– okay, so the world and his dog carried mobiles around these
days, but it still secretly gave Jake a thrill – and arranged for
the ad to run every night for a week. He'd had two calls
already, from a girl offering exotic personal services and from
a man called James who would be more than happy to change
his name to Tom. So long as the money was good, he
explained matter-of-factly, he'd answer to any name Jake
liked.

'Fancy a trip to the cinema?' asked Poppy, who was
missing Caspar and Claudia dreadfully. The big house felt
strange without them and the weekend loomed emptily
ahead. She sat on a George III giltwood armchair with her
feet tucked under her and prodded Jake's copy of the
Standard. 'Whenever you like, tonight or tomorrow night.
Go on, have a look and see what's on. You can choose.'

'Can't make it,' said Jake, imagining his mobile phone
ringing in the middle of the film. He had already decided he
had to stay at home in order to take the calls that were bound
to flood in. 'Sorry, I'm . . . er . . . pretty busy just now.'

Jake never went anywhere in the evenings. Poppy
wondered if he was cinemaphobic.

'Okay, never mind seeing a film. How about coming round

to my place and letting me cook dinner? Nothing too glamorous, just chilli or something, but we could play Boggle, open a bottle of wine . . .'

Jake had compiled a series of questions to ask the potential Toms who phoned up, in order to weed out the cranks. The questionnaire was his version of Cinderella's glass slipper and he could hardly put it to each caller with Poppy there, her ears out on stalks.

'Sorry. I really am busy. Maybe another time.'

Poppy nodded without speaking. She tried not to feel hurt. Jake's manner had become almost abrupt; he clearly had better things to do these days than socialise with her.

I smartened him up, she thought with a twinge of resentment, and now I'm paying the price. Jake isn't busy, he's just seeing someone else.

As if on cue, two women who were regulars at the market approached Jake's stall. Hunched low in her chair pretending to read next week's Bonham's catalogue, Poppy watched them flirt gently with Jake. In the old days he would have blushed, stammered out some lame excuse and disappeared before you could say white rabbit.

To look at him now you wouldn't believe it. He was coping beautifully, taking their attentions in his stride and well on his way to making a sale. He wasn't flirting back at them, Poppy noticed, but he was certainly letting them think he might.

And all thanks to a new image.

Jake had discovered self-confidence and it suited him.

Poppy, whose weekend was looking emptier and more gloomy by the minute, thought: Fat lot of good it's done me.

Feeling faintly guilty, even though all she was doing was phoning a friend for a chat, Poppy rang Dina in Bristol.

'. . . it's so weird, I'm never usually like this. Six o'clock on a Friday evening and I'm already bored out of my skull.

You wouldn't believe how quiet the house is. Every room is so *empty*.'

'What do you look like?' Dina, ever practical, thought it best to check.

'Eh?'

'Your face. D'you still look like a gargoyle?'

'Oh! No, that's all gone down.'

'So you can be seen out in public?' In Bristol, Dina fluffed her hair up in front of the mirror and gave her reflection a knowing grin.

Poppy pretended not to understand. 'What are you getting at?'

'Come on! I can be there by nine. And if Claudia's not there I can't upset her, can I? While the cat's away and all that. We'll have a ball!'

Poppy felt guilty again.

'What about Ben? And the baby?'

'They'll manage,' Dina breezily dismissed that problem. 'You know Ben. If I'm happy, he's happy. He won't mind. And as for Daniel, he won't even notice! Tell you what, hang on a sec and I'll just square it . . .'

She was back on the line moments later.

'Get your kit on, girl. And do yourself up. This weekend is going to be wild!'

Chapter 37

Deciding to go for it was easy enough; actually going through with going for it was another thing altogether.

Hopelessly out of practice, Poppy took a leaf out of Dina's book and tripled her usual amount of make-up. Heaps of black around the eyes, more blusher and *gallons* more mascara. Rifling Claudia's dressing-table drawers in search of big earrings she came across a nice bronzy-looking lipstick and put it on. Bronze was good, it went with her hair and wouldn't make her look a complete tart.

Poppy stared at herself in Claudia's mirror as within seconds bronze turned to crimson. She looked at the label on the base of the lipstick. Damn, it was one of those Ultraglow indelibles.

Now she looked a complete tart.

'Hey, Morticia!' gurgled Dina when Poppy pulled open the front door at three minutes past nine.

By midnight Poppy's mouth was magenta. The lipstick, which couldn't be scrubbed off, not even with a Brillo pad, got darker the hotter you got. And Poppy was hot.

Matching Dina drink for drink had seemed the only way to banish the demons. By eleven o'clock they had jostled and scrummed their way through half a dozen packed-to-the-rafters South Ken wine bars. Poppy found herself drinking tequila and exchanging banter with a crowd of city types ready to celebrate the start of the weekend. Dina, whose skirt barely covered her bottom, kept rounding on innocent men shrieking, 'You pinched my bum! Right, you

250

can buy me a drink for that. *And* one for my friend.'

When they eventually moved on to a club it was with half a dozen or so stockbrokers still in tow. Poppy, purple-lipped and light-headed, wondered if the tall one called Neil was really as good-looking as she was beginning to think, or just the best of an extremely average bunch.

Dina was dancing with B.J., the one who had started all the bottom-pinching in the first place. Poppy danced first with Tyler, then with Ken, then with an Austrian called Hans who galloped around the crowded dance floor like a camel. Feeling sorry for him, because everyone else was laughing and pointing him out to their friends, Poppy galloped like a camel too. By the time Neil managed to battle his way back from the bar she had worked up a raging thirst.

'Steady,' said Neil. 'Don't want you passing out cold.'

Poppy eyed him over the rim of her lager glass – well, maybe not *her* lager glass exactly, but the one she was drinking out of.

'I'm all right. I've got hollow legs.'

Weird, but true. Tonight, she decided, they were definitely hollow.

'You've got gorgeous legs.' Neil had an engaging lopsided grin and endearingly curly earlobes.

'You've got gorgeous ears,' Poppy heard herself say.

The grin broadened. 'You have . . . um, stupendous eyes.'

She wagged a finger at him. 'Are you making fun of me?'

'Absolutely not. Your eyes are stupendous. So's the rest of you.' His appreciative gaze flickered over the little white Lycra dress which clung lovingly to Poppy's every curve. 'I just wish you weren't so plastered. I'd really like to see you again.'

About time I got myself a boyfriend, Poppy thought. She nodded approvingly. Yep, that was what she needed. To sort herself out and settle down with someone nice. Normal and nice. She gave Neil an encouraging look and wondered if he squeezed the toothpaste in the middle. She hated people who didn't do that.

'The thing is, you're going to wake up tomorrow not even able to remember tonight.' He looked wistful. 'When I phone, you won't know who I am. You'll be too embarrassed to meet me . . . we'll never see each other again . . . bang goes our great love affair. We're *doomed*.'

Poppy thought at once of Tom, of the great love affair that had never happened. Thanks to her. Damn, how could she have been so stupid?

'Oh God, don't cry!' Neil was filled with dismay. 'Come on, cheer up. Have another drink.'

Poppy couldn't remember afterwards whose bright idea it was that the impromptu party should be carried on at Cornwallis Crescent. She vaguely recalled everyone piling out of three cabs, loaded down with bottles from an all-night off-licence, and staggering noisily up the front steps to the house.

Boisterous games were the order of the night. Dina, a Club 18–30 devotee, appointed herself games mistress and bullied everyone into teams. In her element, she demonstrated with B.J. how to play pass-the-banana. B.J., who was like someone out of *Baywatch*, kept whispering, 'Wait till this lot have gone. I know better games than this.' Dina shivered with pleasure; she could hardly wait.

Poppy knew if she sat down for a second she'd crash out, so she didn't sit down. If she was going to have a monumental hangover tomorrow – and really, there was no 'if' about it – she was jolly well going to get maximum enjoyment out of tonight. And if playing wheelbarrows around the sitting room – picking up matchboxes in your teeth along the way – wasn't sophisticated, so what? Who cares, thought Poppy as she was hoisted onto Ken's shoulders for the start of the next game. I'm having fun.

'Stop wobbling,' Dina shouted across the room. 'Don't hit the lights. And smile.'

A flash went off. Then another. Dina grinned and threw the camera to Hans. She grabbed B.J. 'Come on, now take one of us. *Ouch –*' she yelped with laughter as B.J's hand slid downwards – 'you sod, I told you not to pinch my bum again! I'll be black and blue tomorrow. What's my old man going to say when I get home?'

Waking up the following morning was awful. As soon as Poppy realised how bad she felt, she tried to go back to sleep.

But how could you possibly sleep when you felt this ill?

'Here,' said a male voice over her shoulder. Poppy jumped as a mug of hot tea was pushed into her hand. When she turned her head – ouch, *ouch* – she realised she wasn't in her own bed.

'I live here,' she groaned up at Neil, who had made her the tea. 'How did I get landed with the sofa?'

'It was more a case of you landing on the sofa,' Neil explained. 'Once you did, you were out cold. To be honest, none of us wanted to risk carrying you down the stairs to your room.'

'Oh.' Poppy thought for a moment. 'So who slept in my bed?'

Neil looked nervous. 'I did.' Hurriedly he added, 'I kept my clothes on.'

'What about everyone else?'

'Um . . . B.J. and your friend Dina disappeared upstairs. Tyler fell asleep on the bathroom floor – he always does that – and Ken's behind the sofa.'

'Ken,' said Poppy, 'are you behind the sofa?'

No reply.

'I can see his feet sticking out,' Neil explained. 'I didn't say he was conscious.'

'Hans,' mumbled Poppy.

'No, his feet.'

'*Hans.*' She tried to remember who else had been at the party. A couple of blonde girls, but they had caught a cab around four. Her last memory of Hans was of him dancing that astonishing dance again, round and round the sitting room like a wasp in a bottle . . .

Neil shrugged. 'Maybe he left.' His earlobes turned red. He cleared his throat and sat down on the far end of the sofa. Poppy shifted her feet over to make room. How embarrassing, had she really been irresistibly drawn to those glowing ears? Had she actually told him they were gorgeous?

In the harsh light of the morning after, it was immediately obvious that Neil wasn't the boyfriend she'd been looking for. Last night he had been good fun, really quite handsome, and flatteringly attentive. Today he was looking thin and gangly. He had adopted one of those eager-to-please, you-do-still-like-me-don't-you expressions that were always, as far as Poppy was concerned, an instant turn-off.

As for the ears: frankly, they were weird.

Guiltily, Poppy dropped her gaze. Since she wasn't looking so hot herself, there was every chance Neil was thinking the same about her.

But it was still embarrassing, having him perched at her feet like a puppy. She had had too much to drink and led him on. Shamelessly. She wondered if she could off-load the blame onto Dina.

'Well,' Neil joked feebly, 'at least you remember me. I was worried you wouldn't.'

'Oh, I remember.'

Sensing her discomfort, his shoulders sagged a good couple of inches.

'But now you're sober and you're having second thoughts.'

Defeated wasn't the word for it, Poppy decided. The boy looked positively trounced.

'Sorry and all that.' She felt rotten, but what else could she say? 'We had a great time last night. But really, to be honest—'

'You don't fancy me, you don't want to see me again, it isn't going to be the romance of the century after all.' Neil shrugged and managed a self-deprecating smile. 'It's okay,

I've heard it before. Story of my life.'

'Oh come on, it can't be that bad.'

'It can.' He was making light of the situation, but clearly meant what he said. 'That's my trouble, you see. If I meet a girl I like, I start fantasising. Oh, not that,' he added hastily as Poppy's eyebrows went up. 'I start fantasising about us getting married. I actually picture the church service, the whole bit. Then I imagine us with kids. Sometimes I even get as far as grandchildren. I know it's hardly macho.' He glanced, shamefaced, at Poppy. 'It's not what men do. But I can't help it. I want to live happily ever after. That was why I couldn't let you disappear last night. You might have been the one I'm looking for. I can't wait for it to happen,' he said sadly. Then, with a rueful smile, 'Of course it never does, because I scare girls off.'

Poppy said nothing. She was thinking about Tom again. And wondering if the magic of their all-too-brief encounter would really have survived.

It was a horrible feeling, like being six again and having to listen to the school bully jubilantly telling you Father Christmas didn't exist.

Poppy had believed unswervingly in Father Christmas, just as she had always believed in love at first sight.

Now, thanks to Neil, she was beginning to wonder if even that existed.

God, this was depressing. She pulled herself together and looked across at the lanky figure perched on the end of the sofa.

'You'll meet someone. One day it'll happen.'

'Yeah.'

'Truly. Loads of girls would kill for a man like you.'

'Yeah.' His tone was unconvinced.

'I mean, look at all the bastards out there who run a mile from any kind of commitment.' As she said it, Poppy thought of Caspar.

'Like B.J.' Neil nodded in agreement. 'He thinks I'm mad.

He says women are only good for two things and one of them's ironing shirts.'

'I'd iron B.J.'s shirt on one condition,' said Poppy.

'What?'

'That he stays in it.'

Chapter 38

Upstairs, Dina slowly regained consciousness. She listened for several seconds, bemused by the fact that the breathing she could hear appeared to be in stereo.

She turned her head to the left. B.J. lay with his smooth brown back to her. His dark hair stuck up at angles. Each breath he took was deep and regular, almost but not quite a snore.

Dina turned to the right. Another back, paler than the first and bonier around the shoulders. This time the hair was sandy-blond, finely textured and floppy like a child's.

Just to make sure, Dina levered herself up on one elbow. She peered over at the sleeping profile of Hans.

Blimey, thought Dina, don't remember that happening. She lay back down again and tried to rack her aching brains, in case it had. But the bedroom door was wide open, and Hans – another quick check revealed – was wearing trousers. He had most likely stumbled into the room in the small hours in search of something more comfortable to sleep on than a floor.

Dina wouldn't have minded a three-in-a-bed situation, but it would have been a shame not being able to remember it.

Reassured that she hadn't missed anything, and dealing with her hangover in the only sensible way, she closed her eyes and went back to sleep.

Tyler was something of a connoisseur when it came to bathrooms. He didn't know why, he certainly didn't do it on purpose, but every time he went to a party he woke up the next morning on the bathroom floor. Carpet if you were lucky, lino if you weren't.

Student flats were the worst.

No, correction: all-male student flats were the worst.

But waking up in a bathroom had its advantages. You could relieve your bursting bladder, splash cold water over your face and clean your teeth before anyone saw you and took fright. Tyler, who never went out on a Friday evening without a folding toothbrush in his back pocket, did all these things now. There, he felt better already, and the bathroom had been a positive pleasure to spend the night in. Thick carpet, he noted approvingly, a good quality bath towel that had rolled up to make a comfortable pillow, and plenty of expensive, girlie-smelling soap to wash with.

Tyler screwed the top carefully back on the toothpaste, replaced his folding toothbrush into its plastic case and slid it into his back pocket.

Halfway along the landing on his way to the stairs he passed an open bedroom door. Inside, in a row like the three bears – except these were all in the same bed – lay B.J., Dina and Hans.

They were all fast asleep. Hans had his arm around Dina, who in turn had her arm flung across B.J. B.J., stubbly-chinned and handsome, was snoring into his pillow like a train.

Tyler experienced a stab of envy. How did that lucky sod B.J. do it? How did chaps like him always manage to pull? Why did some blokes go through life effortlessly getting the girls while others spent their nights alone on the bathroom floor?

Still, that was B.J. for you. The man knew how to operate. Spotting a camera on the carpet beside the bed where it was likely to get trodden on, Tyler picked it up.

It was a good camera, an Olympus. Only one picture left before the film was used up. For Tyler, who was tidy by nature, it was as irresistible as the last window on an advent calendar.

He stepped back, took the photograph and rewound the film. He liked finishing things, rounding them off.

When the camera had stopped whirring he placed it on a chest of drawers where it couldn't get stepped on and went downstairs.

In the sitting room he found Neil talking to Poppy. From behind the sofa, Ken's feet stuck out.

'There was me thinking I was the first one up,' Tyler grinned at Poppy. 'And look at you, with your face done already.'

Poppy flew to the mirror over the fireplace. She clapped her hands in despair over her aubergine lips.

'I don't believe this stuff,' she wailed. 'It's still *on*.'

By Sunday night Jake had taken fifteen calls on his mobile phone and was no longer feeling like a secret agent with a walkie-talkie. The novelty had soon worn off. He was an old hand at this now. A pro.

The phone calls had been a let-down though. Mostly they had come from men claiming to be Tom.

'Yeah, mate, that's me. Met this bird down the disco, like your advert said. What's her name? Poppy, yeah . . . right, so I'm phoning you up, like you said. What do I get, like, a reward or something?'

Some made a better job of it than others, but all Jake needed to do was ask what colour Poppy's hair had been to prove they weren't the Tom he was looking for. 'Blonde,' most replied. 'Brown,' said two. 'She was so beautiful I didn't notice,' claimed one gallant soul.

'Okay,' Jake gave him another chance, chiefly to relieve the boredom. 'How did the two of you meet?'

'We were standing next to each other at the bar. I tipped out a handful of ice cubes and crushed them with my bare fist. I turned to her and said, "Now that we've broken the ice . . ." '

None of them had been the right Tom. Jake was far more disappointed than he had imagined and impatient to try again. He began to compile a new list. Plan B. The same ad, but this time all the papers.

He wasn't going to give up now.

Dina was smitten with B.J.

'Should you be doing this?' asked Poppy, as Dina punched out his number for the umpteenth time on Sunday afternoon.

'Of course I should.'

Poppy was beginning to feel like an old record.

'But what about Ben and Daniel?'

Dina heaved an impatient sigh. 'That's different. They're in Bristol, I'm here. Look,' she struggled to explain, 'B.J. and I just clicked. Really, we clicked. What happened on Friday wasn't a one night stand. There was more to it than that— Oh hi! Is B.J. there?'

He wasn't. Dina left yet another message for him to call her as soon as he got in, even though she had to leave in less than two hours.

'That was his flatmate again,' she said casually when the message had been relayed.

'Has it crossed your mind,' Poppy was exasperated, 'that he might be avoiding you?'

'I've already said, haven't I? It wasn't like that with us.'

Back in Bristol on Monday afternoon Dina was unbelievably restless. She was twitchy, too hyped up to relax. Poppy, who had promised to phone as soon as B.J. got in touch, wouldn't even be home from work before six.

But it was only three o'clock now and Dina was beginning to wonder how she was going to last. Margaret McBride had already popped-round-for-coffee and proceeded to deliver a pointed lecture on young women who don't know when they're well off. Dina, bored rigid by her mother-in-law's barbed comments about duties and responsibilities and the importance of the family – very *EastEnders* – hadn't been able to get rid of her fast enough.

Daniel, who was teething, had hardly stopped screaming all day, getting right on her nerves.

Ben had too. Placid, easy-going Ben. All he had said to Dina about her weekend away was, 'So long as you had a good time, love. That's all that matters.'

Dina wondered what she had to do to get a reaction out of Ben these days. If she told him what had actually happened to her in London on Friday night, would he even care?

By five o'clock, like a junkie no longer able to hold out for a fix, she fell on the phone and dialled B.J.'s number.

As it rang, Dina felt the fix begin to take effect. Even if he wasn't there it didn't matter; she felt better already, just knowing she had made the phone ring in his flat.

On the fifth ring, magically, the call was answered. Thrilled, Dina felt her heart leap into her throat. Adrenalin hurtled through her body. Her hands were all slippery with sweat.

She opened her mouth to say, 'Hi, it's me!'

But the voice at the other end continued. The laid-back drawl belonged to B.J. but his message was being relayed via an answering machine. Swallowing disappointment, Dina listened.

'. . . afraid neither B.J. nor Adam are able to take your call right now, but if you'd like to leave a message, feel free after the tone . . .'

Right, thought Dina, her eyes bright and her pulse racing, that's what I'll do. Just leave a friendly message reminding him he hasn't called me back—

'. . . unless, that is, you're the slag from Friday night,' B.J.'s voice went on, evidently amused. 'Nina or Dina or whatever your name is. The little tart, anyway, who keeps pestering me to phone her. If that's you, we'd much prefer you to hang up now. And please don't bother calling this number again.'

Ben, home early from work, came in through the kitchen

door and found Daniel alone, strapped into his pushchair. He unbuckled him and lifted him out, throwing his son up into the air to make him giggle and swooping him from side to side like an aeroplane. Then, with his elbow, he nudged open the door separating the kitchen from the hallway and aeroplaned Ben all the way through to the living room.

He found Dina sitting bolt upright on the sofa with tears streaming down her face. She was clutching the phone.

'What is it, is someone ill? Is someone dead? Oh my God, not Mum—'

'Nobody's dead.'

Dina wiped her wet face on her sleeve. She hadn't heard Ben arrive home. Damn and blast . . . that *bastard* B.J.

'So why are you crying?'

I don't know, I can't think of a good reason, Dina thought wearily. She didn't know if she could even be bothered to come up with one.

Ben, still holding Daniel, stared down at her. 'Tell me why.'

'Bloody double-glazing people.' She found a tissue up her sleeve, the one she'd used earlier to wipe puréed rusk off Daniel's face. 'Five calls in the last hour, from different firms, all trying to sell me bloody windows.' Dina mopped at her eyes with the Farley's-encrusted tissue. 'I'm sorry, it just gets me down.'

'Oh, love.'

Ben put Daniel down on the floor and placed an awkward arm around his wife. 'You can't let double-glazing salesmen reduce you to this. Maybe you should see the doctor. You could be depressed.'

I am, I'm *bloody* depressed, thought Dina, beginning to howl again.

Chapter 39

The house wasn't as much of a tip as Claudia had been expecting. When she arrived home, bronzed and glowing after six heavenly days in the Canaries, the place was actually clean. It was also empty. Poppy and Caspar must both be out. This was a big shame, because she was bursting to show off her glorious tan, but at least it meant she could lie in the bath, give her sun-bleached hair a hot oil treatment and unpack in peace.

After her bath, feeling extremely efficient, Claudia emptied her suitcases and sorted her washing into whites and coloureds. She loaded the washing machine, chucked her espadrilles into the sink to soak and lugged the empty cases upstairs. Since getting them back on top of the wardrobe was always a hazardous occupation – so much harder than getting them down – she left that task to Caspar. It was a job for a man.

Spotting Caspar's camera on her dressing table reminded Claudia that she had a film to be developed. What Caspar's Olympus was doing in her room was anyone's guess but that was Caspar for you; the other week she had found his sunglasses in the fridge. Caspar's film was used up too, Claudia noticed. He was so hopeless it would be months before he got round to doing anything about it. May as well take both rolls down to the chemist together, she thought a trifle smugly. Goodness, doing favours, I *must* be in a good mood . . .

* * *

263

She picked up both sets of prints two days later. Just to make sure they were Caspar's, Claudia flipped through the first few – taken at a friend's exhibition at some new gallery in Soho – and was soon bored. Modern art wasn't her scene. Shovelling the photos back into their envelope, she ran upstairs and drawing-pinned it to Caspar's attic door along with the rest of his mail, ready for when he arrived home. Claudia was far more interested in her own photos, the ones of her basking on the terrace by the hotel pool. She had been browner, blonder and bosomier than Marilyn and it hadn't escaped the hotel waiters' notice. She'd been whistled at nonstop.

Wait until Jake sees me looking like this, Claudia thought happily as she pored over the various pictures of herself, bikini-clad and positively oozing sex appeal. She was going to knock the unappreciative bugger's socks off.

Caspar had spent the first half of his holiday doing so much thinking it made his head ache.

Poppy was right; he knew that now. Keeping three girls on the go at one time was ridiculous. Disastrous. He might not be hurting himself but he was certainly hurting them.

And why? Caspar hadn't a clue. It wasn't as if he even enjoyed the subterfuge.

It was all so pointless too. None of them was exactly the romance of the decade. He wasn't madly in love with any of them.

He thought he was probably in love with Poppy.

He wasn't sure about this, not completely. It was a pretty bizarre situation, Caspar felt. Could you actually *be* in love with someone you'd never even kissed?

Anyway, that hardly mattered; it was beside the point. Because Poppy had made it abundantly clear to him that he was just about the least fanciable man on the planet. In her view, any girls interested in him needed their empty heads examined. Or, as Poppy had rather cruelly put it, if their IQs were any lower, they'd need watering.

The situation Caspar found himself in wasn't an easy one. The time had come, he decided, to put some distance between himself and Poppy.

Over dinner on the fourth night of the holiday he spoke to Babette.

'I've been thinking about what you said the other week.'

'Oh yes?' Babette knew at once what he meant.

'Have you ever wondered how it would feel, being married?'

They had parted on the chilliest of terms. Poppy, arriving home from work several days later, saw Caspar's car parked outside the house and felt a twinge of apprehension. She had never been one for holding a grudge or keeping a feud simmering. It wasn't in her nature. She hoped it wasn't in Caspar's either.

So how do I do this, she thought, loitering nervously at the foot of the steps. Burst into the house, give Caspar a big kiss and say sorry?

Act as if nothing's happened?

Or wait and see how Caspar handles it and take it from there?

At that moment Claudia pulled up. As usual she parked extremely badly and took an age doing it. Much squeaking of tyre against pavement ensued.

'Caspar's back,' Claudia exclaimed, having also spotted his car. Climbing out, she flashed a great deal of tanned leg. 'Come on, let's see what he's been up to. I'll kill him if his tan's better than mine.'

Poppy felt very much the poor relation. Claudia was brown but Caspar was browner still. And – something she hadn't been expecting – Babette was with him, all dark-haired and glossy and expensive-looking like something out of a Galaxy ad. She was wearing a long silk jersey dress the colour of peanut butter, and a modest smile. Caspar, in a dark blue tee-shirt and battered jeans, poured Bollinger into four un-matched glasses.

He handed one to Claudia.

'What are we celebrating,' she giggled, 'how glad you are to be back?'

Caspar passed the second glass across to Poppy, who was perched nervously on the arm of the sofa.

'Not exactly.' He was speaking to Claudia but his gaze was fixed on Poppy. 'I was given some advice a little while ago. You'll be amazed to hear I took it.'

Poppy glanced across at Babette, who was sitting there looking charming. This was the girl who had told her in no uncertain terms how plain she was. Presumably this meant Caspar had finished with Kate and Jules.

Caspar handed the third glass to Babette.

'And there we were, thinking you'd missed us like mad,' Claudia chirruped. 'We thought you couldn't wait to get home.'

'Actually,' said Caspar. 'I'm moving out.'

Claudia did a double-take.

'What do you mean?' she said finally. 'How can you move out? This is your home. You live here.'

'Like I said, I was given some advice and I took it.' Caspar couldn't help turning to look at Poppy again. 'And no,' he said coolly, 'I didn't go eeny meeny miney mo.'

Poppy felt sick.

'What are you *talking* about?' protested Claudia.

'I can't stand the suspense a moment longer.' Babette smiled and held up her left hand. 'We got married.'

Poppy drank her drink without noticing. She couldn't believe Caspar had done something so stupid. She couldn't believe he was putting the blame for his whim on *her*.

'. . . honestly, Antigua's just so beautiful, such a romantic place,' Babette chattered on, addressing Claudia rather than Poppy because Claudia was so obviously agog. 'The scenery is out of this world. Of course, that's why so many people are

266

getting married out there nowadays. I mean, be honest, where would you rather exchange your vows? On a glorious beach with the sea lapping at your toes and tropical flowers in your hair, or in some musty old register office?'

'Oh well, goes without saying,' agreed Claudia, who would happily have exchanged her vows in a snake pit up to her neck in anacondas. Anywhere, so long as she got married.

'This wasn't planned in advance, you see. We were simply strolling along the beach one morning and we happened to pass a wedding ceremony in progress.' Babette dimpled and glanced across at Caspar, sharing the moment. 'Well, I'd love to be able to say he dropped down on one knee and proposed, but—'

'But I didn't.'

Confidingly, Babette told Claudia, 'He's not really the dropping down on one knee type. But he asked me to marry him and I said yes. So we made our way back to the hotel and spoke to the manager. He's an old hand at this kind of thing . . . he arranged everything.' Babette shrugged and spread her hands, the narrow gold ring on her third finger catching the light. 'Three days later it was our turn! What can I say? It was utterly magical. The most perfect day of my life.'

'It sounds amazing,' sighed Claudia. 'What did you wear?'

'A Liza Bruce swimsuit and an island sarong.' Babette reached for her bag and drew out an envelope. 'I'm sure the only reason Caspar went through with it was because he could wear his cut-off jeans. Here, have a look at the photos. See that confetti? Fresh flower petals. And this is the minister who performed the service.'

'Congratulations,' said Poppy, when Caspar had finished refilling her glass. It wasn't true; she simply couldn't think of anything else to say. Apart from bugger.

'All thanks to you.' He gave her a measured look. 'It was your idea.'

There was definitely no answer to that. Poppy bit the

corner of her mouth. She tried to imagine stamping her foot and yelling, 'Okay, I know it was my idea but I didn't *mean* it.'

Caspar said drily, 'And there was me thinking you'd approve.'

Poppy, all of a sudden dangerously close to tears, changed the subject.

'You still haven't explained why you're moving out. Isn't that a bit stupid? Claudia and I are the ones who should be doing that.'

'Doesn't seem fair, turfing you out.' Caspar shrugged, unconcerned. 'And Babs doesn't want to move. Her flat's her business base. It's easier for me to move in with her.'

Babette's flat, Poppy dimly recalled, was in Soho.

'What about your painting?'

'We'll be living together at the flat. I'll still have to come here to paint. If that's okay with you,' he added with a cool smile.

Poppy didn't smile back. She wanted to hit him. She still couldn't believe he had actually gone and got married.

'Poppy, you aren't looking.' Claudia passed the first handful of photographs across. Numbly, Poppy took them. Caspar and Babette, on the beach, grinned up at her. Their arms were around each other. The minister who had performed the ceremony beamed for the camera. In the second photograph, two small girls in white dresses and flower garland head-dresses stood proudly on either side of them.

'Our bridesmaids,' said Babette, leaning across to see which one she was looking at. 'They're the hotel manager's daughters . . . aren't they simply angelic?'

Poppy turned to the next picture, taken in the hotel's beachfront bar. Caspar was kissing Babette on the mouth. Around them, a crowd of fellow holidaymakers clapped and cheered them on.

Jealousy, like bile, rose in Poppy's throat.

'Our wedding reception,' Babette explained smugly.

'Goodness, that was a party and a half. We sank some booze, I can tell you. Isn't it amazing, how a happy event brings people together? At breakfast we didn't know this crowd from Adam, and by nightfall we were practically best friends.'

'Talking of parties,' said Caspar, 'have we missed any good ones? What have you been getting up to while we've been away?'

Patronising bastard. Poppy handed the photographs back to Babette.

'Nothing. No parties.' She stood up. 'Actually, I think I'll have a bath.'

Claudia and Babette were wittering happily away to each other like new best friends. Caspar left them to it. As he went upstairs he passed the bathroom. The door was shut. Inside, hot water was running, and Bruce Springsteen was belting out 'Born to Run'. For once, Poppy wasn't singing along to the tape.

He wondered if what he had done was the right thing. Poppy had looked quite shaken when he and Babette had broken their news.

For the first time Caspar experienced a twinge of doubt.

When he reached the studio the door was festooned with messages and post. Caspar unpinned a dozen or so envelopes and a folder of photographs, and opened the door. The brown bills he didn't bother to look at. He skimmed through the more interesting envelopes – invitations to exhibitions and parties – then opened the folder. The first fifteen or so photographs had been taken at the Edison gallery. Not exactly riveting stuff.

Then he came to one of Poppy, though for a couple of seconds he wondered if it was really her.

Feeling odd, Caspar flipped through the rest of the photographs.

Looking as he had never seen her look before, Poppy was hoisted Gladiator-style onto the shoulders of some bloke. Her hair was wild, her eyes heavily made up. Her mouth was

269

plastered with dark red lipstick. She looked like something out of the *Rocky Horror Show* and she was laughing uproariously, clearly having the time of her life.

In *my house*, thought Caspar, realising that the picture had been taken in the sitting room.

The rest of the photographs revealed more. Poppy and Dina, dancing with two men he didn't know. A couple of blonde girls kissing a dark-haired chap with a tea towel on his head and a bottle of vodka in each hand. Poppy again, in a wheelbarrow race around the sofa, flashing her knickers into the bargain. Dina, caught unawares, snogging in the kitchen with some muscle-bound hulk. And another one of Poppy lying on the floor shrieking with laughter as a blond guy in a torn tee-shirt tickled the soles of her bare feet.

The last photograph, taken in Claudia's bedroom, was of Dina fast asleep in Claudia's bed, flanked on one side by Mr Muscle and on the other by the blond guy. At the foot of the bed lay a tangled heap of clothes and an empty bottle of Jack Daniels.

So this was Poppy's idea of a quiet time. Caspar flipped through the relevant photographs again. By a process of elimination he worked out who must have shared Poppy's bed; either *him* or *him*. Or maybe they both had. Her bed was only a single, but would that have stopped them? Bitterly he thought, they could have taken it in turns.

Caspar realised he couldn't look at the photographs any more. He shovelled them back into the envelope, wondering if Poppy had used his camera on purpose to make her point. He also wondered if Claudia knew what Dina had been getting up to in her bed.

So much for wondering if he had done the right thing.

There was no going back now, Caspar thought grimly. He would move out tonight.

Chapter 40

Jake didn't care that the adverts he had placed in all the papers had cost him a fortune, but it annoyed him intensely that he wasn't getting a result.

Not the kind of result he wanted, anyway. Just more weirdos and practical jokers and hopeful lonely hearts offering themselves in Tom's place.

On his way into work the next morning he stopped off at his local newsagent for Polos and a ballpoint pen and the latest edition of *Antiques Monthly*. He waited to be served behind an old lady with a shopping basket on wheels, who was counting out change for a *Daily Mirror*.

'And you can take my card out of the window,' she told the newsagent, whom she evidently knew. 'Deirdre's back, safe and sound. Some kind soul rang me last night to say he thought he'd spotted her in Lavender Gardens. I rushed straight over, and there she was! Heaven knows what possessed her, but never mind, she's home with Mummy again now. Aren't you, my precious?'

The old woman lifted the lid of her shopping basket and devotedly stroked the pink nose of an ugly tortoiseshell cat.

'That's good news, Maud,' said the newsagent. 'Mission accomplished, eh?'

Jake looked at the cat. He had noticed the card in the window himself. Privately he had assumed Deirdre must have been run over by a bus.

But luck had been on Deirdre's side. The forlorn little message in the newsagent's window had done the trick.

Jake paid for his magazine and Biro and forgot all about the Polos. He had seen Maud's card; so had the person who had spotted Deirdre in Lavender Gardens; so must practically everyone who came into the little corner shop.

That was it, he thought with rising excitement. People bought newspapers but they didn't necessarily read the personal columns.

Just about everyone, on the other hand, had a newsagent they visited on a regular basis.

'How much does it cost to put a card in the window?' Jake asked.

The man behind the counter said, 'For a week, thirty-five pence.'

'Oh you poor darling,' cried Maud, clutching his arm, 'have you lost your cat too?'

Whoever said there was no point sitting around moping, Rita decided, didn't know what they were talking about. Sometimes a bloody good mope was what you needed more than anything else in the world.

It was what Rita had been doing for weeks, and she was buggered if she was going to feel guilty. She had drunk too much whisky, smoked far too many cigarettes, listened to hour upon hour of Alex's beloved jazz CDs and shed gallons of hot, aching, therapeutic tears.

Weirdly, having always thought she couldn't stand jazz, she now found herself beginning to quite like it after all. She was even getting to grips with Miles Davis. Since not having to listen to all that crappy music any more had been the only thing she had been able to look forward to after Alex's death, Rita thought this typical, and probably his idea of a huge joke.

But moping – or grieving – was something you had to go through and there wasn't a lot you could do to avoid it. Having realised this, Rita had kept visitors to a minimum, preferring to mourn alone. She had her beautiful house and her memories; it was all she needed right now. She was also, thank God, lucky enough never to have to worry about money again.

Unlike the old days, Rita reminded herself, thinking back fondly to the first years of their marriage and the grotty flat in Hackney, with the bucket on permanent drip-duty in the hallway and the rat-infested back yard. Bit different from what they had become used to here . . .

That's another stupid thing people say, thought Rita: Money doesn't buy you happiness. Okay, I might not be feeling that great at the moment, but I'd be a damn sight more miserable if on top of everything else I had to worry about paying bills.

What a load of tosh some people talked.

Today though, she wasn't in the mood for whisky and a mope. Spring had arrived, the sun was out and the temperature outside was on the verge of turning warm. Gazing down from the bedroom window at the daffodils bobbing in the garden below, Rita experienced an urge to embark on a bit of spring-cleaning.

The trouble was, there wasn't any to do. Her super-efficient cleaning women worked tirelessly all year round. Every window sparkled. There was no dust. If she were to drag her dressing-table chair over to the window, climb up on it and run her finger along the top of the curtain track, Rita knew it would come away clean. You could eat your dinner off the curtain tracks in this house.

But the urge to do something wasn't going to go away. If I can't clean up, Rita decided with a new sense of purpose, I'll clear out.

She flung open the fitted wardrobe doors and surveyed her clothes. Rail upon rail of gorgeous dresses. Bright oranges, violets, pinks and greens. Silver lamé. Blue and gold Lurex. Multi-coloured sequins and shimmering fringes. And all with shoes to match.

It was no good. Rita knew she couldn't do it. Alex had

273

helped her choose these outfits. He had loved to see her in them. How could she even think of throwing any of them away?

She slid the doors shut and opened Alex's wardrobe instead. After several minutes of deliberation she chose, for old times' sake, the crimson waistcoat he had worn for their silver wedding anniversary party and a pair of outrageous purple silk pyjamas she had bought for him on last year's happy trip to Lloret de Mar. Weakening briefly, Rita grabbed a favourite blue and yellow striped shirt of Alex's, and a hefty silver-buckled belt with the initials R. and A. intertwined.

Then, because she knew it had to be done, she swept the remaining contents of the wardrobe, hangers and all, into five black binliners. Boots and shoes filled another, sweaters two more.

Rita lugged the bags downstairs to be sent to Oxfam. Still bursting with energy she ran back up to the bedroom and dragged a motley collection of suitcases from the back of the wardrobe. Packed inside was everything they had brought with them when they had moved but hadn't known what to do with.

Now this, Rita thought with satisfaction, was stuff worth throwing out. A bag of tangled braces, years old, from when Alex had gone through a phase of wearing the things. A whole suitcase full of back copies of *Jazz Journal International*. Another case had been crammed with bits of a rusted old drum kit. The last one, with FRAGILE scrawled across it in green felt-tip pen, was stuffed with records in battered paper sleeves, old seventy-eights by ancient wrinkled Mississippians with names like Smokin' Joe Swampfoot.

Kneeling down, Rita sifted through them, deciding that rather than Oxfam she would drop these round to the Cavendish Club. Anyone who wanted the crappy things could have them. And the magazines.

At the bottom of the case, beneath the seventy-eights, were half a dozen hardback books, also to do with jazz. They looked deadly boring and as old as the records. Rita flipped though a few of the yellowed pages, wondering idly if Poppy would be interested in selling them on the stall. The date at the front of this one was 1954. Blimey, practically an antique.

When Rita picked the book up, a photograph fluttered out onto her lap. A small black and white snap, it was as discoloured with age as the pages it had been sandwiched between. With only mild curiosity – she was by this time heartily sick of all things jazzy – Rita turned the photograph over and took a closer look.

She knew at once when it must have been taken. She had bought Alex that patterned shirt the week before he'd left for Bristol, to spend the summer working at the Ash Hill Country Club. When she had broken her leg and Alex had come rushing back to London, he had turned up at the hospital wearing it. It had been bright green, with black Scottie dogs printed all over it. Each dog had been wearing a white collar. Rita, about as handy with a needle as a hippo, but so in love it hurt, had devotedly embroidered each dog's collar a different colour. It had taken hours but she'd done it anyway, and when she'd given him the customised shirt Alex had been thrilled.

So thrilled, thought Rita, that he'd worn it on an awayday to Weston-Super-Mare.

Or wherever it was. It might have been Weston, it might not. All Rita knew was that it was the seaside, somewhere with a pier. Alex was sitting on the beach, grinning broadly.

And he wasn't alone.

It had to be her. This time Rita didn't have any doubts. The way they sat together, her left knee brushing his right one, was a dead giveaway. Those knees said it all.

So this was what her rival had looked like. After years of wondering, it was a relief to find out – like finally managing the last clue in a crossword puzzle that's been niggling away in your brain. Rita, still on her knees in front of the wardrobe, held the photograph up to the light.

The woman was nothing special. Okay, she was pretty, but nothing amazing. Having envisaged everything from Liz Taylor in her heyday to Brigitte Bardot, this came as a relief. The woman Alex had had an affair with had long curly hair, a heart-shaped face and a captivating smile. She was wearing a calf-length pleated skirt and a short-sleeved white blouse. Her feet were bare. There was a ring on her wedding finger.

Rita was surprised how calm she felt. What did it matter now anyway? Her curiosity had been satisfied, that was all. Alex's fling had ended twenty-three years ago and their marriage had been happy to the end. In a funny way, knowing about it – realising that she *could* have lost him to another woman – might even have helped the marriage.

Maybe I appreciated him all the more, thought Rita, gazing at his dear face in the photograph. There, that's female logic for you.

About to crumple the photo up and lob it into the waste-paper basket, she stopped and looked at it again. It was odd, but somehow she didn't have the heart to throw it away.

Instead, she slid it back inside the pages of the book and put the book on a high shelf right at the back of the wardrobe.

Then, suddenly fancying a gin and tonic and a nice fag, she went downstairs.

Chapter 41

'Do you have any idea how many newsagents there are in London?' demanded Claudia, when Jake arrived on Saturday morning at the house. She was dressed and ready to go but it didn't mean she was happy about the idea. In her opinion it sounded like the flimsiest of long shots. It was also a dismal way to spend a Saturday. She normally stayed in bed until lunchtime at least.

'That's why we're going to concentrate on Notting Hill,' said Jake. 'Here, I've got a map. We'll start at the centre and spiral out. With two of us, one can sit in the car and the other can zip into each shop. It'll save having to find parking spaces. Come on,' he added persuasively – heavens, thought Claudia, Jake's being *persuasive* – 'it'll be fun.'

'Sounds like *The Getaway*.' Having always longed to look like Ali McGraw, she began to weaken.

'Only with fewer bullets.'

'I hope you don't drive like Steve McQueen.'

'No, but I don't get chased by so many police cars either.'

Claudia began to forgive him for bullying her out of bed on a Saturday.

'You hope,' she said.

By one o'clock they had visited twenty-three newsagents, some smart, some unbelievably seedy. The cards Jake had had printed – on an eye-catching purple background – were pinned up alongside Megan-the-magnificent-masseuse type ads, rooms to let, sofas for sale, guitar lessons for aspiring rock stars and enough lost pets to fill a zoo.

Jake took Claudia to a wine bar for lunch. Okay from the outside but with an air of shabbiness inside, it served meals-in-a-basket at wonky tables. On each table stood a vase of plastic flowers. Claudia tried to control her upper lip, which wanted to curl in disdain. Jake, who had been doing so well all morning, spotted the lip. His confidence promptly ebbed away.

The bar manager had already handed them the menu (Today's Special, Spahgetti Bollonaise with mushroom's and chip's). Should he hand it back, say sorry they'd changed their minds and leave? If he did that, he would have to find somewhere else to eat, and knowing his luck it would be somewhere even worse. He wanted to appear assertive but he didn't know the area. Staring blindly at the menu, wondering what to do for the best, Jake reached nervously for the bowl of free peanuts on the bar. The moment the first one was in his mouth his panic intensified. Oh God, he'd eaten a free peanut. They couldn't leave now, they were trapped.

'Um, I'll have the lasagne,' he mumbled. Hopefully, the chef cooked better than he spelled.

By the time their food arrived, fresh from the microwave and cardboardy at the edges, the wine bar had begun to fill up. Jake, who was starving, chewed manfully and tried to pretend it was fine.

The spaghetti was the consistency of shoe laces and there was a dried lump of something hideous welded to the underside of Claudia's spoon.

'This is awful.' She laid down her fork. 'I can't eat it.'

'I'm sorry.' Jake looked miserable. 'We shouldn't have stayed.'

'It doesn't matter.'

But it did, and tact had never been Claudia's strong point. Petulantly, she moved the fake freesias away.

'I'm just surprised you come to places like this, when you could afford to eat anywhere.'

Lunch at the Ritz was hardly Jake's style, but he realised she was miffed.

'I didn't know it was going to be like this.' Falteringly, he tried to explain.

'You mean you saw a few plastic hanging baskets outside and thought, Oh well, this'll do, it's good enough for Claudia. Thanks.' She pushed her plate to one side. 'Excuse me if I'm not flattered.'

Jake could feel his neck reddening.

'Look, it's not as if we're out on a . . . a date. If we were, of course I'd take you somewhere nice. But we aren't.' The awful flush was creeping up to his face. He ran his fingers distractedly around the collar of his shirt. 'This was only supposed to be a quick working lunch. If I'd been on my own I'd have had a packet of crisps in the car. Okay, I wish we hadn't come here and yes, it's awful, but I . . . I really didn't think it mattered.'

As Jake spoke, a middle-aged man in a holey grey sweater was approaching their table. The next moment Claudia almost jumped out of her chair as he tapped her on the shoulder.

'It is you,' said the man, evidently delighted. 'I thought it was but I couldn't be sure. As the saying goes, I hardly recognised you with your clothes on!'

Claudia gazed at him, dumbfounded. It was her turn to blush. Unlike Jake's stealthy creeping redness, her face turned crimson in a flash.

'Mike Cousins, from the life class at St Clare's,' the intruder prompted jovially when she didn't react. As if she needed prompting after a remark like that.

'Of course,' murmured Claudia, not jovially at all. She was seized with the urge to strangle Poppy and Caspar all over again. The only way she had been able to endure those nightmarish classes was by telling herself she would never set eyes on any of its pupils again as long as she lived.

'Well, well, what a coincidence.' The beastly man, who

had never uttered so much as two words to her before, was now beaming matily across at Jake. 'This is some girl you've got there, if you don't mind me saying so. Splendid body. Rubensesque. You're a lucky chap.'

Jake, traitorously, was biting his lip and trying not to laugh. Claudia stood up, chair legs scraping noisily against the black and white tiled floor.

'Actually, we were just about to leave—'

'Bit of luck, too, bumping into you like this! Only last week I finished that oil I was working on . . . you know, the one with you lying on your side reading a book?' He mimed the pose, propping one hand dreamily beneath his chin. 'That one, remember? Bit of a success, if I say so myself. Thing is, I wondered if you'd like it. As a kind of memento—'

'No thank you,' gasped Claudia, snatching up her jacket and making for the door. 'Jake, we must *go*.'

'To remind you of your happy time with us at St Clare's,' Mike Cousins persisted, bemused by her reaction to his well-meant offer.

'Jake,' she almost shrieked, 'come *on*. NOW.'

Back in the car, Jake wisely made no reference to the incident. For the next three hours he and Claudia drove around Notting Hill placing another twenty-eight cards in newsagents' windows.

He dropped her off at Cornwallis Crescent at five o'clock before Poppy, who had been left running the stall single-handed, could arrive home and demand to know what the pair of them had been getting up to.

'Sorry about the pervert,' Claudia muttered as she undid her seatbelt.

'Sorry about lunch.'

Her lips tightened. 'Pretty disastrous all round.'

Jake took his courage in both hands.

'Look, I meant what I said earlier. If we went out . . . you know, properly, on a *date* date, I would take you somewhere nice.'

She stopped fiddling with her front door key.

'How nice?'

'As nice as you want.' Encouraged by the question, Jake said, 'Tablecloths, the works.'

Claudia very nearly smiled.

'Heavens, how posh.'

'Anywhere. You could choose. Any restaurant you like.'

'The thing is . . . is this a hypothetical question or are you actually asking me?'

Jake looked at her. 'That depends on whether or not you'd say yes.'

'I'd say yes,' she murmured, 'if you took me to Chez Nico.'

'Sure it's expensive enough for you?' Even Jake had heard of Chez Nico.

Claudia had got what she wanted. This time her smile was triumphant.

'You can afford it.'

Chapter 42

Jake, back from a spectacularly unsuccessful car boot sale in Chigwell, sat peacefully in front of the TV eating a Birds Eye frozen dinner for one. Claudia would not have been impressed.

Jake didn't care. It was Sunday afternoon. The Birds Eye roast-dinner-on-a-plate was actually quite edible, especially when you were as hungry as he was after a long day sifting through boxes of Barbie dolls with matted nylon hair, bent cutlery, dodgy electrical items and chipped tea sets. And he was watching *The Antiques Roadshow*, one of his favourite programmes. What more could a man want?

One of the furniture experts was assessing a French provincial chestnut armoire carved with vines and acanthus scrolls. The owner was pretending to be interested in the age of the piece. Lying through her buck teeth, she said, 'Well no, we never have,' when the expert asked if she'd ever wondered about its value.

'Two thousand six hundred,' muttered Jake, chasing the last potato around his plastic plate. 'Maybe two eight.'

'Well,' said the expert, prolonging the agony, 'it is a particularly charming example of the period.'

'Come on, come on,' Jake urged.

'On the other hand, this split in the wood will obviously have an effect on the value.'

'Okay, two four,' amended Jake. He cursed as the phone rang. Didn't these crank callers have any sense of timing?

The owner of the armoire was looking mulish. 'Actually,

I'm sure that split wasn't there this morning. Are you sure your cameraman didn't do that when he bumped into it just now?'

Great, a fight.

'Hello,' said Jake, answering the phone. If it was yet another nutter he was hanging up.

'Oh . . . hi.' The male voice at the other end of the line sounded briefly taken aback. 'I was kind of expecting to speak to Poppy. Is she there?'

'No.' Jake's tone was brisk. He had dealt with enough of these dirty phone callers by now. 'And before you say anything else, your number can be traced.'

'Just as well.' This time the voice sounded amused. 'That's rather the point of the exercise, isn't it? To trace me. Besides, if I didn't want to be found, would I be ringing you now?'

He didn't sound like an obscene phone caller. Adrenalin began to fizz through Jake.

'Are you Tom?' He spoke cautiously, hardly daring to believe it could have happened at last. 'Are you really *that* Tom?'

'Of course I am,' said the voice. 'I fell in love with Poppy when she fell down that flight of steps. When she didn't turn up at Delgado's I thought that was it. I couldn't believe it when I heard she'd cancelled the wedding.' He paused then added drily, 'I suppose that dippy friend of hers didn't pass on my address.'

'My God, it is you.'

'If you like, I can tell you about the hat she was wearing.'

'It's okay.' Jake glanced at the television, where the credits were rolling up the screen. The jolly signature tune signalled the end of the show; now he would never know how much that armoire was worth.

'Anyway,' said Tom, 'if it isn't a rude question, who are you?'

'Jake, you just caught me.' Poppy sounded pleased to hear

283

from him. 'I was about to jump in the bath.'

'You still can. Claudia's the one I want to speak to.'

'Oh charming. What's she got that I haven't?'

Exhilarated by success, Jake grinned and said, 'Big boobs for a start.'

But Poppy had already chucked the phone over to Claudia, who was on the floor doing sit-ups. Mike Cousins' remark about her Rubensesque figure had hit a nerve.

'Thanks a lot,' said Claudia. Jake, who was managing to offend everyone, didn't even blush.

'Listen, we did it. He phoned. Just now. We've *found* him.'

'You mean—?'

'Don't say it! Yes, Tom of course – who else? But not a word to Poppy, okay? We want it to be a surprise.'

'So what was that about?' Poppy asked nosily when Claudia had hung up. 'Is something going on between you and Jake that I should know about?'

Claudia fished around for inspiration. 'He just rang to say he was looking forward to tomorrow night.' She looked vague. 'You know, at . . . um . . .'

'Chez Nico,' Poppy supplied, straight-faced. As if Claudia had forgotten. She still found it hard enough to believe Jake was taking Claudia somewhere so smart. And now . . . luurve messages, no less. He was actually phoning, in true teenage fashion, to say he couldn't wait.

Something was definitely up.

When she didn't move, Claudia said, 'I thought you were having a bath.'

'Just wondering what kind of hat to wear at your wedding.'

'Typical.' Claudia resumed her sit-ups. 'You always have to make fun of people. You're only jealous because nobody ever takes you out, let alone anywhere nice.'

She was pleased with this bit of jokey repartee. Knowing that Tom had been found – and that Poppy would at last have a love life of her own – made it extra amusing.

Poppy, who didn't get the joke, was less amused. Since

Caspar had moved out she hadn't been in the greatest of spirits. A twittery, about-to-sit-an-exam kind of feeling had taken up more or less permanent residence in her stomach, a sensation so weird that if she'd had sex any time in the last century she might have wondered if maybe she wasn't the tiniest bit pregnant.

But she hadn't, so she definitely wasn't that.

Cheers Claudia, Poppy thought, for reminding me what an empty, wizened-old-spinster life I lead. In case I'd forgotten, thanks for pointing it out.

'. . . forty-seven, forty-eight, forty-nine, fifty,' fibbed Claudia, collapsing on her back with a groan. 'God, why do sit-ups have to hurt so much?'

'All this,' Poppy mocked, 'for Jake's benefit.'

'No. Well . . .'

'Don't tell me. He's *so* much more attractive now he's got money to throw about.'

What was Poppy implying, that she was a fortune hunter?

Huffily, Claudia said, 'That's not true.'

'You mean you'd be just as happy eating fish and chips in a bus shelter?'

Even Claudia didn't have the nerve to lie her way out of this one. Instead, as if the question simply wasn't worth answering, she sighed and stretched her arms lazily above her head. 'Oh please. You're not happy so you can't bear anyone else to be, is that it? I don't know what's got into you tonight.'

Nothing, thought Poppy. Not for ages. Maybe that's the trouble.

'I'm just warning you. Jake's my friend.' She spoke through gritted teeth. 'And I don't want to see him get hurt.'

'. . . I'm not trying to be a killjoy, okay? I'm just saying bear it in mind.'

Hoping she hadn't upset him, Poppy offered Jake her last Juicy Fruit.

He shook his head. 'No thanks. Should you be eating that now?'

Jake was far too hyped-up to pay much attention to Poppy's lecture. Tom was due any minute now and he wanted Poppy to make a good second impression. Sartorial elegance might not be Jake's forte, but even he knew the sight of someone chewing chewing gum wasn't the ultimate turn-on.

'Why not?' Poppy stared at the unwrapped stick.

'Um . . . won't it ruin your appetite?'

She broke into a grin and folded the gum expertly into her mouth. 'Jake, five doughnuts and a chip sandwich don't ruin my appetite.'

'Oh well, suit yourself.'

Jake was definitely odd today. Poppy guessed he was on edge about dinner with Claudia. She waited until a pair of Americans had finished examining a pewter mug ('Look at that silver, Herman, you'd think they'd take the trouble to polish it') before trying again.

'Jake, were you listening to me? I know it's only a dinner date, but I'm just saying don't get too carried away.'

'Hmm?' Jake couldn't stop glancing across at the main doors. What if Tom didn't turn up?

'Tonight. Claudia. The thing is, I know you like her and you think she likes you because she's having dinner with you—'

'You're chewing and talking at the same time.'

'Sorry. Look, what I'm trying to get across is, Claudia's always gone on and on about how when she gets married it's going to be to someone seriously rich.'

Was Jake listening to her? Or was he only pretending to ignore her because she was telling him something he didn't want to hear? Dramatically, Poppy launched into the next phase, 'And when she *does* finally land some dopey rolling-in-it idiot, she's going to murder him the minute the honeymoon's over. I'm serious, Jake, she told me so herself. A quick splash of weedkiller in the casserole, that's how I reckon she'll do it. With Claudia's cooking, who'd notice?'

'Stop wittering, Poppy,' said Jake, 'and serve the customer.'

The customer said, 'I'd like three condoms, please, and a stupid hat.'

Chapter 43

She turned her head in what felt like slow motion and there he was. Those dark, dark eyes, thickly lashed and as bright as coal, were watching her reaction. The tangled black curls were damp from the rain. He was wearing a dark grey sweater and faded jeans and he smelled exactly the same as he always had in her dreams.

Poppy wondered if she *was* dreaming, but no, she was fairly sure this was real.

Oh damn, she thought vainly, why didn't I listen to Jake? What kind of a gormless Gertie do I look like with my mouth hanging open and my chewing gum on show?

But it was no good wishing she'd got make-up on, or that her hair could be looking a bit more glam, a bit less as if it had been given a brief going over with an egg whisk. This was the day the extraordinary coincidence she had waited for for so long had actually happened. She was wearing a battered sweatshirt and her least flattering leggings – the ones with the exhausted Lycra, that gave her wrinkled knees like an elephant's – but it was no good panicking because there wasn't a damn thing she could do about it.

By some miracle, at least Tom had still recognised her.

Hastily, before it fell out of her open mouth and put him off completely, Poppy swallowed her gum.

'My God, it's you! How amazing . . . Jake, this is someone I haven't seen for ages . . . his name's Tom . . . and this . . . this is Jake . . .'

Poppy's voice trailed away. Introductions always floored

her; she could never remember the proper way, which had something to do with age, but how were you supposed to go about it if you didn't know who was the eldest, ask to see their driving licences before you began?

'I think she's in shock,' said Jake. 'Poppy, are you okay? Do you want to sit down?'

'I really wish I'd thrown these leggings away now,' said Poppy. She gripped the sides of the cashbox until her fingers ached, and forced herself to concentrate. She needed to pull herself together, fast. What must Tom think?

'It's – it's great to see you again,' she heard herself stammer idiotically. 'Is there something you're in-in-interested in, or are you just having a browse?'

Tom said, 'Oh no, there's definitely something I'm in-in-interested in.'

He was teasing her. It struck Poppy that he didn't seem nearly as astounded to see her as she was seeing him. She tried to say something sensible, without stammering, but her chewing gum had got itself wedged at epiglottis level. This time all that came out was a mousy squeak.

'Lost for words,' observed Jake. 'Now there's a first.'

'And here we are, making fun of her.' Tom grinned and ran a finger lightly over her knuckles, white where they still clutched the cashbox. 'I suppose we aren't being very fair. Poppy, this isn't a coincidence. I didn't just happen to be passing. Jake found me.'

This was getting more bizarre by the minute. Behind Tom, an old dear in an ochre Pakamac was hissing crossly, 'If you'd move out of my way, young man, I'd quite like to have a look at that Staffordshire pig.'

Poppy swallowed again. This time the chewing gum went down and stayed down.

'Jake what? What d'you mean, *found* you?'

With some pride, Jake said, 'I advertised.'

Was this how it felt to be Tango'd? Poppy shook her head. 'Advertised how?'

'In all the papers. But that didn't work.' Jake was beaming like a new father. 'So we tried newsagents' windows. And bingo.'

She knew she was parroting everything they said, but it was all she was capable of just now.

'You put an advert in a newsagent's window,' Poppy said carefully. She turned to Tom. 'And you *saw* it?'

'Well, the girl who lives in the flat downstairs saw it, and remembered me telling her about the night we met.'

He'd told other people about her . . .

'And it wasn't actually me who put the ad in that window,' said Jake, not to be outdone. 'It was Claudia.'

Tom took Poppy to a tiny restaurant just off Kensington High Street. Like a sleepwalker Poppy allowed herself to be helped into her seat.

'Jake was right, by the way, about me being lost for words. I'm not usually like this.'

'Look,' said Tom, 'maybe there's something we should get straight before we go any further. Is my turning up out of the blue a nice surprise or a bloody awful shock? Are you happy about it, or not?'

'God yes, of *course* I'm happy.' Flustered, Poppy realised she sounded like some hopeless lovestruck groupie. 'I mean . . . I mean . . .'

'Good.' Beneath the table, Tom's foot touched hers. His smile reassured her. 'Seeing as Jake's been to all this trouble. Imagine how offended he'd be if we took one look at each other and went Ugh!'

'Dina told me she'd bumped into you. She lost your address. I wanted to kill her!'

'Don't worry, I'll do it when we next see her.' He lit a cigarette and exhaled with relief. 'It'll make up for all those weeks afterwards, twitching every time the phone rang and being disappointed when it wasn't you.'

'I saw you, just before Christmas.' The words began

tumbling out. 'At a petrol station. I tried to get your attention but you disappeared so fast—'

'What I don't understand,' said Tom, 'is why you didn't turn up at Delgado's that night. Did you think I wouldn't be there?'

'I knew you *would* be there. I did turn up. I saw you, at that table in the window.' There was so much to say, so many things to explain. A waitress was hovering behind them. Poppy glanced at the menu in her hand, knowing she wouldn't be able to eat.

'It's okay, you choose,' Tom told the waitress. 'Anything you like. And a bottle of something to go with it.'

'I panicked,' Poppy admitted when they were alone once more. 'I was meant to be getting married. Meeting you wasn't supposed to happen.'

Tom grinned. 'I think it was. Anyway, you didn't get married.'

'I couldn't.'

'Can't have been easy.'

'It was awful. Like the end bit of *The Graduate*, but without anyone to jump on the bus with. In the end I jumped on by myself,' Poppy said drily, 'and came to London. Before I could be burned at the stake.'

'What about your family?' Tom stubbed out his cigarette, half-smoked. 'Were they okay about it? Did you ever regret calling off the wedding?'

'Not for an instant.' He was running an index finger idly over the veins on the inside of her wrist. Distracted, Poppy trembled with pleasure. 'As for my family . . . I would never have found my real father if it hadn't been for you.'

Tom frowned. 'You've lost me.'

'It's a long story. And no, I haven't lost you,' said Poppy, realising that there was simply no point in being coy. 'I've found you. God, that sounds naff.' Laughing, she buried her face in her hands. 'I can't believe I just said it.'

'Here comes the food. We're going to have to pretend to eat.'

Their eyes locked. Over the worst of the shock now, Poppy had begun to relax. The last time they had met, it had been the middle of the night, pitch-black and tropically warm. Ever since, trying to conjure up a mental image of Tom, she had only been able to picture him in darkness.

Now, almost a year later, it was daylight. Unforgiving drizzly grey daylight at that. It was a huge relief to discover he was as breathtakingly handsome as she remembered. The sight of him still made her stomach disappear.

The magic was still there. Remembering her elephant-kneed leggings and out-of-control hair, Poppy amended that. It was still there, on her side at least.

'What's the matter?' said Tom.

'I wish I wasn't wearing these clothes.'

'You look fine.'

'I can look better.'

'I know.' That knee-trembling grin reappeared. Heavens, he was gorgeous.

'Everything all right?' enquired the waitress, who evidently thought so too. She was addressing Tom. Poppy, watching the way she looked at him, spotted the quick glance down at his left hand. The ring-check, every single girl's reflexive response to a good-looking man . . .

Poppy followed the waitress's gaze.

'Oh bloody hell, I don't believe it,' she wailed. 'You're married!'

Chapter 44

'No I'm not,' said Tom.

'Yes you are.' Poppy jabbed an accusing finger at his hand. How could she not have noticed it before? After all those things she'd said, too. How embarrassing.

'No he isn't,' said the waitress, looking at Poppy as if she were mad. 'That's his right hand.' Nodding at the other half of the pair she added kindly, 'That one's his left.'

'Sorry.' Poppy tried to shrink into her chair. 'I'm dyslexic.'

'The thing is,' said Tom when the waitress had sauntered back to the kitchen, 'I'm not married. But I am kind of . . . well, involved with someone.'

Buggeration. In an effort to appear laid-back, Poppy picked up her glass and swilled the wine before sipping it. Sadly it swilled out of the glass and onto the white table-cloth.

'I see.' So much for laid-back. 'How involved?'

'On a scale of one to ten? Five. Maybe six.' He watched her mop ineffectually at the wet tablecloth and smiled. 'But at least I won't have to get a divorce.'

'I'm single. Unattached, I mean.'

'I know. Jake told me.'

'What else has he said?' Poppy wondered if she wanted to hear this. If Jake had made her out to be some kind of sad charity case she would die. Her heart skipped a couple of uncomfortable beats as another thought struck her. 'My God, he didn't pay you to come and see me, did he?'

Tom burst out laughing.

293

'This is getting less romantic by the second. Do I look like a gigolo?'

The thing was, he was so gorgeous, he did rather.

'You could be.' Poppy felt herself going pink. 'I'm sorry, I'm a bit confused. I keep wondering if this is a huge joke. I don't know what's supposed to happen next.' She glugged down the remains of her wine. 'I feel like I've been given an instruction manual and it's in Japanese.'

'Not that bad.' He was teasing her again. 'At least I speak English.'

'I don't even know your surname.'

'That's an easy one. Kennedy.'

'Are you really a doctor?'

'Did you think I was?' Tom grinned. 'No, it was all I could come up with at the time, to explain away the fact that your foot was in my lap. Somehow chiropodist didn't have the same ring.'

'You're a chiropodist?' Poppy bit her lip. She didn't know if she could fall in love with someone whose life revolved around other people's feet.

'I'm an architect.' His smile broadened. 'Is that all right with you?'

Phew. 'Oh yes, much better.'

'Next question.'

The waitress returned with more wine, giving Poppy time to gather her scattered thoughts. Her lamb cutlets looked heavenly but she hadn't been able to eat a thing.

'Go on,' prompted Tom while she dithered with her napkin.

'That night. What would have happened if I'd met you in Delgado's?'

He grew serious. 'We wouldn't have wasted the past year.'

It hadn't been wasted. She had found Alex. Still, Poppy held her breath.

'We might not have got on.'

'You felt the same way as I did. How often does that kind of thing happen?'

Helplessly she said, 'So . . . what now?'

'We make up for lost time.' His dark eyes were intense. 'We aren't going to eat this, are we? I'll get the bill.'

'But . . . this girlfriend of yours.'

Tom shrugged. 'It's over.'

'Oh God, won't she be upset?'

Taking Poppy's hand, he drew her to her feet and kissed her full on the mouth. Almost instantly he pulled away.

'No, not here. I can't kiss you how I want to kiss you. Of course she'll be upset. I imagine your chap was upset when you called off the wedding. But you and me . . . when these things happen, they happen.'

Quivering, Poppy said, 'Yes, but—'

'Don't argue. It's destiny. I'm not going to lose you again.'

Tom settled the bill. Outside, he hailed a cab. It was still raining.

'You don't have to go back to work, by the way.' He brushed droplets of rain from her flushed cheeks. 'Jake's given you the rest of the day off.'

'That's even more of a miracle than you turning up,' Poppy joked feebly.

The cab had drawn to a halt in front of them.

'I know how I'd like to spend the afternoon,' said Tom as he helped her in, 'but say if it's too soon. I don't want to pressure you.'

'Are you kidding?' Poppy was practically melting with lust. 'I thought you'd never ask.'

'Right, it's make your mind up time,' said the world-weary driver. 'Your place or his?'

So the nosy cabbie couldn't hear, Poppy whispered, shame-faced, 'I've only got a single bed.'

Tom squeezed her hand. 'That's nothing. I've got a girl-friend with a key to my flat.'

The house was empty when they reached it. Claudia was at work and there had been no sign of Caspar for days. Poppy, who knew what a state the kitchen had been in when she'd raced out of the house that morning, took Tom straight downstairs.

'Welcome to my rabbit hutch.' She gestured around the tiny, messy room. 'If I'd known you were coming I'd have made the bed.'

Tom took her into his arms.

'Are you nervous?'

'Of course I'm nervous. Would I be making this many bad jokes if I wasn't?'

'Sshh.' He pulled her closer. 'No more jokes. Time for that kiss I couldn't give you earlier.'

The one good thing about horrible clothes, thought Poppy, was you couldn't wait to get them off. And they made your body look better by comparison.

'You are beautiful,' said Tom. 'I mean it.'

'Don't sound so surprised.'

'Well, you never know. Some girls look stunning until you see them naked. Then you realise it was all industrial-strength knickers and Wonderbra. One minute they're up here, the next . . . whoomph. Talk about a let-down.'

Poppy glanced at her own modest breasts. 'I don't have enough to let down.'

'I said no more jokes.' His dark eyes softened. 'You're perfect.'

'Well,' said Poppy an hour later, 'that was definitely perfect.'

'Not to mention long overdue.'

She lay in his arms and gazed around her room, seeing it as Tom must see it.

'Sorry. This place is such a tip.'

'Never mind, I'm here now.' He raised himself up on one elbow and planted a necklace of kisses around her throat. 'I'll take you away from all this.'

'That won't help.' Poppy closed her eyes, squirming with pleasure as he ran warm fingers across her bare stomach. 'I

296

can be untidy anywhere. It's pro rata. The bigger the space, the more mess I make.'

'Sshh.' Tom kissed her again. Then he made love to Poppy a second time, slowly and thoroughly, until overcome by the events of the day she sobbed with joy.

A sheen of perspiration covered Poppy's body. The duvet cover was sticking to her hips.

'A bath.' She reached over Tom, peering at her wristwatch on the bedside table. 'That's okay, only four o'clock. Claudia won't be home for ages yet.' She double-checked the time. 'How amazing.'

Tom seized her arms and pulled her down on top of him.

'What?'

'It's only four o'clock,' Poppy sighed between kisses. 'I feel as if we've been in bed together for days.'

Shaking off rain like a dog, Caspar let himself into the house. Getting away from London for the weekend was all very well – he and Babette had driven down to the Cotswolds and stayed in an hotel teeming with golfers in loud sweaters – but his commissions were piling up. Back in the real world he had work to do.

Incredibly, Bella McCloud had decided to forgive him. Now back in the country following a triumphant appearance at La Scala, the diva had instructed her manager to re-schedule a series of sittings with the so-handsome young artist who had had the audacity to stand her up.

She was meeting him here in – Caspar checked his watch – twenty minutes. He lit a cigarette, since her manager had already warned him he wouldn't be able to smoke in La McCloud's presence. Wondering if this meant opera singers *never* went into pubs after a hard day's warbling, Caspar made his way slowly upstairs.

When he reached the first-floor landing he realised the house wasn't empty, as he had first thought. Something was going on in the bathroom. And whoever was in there clearly wasn't alone.

Claudia? Had she and Jake got it together at last? Or was she here with her new boss, having sloped out of the office for a naughty afternoon off? Amused by this idea – giving Claudia a lift into work the other week, he had seen her middle-aged boss ogle her across the car park – Caspar listened to the sounds of shrieks and splashing filtering through the bathroom door.

Then he heard Poppy, helpless with laughter, scream 'No, no, not the cold water – oh you sod!'

Not Claudia. Poppy.

Caspar's blood ran cold. What the bloody hell did she think she was playing at? Even more to the point, who was she *with*?

More giggles and shrieks. Caspar felt his hands curling into angry fists. Of course he knew who Poppy was with. It had to be that prat from the photographs, the lanky one with the inane grin Poppy had so boisterously entertained here while he and Claudia had both been away.

Without stopping to think what he was doing, Caspar marched up to the door and hammered on it. The door, which had been left unlocked, burst open.

298

Chapter 45

'Jesus!' exclaimed a dark-haired, dark-eyed Adonis he had never seen before in his life.

'Aaargh!' screamed Poppy, who had streaked along the landing earlier to grab a couple of dry towels from the airing cupboard and forgotten to re-lock the bathroom door. Like a scene from a Whitehall farce she made a lunge for the nearest towel, which was slung around the Adonis' hips. He hung onto it. Yelping, desperately trying to cover herself with her hands, Poppy scuttled sideways and snatched the other towel from the rail.

If he hadn't been so furious Caspar would have found it funny.

'What are you *doing* here?' Poppy shouted, her face burning with embarrassment. She clutched the yellow towel to her chest like a toddler's security blanket.

'It's my house.'

'How dare you come barging in! You must have heard us,' she seethed. 'Couldn't you have knocked?'

'I did. I thought you'd have locked the door.'

'I forgot!'

'And I heard you screaming.' Caspar looked pointedly at her companion. 'What was I supposed to do? How did I know you weren't being murdered?'

'Oh, please.' Poppy's eyes were like chips of ice. 'Now I've heard bloody everything.'

'Look—' began the bloke in the towel.

'No, *you* look.' Ignoring him, Caspar pointed an accusing

finger at Poppy. 'Listen to me for once in your life. I'm not talking morals here, just plain common sense. Picking up total strangers and bringing them back to an empty house is a dangerous hobby. You're not stupid, Poppy. You read the papers. Girls get attacked. They get raped, murdered—'

'You've got a nerve!' Poppy was so agitated she almost dropped her towel. 'How many girls have you brought back here? I bet you didn't lecture them about how stupid they were being! Anyway,' she yelled, 'I haven't picked up a total stranger. This is Tom. Tom Kennedy.'

'Oh well done, you know his name,' Caspar's voice dripped sarcasm. 'He actually bothered to introduce himself. That's okay then, he can't possibly be a psychopath.'

But as he spoke, the significance of the name sank in. Tom. This was *that* Tom. Jake's hare-brained scheme to find him must actually have worked. He was here with Poppy and things were obviously going with a swing.

Great.

'Okay?' demanded Poppy. 'Does it all make sense now?'

Caspar was buggered if he was going to apologise.

'So you met him once before. Big deal. You still don't *know* him.'

'I know enough,' Poppy countered hotly.

'Please,' said Tom, who was far too handsome for Caspar's liking, 'could we all calm down? I'm really not a psychopath.' He turned to Poppy. 'But you can see Caspar's point. He only has your best interests at heart.'

'Like hell he does.' Poppy glared at Caspar. 'He's just pissed off because he thinks he's the only one around here allowed to have any fun.'

'Now you're being stupid,' Caspar snapped back.

'If you had my best interests at heart, you'd be happy for me.' Poppy was startled to find herself thinking that if he'd had her best interests at heart he would never have married Babette Lawrenson. 'If you *really* had my best interests at heart,' she shouted, 'you'd get the hell out of

300

this bathroom and leave us to get dressed in peace!'

Bella McCloud had a disappointing afternoon. Having looked forward to meeting and being gently flirted with by the famously attractive Caspar French, she was feeling deeply let down. Oh, he had been polite enough, and the preliminary drawings he had done of her couldn't be faulted – if you didn't count the fact that he had insisted her hint of a double chin stayed in – but that had been as far as it went. Where was the charisma, the easy charm Bella had heard so much about? Caspar French had been quiet, almost abstracted. He had simply got on with the job. Not a flirtatious grin in sight.

In the back of the cab as it took her back to her hotel, Bella McCloud dug in her bag and flipped through her diary. She tapped a long red fingernail thoughtfully against the number of the Harley Street surgeon all her friends had been raving about. Maybe it was time for that face lift after all.

Tom's flat was on the third floor of a huge Victorian house in the smarter section of Notting Hill.

'Well? Do you approve?' he asked when the guided tour was over. She had seen the kitchen, the living room, the bathroom and both bedrooms.

'Very smart.' Poppy ran her hand over the matte black wooden shelving. Recessed lights cunningly illuminated a selection of steel-framed black and white prints. The walls were pale grey, as was the almost futuristic sofa. 'Very . . . architecty.'

He looked amused. 'I don't like clutter, if that's what you mean.'

'I don't think you and Laura Ashley would have hit it off.'

'Judith, the girl who lives downstairs, calls it stark. She hates my kitchen, says it's like being on board a bloody spaceship.'

'It's not stark,' Poppy lovingly assured him, 'it's manly.'

Tom put his arms around her. 'I know. Maybe what it needs

301

is a woman's touch. I've just been waiting for the right woman to come along.'

He's probably envisaging fresh flowers, thought Poppy; five perfect irises faultlessly arranged in a conical vase. Since her version of a woman's touch was more likely to be cake crumbs all over the pristine kitchen worktops and blobs of mascara on the bathroom mirror she realised she was going to have to buck up her ideas pretty damn quick.

'Right, down to business.' Tom glanced at his watch as the oven timer in the kitchen went ping. 'Sit down, sweetheart. Make yourself at home. I have a phone call to make.'

Thinking he meant work-type business, Poppy happily made herself comfortable on the grey sofa and chose a magazine from the coffee table. Called *Architecture Today*, it made her feel jolly intelligent.

She was gazing at a picture of an office block when she realised to her horror that Tom wasn't phoning the office at all.

'. . . no, it's better if you don't come over. Jan, listen to me. I'm sorry, really I am, but we can't see each other any more. Hang on, let me explain . . . Jan, please . . . I've met someone else. It's serious. This is the real thing.'

He was standing with his back to Poppy, looking out of the window. Even from ten feet away she could hear the anguished wail on the other end of the phone.

Poppy squirmed. Tom listened in silence for several seconds. Then he said, 'Jan, calm down. I know it isn't fair but there's nothing I can do about it. Yes, yes, I know that too. I'm a bastard. And a shit. What else can I say? I *am* sorry. If we could be friends, that'd be great. Look, can I ask you to do something for me? Post your key back? No, just send it in the post . . .'

Cringing, Poppy watched him listen for a few moments more. When he had put the phone down he turned round.

'She doesn't want to be friends.'

'Oh, I feel terrible! That poor girl,' Poppy gasped. 'She sounded dreadfully upset.'

'She'll be fine.' Tom's smile was rueful but dismissive. 'It just came as a shock, that's all. She wasn't expecting it.'

'Neither was I.'

'Come on, it's over now.' He drew her to her feet and kissed her again. 'We can't have you feeling sorry for Jan. It's not as if it was the love affair of the century. We weren't even living together.'

'Why did she have a key?'

He led her through to the kitchen. Through the smoked glass door of the oven a casserole was in the process of being heated up.

'It made life easier,' said Tom. 'Jan finished work an hour before me. She used to let herself in and make a start on the evening meal. She made this this morning,' he went on, 'before she left. Actually, she's a bloody good cook.'

He was taking plates down from a steel-fronted cupboard. Then he slid open the cutlery drawer and began picking out knives and forks.

Poppy blurted out, 'I can't eat that casserole!'

'Oh God, you're not a vegetarian?'

'No! I mean I can't eat something your girlfriend made for the two of you to share tonight!'

Tom frowned. 'Ex-girlfriend.'

'Okay, ex-girlfriend.' Poppy started to laugh. Men, honestly. 'Don't you see? All the more reason why I can't eat it.'

'Oh.' He nodded. 'Right. Bugger, I'm starving.'

She decided to take the plunge. He was going to have to find out sooner or later. 'We'll make something else. Except . . . I have to warn you, I'm a pretty hopeless cook.'

'So am I.' Tom held her face between his warm hands. 'It doesn't matter. Nothing else matters, Poppy. I love you.'

'You're in a grumpy mood,' observed Babette. Since

emerging scented and revived from her bath an hour earlier, Caspar had hardly said more than two words. She rubbed the last vestiges of moisturiser into the backs of her fingers and glanced at her diary, lying open on the sofa. 'What was Bella McCloud like, a pain in the neck?'

Caspar stopped pretending to watch whatever was on TV. He gazed across the room at Babette, who had now finished efficiently rubbing in hand cream. She fished in the pocket of her white silk dressing gown, clipped her watch briskly onto her wrist and slid the narrow gold wedding ring back into place.

'Pain in the chin, if anything.' He shrugged. 'She was okay.'

'Well, something's bothering you.' Picking up her diary, Babette came over to his chair and draped her arms lovingly around his neck. 'Cheer up, darling. Look who I'm seeing tomorrow.' She pointed with pride to the name she had underlined in red, belonging to the owner of one of the smartest galleries in Knightsbridge. 'He wants me to promote his next exhibition. Is that a coup or what?'

Becoming known as Caspar's wife had done Babette's career no harm at all. There had been a flurry of interest in the media and Babette had handled it superbly, in interviews playing up the differences between the super-organised businesswoman and the laid-back artist. Their marriage certificate, Caspar joked, had been photocopied in triplicate and filed away in her office under M for marital status.

'Great.' He forced a smile. She was right, he was being grumpy and it wasn't her fault. 'Sorry. Headache.'

'You don't get headaches. Come on, something's up.' Babette slid onto his lap. 'Isn't this what wives are for? You can tell me.'

'Nothing to tell. Poppy's taken up with some old flame, that's all.' Caspar didn't want to elaborate; this was close enough. 'She thinks she's in luurve. I just hope she isn't making a horrible mistake.'

Babette checked her watch. It was early yet; if they made love now she would still have plenty of time to work on tomorrow's presentation.

'If it's love, you could soon be losing yourself a lodger,' she pointed out. 'That's good news.'

'Why is it good news?'

'No need to jump down my throat! I mean if Poppy moves out, maybe Claudia will go too. You'd get more money renting the house out to a family. Financially it makes far better sense.'

Caspar grinned. 'So organised. So efficient.'

Babette shifted position on his lap and began undoing his shirt.

'Not to mention,' she said happily, 'so great in bed.'

Chapter 46

Jake didn't know what he'd eaten, but something was doing its damnedest to wrench his stomach inside out.

'I'm sorry, this evening's off,' he told Claudia. He felt so dreadful it was a struggle even to hold onto the phone.

'Food poisoning?' Claudia had spent enough time working in offices to know this was the oldest and least original excuse in the book. Along with funerals. 'Sure it isn't a funeral?'

'What?'

She looked at her glamorous reflection in the mirror above the fireplace. All that make-up, all that careful hair tonging, all for bloody nothing.

'Are you really ill?'

Jake closed his eyes. His stomach was churning ominously.

'Of course I'm ill. Why would I invite you to dinner and then cancel?'

Claudia's self-confidence was deserting her. All she knew was that she was being stood up. Insecurity flooded through her like poison.

'Maybe you found out how much dinner was likely to cost.'

'Oh come *on* . . .'

'Okay, I know. I'll drive over. I can look after you.'

Jake hadn't been sick for almost fifteen minutes. Sweat prickled across his icy skin, reminding him it was time he headed for the bathroom again.

'Please don't,' he said urgently. The prospect of having

Claudia here to witness his condition was too awful to contemplate. 'I mean it. You mustn't.'

You mean I mustn't come over and find out you aren't really ill, thought Claudia. Mentally she was ten again, in an unflattering pinafore dress, and Angie was trilling to all and sundry, 'With hips like mine, I can't imagine how I managed to produce such a gawky great lump of a girl!'

'You won't, will you?' Jake had to double-check.

'Of course I won't,' Claudia snapped back.

A great wave of nausea swept through him. Jake lurched unsteadily to his feet. 'Sorry, got to go—'

It gave Claudia the tiniest amount of satisfaction to hang up first. She kicked off her high heels and stomped barefoot through to the kitchen. No Caspar, because he was too busy being happily married to Babette. No Poppy because she was busy being even happier with Tom.

No Chez Nico.

And no Jake.

Claudia, whose own stomach was growling with hunger, peered at the contents of the fridge. I'll have scrambled eggs on toast, she decided, trying hard to be brave. And lemon pudding.

Then she burst into tears.

Ben McBride took the message on Friday afternoon while Dina was out at the supermarket. Returning weighed down with nappies, she spotted the brief note propped against the phone.

'Poppy rang! What did she say? What's this bit?' Dina dropped the nappies and wandered into the kitchen, where Ben was mending the toaster. 'Your writing's in a world of its own. She's found what? *God*?'

'Tom.' Ben was poking and prodding amongst the wires with his screwdriver. 'She said to tell you she found Tom. Whoever he is.'

Dina didn't tell him. Tom was, after all, the reason why

Poppy hadn't married Ben's precious brother.

'He's an old friend. That's brilliant news.' It was like giving up smoking, then breathing in the seductive whiff of a cigarette; the urge to zip up to London came over her in an instant. Eyes shining, she turned to Ben. 'You aren't working this weekend, are you?'

He gave her a weary look.

'What does that mean? You, buggering off again, leaving me stuck here with the baby?'

'Poppy's my friend.' Dina's arms were crossed, which meant she wasn't going to give up without a fight. 'She's had some good news. Is there anything wrong with seeing a friend, helping her celebrate?'

The look of defiance on her face was what Ben couldn't bear. Dina always made him out to be some kind of ogre, the boring grown-up out to spoil her fun. And all he wanted was for them to have fun together . . .

'Go,' he said stiffly, 'if that's what you want.'

'Thanks.' It was so easy to twist him round her little finger. Dina dropped a triumphant kiss on top of his head. Now she could ring Poppy and fix things up.

She pulled a face when Claudia answered the phone.

'Poppy's not here,' said Claudia in a 'so-there' voice. 'She'll be at Tom's flat. And no, I don't have the number. Sorry.'

Bitch. But Dina's weekend was at stake, so she forced herself to sound friendly.

'Great news, isn't it, about Tom? Actually, Poppy suggested I came up this weekend—'

'She isn't here,' Claudia repeated.

'Yes, but I can still crash in her room, can't I?' Dina's manner was confident, all-girls-together. 'I mean, I don't want to play gooseberry at Tom's place.'

'Look, I'm just on my way out. Staying here isn't really on, I'm afraid. Maybe you should make other arrangements.'

Bitch, *bitch*. Claudia was giving her the kind of brush-off normally reserved for double-glazing salesmen. Except double-glazing salesmen weren't allowed to bite back.

'Okay, no problem,' said Dina breezily. 'I'll give Jake a ring.'

It was a shot in the dark, but Poppy had told her Claudia was keen on Jake.

'Jake? You can't do that! You've never even met Jake.'

Dina grinned. Bingo. The bitch was rattled.

'So?' she countered innocently. 'He's a friend of Poppy's, isn't he? I bet he'd put me up.'

'My God, you have a nerve.'

'Anyway, I've been looking forward to meeting him for ages. Poppy says he's lovely. And now he's got all that money stashed away—'

'He's not going to want you turning up on his doorstep,' Claudia interrupted furiously. 'I'll tell you that for nothing.'

Before putting the phone down Dina purred, 'Want to bet?'

Ben had finished mending the toaster. Testily he said, 'What was all that about?'

'Poppy shares a house with a complete cow.'

His face reddened with suppressed rage. 'And who the bloody hell's Jake? Dina, you're not going up to London and staying at some bloke's house. Not some bloke you've never met. I won't have it.'

'Don't get your knickers in a twist. Of course I'm not going.' She didn't even know where Jake lived. The weekend was off. Upstairs, Daniel began to wail. With bitter satisfaction Dina said, 'I was just geeing her up.'

Claudia, who had been lying about going out, was so angry she couldn't even manicure her nails straight. She gave up and ran a bath instead, tipping in half a bottle of hair conditioner by mistake.

It was four days since Jake had cancelled their date and there had been no word from him since.

If I phone to warn him about Dina, she thought miserably, he'll think it's just a pathetic excuse to speak to him.

It wasn't as if they'd parted on the sunniest of terms. Oh, but if that slut Dina really did have plans to get her claws into Jake, how could she *stand* it?

The bath water was weirdly slippery. Unable to relax, Claudia climbed out and ran downstairs. She found Jake's number in the phone book, picked up the receiver and dialled. Then, her courage failing her, she put the phone down after the first ring. Jake hadn't bothered to make contact all week. She would sound so obvious, so . . . desperate.

Claudia forced herself to sit through *Coronation Street* and *The Bill* in her dressing gown. By eight thirty her agitation was at fever pitch and most of the nails she had lopsidedly manicured earlier were bitten to the quick. If Dina had caught the coach straight up to London she'd have arrived by now. She would be wearing a skimpy top and an up-to-the-bum skirt, and carrying a change of clothes in that cheap leather-look bag of hers. With her cat-like smile and sickeningly tiny figure, Claudia realised, Dina was a low-rent version of her mother. Except even Angie didn't have quite that much barefaced cheek.

By nine o'clock she couldn't stand it any more. Not knowing what was happening was the worst torture of all. Leaping to her feet, Claudia raced back upstairs and pulled on a white sweater and pale green trousers. Moments later she tore them off and changed into a black sweater and black jeans. It made her look like something out of a Milk Tray ad, but maybe that was what she needed . . .

She was so nervous she could hardly drive. By the time she reached Jake's road she had taken four wrong turnings and her *A-Z* was practically in shreds.

Trembling like a leaf, Claudia parked four doors away and switched off the ignition. The lights in Jake's house were on and the living-room curtains had been drawn, but carelessly. One of the curtains had got hooked up against a pile of books on the windowsill, leaving a smallish triangular gap.

There could be no backing out now. She had come this far and she had to know. Fuelled by jealousy, Claudia slid out of the car and crept, Milk Tray-style, across the road. Thankfully, there was no one else in sight.

Not so good was the way the house had been designed. Five steps led up to the front door and the minuscule front garden, surrounded by railings and planted as a rockery, was eight feet below the window-ledge. If she clambered over the railings and onto the rockery, there was no way she could see into the window. If she mounted the steps and leaned across as far as she possibly could . . . well, she would fall over.

Claudia hovered agonisingly on the pavement wondering what to do next. She jumped as a front door opened and shut at the far end of the street, and watched a fair-haired man climb into a van and drive off. Moments later, realising what the van had been parked behind, she experienced a surge of adrenalin and raced up the road to investigate.

The skip was three quarters full, packed mainly with builders' rubble and planks of rotted wood. But thrown in on top, by some miracle, was a dining chair. Granted, a chair with the seat missing and only three legs, but enough to do the trick.

Joyfully, Claudia hauled herself into the skip, seized the chair and eased herself out onto the pavement. She ran with it back to Jake's front garden, climbed over the rusty railings and wedged the chair against the front of the house with the missing leg nearest the brickwork to keep it secure.

The street was silent. All she could hear was her own breathing. Balancing herself carefully, one foot at a time, on the frame of the chair to which the seat had once been attached, Claudia edged her bitten fingernails up the wall. She was safe, she wasn't going to topple over, all she had to do now was grab the window-ledge and pull herself from a crouch to a standing position—

'Oi, you!' yelled a voice from the other side of the road, 'Stay right where you are! Smash that window and I'll smash your head in.'

Claudia almost wet herself. Whimpering with fear she tried to climb down. Her fingers scraped against the wall, losing what feeble grip they might have had. One knee gave way. The chair wobbled in the opposite direction and cracked under the strain.

She landed in the rockery with a scream and a bone-crunching thud.

Chapter 47

'Don't move!' ordered the rough male voice, now close behind her. 'Thieving bastard, I hope you've broken both your bloody legs. Don't you move a muscle. Jake, GET OUT HERE!'

It was a nightmare. Everything hurt. Too appalled to cry, Claudia lay in the darkness amongst the rocks and splintered chair legs wishing she could at least have been knocked unconscious. Anything to be spared the humiliation of the next few minutes.

Above her Jake's door opened, spilling out light.

'What's going on?'

'Bloody cat burglar. Saw him from our bedroom window. It's okay,' the rough voice declared with satisfaction, 'I've already phoned the old Bill. They're on their way.'

Not okay. Not okay at all. Struggling to raise her head from the ground Claudia heard herself moan pathetically, 'Oh please, not the police.'

'Flaming Nora,' the rough voice exclaimed, 'it's a bird.'

'Jake, it's me. Make them go away. Not the police, *please*.'

'*Claudia*?' Jake leapt over the railings in amazement and appeared beside her. 'Are you hurt? Can you move?'

'Ouch, I think so. Oh no—'

The wail of a police siren shattered the night. Gritting her teeth – at least they were all still there – Claudia let Jake help her slowly into an upright position. Somehow, between them, he and the man from across the road managed to lift her back over the railings. She sat on the steps of the house with her head buried in her hands and listened to Jake explaining to the police officers that she wasn't a burglar; it had all been a mistake.

You're telling me, thought Claudia, hot tears of self-pity seeping through her aching eyelids and dripping onto her wrists.

'Well, well, you're a dark horse and no mistake,' marvelled his neighbour when Jake had persuaded the police to leave. 'Never had you down as the type to have a fan club, Jake. What are you, some kind of rock star in your spare time?'

'His name's Dan. He's very into Neighbourhood Watch.'

One way and another, Claudia thought morosely, Jake's Neighbourhood Watch scheme was out to ruin her life.

'Now –' he put a mug of coffee into her hands – 'are you sure you're all right?'

'Is that meant to be a joke?'

'I mean if you want to see a doctor I could drive you to casualty.'

Claudia shook her head. The last thing she needed was a gaggle of medical students with smirks on their faces prodding her bottom. By tomorrow it would be one huge bruise. The least she could do was keep it to herself.

'Sorry about the chips,' said Jake, breaking the silence.

'What?'

He pointed to the mug she was holding, chipped around the rim.

'I'd have thought you could've treated yourself to new ones,' said Claudia. 'Now you can afford it.'

It wasn't the first time she had made that kind of remark. Jake really wished she wouldn't. He wished he didn't keep remembering Poppy telling him that Claudia was only interested in men with more money than sense.

Ironically, it was probably thanks to Claudia that he was still living here. The more digs she made, the less keen he became on the idea of moving to a smarter address. And it wasn't as if he was cutting off his nose to spite his face, Jake reassured himself. There was no rush, and he'd always been happy here. He loved this house.

He glanced briefly around his cluttered, comfortable-but-shabby living room, seeing it through her eyes.

'Would you like to criticise my home too, while you're about it?'

Claudia shook her head. The room was actually quite cosy, though clearly the domain of someone whose priority in life was not interior design. The carpet was threadbare in places, the furniture old and functional rather than elegant. Those striped blue and green curtains didn't match anything else in the room . . .

Bloody curtains, she thought crossly. If he'd only taken the trouble to draw them properly there wouldn't have been that enticing gap and she wouldn't be here now, nursing a bruise the size of a pizza and looking a complete prat into the bargain.

'So what *were* you doing outside my front window?' asked Jake at last.

Claudia couldn't look at him.

'I wanted to find out if Dina was here.'

'Who?'

'Poppy's friend. From Bristol.' Painfully, she forced herself to meet his astonished gaze.

'I've never even met Dina!'

'I know. But I wouldn't let her stay at the house tonight so she said she'd ask you instead. She told me you wouldn't turn her down and anyway, from what she'd heard, you sounded right up her street. She's a shameless uppity trollop.' Claudia was indignant. 'And a gold-digger to boot.'

Mildly, Jake said, 'Well, she isn't here. You came up my street instead. If you were so worried, why didn't you just phone?'

'After you'd stood me up on Monday and hadn't bothered to get in touch all week? You'd have thought I was chasing you,' Claudia snapped. 'That would have looked great.'

'You lying splattered all over my front garden didn't look that great,' he pointed out. 'A phone call would have been easier. Anyway, why would I think you were chasing me?'

'Oh come on! It happened to Caspar all the time. He spent his life getting us to field phone calls from besotted girlies.' Her lip curled. 'They were a standing joke.'

As opposed to a flat-on-your-back-in-the-rockery joke, thought Jake. Diplomatically, he didn't say so.

'I'm not Caspar.'

'No.'

'I'm not anything like Caspar.' Drily he added, 'And I've never had a phone call from a besotted girlie in my life.'

Claudia thought it was just as well everyone wasn't like Caspar. Imagine a world full of them . . .

'What, never?'

Jake shook his head.

'Why not? You aren't that ugly.'

'Thanks.'

Flustered, Claudia said, 'I didn't mean it like that.'

He smiled slightly. 'You should have seen me as a teenager. When you're awkward and shy *and* you wear NHS specs, girls don't exactly swoon at your feet.'

'But you must have had a girlfriend at some stage.'

'I had a girlfriend for five years. Emily. She wore glasses too,' said Jake. 'The first time I kissed her, at the school Christmas disco, it was like antlers clashing. Everyone saw us go clunk.' He mimed the jarring action. 'We didn't live it down for months.'

'Yes, but you were together for five years, so it must have been serious. What happened?' Claudia was burning with curiosity.

'She had cystic fibrosis. She died.'

Claudia's hands went up to her mouth. 'No! How awful. God, I'm sorry . . . Poppy never told me.'

'Maybe because Poppy doesn't know.'

'But that's so sad—'

'It was a long time ago.' Jake shrugged off her sympathy. 'Do you want another coffee? If you want to use the bathroom to tidy yourself up, feel free.'

It was pretty galling, being told to tidy yourself up by Jake – rather like Harold Steptoe suggesting your teeth could do with a scrape and polish – but when she reached the bathroom Claudia saw what he meant. The rubble in the skip had left a layer of grey dust over her black sweater, and her hair was thick with it too. There were twigs in her fringe and a smudge of mud across one cheek.

What a fright.

'I'd better go,' she said when she had made her way back downstairs.

Jake, rather touchingly, was emptying a packet of peanuts into a dish. Next to it stood a bowl of Ritz crackers.

'Do you have to? I still don't know why you came.'

You blind bat, can't you see I was jealous? Why else would I leap about in a skip like a demented monkey? Why else would I try and climb up the outside of your house?

Claudia couldn't say it. She gazed hard at a frayed patch of carpet and wondered why getting it together with someone you fancied had to be so fraught. Why couldn't she make something approaching a first move? If Jake really did like her, why couldn't *he*?

For a mad moment she wondered what he would have done if she'd come back downstairs naked, if she'd just ripped off all her clothes and presented herself to him in all her wondrous glory.

But if she had, she would have looked a berk, what with all the crease marks on her stomach from wearing too-tight jeans, not to mention the whacking great bruise on her bottom.

Wondrous glory was hardly the phrase most likely to spring to Jake's mind.

'Here,' he offered her the dish, 'have a peanut.'

I'm such a failure, thought Claudia miserably.

The peanuts were stale. They tasted disgusting.

'Come on, sit down,' Jake urged. '*Raiders of the Lost Ark* starts in a minute. You know, with Indiana Jones.'

Indiana Jones. Wild, brave, reckless and passionate. Claudia, her imagination running riot, wondered if some of that recklessness and passion might rub off on Jake. She sat down cautiously – ouch – at one end of the sofa.

'You'll be more comfortable if you stretch out,' said Jake. 'Put your feet up. Here, have a cushion.'

She uncurled her legs a few inches, wondering if he was inviting her to rest her feet on his lap.

'Am I taking up too much room?'

'Don't worry about me. You're the invalid. I'll sit on the chair.'

'Eh up,' said Poppy at work the following week when Jake accidentally let slip that Claudia had spent Friday evening at his place. 'I saw Claudia yesterday and she didn't mention any of this! Come on, tell. Are we talking true romance here or what?'

'Actually, we're talking about watching *Raiders of the Lost Ark* and sending out for a Chinese. That's all.'

'What? Claudia hates takeaway Chinese! She calls it repulsive slop.'

Jake flushed. This explained why Claudia had left most of hers. Probably not expensive enough for her; he should have ordered a takeaway from the Savoy Grill.

'You aren't telling me everything,' Poppy persisted annoyingly. Her own current state of bliss had got to her like religion. She longed for the rest of the world to be as happy as she was with Tom.

If she'd been a Jehovah's Witness, thought Jake, he could have closed the door in her face. But she wasn't, she was here on the stall, with an awful gleam in her eye.

'Jake, I have to know! Did she stay the night?'

'No!'

'Oh well, maybe that's too much to hope for.' The gleam was still there. 'How about heavy petting?'

'Poppy, stop it.'

'Snogging, then. You must have kissed her.'

There might not be a door to slam in Poppy's face but there was a cash register he could bring down on her head. Taking off his glasses so at least he couldn't see her any more, Jake said wearily, 'No.'

'Not even a weeny one? On the doorstep? A goodbye peck on the cheek?'

Of course he had kissed her, a million times and a million different ways . . . in his dreams. All the time Harrison Ford had been swashing and buckling his way across the screen, sweeping his heroine masterfully into his arms, Jake had imagined doing the same to Claudia. The trouble was, the more he had wanted to, the more firmly he had remained welded into his chair. Crippled with uncertainty, he hadn't dared move so much as a muscle. What if he tried it and she screamed? Or laughed? Or slapped his face?

As for the dreaded saying-goodbye-at-the-front door scenario (surely the ultimate doorstep challenge) . . . well, he *had* been gearing himself up to it. A friendly kiss on the cheek, Jake had assured himself, wouldn't be out of order. Not a slapping offence, at least.

But as Claudia had hovered and he had wavered, a motley crew of lads from the Crown and Feathers had been making their way noisily up the street. Spotting Jake and Claudia in the lit-up doorway they had passed by chanting, 'Give her one, give her one, give her wo-on,' and that had been that. Chance blown.

Hugely embarrassed, realising he couldn't possibly kiss her now, he had taken a step back.

With an awkward little wave Claudia had scuttled across the road to her car and driven off.

Jake looked so sad, Poppy rushed to reassure him. 'Oh

well, never mind, she was only interested in your bank account anyway. And imagine, if you married Claudia, you'd have Angie as a mother-in-law.' She giggled. 'She'd have your Y-fronts off in a flash.'

'How's Tom?' said Jake, because Poppy was easily diverted these days and he didn't want to imagine marrying Claudia.

Poppy heaved a besotted sigh.

'What can I say? He's wonderful. I'm so happy I could burst. The more we get to know each other, the better it gets. I'm meeting all his friends, and he's so *proud* of me.' Dreamily she shook back her hair. 'I know it sounds sick-making, but I had no idea it was possible to feel so . . . so *special*.'

Poppy had got it bad and Jake was glad for her. He just wished it didn't make his own life feel so empty in comparison.

Chapter 48

Tom emerged from the shower drying his dark hair with a towel. He came up behind Poppy, who was sitting cross-legged on the bed doing her eyes with the help of a shaving mirror.

'You look gorgeous. Take that dress off.'

It was Poppy's favourite dress, one of her charity shop bargain buys from Help The Aged. When Caspar had first seen her in it he had whistled and said, 'Help the Aged on their way to a heart attack, more like.'

She grinned at Tom's reflection in the mirror.

'No time for that now. We're supposed to be meeting your friends at eight.'

'Dress,' murmured Tom, unzipping it in one smooth movement, 'off.'

'Oh God, we'll be horribly late.'

But instead of ravishing her body, Tom was pulling a carrier bag out of the wardrobe.

'Surprise.'

Poppy realised he wanted her undressed for quite a different reason. He wanted her out of her short white strapless number with the flirty hem and into a far more elegant affair in navy blue crêpe, with a high neckline and below-the-elbow sleeves. It was calf-length, clearly expensive and extremely grown-up.

'It's beautiful,' she said, touched by the trouble he had taken. If you didn't count the Motorhead tee-shirt Rob had once given her for Christmas, no man had ever bought her clothes before. 'Um . . . do you think it's quite me?'

'This one's nice,' Tom picked up the white dress, then pointed to the navy one Poppy was wriggling into, 'but that one's better.' His dark eyes softened as she zipped herself into it. 'There, see the difference.'

Poppy saw. She looked positively nun-like.

'Don't you like it?' He sounded concerned.

Hastily she looked ecstatic.

'Oh yes, yes! It's just the length. I'm not used to . . . well, so much material.' She kissed him. 'All my dresses are short. But this is . . . it's brilliant.'

He smiled, reassured.

'I prefer long. You're mine, Poppy. I don't want other men ogling your body.'

'Sure you wouldn't like me to sling on a yashmak?'

'No, that's okay. They can ogle your face.' Tom looked amused. 'I'd just rather keep the rest of you to myself.'

They were meeting his friends at a restaurant in Hampstead. Richard Mason worked with Tom and his wife Anna stayed at home to look after their two children.

'You'll like them,' Tom assured Poppy. 'Better still, they'll like you.'

As usual, he was right.

'We've heard so much about you,' Anna told Poppy when they were seated at their table. 'We couldn't believe it when we heard Tom had found you again. It's just so romantic, like something out of a film. Not like Richard and me.' She pulled an unromantic face. 'All we did was get pissed and crash into each other one night in a pub.'

'Ah, but we had a happy ending,' Richard put in. 'I made an honest woman of you, didn't I? And now here we are, two kids and a gerbil later.' He gave Anna's hand a squeeze. 'It might not be the stuff of film scripts but we're a good team.'

When they had ordered from the menu Richard went on, 'Anyway, talking of happy endings. How long before we can expect a bit of knot-tying from you two?'

'Oh yes,' Anna exclaimed with longing, 'I could buy a new hat!'

Poppy gulped a lungful of wine and spluttered into her hand.

'We've only known each other a month.'

'Listen, when Tom met you last year he told me he knew in an instant you were The One for him. The other week he said This Is It, Together Forever and other such tosh.' Richard, who played rugby and didn't much go in for soulful declarations of love, mimed sticking his fingers down his throat. A nearby waiter looked alarmed. 'I wouldn't ask, only it's going to be fun watching the secretaries in the office hold a communal wake.'

'Stop it, you're embarrassing Poppy,' said Anna. She leaned across the table, bright-eyed. 'He's such a nosy bugger. Don't tell him, okay? Tell me.'

'Of course we'll be getting married,' said Tom. In his right hand he held his glass. Beneath the table his left hand stroked the inside of Poppy's thigh. 'But big weddings take time to organise. Besides, this is the nineteen nineties. These days it's pretty much compulsory to live together first.'

Poppy turned to stare at him. They had talked about it, of course, but only in a desultory fashion. No definite decisions had been reached.

'You mean . . . ?'

'As Richard says,' Tom grinned, 'why wait? It's what we both want.'

'Fab!' Anna clapped her hands. 'Can we order champagne?'

'You really want me to move into your flat?' Poppy was thrilled but nervous. 'Are you sure? I'll turn it into a terrible heap.'

Tom started to laugh. 'No you won't. It's just a matter of getting you house-trained. Anyway, once you give up work you'll have more time to clear up after yourself.'

Richard was busy ordering two bottles of Bollinger. At the same time, their food arrived.

'Give up work?' echoed Poppy. This was definitely news to her. 'What, and be like a . . . a *housewife*?'

'Why not?' Tom's fingers were still caressing her leg. He looked pleased with himself. 'I can afford to support both of us. Darling, you don't *need* to work.'

'She's in shock,' said Anna. 'Poppy, don't look like that . . . you'll love it! Take it from me, not having to go out to work is the best thing ever.'

Stunned, Poppy glugged down more wine. This wasn't something she had ever considered. Surely, giving up work was what you did once you had children.

'I'm not pregnant,' she blurted out, in case Tom thought she was.

'Give me a chance.' His dark eyes regarded her with affection. 'It's only been a month.'

'Think about it,' Anna went on enthusiastically, 'you'll be a lady of leisure! No beastly early mornings battling through the rain, getting crushed to a pulp on the tube, never having enough time to do lovely things like shopping for clothes because you've got to work instead. I used to be a nurse.' She pulled a face. 'The sister in charge of our ward was a right cow. I tell you, jacking in my job was the best move I ever made.'

The conversation moved on to Bastard Bosses each of them had been forced to work for over the years. Since Jake wasn't a bastard, Poppy used the breathing space to turn Tom's suggestion over in her mind. Okay, she liked her job, but maybe Anna had a point. To be unemployed and forced to survive on some miserable dole cheque was depressing beyond belief, but giving up work knowing you were financially secure was surely the height of luxury. It was why people did the pools, wasn't it? Instead of slaving your life away in some smelly office you actually got to sit back and enjoy all those acres and acres of delicious free time.

I could go to the theatre, thought Poppy, who had never

been to a theatre in her life. I could take long walks, go to coffee mornings, meet friends for lunch, join a health club like Princess Di, have – what were they called? Oh yes, that was it – *pedicures* . . .

'What are you thinking?' Tom whispered, his mouth brushing her ear.

It was Poppy's turn to squeeze his leg. He was so perfect for her; he knew her better than she knew herself.

'Just how clever you are,' she murmured back. 'I think I could enjoy giving up work.'

'I love you. I want to look after you.'

It was such a novelty. No one had ever said that to her before. Poppy felt dizzy with desire.

'I love you too.'

It wasn't exactly the surprise of the century but that didn't mean Caspar had to like it.

'I'm moving in with Tom,' Poppy announced, almost bashfully. Her eyes were bright and there were spots of colour high up on each cheekbone.

Tom, who was holding her hand, said easily, 'You've had her long enough. My turn now.'

Haven't had her at all, thought Caspar, hating the way Tom's fingers stroked the inside of Poppy's wrist almost as much as he hated the aura of blissful happiness surrounding them like ectoplasm.

'First you and Babette,' said Poppy, 'now us. It must be catching!'

'Yeah, well, that's great.' Caspar knew he didn't sound as thrilled as he was supposed to sound. 'When are you off? Straight away?'

'Well, Tom's having the bedroom redesigned. The decorators arrive tomorrow and they reckon it'll take a week. So if it's okay with you, I'll move out next Saturday.'

Tom said, 'It'll be chaos until then.'

'It'll be chaos when I move in.' Poppy grinned.

'No it won't. I told you, it's simply a matter of getting you trained.'

Caspar tried to imagine the new, improved, fully house-trained Poppy Dunbar, the perfect Stepford Wife.

'Are you okay? I know it's not much notice,' Poppy put in hurriedly, 'but I can still pay the rent up to the end of the month.'

She was beginning to look hurt. Caspar pulled himself together.

'Don't be daft. Sorry. I was miles away.' He broke into a smile. 'Trying to figure out who we can invite to your leaving party.'

She brightened. 'Oh, you don't have to—'

''Course we do. Next Saturday. It's about time we had another party anyway. It'll be a bloody good bash.'

Poppy looked excited. 'Can I invite everyone from the antiques market?'

'Actually,' said Tom, 'I was planning something for next Saturday. Dinner with the head of our firm. Perhaps you could hold your party on the Friday?'

'Afraid not,' Caspar lied smoothly, for the hell of it. 'I'm busy then. You'll just have to put your boss off.'

Chapter 49

'Daddy! I didn't know you were in London! When did you sneak back?'

It was Saturday afternoon and the phone had been ringing incessantly all day. As word spread that Caspar was holding another of his infamous parties, friends and friends-of-friends had been calling up out of the blue on the off-chance of being asked along.

'Last night.' Hugo Slade-Welch's deep hint-of-Edinburgh voice was as unmistakable as ever. He sounded amused. 'And I don't sneak anywhere. I'm staying at the Hyde Park Hotel for a few weeks, taking a break between films. I wondered what you were doing this evening. Thought I might take my little girl out on the town.'

Claudia melted when her father called her his little girl. He was such a hero in her eyes, not least for having put up with her mother for as long as he had. And it was such an age since she'd last seen him, not since Christmas in fact, when Angie had given him that nude portrait of herself and he had carted it back unwrapped through customs at Heathrow, telling the press he couldn't have hoped for a better Christmas present, his old dartboard was worn right out.

'Oh Daddy, I'd love to see you. But Poppy, who's been living here with us, is moving out tonight. Caspar's holding the most massive party.'

'Is he indeed? What, young people only or are old fogeys allowed in as well?'

'Of course you could come!' Claudia swivelled round as

Caspar, lugging two crates of wine, pushed the hall door open with his elbow. 'It's my father. He'd like to come tonight.'

'Just what we need, more bloody gate-crashers,' said Caspar loudly. 'And a struggling no-hope actor at that.' He dumped the crates and grabbed the receiver.

'Hello, you old bugger. When are you going to get yourself a proper job?'

'Daddy?' said Claudia, when she had wrestled the phone back. 'No, of course you don't have to bring a bottle. I just wondered, are you bringing anyone else?'

'You mean Alice, presumably?' Hugo's tone was dry. 'No, Alice and I have had a parting of the ways. When I left Bel Air she was throwing all her shoes into cases. Shouldn't take her more than a week. By the time I get back next month she'll be gone.' He didn't sound too upset. 'Ah well, at least we weren't married.'

Alice was a silicone-boobed aspiring actress who had once had a walk-on part in *Baywatch*. Or as Hugo had once been heard to remark, a bounce-on part.

'Well, she was too young for you, Daddy.'

'I know, I know. Women are like cigarettes, I guess. A hard habit to break.'

'She was quite fun,' Claudia admitted.

'Oh, Alice was okay. Drew a moustache on that expensive painting Caspar did of your mother.'

'Did she?'

'Mm.' Hugo chuckled. 'And it wasn't on her face.'

By nine o'clock the house was filling up fast. In the sitting room, now minus most of its furniture, music blared. As usual the kitchen was bursting at the seams.

Another crowd of guests piled in through the front door. Luckily it was a warm dry evening, which meant the garden – even if it wasn't the best tended in Cornwallis Crescent – could be pressed into service to take the overspill.

Caspar was watching Poppy introduce Tom to her friends

from the Markham Antiques Market.

'No wonder she's so besotted,' said Babette, holding out her glass for a refill of Chablis. 'He's definitely gorgeous. Looks like Rufus Sewell.' She raised her brimming glass to smiling lips. 'In fact he's nearly as handsome as you, darling one.'

'What I don't get,' said Caspar with a touch of irritation, 'is the first time he saw Poppy she had her skirt up round her ears. He obviously liked what he saw. So what's with this new look?' He nodded in the direction of Poppy who was wearing yet another long dress bought for her by Tom, a high-necked black jersey affair with a bias cut skirt that swirled just above her ankles. It had clearly cost a great deal and would have suited any number of women to a tee, but it still wasn't Poppy.

'Maybe he wants to make sure it doesn't happen again,' Babette said calmly. 'Some men are like that. It's the whore-madonna thing. They don't mind seeing other girls with their bits on show, but their own wives and girlfriends are another matter.'

Crossly, Caspar said, 'I know that, but what the hell's Poppy doing, going along with it? She looks about forty.'

'She's flattered.' That was the thing about Babette; she had all the answers. 'He adores her and she loves it that he cares. It's why some women stay with their men, even when they're being battered senseless every Friday night. They think it shows they care.'

'Christ.' Caspar wondered wildly if that was why Poppy was keeping her legs hidden. Maybe beneath all those yards of exquisitely draped jersey her thighs were beaten black and blue. He experienced a sudden urge to rush up to Poppy and do a Bucks Fizz, rip her skirt clean off . . .

Thinking better of it, he poured himself another drink. It crossed his mind that Tom Kennedy was clearly the possessive type and that upstairs in his studio he still had, somewhere, the interesting selection of photographs taken of Poppy getting up to all sorts while he and Claudia had both been away.

Caspar shook his head. Bloody hell, what was the matter with him tonight? As if he didn't know. He was more jealous than he'd ever been in his life and it wasn't a happy experience. Of course he wouldn't stoop so low, shatter Poppy's newfound happiness . . .

It would just be nice if someone else did.

'Look, there's Claudia,' said Babette excitedly. 'With her dad. Now that would be a catch. Imagine handling *his* PR.'

'Oh no, what's *she* doing here?' wailed Claudia as Angie, in a flesh-coloured chiffon dress and the highest of high heels, made her impressive entrance at nine thirty. She looked more burnished and golden than ever and her perfume was apparent even at twenty paces. Before she had time to do more than wave gaily across at her daughter and ex-husband she was accosted by Caspar's sculptor friend, all but foaming at the mouth with lust.

'Darling, I assumed you'd invited her. When she rang me this afternoon I mentioned I was coming along to your party tonight. All she said was fine, we'd bump into each other then.' Hugo's smile was rueful. 'Should've known better, I suppose, after all those years of practice. My dear ex-wife evidently hasn't lost her touch.'

'She'll tell me I've put on weight.' Claudia, who had, looked miserable. For weeks now she hadn't been able to stop thinking about Jake. Unfortunately she hadn't been able to think about him without reaching for the biscuit tin. She had put on a terrifying seven pounds and the bugger of it was, he still hadn't phoned.

When an extremely famous person puts in an appearance at a party, the non-celebrities generally pretend they haven't spotted him. Only when they know for sure he can't see them will their eyes swivel furtively in the VIP's direction.

Not Dina.

'Oh wow, you're Hugo Slade-Welch!' she squealed, charging up to him and all but ricocheting off his broad chest. 'Am I a big fan of yours! I've seen all your films. You were brill in *Black Thursday*. I'm Dina, a friend of Claudia's – hi, Claudia – God, I can't believe I'm standing here talking to you, I've never met a film star before! Here, have a fag.'

Claudia glared at Dina, who was thrusting a crumpled packet of Embassy Regal practically up her father's nose. This girl really did have an endless supply of nerve. And to say she was a *friend* of hers . . .

Hugo, looking amused, said, 'Actually, I don't smoke.'

'Oh well, never mind. You can still autograph the packet.'

'Daddy, why don't we—?'

'Hang on, not so fast. Who's got a pen around here? Hugo, how about you?'

Claudia was about to spontaneously combust at the chummy use of her father's Christian name when she realised Dina was actually pulling open his jacket. Locating a fountain pen in Hugo's inside pocket, she whisked it out.

'Ooh now, there's posh! I might have known a big star like you would have a real ink job. And feel how heavy it is! How much did that set you back?'

'Dina—'

Claudia's eyes were almost as narrowed as her mouth. Snotty bitch. Dina refused to be cowed.

'Okay, no need to get your knickers in a twist. I'm not going to nick it. Here –' she offered the uncapped pen back to Hugo – 'tell you what, real ink won't work on the fag packet. How about autographing me instead?'

Dina was wearing a sequinned boob tube and skin-tight blue satin trousers. She thrust her chest forward and pointed to the area midway between the top of the tube and her left collarbone.

Outraged, Claudia hissed, 'Do you have any idea how stupid you're making yourself look?'

'Come on, it's only a bit of fun! Everyone'll think it's a tattoo.'

'Leave my father alone.'

'It's okay, really,' Hugo placated his angry daughter. In an attempt to defuse the situation he smiled and winked at both of them. 'I've been asked to autograph stranger parts of the anatomy in my time. Claudia, would you be an angel and fetch me another drink?'

All Claudia wanted to do was slap Dina's ridiculous over-made-up face, but her father was clearly anxious to avoid a scene. She stomped off, cannoning into people on all sides, unaware that Dina's cigarette had burned a neat hole in the back of her dress.

'Please excuse my daughter,' said Hugo, his famously blue eyes twinkling. 'She is rather protective.'

'Jealous, more like. What with your last girlfriend being exactly the same age as me. And I'm very into older men,' Dina told him, cleverly blowing her cigarette smoke out sideways so it didn't go straight in his face. 'You can under-stand why she's worried. If we got married, I'd be her step-mother.'

'Now there's a thought.' Since Dina was still pointing to her chest, Hugo leaned forward and signed his name with care. 'You aren't married yourself then, I take it?'

'Well . . . kind of. But you know how it is. If a better offer came along it wouldn't be a problem.'

'That can't be easy for you.' Hugo was sympathetic. 'I mean, a lovely young girl such as yourself must receive offers all the time. I daresay they're hard to resist.'

He's chatting me up, thought Dina, so dizzy with excite-ment she could hardly breathe. Here I am, in London, at a party so glamorous you aren't even expected to chip in for the booze, being chatted up by an honest-to-goodness movie star.

In an instant her mind conjured up a whole series of thrilling fantasies: Dina and Hugo whizzing round the world on their private jet . . . sunning themselves on the deck of a yacht . . . arriving at the Oscars ceremony hand in hand . . . being photographed for *Hello!* magazine . . .

'So Hugo, what kind of car do you drive?'

'Well—'

'D'you know what I'd have, if I was loaded? A bright green Rolls Royce.'

'Well now, that sounds a wonderful choice.' He smiled down at her. 'I did own a Silver Shadow many years ago—'

'Are they good? I'd still rather have a Rolls. Tell you what,' said Dina, slipping her arm through his, 'why don't we go out into the garden? Before that old crosspatch Claudia gets back.'

Chapter 50

Claudia wasn't in any hurry to get back. If her father was so set on humouring Dina – and he was famous for his patience with members of the public when they took the liberty of introducing themselves – she didn't want to be around to witness it. Serve the silly old fool right.

She had just finished pouring Hugo a quadruple Scotch when Angie materialised at her side.

'Darling, you forgot to send me an invite! If Hugo hadn't mentioned it this afternoon I'd have missed the party altogether.' Ostentatiously reaching up on tiptoe she kissed her daughter's rigid jaw. 'And look at you in a pretty new dress. Such a shame about the cigarette burn.'

'Where? Oh *no*!'

'Never mind, make a few more holes and pretend it's the latest Vivienne Westwood. Where's Hugo?'

'Talking to some little tart.'

'Oh well, what's new?' Angie looked amused. 'You don't look terribly cheerful, my darling. If there's some kind of problem, tell Mummy.'

Well Mummy, you see the thing is, I'm completely besotted with someone and I don't know if he likes me and I'm way too embarrassed to ask and he's really shy so he might fancy the pants off me but he keeps his feelings so much to himself it's just about impossible to tell.

'I'd rather die,' Claudia said aloud. 'Since when were you interested in my problems anyway?'

'I love hearing about problems! I'd make a wonderful

agony aunt,' Angie protested, laughing. 'If only people would have the nerve to take my advice.'

Nerve was what Angie possessed in abundance. Claudia definitely didn't want to be Angie but she wished she could have inherited a bit more nerve. It was a handy thing to have around. Especially right now.

Jake was heading almost straight for them. He was wearing the plain dark blue sweater and a pair of the well-cut trousers Poppy had chosen for him. His dark hair, freshly washed, was flopping onto his forehead. Behind the tinted gold-rimmed spectacles his dark eyes searched the room. He looked so smart and so quietly handsome Claudia felt her heart leap into her throat like a fish. And he had come in search of *her*.

'Jake,' she said, because he was in danger of veering off to the left.

'Oh. Hi.' He stopped dead and the look on his face told Claudia he hadn't been searching for her at all. 'Um . . . I thought Marlene would be in here. How . . . how are you?'

'Oh, I'm fine. Yes, fine.'

Jake hesitated then said, 'Fallen off any good windowsills lately?'

It was meant to be a light-hearted quip, an ice-breaker, and it was clearly a line he had prepared earlier, like a Delia Smith soufflé.

Except Delia's soufflés never fell this flat.

Angie, her tinted eyebrows up in her hairline, said, 'Heavens, I *am* intrigued.'

Claudia took a gulp of her drink, clean forgetting it wasn't her drink. She had never been able to get to grips with Scotch.

'Aaargh.' Spluttering helplessly, unable to swallow the burning liquid, she was forced to spit it back into the tumbler. Her eyelids felt as if they were on fire.

'You must excuse my daughter,' Angie said smoothly, 'she has the manners of a wart-hog. I'm Angie, by the way. And of course I've heard all about you! Now Jake, what an

335

enthralling remark. There must be a story behind this. Do tell.'

'Mother—'

'Claudia, throw that Scotch-and-saliva away before someone else drinks it. And go and clean yourself up, you've got dribble on your chin.'

In desperation Jake said, 'Actually—'

'No, no, I insist,' Angie lowered her voice a conspiratorial octave. 'I can't wait to hear what my daughter gets up to on windowsills when I'm not around.' Reaching up, she smoothed a section of hair behind Jake's left ear. 'There, that's better. It was sticking out. Goodness me, what glossy hair you have, you must take tremendous care of it. And I adore your aftershave.'

'I'm not wearing any.' Jake looked nervous. 'It must be deodorant.'

'Mum, please.'

'No, it's definitely not Mum. And Claudia, what did I just tell you to do? Chin, darling. Chin.'

'It's going to seem weird here without you,' said Caspar. Tom, who had barely left Poppy's side all evening, was deep in conversation across the room with one of Caspar's artist friends, who had once been an architect. 'We'll miss you.'

'Me too.' Poppy grinned. 'Listen to us. Anyone would think I was disappearing up the Amazon. We'll still see each other.'

'Yeah.'

'We will! Tom's already said we must have you and Babette over for dinner.'

'Well,' Caspar struggled for something to say, 'that sounds . . .'

'Like your idea of the dinner party from hell,' Poppy suggested drily. 'I know. Babette and I haven't exactly hit it off. And you and Tom didn't get off to the greatest of starts. But he did say he liked Babette.' She pulled a face. 'She's got her act together, apparently. Tom approves of people whose acts are together.'

Now there was a thought. Caspar glanced across the room at Babette, chatting animatedly to a tall antiques dealer. Poppy followed the direction of his gaze.

'Can I ask?' she said suddenly. 'Why *did* you marry her?'

But Caspar's expression was unreadable. He raised his glass of Beaujolais to the light, apparently studying the colour.

'Because you told me to.'

'Really?'

'I thought it would simplify matters. And I wanted to know what being married would be like.'

'And has it? Simplified matters?'

'Of course.' Was Caspar mocking her? It was impossible to tell. 'Only one notch on my bedpost nowadays. I'm a respectable married man.'

'You must still get chatted up.' Poppy was disbelieving. 'That hasn't stopped, it can't have.'

Caspar broke into a grin. 'Oh, I get my share of offers. But being married is a great excuse for saying no. They don't get offended. Some of them are even impressed.'

'I'm definitely impressed.'

'So how about you?' Swiftly Caspar turned the tables on her. 'Are you happy? Sure you're doing the right thing?'

Poppy gave him a strange look.

'Of course I'm sure.'

'Because—'

'What a bloody stinking awful pig of a party,' howled Claudia, barging up to them. 'If there wasn't such a queue for the bathroom I'd slash my wrists.'

Caspar said, 'Don't tell me. Someone else has turned up wearing the same dress as you.'

Claudia commandeered his glass and downed the contents in one.

'My unspeakable mother is chatting up Jake. My father is

337

being chatted up by your even more unspeakable friend Dina. And some total bastard has burned a sodding hole in my dress.' Gathering up material from the back, Claudia showed them the evidence. 'If I find out who did it, I'll kill them.' Her eyes narrowed to slits. 'Does that look like the kind of hole an Embassy Regal would make?'

Poppy left them to it. She had spotted Rita in the doorway.

'I'm so glad you're here.' She hugged Rita, who was wearing an orange and white polka-dotted frock and matching shoes. 'I thought you weren't coming.'

'Said I would, didn't I?' Rita lit a cigarette. 'Never been one to miss out on a good party. How's it going?'

'If you don't want to be depressed, steer clear of Claudia.' Poppy took her arm. 'Come on, let me introduce you to some people.'

'Don't worry about me, love. I don't need looking after. Just point me in the direction of the drinks. When I see someone I like the look of, I'll introduce myself.'

It was dark outside in the garden, apart from the coloured lights Caspar and Poppy had strung up somewhat haphazardly in the trees.

'Aren't they pretty?' sighed Dina, gesturing dreamily with her cigarette at a ball of lights Caspar hadn't been able to untangle. 'It's like a fairytale. Like . . . Cinderella.'

'Mind your glass slippers don't get stuck in the mud.'

She looked down at her stiletto heels, ringed with earth and leaves.

'That's not very romantic. Fine Prince Charming you'd make.'

Hugo smiled. 'I'm rather afraid my Prince Charming days are over. Far too old.'

Dina's stomach did a cartwheel. She flicked her cigarette into the bushes and turned to face him.

'I don't think you're too old. I said, didn't I? I like older men. Especially you.'

She half-closed her eyes, waiting for him to kiss her. They were away from the house, unobserved. All he had to do was take a step forward and pull her into his arms.

But Hugo tilted his head to one side and gave her a look of affection mingled with genuine regret.

'Oh, my dear. It's delightful young things like you who get men like me into trouble.'

'I wouldn't.' Dina shook her head eagerly. 'Honest. I'm on the Pill.'

Hugo's mouth twitched.

'You're very sweet. Nevertheless, maybe we should be making our way back to the house. Before people start to wonder where we are.'

Claudia waited until Jake had taken her mother's empty glass and disappeared in search of a refill. She was over in a flash.

'Hello darling, fancy bumping into you again so soon,' said Angie. Claudia had been scowling at her from a distance for the past ten minutes. She unclipped her evening bag, took out a mirror and calmly re-did her lipstick. 'I must say, I can quite see why you're so keen on Jake. What a poppet.'

A *poppet* . . .

'You always have to ruin everything,' hissed Claudia, 'don't you?'

'Ruin everything?' Angie looked surprised. 'Baby girl, I had no idea there was anything to ruin. I assumed he was a free agent. I'm sorry, are you saying you and he are a couple?'

'You know I'm not!' Claudia spoke through gritted teeth. 'You just come out with the most embarrassing remarks, like, "I've heard all about you." Viciously she imitated her mother's words. 'That was a lie for a start. I've *never* told you about Jake.'

Angie's smile was pure Cheshire Cat.

'I didn't say you had. Caspar did, while I was sitting for my portrait. He told me all about your crush on Jake.'

Bloody Caspar.

339

'But that was months ago,' Angie shrugged. 'Let's face it, sweetheart, if he was interested he'd have made his move by now.'

Since there was no answer to that, Claudia scowled and said instead, 'So what were you talking about?'

'Oh, money mainly. Jake's little windfall . . .'

'How typical.'

'. . . how to spot gold-diggers . . .'

'Well, you'd know about that,' Claudia said bitterly.

Angie looked at her. 'You should try smiling occasionally, darling. It does wonders.'

'Don't—'

'Just a suggestion. Ah, there's your father. Speaking of gold-diggers, who *is* that frightful creature with him? He looks as if he needs rescuing.'

As Angie drifted away, Claudia wondered if the evening could possibly get worse.

Chapter 51

Bursting for the loo, Dina excused herself seconds before Angie reached them. She slipped into the downstairs cloakroom, relieved herself, then studied her flushed reflection in the small mirror above the basin.

Hugo Slade-Welch had called her delightful. And sweet. He fancied her like mad, she knew, but was holding himself back because he thought it was the gentlemanly thing to do.

Dina, whose maxim when it came to make-up was more-is-more, rummaged around in the bottom of her shoulder bag. She applied an extra layer of metallic Bahama Blue eyeshadow, another generous coat of blue mascara and re-did her lipstick. When someone tried the door handle she called out, 'Hang on a sec,' but as her mouth was in lipstick-receiving mode at the time, the words came out oddly. Hey, Dina marvelled, I sound dead posh.

But there were evidently two people on the other side of the door. A woman, in a low voice, was saying '. . . but darling, where on earth did you find her? Talk about Girl at C & A. I can't believe you brought her over with you from the States! I mean, she'd still be in quarantine . . .'

When Dina heard Hugo's unmistakable laugh, she froze.

'Angie, didn't anyone ever tell you? You're supposed to mellow with age.'

'I am being mellow. I could think of far worse things to say about her. Come on, Hugo, spill the beans. Who is she and where *did* you pick her up? King's Cross?'

Dina's hands were shaking so hard she almost dropped her lipstick in the basin.

'Do I look as if I found her anywhere?' she heard Hugo reply with amusement. 'She found me. I hadn't been here more than ten minutes when she latched herself onto me. Her name's Dina, she knows Poppy and Claudia and she's spent the last hour telling me how much she loves older men, especially ones who star in Hollywood movies. She made me autograph her chest, she told me I should try a splash of Pepsi in my Scotch. As for Girl at C & A,' he added drily, 'you couldn't be more wrong. She told me herself, her boob tube cost seventeen pounds ninety-nine at Top Shop.'

Dina didn't know why this should be so funny but it clearly was. Angie snorted with laughter and Hugo joined in. She clutched the sides of the basin as Hugo, recovering himself, went on, 'And when I said I was due to play Othello at the Royal Court next year, she said yeah, Charles Dickens is brill, she's seen all his films but *Oliver!* is her favourite.'

Dina didn't move. Eventually she heard Angie say, 'Darling, whoever's in that loo has obviously died. Could you be an angel and find me another drink? I'm going to have to run upstairs.'

When they had both gone, Dina looked up again at her face in the mirror. Bahama Blue tears ran down her cheeks and plopped steadily into the basin.

When the door bell rang at ten thirty, Caspar answered it.

'Bloody late as usual,' he grinned at Patrick Dennehy, who was lugging a huge canvas-shaped parcel tied up with brown paper and a lot of frayed string. 'What's this, homework?'

Patrick was the evening class tutor at St Clare's, which wasn't the kind of career he'd dreamed of during his art student days but was still better than the dole. Since his arms were aching, he thrust the parcel at Caspar with some relief.

'Kind of. Here, you can take these through. Presents for the girls.'

'Great,' lied Caspar. Patrick was an old friend but his paintings were crap, hopelessly modernist and quite without meaning. Still, it was a kind gesture. Caspar just hoped Claudia would be diplomatic when the paintings were unwrapped.

He had to clear a space in the sitting room for the opening ceremony. Neither Claudia nor – more surprisingly – Poppy seemed overjoyed to see Patrick there.

'Try and look thrilled,' Caspar murmured in Claudia's ear. 'It's probably three black splashes and a blue triangle. Patrick's only ever sold one painting in his life. And that was to his mother.'

It was like pass-the-parcel. Both paintings had been extremely thoroughly wrapped. By the time the last layers were ready to come off, the carpet was strewn with brown paper and a sizeable crowd had gathered to watch.

Claudia, who had thought the night couldn't get any worse, realised it could. She screamed and tried to cover the painting up with a crumpled sheet of paper which had unaccountably shrunk.

A howl of protest went up from the audience.

Next to her, Poppy froze. 'Oh shit.'

'You bastard,' wailed Claudia, swinging round to glare at Patrick.

'You didn't paint those,' said Caspar, starting to laugh.

'I didn't say I had.' Deeply offended by such a suggestion, Patrick failed to see what all the fuss was about. 'One of my students did them. Mike Cousins. When I mentioned I was coming here tonight, he asked me to bring them along.' He turned back to Claudia. 'Mike bumped into you the other week, right? He was worried you might have got the wrong idea and thought he'd wanted you to buy the picture. He didn't mean that at all, he just wanted you to have it.'

Claudia just wanted to die. One of Caspar's friends had whisked the brown paper from her grasp, leaving the painting exposed for everyone to see.

And, dreadfully, everyone had. Some people were laughing, others applauding. Next to her, pink to the hairline and similarly humiliated, stood Poppy.

'Mike wanted you to have yours too,' Patrick assured her. 'You don't have to buy it. It's a gift.'

To add insult to injury, Mike Cousins was an enthusiastic artist rather than an accomplished one. He had given Claudia a hint of a squint and a right breast larger than the left.

Poppy hadn't fared much better – one arm was longer than the other and her hair looked like a wig put on in a rush – but at least she was thin. Depressingly, one aspect of Claudia's figure Mike Cousins had got off to an absolute tee was her awful undulating stomach.

Caspar came up and stood between them. He put his arms around Poppy and Claudia and said, 'You both look great.'

Jake, over by the doorway, agreed. Seeing Claudia naked was something he had dreamed of. And he wasn't disappointed. She looked beautiful, even more beautiful than he had imagined. He adored every curve, every perfect voluptuous inch of her . . .

'Christ Almighty, who's the blob?'

The voice, loud and slurred, belonged to a late arrival. Jake didn't know him but he appeared to have tagged along with a group of Caspar's friends. He leaned in the doorway, his arm draped around the waist of an anorexic-looking brunette.

'Shut up,' said Jake.

The bloke grinned. 'Come on, look at it! What a whale! Imagine getting trapped under something like that.'

The room fell silent. Glancing across at Claudia, Jake saw the anguish in her eyes.

'Move,' he instructed the skinny girl.

She looked blank. 'What?'

Jake placed her to one side and punched the smirking heckler so hard he was catapulted through the doorway. Out in the hall, sprawled on his back on the floor, the man

344

groaned loudly and clutched his face.

'You've broken my nose . . .'

'Good,' said Jake. He wrenched open the front door, surprising two more late arrivals on the doorstep. 'Now get up and get out. You too,' he told the skinny brunette, who was kneeling beside her boyfriend, using the hem of her cheesecloth skirt to wipe the blood from his face. 'Come on, out you go.'

The open-mouthed couple on the doorstep stood aside to let them past. When they had gone Jake said, 'Sorry about that. You can come in now.' To be on the safe side he added, 'You're friends of . . . ?'

'We aren't really friends of anyone,' replied the girl, who was plump and sensibly dressed. 'We're just looking for someone. Maybe you can help us,' she went on, sounding like an efficient policewoman making enquiries. 'Her name is Dina McBride.'

Claudia had disappeared upstairs. Caspar gathered up the offending paintings and dumped them in the broom cupboard out in the hall.

'Well,' said Tom icily, 'that was fun. Anything you'd like to do as an encore? Rip your dress off, maybe, and dance on the table? After all, it's hardly going to make a difference now. Everyone here already knows what you look like.'

His eyes glittered, reflecting his disgust.

Since there wasn't much else she could do, Poppy attempted to brazen it out.

'It was just a bit of life-class modelling,' she said lightly, with a shrug. 'I don't do it any more. I needed to earn some money to pay the rent. I thought I'd *told* you about St Clare's.'

She hadn't, of course she hadn't. For this exact reason.

'No, you never did. I think I might have remembered.' Tom's jaw was set like concrete. 'Jesus. I wondered how you could afford to live in a house like this. How long ago did you stop doing it?'

'February. Three months ago. Before I met you.'

'And how have you been managing to pay the rent since then?' His gaze flickered dangerously in the direction of Caspar. 'In kind?'

After the von Kantz had sold at auction, Jake had doubled her salary. Tom knew that.

Poppy looked at him.

'What are you trying to say, you don't want me to move in with you? It's all over between us? You don't want to see me any more?'

Tom didn't speak for several seconds. Finally he shook his head.

'Don't be stupid, of course I still want you to move in. I love you, Poppy. More than words can say. You know that.'

The tiny hairs at the back of Poppy's neck were standing to attention. Abruptly a lump came into her throat.

'But—'

'Come here,' murmured Tom, drawing her to him and wrapping his arms tightly around her. 'You silly thing. If I didn't love you I wouldn't care, would I? But I do care. You're mine and I want to be the only man who sees you without clothes.' He kissed her, lingeringly, then stroked her pale cheek. 'I want to keep you all to myself.'

'Um . . . excuse me,' said Jake, embarrassed to be butting in. 'Poppy, some people are here looking for Dina. I can't find her. Any ideas?'

Extricating herself from Tom's embrace, Poppy turned and came face to face with the man she had once so nearly married, Rob McBride.

Chapter 52

'Rob!'

'Hello, Poppy.'

She felt her mouth drop open. This party was in danger of becoming seriously bizarre. Who was going to turn up next, Elvis?

Rob was suffering from something approaching shell-shock himself. The last time he'd seen Poppy had been on the morning of their supposed wedding. When she had scuttled off to London he had imagined her living in some godawful bedsit. He'd certainly hoped it was godawful anyway.

But he had been wrong. Instead she was here, in this palatial house where wild parties were held, huge parties where gate-crashers got their noses broken and good-looking men strolled through the hall, clutching paintings of the girl he had once almost married. Only the one glimpsed by Rob had been no ordinary painting . . . in this one Poppy had definitely been *naked*.

To add to the air of surreality, he was almost sure the middle-aged man standing less than three feet away from him was the film star Hugo Slade-Welch.

'Rob. It's nice to see you again.'

He pulled himself together.

'Yeah, you too.' A small lie. It was downright weird seeing Poppy again. And that bloke over there definitely *was* Hugo Slade-Welch. 'Sorry . . . uh, this is Alison.' Awkwardly he made the necessary introductions. 'My fiancée.'

Poppy smiled and nodded and said 'Hi.' Dina had told her all about Alison, the nurse with the unfortunate ankles. Unable to help herself, she glanced anklewards. Yep, there they were. Alison's legs, encased in woolly blue tights, went straight down. She was wearing sensible shoes with real laces.

'Sorry, I'm a bit confused,' said Poppy. 'Did Dina invite you along to the party?'

'I'd better explain.' Rob was still staring goggle-eyed at Hugo Slade-Welch so Alison put herself in charge. It was what she was good at. 'Ben didn't want Dina to come here tonight. They had a major row and she stormed out. The thing is, as far as Ben's concerned, this is the last straw. He's in a dreadful state, but absolutely determined. If Dina doesn't come home tonight, their marriage is over. He'll divorce her. He says he never wants to see her again and he'll fight for custody of little Daniel.' Alison paused for a second. Ever practical, she added, 'He probably won't win, of course. The courts almost always favour the mother. But he does mean it. If we can get Dina back tonight, they can try again. Otherwise that's it; Ben's had enough.'

'Oh Lord.' Poppy bit her lip. If the remarks Dina had been making recently were anything to go by, they might as well book the solicitors now. She had a sneaking suspicion Dina would declare this the best news she'd heard all year.

'So you see why we had to come. Sorry to have intruded on your party. We tried phoning a few times but it was always engaged. In the end we thought we'd better drive up.'

'Alison found the address in Dina's diary,' Rob put in. He didn't add what else they had found in the diary. 'Ben doesn't know we're here.'

Poor Ben. Poppy peered in desperation over the heads of the milling guests. She hoped Dina wasn't nearby doing something horribly indiscreet.

'She could be anywhere. Why don't you two help your-selves to a drink now you're here? Let me go and look.'

But she found Dina almost straight away, sitting on her

own on a wooden bench at the bottom of the garden.

'What happened to your make-up?' said Poppy, joining her. Dina was sitting very still, gazing blankly ahead.

'Washed it off.'

'Have you been crying?'

'No.'

Since it was obvious she had, Poppy proceeded with care. 'Rob and Alison are here. They want to take you back to Bristol. Look, I heard about your fight with Ben. If you don't go home tonight, he's going to divorce you.'

'Okay.'

'Okay what?' Poppy leaned closer. Dina didn't even sound like Dina. 'Okay you'll go back or okay he can have a divorce?'

Dina heaved a long sigh. 'I'll go back.'

This was so unlike her Poppy thought there must be a catch.

'Really?'

As Dina took out a cigarette her hands trembled. The brief flare of the match lit up her face. Fresh tears slid down her white cheeks.

'Oh Poppy, I thought I could do it. I thought I could change my life, like you changed yours . . . for the better. But I can't. It's no good, I just bloody can't. It worked out for you but it wouldn't work for me.'

'I don't get it.' Poppy frowned; an hour ago Dina had been in tearing spirits. She couldn't imagine what must have happened to knock her down like this. 'Has somebody said something to you?' Claudia, perhaps? Surely not Caspar . . .

'Not to my face.' Dina's voice wavered. 'But it's what they say behind your back that counts, isn't it?'

'Who?' For a wild moment Poppy wondered if Caspar had been leading Dina on.

'Doesn't matter who. Everyone probably. Anyway, sod them.' Dina ground her cigarette out with her heel and stood up. 'I don't care any more. I've got a husband who loves me. And a baby. I may as well go back home.'

349

Worried, Poppy said, 'Do you love them?'

'Of course I do.' Dina's answering smile was bleak. 'Oh, I know I said I was sick of it all, but that was when I thought I could find something better up here. Meet someone richer, more exciting. Like you did.' She shoved her cigarettes and matches into her bag and looked down at the angry red mark on her chest. Hugo Slade-Welch's scrawled signature had taken ages to scrub off. 'But now I know I can't, I'll be all right. Might even have another baby. Ben's been going on about a little brother for Daniel for months.'

'You might have a girl.'

'Yeah.' As they made their way back to the house, Dina gave Poppy's arm a squeeze. 'Poor kid, if we do. We'll just have to hope she doesn't take after me.'

'Now there's a blast from the past,' remarked Hugo, inhaling pleasurably as he found himself next to Rita. 'That takes me way back. All of a sudden I'm twenty-five again.'

'In your dreams,' replied Rita good-naturedly.

'Mitsouko. Guerlain. I'm right, aren't I?'

She nodded. 'My husband bought it for me.'

'I haven't smelled it for years. Reminds me of a beautiful woman I once knew, back in Edinburgh. I was madly in love with her.' Hugo's eyes crinkled. 'Sadly, her husband had bought her that scent too.'

'Did you have an affair with her?'

'Even more sadly, no. She wouldn't. I was a penniless drama student, not much of a catch. And she was a lady of expensive tastes.'

'I bet she was gutted when you became famous.' Rita looked entertained. 'Did you ever hear from her again?'

Hugo shook his head.

'But for years, every time I was interviewed on television, or one of my films was being shown, I imagined her sitting at home watching me. And hoped, of course, that she was . . . gutted.'

'If she'd really loved you she wouldn't have minded you being skint. When I met my husband he didn't have a bean.'

Unlike Poppy, Hugo was able to tell real diamonds from fakes.

'And what does he do now?' he enquired with genuine interest.

'Nothing much. He died in January.'

Hugo was appalled. 'I'm so sorry.'

'On the other hand,' Rita went on easily, 'he could be getting up to all sorts. We don't know, do we? He might be having a high old time, banging away on some piano, vamping it up with Louis Armstrong and Count Basie, playing up there in the clouds where the bar never closes, the beer's free and the audience always knows when to clap.'

'Your husband was a jazz pianist!' Hugo looked delighted. 'I'm a bit of a jazz buff myself. Would I have known him?'

'He wasn't famous. Alex Fitzpatrick. I shouldn't think you'd—'

'Alex Fitzpatrick? I have heard of him! I even saw him playing once, many years ago, at a club in Soho. He was excellent. I say, what a small world.'

'Bugger it!' exclaimed Rita as a blonde trailing a handbag squeezed past. Looking down, she saw that the clasp on the girl's handbag had caught against her tights. When she bent her knee to examine the hole, a ladder promptly slithered the length of her leg. She rolled her eyes at Hugo Slade-Welch. 'Shit, don't you just hate it when that happens?'

He started to laugh. 'Where are you going? Don't disappear . . . we've only just met. I don't even know your name.'

'Rita. And if you want to make yourself useful, find me another gin and tonic.' She moved away, trailing Mitsouko. 'That way you can guarantee I'll be back.'

'Sorry to interrupt, pet, but look at the state of my tights. Is there an all-night garage anywhere near here, or a late-opening corner shop?'

'I've got a spare pair.' Poppy, who had just waved off Dina, Alison and Rob, was talking to Jake. Luckily, Rita's torn tights were Barely Black. 'Same colour, one-size-fits-all, still in the packet.' Feeling madly efficient she said, 'You can have those. Hang on a sec, Jake . . .'

'Don't worry, I can get them. Just tell me where to look.'

Following Poppy's directions Rita made her way downstairs. The tiny bedroom Poppy had occupied for the past eight months was almost empty now, most of her belongings having already been packed into suitcases and moved into Tom's flat. The narrow bed was stripped, the wardrobe empty. Only an overnight case remained, crammed with toiletries and the contents of the bedside table. The tights, Poppy had explained, were somewhere in the case.

Rummaging carefully, Rita found them near the bottom. As she slid the oblong pack out, her rings clunked against glass. Silly girl, thought Rita, glimpsing the silver edge of a photograph frame squashed against a can of hairspray, that could get broken.

She pulled an ancient pink tee-shirt out of the bag, to wrap around the glass and keep it in one piece. Then she levered the photograph frame upwards.

The woman in the photo, smiling up at her, was instantly recognisable.

She stood in a small garden, holding a newborn baby in her arms.

She was wearing a white blouse and a full, flower-patterned skirt, and her curly hair was tied back from her face with a white scarf.

She was, Rita realised, Poppy's mother.

And although there was no date on the back of the photograph Rita also knew when it must have been taken.

Nine months, give or take a few weeks, after she had broken her leg.

Chapter 53

Jake knocked on Claudia's bedroom door.

'Go away.'

'No.' Standing his ground he said firmly, 'It's me. I want to come in.'

When Claudia opened the door, her eyes brimmed at the sight of him.

'What a fiasco. Has everyone stopped laughing yet?'

'No one's laughing. Nobody has laughed. Why would they?'

'Oh come on.' She rubbed her face with the sleeve of her dressing gown. '*I* would have, if it hadn't been me. As my mother once so thoughtfully pointed out, I've got more spare tyres than Kwik-Fit.' Almost as an afterthought Claudia added wearily, 'Thanks, by the way. For punching him.'

Exasperated, Jake said, 'Why do you suppose I did?'

'Because there are some things it's kinder not to say.'

'Dammit, what's the matter with you?' shouted Jake. 'I punched him because what he said wasn't *true*.' Reacting physically had unleashed something in him; the adrenalin was still pumping, making it easier to say what he had never before had the courage to put into words. His dark eyes were alight with almost missionary fervour. 'You looked beautiful . . . dammit, you *are* beautiful. If you don't want the painting, I'll have it. I could happily look at that portrait of you every day for the rest of my life.'

Masochistically, Claudia whispered, 'But he called me a blob.'

'And did you see that stick of celery with him? That scrawny girlfriend of his? Some men like shrimps,' Jake declared with reckless abandon. 'Others prefer . . . well, langoustines. Stop *looking* at me like that,' he went on, close to despair. 'I wouldn't say it if I didn't mean it. And I don't make a habit of punching people, either. I've never done it before . . . oh, don't cry. He isn't worth it. He deserved to be punched.'

'I'm not crying because of him,' Claudia sniffed. Her dressing-gown sleeve was really quite soggy now. 'I'm crying because I'm h-h-happy.'

I will never, ever, understand women, thought Jake.

But Claudia, who had made up her own mind, moved towards him. If she was going to do anything, it had to be now. Jake had rushed to protect her earlier. He had called her beautiful. He had even – well, it was the thought that counted – told her he preferred langoustines to shrimps.

She kissed him. On the cheek. Just a peck.

Jake stopped being angry. Instead he looked nervous. Not very romantically he said, 'What was that in aid of?'

'I just wanted to do it.'

'Why?'

This was make or break time. Claudia heard the sound of her own blood drumming in her ears. She took a shuddery breath and threw herself into the breach.

'Why d'you think? Because I've wanted to do it for months but I never knew if you liked me, but now I think maybe you do after all. Because *you* never kiss *me*. Because . . . because you're hopeless and it's about time one of us did something. Now, shall I try again or would you rather I didn't?'

There, she'd said it. God, thought Claudia, I feel sick.

Jake smiled.

'Try again. Definitely try again. I'd much rather you did.'

'You came back.' Evidently relieved, Hugo Slade-Welch

354

handed Rita the gin and tonic he had been holding onto. 'You've been ages. The ice has melted.' He glanced down at her shapely legs. 'All okay now?'

'What? Oh . . . yes. All okay.'

'You're looking more cheerful.'

'I've just made a discovery.' Rita nodded. 'You know that feeling you get when the last piece of the jigsaw slots into place?'

'I'm not a great one for jigsaws,' Hugo admitted. 'I like crosswords though.'

There was laughter in Rita's eyes.

'Either way. It's a great feeling, isn't it? Suddenly figuring everything out?'

Hugo nodded. He didn't have a clue what she was talking about, but he knew what he wanted to say next. He had spent the last ten minutes rehearsing his lines.

'Look, I'm staying in London for a while. Say if you don't feel up to it, but would you like to come out with me one evening? Have dinner, maybe, and visit a jazz club afterwards?' He glanced across, trying to gauge her reaction. 'We could go to Ronnie Scott's.'

'It's a funny thing,' Rita mused, 'all those years with Alex, I used to think I couldn't stand jazz. It wasn't until he died and I found myself going through his old LPs I realised I'd got to like the stuff after all.'

'Is that a yes?'

She looked tolerantly at Hugo. 'What is this, a set-up? Did Poppy tell you to be kind to me? There's no need, love. Really. I'm fine as I am.'

'I'm not being kind. I'd like to get to know you better, that's all.' Hugo was wounded. 'And I've never been turned down before. Please say yes, for the sake of my ego if nothing else.'

'Tights all right?' said Poppy, joining them.

'They're fine.'

Rita's smile was affectionate. There was no hurry; she

could tell Poppy about her discovery another time. And she could give her the other photograph too. It would mean a lot to her—

'Poppy, do something,' Hugo pleaded. 'I've invited this lady to have dinner with me and she's making excuses. I'm on the verge of rejection here. Help.'

'It's too soon, love. Nothing personal, I just wouldn't feel right. Ask me again in a year.' Rita patted his arm equably. 'That's if you aren't married again by then.'

'But—'

'Don't try and argue,' said Poppy. 'Not with Rita. She had the best husband in the world. You can't compete.'

The party finally broke up in the early hours. Caspar stood in the lit-up doorway seeing out the last of the guests. Earlier he had watched Tom carry Poppy's overnight case to the waiting taxi, and had thought how like an amicable divorce it felt as Poppy, hesitating on the doorstep, had slipped her still-warm front door key into his hand.

'Thanks for everything,' she had whispered almost shyly, brushing Caspar's cheek with her lips. 'And the party. See you soon.'

'Darling?' Babette appeared behind him, holding his leather jacket. She had to be up at six, for a breakfast meeting with a new client. 'Ready?'

'You go.' Caspar knew he wouldn't sleep. 'I've got some work to do. A painting to finish.'

Babette raised her eyebrows sympathetically. 'Sure?'

'Sure.'

'Okay darling. Make it a masterpiece.' She lifted her face up to his for a kiss. 'See you when I see you. 'Night.'

Caspar took a half-full bottle of warm Chablis up to the studio with him and began to paint. He wasn't in the mood but anything was better than sleeping. Or thinking.

He especially didn't want to think.

* * *

At four o'clock in the morning the phone rang. Caspar picked it up.

'Hello?'

'What are you doing still there?' whispered Poppy. 'I wanted to speak to Claudia.'

'Bit of an odd time for a girly gossip, isn't it? What's wrong, did nobody ever tell you the facts of life?'

Clearly put out, she hissed, 'I wasn't expecting you to answer the phone.'

'I'm working. And Claudia isn't here. She left with Jake and a terrifying smirk on her face.'

'Oh.'

'Won't I do?' asked Caspar.

Sounding nervous, Poppy whispered, 'This is embarrassing.'

'What's it about? Contraception? Come on, you were going to ask Claudia. Ask me instead.'

'Okay.' He heard her rapid breathing. 'I was going to ask Claudia to leave a key under the mat.'

'Who for?' Caspar was less than enthusiastic. 'Not Dina again.'

'No. Oh Caspar.' For the first time, Poppy's voice broke. 'Can I come home?'

Back on the front doorstep, Caspar watched as the taxi pulled up at the kerb and Poppy – this time carrying her own cases – jumped out. It was like déjà-vu on rewind.

At least the long black dress had gone. Poppy's hair swung loose around her shoulders and she was wearing a white shirt tucked into tightly belted Levi's.

'Get inside,' said Caspar, taking the two largest cases from her. 'What was that business with the bracelet?'

The silver bangle she always wore had disappeared with the taxi driver.

'Couldn't pay my fare.' Poppy avoided looking at him. 'Oh God, I'm sorry about this. Am I a prat or what?'

In the sitting room Caspar plonked her down on the sofa

357

amid the party debris and pushed an abandoned drink into her hand. Her face seemed okay, but you could never tell.

'What happened, did he hit you?'

'Hit me?' Poppy looked amazed. Then she sank wearily back into the sofa. 'He didn't hit me. I almost wish he had. It'd make all this a damn sight easier.'

'All what?'

Poppy pushed her fingers through her hair. Her sigh blasted a layer of ash from a nearby ashtray.

'It's no good, I can't do it. Tom . . . *worships* me. I know how stupid that sounds, but he does. And it's too much. He loves me too much. If I stayed with him I'd . . . well, I'd drown.'

'He doesn't love you too much,' said Caspar. 'He's just possessive. Jealous. Desperate to keep you to himself. If he loved you,' he added, unable to resist pointing it out, 'he'd have bought you a dress that suited you. Not a bloody marquee.'

'I was flattered,' Poppy said sadly. 'Nobody's ever cared that much before. I thought it was so great . . . so romantic.'

'So you've left him.'

'It's a good job I wasn't expecting you to be sympathetic.'

Poppy's look of indignation was adorable. Bottle it, thought Caspar, and you'd make a fortune.

'Is that what you want? Sympathy?'

She lifted her face to him. 'I know. I'm sorry. The party must have cost a bomb.'

'Sod the party. Your moving out was only an excuse to throw one,' said Caspar.

'And now I want to move back in.' She bit her lip. 'Can I?'

'Am I likely to say no?'

'Thanks.' Poppy drank her drink and pretended she hadn't really been nervous at all. After a while she said, 'I've been so stupid, kidding myself everything was all right.'

'Why?'

'Because I desperately wanted it to be, I suppose.'

'Should have listened to me,' Caspar said lightly. 'I knew he wasn't right for you.'

Poppy heaved a sigh.

'The trouble is, I knew it too, practically from the start. I just wouldn't admit it to myself.' She paused, lost in thought, then glanced up again at Caspar. 'He was jealous of you, you know.'

Caspar grinned. 'Surely not.'

'He said did I have to snog you in front of everyone, as we were leaving earlier.'

'Oh yes?'

'I said it wasn't a snog, and anyway I'd been living here since last September, if anything was going to happen between you and me it would have happened by now.'

Caspar felt his heart begin to race. He picked up an abandoned cigarette packet; annoyingly it was empty.

'Would it?'

'Well, before you got married, anyway.'

He spotted a crumpled Marlboro pack behind a cluster of glasses on the mantelpiece and went to investigate. Bingo, three left. His hand unsteady, Caspar lit one.

'Poppy, listen to me—'

But when he turned to face her, she was crying.

'Shit, what a mess. I've done it again, haven't I? Run away.'

'But it was the right thing to do.'

'All I ever wanted was to be happy.' Poppy grabbed a crumpled-up napkin and sobbed into it. 'God, I'm such a failure. There must be something horribly wrong with me. Why can't I meet someone like you did? Why can't it be for me like it is for you and Babette?'

'Poppy, stop crying and listen—'

But when she started, Poppy didn't stop easily. With a wail she held a cushion over her face.

'Mmf Tom mmmff mff furry mmf . . .'

'What? I can't hear you.' Leaning across, Caspar whisked the cushion away. '*What* did you say?'

Red-eyed and miserable, she gazed up at him.

'I said Tom's going to be furious when he finds out.'

Chapter 54

Furious wasn't the word. Caspar, enjoying every moment and making only a token effort not to show it, lay across the sofa with his feet up pretending to watch The Open University.

Poppy stood with her back to the bottle-strewn fireplace. Tom endlessly paced the room.

'Can't we at least have some privacy?' he demanded, glaring at Caspar's suntanned feet. The fact that they were propped up on the arm of the sofa seemed to annoy him more than anything else. 'This is ridiculous. Does he have to be here?'

'I want him to stay. I'm not going to change my mind,' said Poppy. 'You shouldn't have come. I told you not to.'

'Shouldn't have come?' Tom stared at her in disbelief. 'Are you mad? You left me a *note*, Poppy. I woke up this morning and found a fucking note, telling me it was all over. Did you seriously expect me to leave it at that?'

'Well, yes.' Poppy deliberately didn't look at Caspar, who was half-killing himself trying to keep a straight face. 'It was what you did, to Jan, after you met me. The only difference is you did it on the phone. I heard you, remember?'

'That was different,' he shouted. 'That was only Jan. We weren't even living together.'

Poppy stood her ground. 'Neither were we. Two and a half hours doesn't count.'

'But we were going to get *married*,' Tom raged, unable to understand why he wasn't getting through to her. 'This is ridiculous. Poppy, you can't *do* it.'

'I can. I have. It wouldn't work,' she told him simply. 'I'm staying here.'

Tom's black eyes blazed.

'Who put you up to this?' Furiously he jabbed a finger in Caspar's direction. 'Him? What happened when you were making that exhibition of yourself on the doorstep last night – did he make you a better offer?'

'Now you're just being stupid,' Poppy wailed. 'I told you before, there's nothing going on between Caspar and me. He's *married*.'

Caspar, gazing steadily at a sociologist in flares being witty on the TV screen, thought, So I am; I nearly forgot.

'Oh my God,' shouted Claudia, jerking awake and clapping her hands over her ears as an alarm clock three inches away from her head exploded into life. 'Turn that thing OFF!'

'Sorry.' Leaning across, Jake silenced the terrible jangling. He hadn't even been asleep. For the past hour he had been watching Claudia beside him, reminding himself that last night really had happened and wondering if it was humanly possible to be happier than this.

She groaned aloud and squinted at the clock.

'It's eight o'clock. On a *Sunday*.'

'There's a car boot sale in Hertfordshire.'

'A car boot sale . . .'

The look of undiluted horror on Claudia's face brought Jake out in goosebumps.

'I won't go. It's just what I normally do on Sundays. I set the alarm yesterday, before the party. Before . . . oh hell,' he shook his head in resignation, 'this is a good start.'

Claudia lay back against her tartan pillow, overcome with remorse. I'm so used to feeling miserable, she realised, I've forgotten I don't need to be any more.

'My fault. I'm a terrible grouch.' Her fingers brushed Jake's bare shoulder, cold to the touch because in her sleep she'd managed to hog most of the duvet. How typical of him, she thought with a rush of love, not to have grabbed it back.

By the time Jake had finished making the coffee and carried it upstairs, the bed was empty and the shower was going full pelt next door. When Claudia emerged ten minutes later she was fully dressed.

Having rather hoped for a repeat performance of last night, his face fell.

'You're going?'

'Not unless you want me to.'

'I don't want you to.'

Claudia took one of the mugs from him. Crossing the room, she drew back the faded blue curtains. Sunlight poured in. 'It's morning. Sure you still respect me?'

Jake said quietly, desperately, 'I *love* you.'

'Oh Jake.' Claudia bit her lower lip, willing herself this time to say the right thing. 'If you truly mean it, then I love you too. But you'll have to be patient. I'm not used to being happy and I'm not used to being nice. I'm especially not used to men being nice to *me*—'

Clumsily, since they were both still holding brimming mugs of coffee, Jake kissed her. He felt Claudia's mouth begin to tremble against his own.

'Come on. You aren't going anywhere.' With his free hand he began unbuttoning her navy cashmere cardigan. 'Let's go back to bed.'

Claudia wanted to, like anything, but the urge to start being nice – to show Jake she could be if she really tried – was overwhelming.

'No.' She pulled away, wincing as hot coffee slopped over the back of her hand. 'I want you to take me to a car boot sale.'

Jake, who would a million times rather have stayed in bed, said, 'But—'

'I mean it. Get dressed,' Claudia told him firmly. 'We're going to Hertfordshire.'

* * *

'Well well, it just goes to show the quiet ones are always the worst.' Angie, phoning up for a post-party gossip, sounded amused. 'We did wonder what had happened to you after that thrilling punch-up. And what a very Clint Eastwoody thing to do! Who'd have thought dear old Jake had it in him?'

'Mum—'

'And how wildly romantic, darling! What did he do, carry you off into the sunset on his white Vespa?'

'Don't you dare make fun of Jake,' said Claudia, her knuckles turning pale around the receiver. 'I mean it, don't start. I love him and he loves me. I'm happy. Just this once, don't try and ruin everything, okay?'

'Sweetheart, as if I would!' Angie sounded contrite. 'Baby girl, I *want* you to be happy. Daddy and I were discussing it at the party, in fact – saying wouldn't it be wonderful to see you off that lonely, dusty old shelf.'

Pride mingled with recklessness.

'Yes, well, maybe I'm off it now.'

Claudia had to hold the phone away from her ear. For a small woman, Angie had a loud laugh.

'What's so funny?'

'Oh sweetheart, have a bit of fun with Jake by all means. But you can't seriously want to spend the rest of your life with him!'

'Why not?' Claudia countered hotly. It was what she wanted more than anything.

'Darling, darling.' At the other end of the line Angie was still gurgling merrily away. 'Jake's a nice enough lad, bless him. But let's face it, he's hardly going to set the world alight. He's not exactly a thrill-a-minute merchant, is he?'

'For God's sake, I don't want—'

'Listen to me, Claudia, I'm your mother. I know you and I know the kind of man you need. A risk-taker! Someone to make your pulse race! Someone,' Angie declared passionately, 'who rides a Harley Davidson, not a Vespa.'

Claudia howled, 'Jake doesn't have a Vespa!'

'I know he doesn't. I talked to him on Saturday night, remember?' Her mother's tone was cutting. 'He drives a van.'

Claudia was still boiling with rage when Jake and Poppy arrived at the house an hour later. Jake, who had given Poppy a lift home from work, was looking forward to taking Claudia out to a popular new Italian restaurant in Fulham. Now, to his dismay, Claudia was insisting she was too wound up to eat.

'You can share my Welsh rarebit,' said Poppy, who knew Jake was ravenous. She offered him the least burnt slice, which he wolfed down in seconds. Generously – because she was hungry too – she gave him the rest.

'My mother is the bitch of bitches,' Claudia seethed.

Poppy tore open a packet of chocolate digestives and emptied them onto a plate.

'Yes, but what exactly did she say?'

'I can't tell you.'

'Why not? Was it something awful about me?'

'No.'

Jake finished the last of the incinerated Welsh rarebit and reached for a biscuit.

'I expect it was about me.'

Claudia didn't deny it, so he knew he was right. He shrugged and helped himself to another biscuit.

'Don't let her get to you. It doesn't bother me.'

'She just doesn't want me to be happy. She always has to stick her oar in.'

If Jake wasn't bothered, Poppy didn't see why they couldn't all know what Angie had said to upset Claudia so much.

'Go on, you may as well tell us,' she wheedled. 'What *did* she say?'

It was a relief to blurt it out.

'That Jake isn't very exciting.'

Jake looked amused. 'I'm not very exciting. I already know that.'

'She said what I needed was a man to make my pulse race. Someone who takes risks. A red-hot chilli pepper,' Claudia recited bitterly, 'not a wet lettuce.'

Jake rather wished he hadn't asked now. He pretended not to mind.

Across the table Poppy sensed his discomfort. Rushing to his defence she declared, 'Chilli peppers make my eyes water and my nose run. And some lettuces are great. You could be a cool iceberg, Jake. Or a drop-dead trendy lollo rosso.'

But Poppy was trying too hard to help. Jake wondered if maybe Claudia was upset because there was an element of truth in what Angie had said.

'*Is* that what you want?' he said quietly. 'A risk-taker? Someone who'd make your pulse race?'

'No thanks. My mother has spent her life making my pulse race.'

Claudia stared hard out of the window. She loved Jake, she really did, but Angie's cutting remarks had unsettled her. Outside, it was raining. A sleek, dark green Lotus shot up the street, the driver tooting his horn in appreciation as he passed a pretty girl in a miniskirt. Across the road, parked beneath dripping plane trees, stood Jake's rusty old van with Landers' Antiques stencilled across the side.

'How about some ice cream?' suggested Poppy brightly. 'I've got Chunky Monkey or New York Fudge Crunch.'

'Vanilla?' asked Jake.

'That's so boring! Come on, live a little.'

Abruptly Claudia turned away from the window.

'We'd better get a move on. Our table's booked for seven thirty.'

'You said you didn't want to eat.' Jake looked startled.

'I changed my mind. I do now.'

'But I've just . . .' he gestured towards the empty plates littering the table. Between them, he and Poppy had finished the whole plate of biscuits. 'I'm not hungry any more.'

'Oh I don't believe this!' shouted Claudia. 'You are so

selfish. All that money of yours and you won't even take me out for a lousy pizza.'

Poppy stared at her.

'Claudia, you said you couldn't eat a thing. You can't blame—'

'It's okay,' Jake cut in, 'we'll go.' He knew why Claudia was so on edge. He just wished she wouldn't drag his money into every argument they ever had.

'Mind your tights, by the way, on the passenger seat,' Poppy called out as they left the house. 'There's a hole in the plastic with a spring sticking out.'

Claudia, who was wearing a cream linen dress and Donna Karan ten-denier stockings, said, 'Your van is the pits. Why don't you buy something decent?'

'I am. I've ordered a brand-new one.' Jake looked pleased with himself.

'I didn't mean another *van*. Why can't you get a Mercedes? Or . . . or a Lotus?' she demanded fretfully. 'You can afford it.'

Chapter 55

'Oh flaming Nora, what are you doing here?' groaned Rita, opening the front door with a headful of fluorescent pink curlers and no make-up.

'I came to apologise.' Hugo modestly inclined his head and handed her a bunch of tiger lilies.

'Blimey, no need to bow. I'm not the Queen.' Grinning, she took them from him. 'Come in. Sorry about the hairdo. Serves me right for thinking you were the milkman. Anyway, what have you got to apologise for?'

'I didn't know if I'd offended you the other night, inviting you out to dinner.' Hugo followed her through the vast wood-panelled hall and into the swimming-pool-sized kitchen. He watched Rita fill a fluted vase with water and begin to arrange the flowers. 'Do you remember what Poppy said, that you had the best husband in the world and that I couldn't hope to compete? Well, I've been a pretty lousy husband in my time and I'm not even trying to compete. But I would very much like us to be friends.'

While not strictly true, it would do for a start. Hugo didn't know why he should have been so instinctively drawn to Rita. She was hardly his usual type. But there was something about her, maybe something that reminded him of the women he had knocked around with back in the old days in Edinburgh, those lusty, straight-talking, honest-to-goodness *real* women he had known – and frequently bedded – before acting had changed his life and the fiendish Hollywood bug had bit.

Rita regarded him shrewdly, her head on one side.

'Friends, eh?'

'Purely platonic,' Hugo assured her.

'All the rage, is it, in California this year?'

He liked the way she made fun of him, refusing to be impressed by his fame. Although with a house like this, he thought dryly, why on earth should she be impressed?

'Oh, absolutely. The latest thing. And so much less painful than body-piercing.'

Rita cackled with laughter, stifled a cough and patted the pocket of her cardigan. 'Bugger, I forgot.'

'Forgot what?'

'Gave up smoking yesterday. I keep thinking it's time for a fag. It's murder.' She pulled a face. 'Can't see me lasting.'

'In that case, what you need,' said Hugo, 'is the help and support of a friend. A non-smoking platonic friend,' he added in his most beguiling tone, 'to take your mind off the fact that you've given up.'

He took Rita, minus fluorescent rollers, to Little Venice. They ate lunch at The Glassboat, a floating restaurant moored on the Regent's Canal, and listened to the jazz being played by a quartet out on the deck. The sun shone and the sky matched Hugo's cobalt blue shirt. Rita's dress, which was peony pink shot through with lilac, clashed exuberantly with the restaurant's Rosie-and-Jim style decor.

Hugo, as deft a storyteller as David Niven, told Rita how utterly hellish each of his marriages had been, and showed her the photographs in his wallet, of his three glossy ex-wives. He carried them with him at all times, he explained with suitable gravity, as a salutory reminder never to do it again.

'Maybe I should carry a picture of a packet of Rothmans.'

To steer the subject away from cigarettes, Hugo said, 'Do you have a photo of your husband with you?'

She shook her head.

'Don't need one. I can remember what he looks like.'

'Tell me all about your happy marriage –' he refilled their

coffee cups – 'and your perfect husband. I want to hear about Alex.'

'He was a wicked old bugger and he made me laugh.' Rita heaped sugar into hers. 'But he wasn't perfect. He was no Jane Asher.'

Hugo raised a quizzical eyebrow. 'Would you have wanted to be married to Jane Asher?'

'She'd be a whizz with home-made Christmas decorations.'

'Ah, but sit her in front of a jazz piano and what would she do?'

Rita roared with laughter.

'Stencil it.'

After lunch they walked along the canal path.

'I want a cigarette.'

'Here, hold my hand instead.'

'Can I smoke it?'

Hugo took her hand anyway.

'Try patches. They worked for my agent and he was a twenty-a-day man.'

Only a lifelong non-smoker, Rita thought affectionately, could think twenty a day was a lot.

'I was a fifty-a-day woman.' She looked depressed. 'Anyway, why d'you suppose I'm wearing long sleeves? I've already got a week's supply slapped on all over me. Underneath this dress I look like Mr Blobby.'

It was five o'clock when they arrived back at Rita's house, almost five fifteen by the time she'd finished deactivating the elaborate security system.

'It's a bugger but you have to have it. D'you want a drink or is it time you were off?'

Hugo, following her into a sitting room so big you'd need binoculars to watch television, realised she wanted him to leave. Feeling distinctly put out, because he'd thought she was enjoying his company – and because nobody ever wanted him to leave anywhere – he made himself comfortable on an indigo velour upholstered sofa.

'I'll have a brandy, thanks.'

He watched Rita pour two incredibly small measures.

'There you go. Cheers.'

Before Hugo had finished saying cheers back, her drink had vanished. She was hovering in front of him, willing him to drink up and go.

'Well, thanks for today. It's been great, really. I've enjoyed it.'

'But,' drawled Hugo.

Rita looked evasive. 'But what?'

'But it's time I left? But it's time for your bath? I don't know,' said Hugo. 'You tell me.'

'I thought you'd have other plans. Places to go, VIPs to see.'

'No.'

'Oh.'

She was jittering; he could see it. If he reached across and touched her it would be like resting his hand on the bonnet of a Volkswagen Beetle.

Hugo said evenly, 'Why do you want me out of here?'

'I d-don't—'

'Unless you have a secret lover tucked away upstairs.'

'Ha ha.' Rita laughed nervously.

'Or, better still, a secret stash of cigarettes.'

'You sod!' She went bright red and covered her face with both hands. 'Oh God, and after all your hard work. I'm so ashamed . . . what must you think of me?'

'I think you're human. And being with you today hasn't been hard work. Go and get them.' Enormously relieved, he added, 'Now, can I stay?'

He insisted on peeling the nicotine patches off Rita's arms first.

'Otherwise you'll overdose.'

'Ouch!' She winced; he was being careful but it still hurt. 'This is worse than having your legs waxed.'

'Sorry. Tenacious little buggers. There, last one. You can light up now.'

'Bliss,' sighed Rita, taking her first toe-tingling drag. 'Right, we'll have a proper drink this time.' She grinned happily at Hugo. 'You pour, I'll forget to say when.'

The level in the brandy bottle went steadily down. Swathed in smoke, Rita relaxed visibly, regaling him with stories of growing up in the East End.

'So when did all this happen?' Hugo gestured around the sitting room, at the three chandeliers, the football-pitch sized carpet, all the gold-plated trappings of wealth. 'And how did it happen?'

'Property deals.' Rita stubbed out a cigarette and promptly lit another. 'Buying, doing up, selling on. That old routine. You know the kind of thing.'

'Yes, but—'

'And then two years ago,' she continued blandly, 'a high-risk deal came off. In Spain, it was. This massive company was so desperate to get their hands on our bit of land, we could pretty much name our price. Alex thought of a number, doubled it, and the daft buggers said yes. We made three million, overnight.'

'Whereabouts in Spain was this?'

'Barcelona.'

'I know Barcelona quite well,' said Hugo, who wasn't an actor for nothing. If Rita could lie through her teeth, so could he. He'd make a far better job of it too. 'Which company negotiated the deal?'

Rita's eyes flickered. She tried to light another cigarette, then realised she already had one on the go.

'God, I can't remember. Los something . . .'

'Loss of three million, I should think.' Hugo leaned towards her, his mouth twitching. 'Come on, you can tell me. What really happened?'

Rita looked even more agitated than when she hadn't been allowed to smoke.

'I can't . . .'

'If it helps at all, I asked Poppy when I rang her to get

your address. She seems to think Alex was something to do with the Great Train Robbery.'

'My Alex? He couldn't have robbed anyone to save his life! Anyway, he got travel-sick on trains.' Flustered, Rita tried to stub out her lighter. She sighed. 'It wasn't anything illegal, okay? Oh hell . . . the thing is, we made a pact never to tell anyone. It just seemed safer, easier . . . people can get so *funny* . . .'

She rubbed the ash off the gold Cartier lighter. Hugo was sitting there looking at her, not saying a word.

But he's come up from nothing, thought Rita; he's got money now, enough to appreciate the problems.

In fact if anyone could truly understand why she and Alex had done what they had, it was Hugo.

'People *do* get funny,' she said again, psyching herself up to confess. 'When you've got money and they haven't, they treat you differently. If you've earned it, at least they can respect you for that. It's when you haven't earned it they really give you a hard time.' She took a gulp of brandy; she'd started, now it was too late to stop. 'Two years ago, me and Alex watched one of those documentary thingies on TV, about people who'd won tons of money and how it had fucked up – sorry, *messed* up – their lives. They didn't know who their friends were any more. They got hate mail. Death threats. They argued about how much to give to their relatives. Their marriages broke up, they wished they'd never won it . . . I'm not kidding, it was real Hammer Horror stuff, the scariest thing I've ever seen.'

Still Hugo didn't speak.

'Well, you can guess the rest,' Rita went on. 'We said right, that was it, no more lottery for us. Except Alex had already bought our tickets for Saturday's draw.' She paused then said simply, 'Three days later, we won.'

Margaret McBride looked as if she'd won the lottery and lost her ticket. When Ben and Dina finally clattered into the sitting room that night, she greeted them with a disapproving glare and her arms tightly folded across her chest.

'It's one o'clock in the morning,' she announced grimly, 'and you promised to be back by eleven. It's downright inconsiderate, that's what it is.'

Dina, clinging to Ben's arm, did her best not to giggle. Ben nudged her in the ribs and tried to look suitably apologetic.

'Mum, we're sorry, we didn't mean to be late—'

'But you are,' his mother interjected, 'and being sorry just isn't good enough. Apart from anything else, the pubs shut at eleven. I can't imagine what you've been doing for the last two hours.'

Dina couldn't help it; a great snort of laughter escaped and she had to hide her face in Ben's shoulder. If Margaret McBride knew what they'd really been up to, she'd have a heart attack. Making riotous love in the bus shelter around the corner simply wasn't what respectable married couples did in their free time.

'Margaret, it won't happen again, I'm really, really sorry.' Dina made an effort and pulled herself together. 'There was a party at the pub, an after-hours thing, that's why we're late. How was Daniel, anyway? Did you manage to settle him all right?'

Her mother-in-law's expression softened. Daniel was the absolute light of her life.

'No trouble at all. Went out like a light.' She looked proud. 'He's always a good boy for his Nan.'

'I don't know what we'd do without you, Mum,' said Ben, because outrageous flattery always went down well.

'The best babysitter in the world,' echoed Dina, secretly sliding her fingers under Ben's shirt at the back and running them up his spine. She stifled a grin as he squirmed and made a dash for the kitchen.

'I'll put the kettle on, shall I? Mum, fancy a cup of tea before you go?'

Margaret McBride hesitated, then smiled and nodded.

'Just a quick one then.' Now why was Dina giggling like that? Still, at least the girl seemed more cheerful these days. 'So you enjoyed yourselves this evening,' she said to her daughter-in-law. They'd apologised for being late; she couldn't be cross with them for long. 'Had a good time, by the look of you.' Not to mention a few drinks.

'Oh yes, we definitely enjoyed ourselves. It was brilliant.' Dina realised as she said it that she meant every word. She nodded happily. Who would've thought you could have so much fun with your own husband? 'We had the best time in the world.'

Chapter 56

'Smile,' said Jake, 'you're frightening the customers.'

Poppy knew she was looking down in the dumps. It suited her mood. Down in the dumps was how she felt.

'I'll read this, then they won't be able to see my face.' She reached for her dog-eared copy of *Miller's Guide* and opened it at random.

Rifling through the pages didn't help. Poppy chewed her thumbnail and gazed morosely at the photographs: a pair of Tiffany peridot and diamond earrings, pairs of candelabra, *endless* pairs of wheelback, ladderback and splatback chairs . . .

With a mammoth sigh she slammed the book shut, making Jake jump.

'What is it?' He knew something was up. Poppy hadn't even been able to finish her mid-morning banana doughnut.

'Nothing. Just . . . oh, nothing.'

'Tom?' Jake looked worried. He wished he'd never tracked Tom Kennedy down now. The fairytale happy ending hadn't taken long to turn sour.

'No.' Sensing his discomfort, she managed an invalid's smile. 'I'm glad I got out when I did. And I'm glad you found him for me. If you hadn't, I would always have wondered. It's just such a let-down,' Poppy said sadly, 'spending your whole life believing in love at first sight then discovering it doesn't exist. It's worse than finding out about Father Christmas.'

The tatty *Miller's Guide* slid off her lap. When she leaned over and picked it up, it fell open at a page of Staffordshire figures, every one a perfectly matched pair.

'Ohhh,' Poppy wailed in frustration, convinced the book was doing it on purpose. 'Couples, couples everywhere I bloody look! It's not *fair*.'

Trying to help, Jake said, 'You'll find someone else.'

Wearily, Poppy turned and looked at him.

'Oh, I've found someone else.'

'You have? Who?' Bewildered, he wondered why, in that case, she was so miserable.

'Doesn't matter who.' Poppy looked evasive. 'He's already one of a pair.'

Jake was shocked. 'You mean he's married? Poppy, are you mad? How could you get yourself involved with a—'

'I'm not,' she intercepted, her cheeks reddening. 'Anyway, he wasn't married when I met him.'

'For God's sake, Poppy.'

'I didn't *want* it to happen.' Poppy rolled her eyes at his stupidity. 'You can't always help who you fall in love with. You of all people,' she added, unable to resist the dig, 'should know that.'

Jake ignored it.

'Look, having an affair with a married man isn't the answer.'

'I'm not having an affair with him. And don't preach at me,' Poppy said sulkily. 'Stop sounding like a Relate counsellor.'

Thank goodness there were no customers within earshot. Jake, determined to make her see sense, said, 'Listen to me, Poppy. Get out while you can. It's for your own good. They never leave their wives. Promise me,' he said urgently, 'please promise me you won't see him again.'

Poppy had finished chewing her thumbnail. She'd chewed so far down it hurt.

'Could be tricky.' She examined her thumb. 'Seeing as I live in his house.'

Up until now Jake had somehow assumed she'd fallen for a fellow trader, most probably the dark-haired, notoriously charming – and married – ceramics expert who was always timing his coffee breaks to coincide with hers.

But Caspar . . .

He opened his mouth to speak.

'Don't,' Poppy blurted out. 'Just don't, okay? I know it's totally pathetic of me. Dammit, I know better than anyone what Caspar's like!' She was twiddling her hair furiously, a sure sign of agitation. 'And you don't have to lecture me – I'm not planning to do anything drastic. It's like measles. I'll get over it.' She winced as a strand of hair got caught up in her earring. More entanglements. Irritably she said, 'Claudia did. I suppose I will too.'

Whoever said confession was good for the soul? Some berk. Poppy was already deeply regretting telling Jake.

He was still looking appalled.

'Does Caspar know?'

'Are you mad? Of course Caspar doesn't know! Nobody knows.' It occurred to Poppy that newly-in-love people had a sickening habit of telling each other everything. 'And you aren't going to tell anyone either. Especially not Claudia.' She gave Jake a deadly, I-mean-it look. 'If you breathe a word, I'll break your new glasses.'

Jake still missed his old, taped-together pair, the ones Poppy had so triumphantly snapped in half.

He looked rueful. 'What's new?'

Claudia was surprised how easy it had been to feel comfortable in Jake's house. Accustomed as she was to opulence, elegance and space, clutter and fraying curtains weren't her line of country at all. But somehow the fact that his style was less *Homes and Gardens*, more *Exchange and Mart*, didn't bother her nearly as much as she expected it to. The effect was cosy, undemanding, as relaxed as Jake himself.

More and more easily, Claudia realised, she could

envisage living here. Threadbare carpets weren't the end of the world. Besides, she thought, once I persuade Jake to part with a bit of money we can buy new ones. Together we could really do this place up.

That evening, having come straight from work to his house, she had made a lasagne and opened a bottle of Chianti. Another thing she loved about Jake was how appreciative he was of her cooking.

'This is terrific. Better than Findus,' he told her as he mopped up the last of the sauce with ciabatta.

This, coming from Jake, was the ultimate compliment. Glowing with pleasure, Claudia caught sight of her candlelit reflection in the big mirror behind him. She looked so bright-eyed and happy, for a split second she barely recognised herself.

'It's Poppy's favourite. She's always nagging me to make it.'

Jake poured more wine.

'Maybe we should have invited her over here tonight. There would have been enough for three.'

'I prefer it like this,' said Claudia. 'Just us. Anyway, Poppy's been such a grouch lately. She even had a go at me last night for leaving my clothes in the washing machine. I mean, honestly, the nerve of that girl! I told her she had a bloody cheek and the next thing I knew, she'd dragged all my stuff out of the machine and dumped it on the floor.'

'She's going through a bad patch,' said Jake, ever the peacemaker.

'Don't start feeling sorry for her! If you ask me,' Claudia pronounced bluntly, 'she's behaving like a spoiled brat. Everything Poppy wants, Poppy gets. Even Tom Kennedy, thanks to all *our* hard work. And then what does she do? Dumps him, for no sensible reason at all. I still can't figure out why. What was wrong with him, for heaven's sake? Nothing, that's what.' With an air of triumph, Claudia waved her fork at Jake. 'Which is why she's being so grumpy now,

I bet you anything. She regrets it. She probably went to see him and begged him to have her back, and Tom told her to take a hike. Well, good for him,' she declared roundly. 'Serves Poppy jolly well right.'

Having a go at Poppy was one thing but elevating Tom to hero status was quite another. Claudia made him sound like Rhett Butler telling Scarlett he didn't gave a damn.

This was so unfair Jake couldn't – simply couldn't – let it pass.

'Look, if I tell you something,' he lowered his voice, 'will you promise, absolutely *promise*, not to breathe a word to another soul?'

Claudia leaned towards him. She adored secrets.

'Jake, you can trust me! What is it? Of *course* I won't tell.'

Chapter 57

Having spent a long afternoon upstairs in the studio, working on a canvas commissioned by a wealthy factory owner – 'Summat blue and green, lad, to hang in t'boardroom' – Caspar was cleaning brushes over the sink.

As Claudia switched the kettle on, the phone rang.

'Oh hi,' said Babette's voice. 'Is Caspar with you?'

'Hang on, he's covered in paint. I'll have to put the phone to his ear.'

'Don't worry, I just called to remind him about tonight.' Babette sounded cheerful. 'We're off to a bash at the Wellington Gallery. Tell him I've got his jacket back from the cleaners, I've booked the cab for eight thirty and if he's hungry there's a dozen oysters sitting here waiting for him.'

'Heavens, you know what they say about oysters.'

'Yes, well, the cab can always wait.' Babette was laughing. 'Damn, there goes my other phone. Blow him a kiss from me, okay? Tell him to hurry home. Byeee.'

Caspar nodded when Claudia relayed the message, and carried on cleaning his brushes.

'She won't keep the cab waiting. Babette's never been late for anything in her life.'

Claudia, who liked Babette, said, 'She's exactly right for you. The perfect wife. I can't imagine what you've done to deserve her.'

He grinned. 'Maybe I'm a perfect husband.'

'Are you?' Daringly, overcome with curiosity, Claudia said, 'Are you faithful?'

'Don't look at me like that. Yes, I am.'

When Caspar had finished cleaning himself up with another spirit-soaked rag, she passed him his coffee. Across the hall, the clock struck six.

'Poppy should be home by now.'

'Been and gone,' said Caspar.

'Really? Where?'

He looked out of the kitchen window at next door's cat launching itself at a starling.

'For a walk, she said.'

'A what?' Claudia was incredulous. 'Poppy doesn't go for walks.'

Caspar shrugged. It had happened the last three or four times he had come to the house. Poppy had made some bizarre excuse or other and promptly disappeared.

'Looks like she does now.'

Claudia watched him drink his coffee. When she sipped hers, she almost gagged.

'This has got sugar in it! You've got mine. Here –' she swapped mugs, gazing at him in disbelief – 'didn't you even notice?'

But Caspar, clearly distracted, only shook his head. Something was on his mind.

Claudia wondered if Poppy had been making a nuisance of herself.

'She's been a bit odd lately,' she ventured. 'Had you noticed?'

Caspar was trailing his forefinger through a pile of sugar he had spilled earlier on the worktop. He drew an unsmiley face.

'Not really. Well . . . maybe a bit.'

He was being evasive. More than likely, Claudia decided, he was playing the situation down in order to protect Poppy. In the past they had always got on so well.

But Caspar was married now. There was Babette to think of.

Claudia had promised Jake she wouldn't tell anyone what he had told her, but what he'd really meant was don't embarrass Poppy by blabbing to all their friends. Surely, she thought, it was only fair to put Caspar in the picture, to give him some warning. Then if Poppy did do anything stupid – like fling herself at him – he'd be able to handle it. He wouldn't be caught off-guard. Better still, aware of the potential awkwardness of such a situation, he could make sure it didn't have a chance to happen in the first place.

'Actually, there's something I think you should know about Poppy.'

Caspar's jaw tightened. When Claudia put on her compassionate face, the news had to be bad.

All of a sudden he knew what she was going to say. In an odd way, he realised, he had been dreading this moment for weeks.

'Don't tell me. She's pregnant.'

Claudia almost dropped her coffee mug. The pain and guilt in Caspar's eyes was unmistakable. He wasn't asking, he was telling her.

'What? You mean she's having your baby?' She gasped and covered her mouth. 'Oh Caspar, how *could* you? Poor Babette . . .'

He frowned. 'Hang on a sec, it's not mine. I thought you meant she was having Tom's baby.'

Bewildered, Claudia said, 'But I didn't even know she was pregnant.'

'In that case,' Caspar heaved a sigh of relief, 'she probably isn't.' His eyes narrowing, he looked at Claudia. 'But why on earth did you think it was mine?'

'I d-didn't really.' Stammering, she tried to explain. 'It . . . it just kind of tied in with what I was about to tell you. The thing is, Jake told me and I thought you should know . . . but then I thought maybe you knew already . . .'

'If I wanted a cryptic crossword, I'd buy the *Telegraph*. Get to the point.'

Claudia took a deep breath.

'Poppy's got a thumping great crush on you. Actually, she told Jake she was in love with you, but you know how Poppy exaggerates. Anyway,' she chided, 'it's probably your own fault. You know what you're like – half the time you flirt without even realising you're doing it. And Poppy's vulnerable right now – she's single again and probably panicking that she'll never meet the right man. Look,' Claudia went on, because Caspar seemed too shell-shocked to say anything, 'I'm just saying watch yourself. The way Poppy's feeling at the moment, you could end up getting pounced on. Don't give her any encouragement, that's all,' she concluded kindly. 'It wouldn't be fair to Poppy or Babette.'

The private viewing at the Wellington Gallery hadn't gone well for the exhibiting artist, who only sold two paintings, but the evening had been a profitable one for Babette.

'Networking, that's what it's all about,' she told Caspar in the cab as they made their way home. She flipped through her Filofax, happily pointing out the names and numbers of influential contacts she had made during the course of the evening. 'Damn, I'm good! Play my cards right and I've got myself another fifty grand's worth of business here. Are you okay, darling? You've been quiet. Come on, cheer up. Play *your* cards right and you could make love tonight to a future Businesswoman of the Year.'

Caspar shook his head.

'Sorry, sweetheart. It's over.' Reluctantly he closed the bulging Filofax and took her hand in his. 'It's been fun, we've had a great time. But I'm moving out tomorrow.'

'Oh.' For a second Babette looked as if she was about to cry. 'Oh, right. Okay.'

'I know this is all rather sudden. I'm sorry, but I can't help it. I just have to go.'

She leaned her head against his shoulder.

384

'Where?'

'Home,' said Caspar.

'To . . . ?'

He nodded. 'Yes. Well, hopefully.' Gazing out through the window at the wet street, he realised the alternative was too horrible to contemplate.

'Oh well, here's to the good times.' Recovering herself, Babette reached up and planted a kiss on his cheek. She even managed a smile. 'After all, we had fourteen good weeks together.' Wryly she added, 'And you did say it wouldn't last.'

Chapter 58

Jake, arriving back from a house auction at four o'clock the following afternoon, found Poppy sitting with her bare feet tucked cosily under her on the bottle green velvet chaise longue he had sold that morning. She was curled over a folded-up copy of the *Evening Standard*, so absorbed in what she was reading she hadn't noticed the top fall off her felt-tip pen. Having clearly spent the last twenty minutes absent-mindedly flicking the pen against her thigh, the leg of her white jeans was now crisscrossed with red ink.

Jake dumped a box of copper jelly moulds on the floor.

'These need cleaning. Have you finished pricing the cutlery?'

Poppy nodded.

'Been busy?'

She shook her head.

Exasperated, Jake picked up a pile of glossy brochures. Poppy hadn't exactly been working her socks off in his absence, even if her feet were bare.

'What are these doing here?'

At last she looked up. 'Claudia came by earlier, dropped them off for you to have a look at.'

They were sales brochures for new cars. BMW. Mercedes. There was even – for heaven's sake – one from the Rolls Royce showroom in Mayfair.

Jake tipped the brochures into the bin.

'Feet off that chaise. The buyer's picking it up at five.'

It's one hundred and fifty years old, thought Poppy. If it

can survive that much action, I don't see what difference another hour of my feet can make.

But she swung her legs down, dumping the paper on top of the jewellery cabinet. Jake looked at the ads she had circled in red.

'What's this? Flats and bedsitters?' He raised his eyebrows at Poppy. 'I thought you didn't want to move.'

'That was then, this is now.' She shrugged and began listlessly unpacking the jelly moulds. 'I thought about what you said and decided you were right. I'd be better off living somewhere else.'

'What happened to getting over it, like measles?'

'It might not be measles,' said Poppy. 'It might be something that goes on for years, like TB.' She took the paper back from him, tore out the page she'd been studying and folded it, tucking it into her shirt pocket.

'You could stay at my house,' Jake offered.

'Claudia would love that. Fifty ways to irritate your lover.' Poppy's smile was dry. 'It's okay, I'll be fine. There's a bedsitter in Peckham that doesn't sound too bad. I'm going round to have a look at it after work.'

'Go now,' said Jake, 'if you want.'

'No hurry. They aren't expecting me until six.' She opened the cupboard, took out a couple of cloths and a tin of Brasso. 'I'll do these first.' Spotting the brochures sticking out of the bin she said, 'Aren't you interested? From the sound of it, Claudia has her heart set on a Merc.'

Not looking amused, Jake said, 'Claudia can take a running jump.'

Poppy was on her knees engrossed in an extra-vigorous bout of polishing when Caspar came through the glass doors.

Jake said, 'Caspar's here,' and the tin slipped out of Poppy's hand.

'Oh fuck.' She let out a wail as escaped Brasso soaked into her jeans. From her position on the floor she glared defensively up at Caspar, who was wearing a blue and white

387

rugby shirt and dark blue chinos. 'What do *you* want?'

'I can see why you employ her,' Caspar told Jake. 'Cheerful, polite, eager to assist the customer—'

'You aren't a customer.' Poppy gazed down in dismay at her now totally wrecked white jeans.

'Yes I am.' Grinning, he waved his wallet. 'I want to buy a ring, a big glittery one. Come on, Poppy, wipe that gunk off your hands and sell me something expensive.'

Poppy guessed it must be Babette's birthday. If past experience was anything to go by, it was probably her birthday today and Caspar had forgotten. Now he had to buy something fast. Guilt always made men spend more.

Jake sat pretending to read the BMW brochure while Caspar studied the trays of rings. To impress Jake, Poppy reeled off dates, carats and settings. She described the way the stones had been cut, and the meaning of the different hallmarks. What she didn't know, she made up.

'This is completely riveting stuff,' drawled Caspar some time later, 'but I'd rather know which one you like best.'

Poppy didn't see why; about the only thing she and Babette had in common was they both had periods.

But, to humour him, she pointed to a diamond gypsy ring, heavy, totally unfussy and worn smooth with age.

'Okay. I like that one. But I really think Babette would prefer this.' Picking up a ravishing solitaire with rose diamond three-stone shoulders, she held it up to the light. 'Look at the cut of those stones. You could send morse code signals across Kensington. Of course it costs fifteen hundred more—'

'Try on the gypsy one,' said Caspar. 'I want to see how it looks. No,' he ordered, 'put it on the third finger.'

Poppy did as she was told. The ring was miles too big.

'Bloody typical,' said Caspar. If this was a film with Meg Ryan in it, it would have fitted.

'Doesn't matter.' Shifting from one bare foot to the other, wishing she didn't reek so overwhelmingly of Brasso, Poppy pointed towards the far end of the market. 'Dennis, over there by the fire exit, does alterations. He can take it down a few sizes. You mustn't just guess, though,' she went on, remembering that Caspar was probably desperate to get the thing home. 'Can you remember what size Babette's wedding ring was when you bought it?'

'No. What size are you?'

'Don't look at my hands,' Poppy said irritably. 'Babette's fingers are fatter than mine.'

Caspar burst out laughing. 'Oh, you bitch.'

'I'm not being bitchy, I'm just stating a fact. She isn't going to be thrilled if she can't get the bloody ring *on*.'

He was still shaking with laughter.

'Poppy, now listen. Do you love me?'

For a moment Poppy thought she must have misheard. How embarrassing, for a moment there, she thought he had said love.

Poppy's mind worked feverishly, struggling to figure out what he had actually said.

Try as she might, she was unable to come up with another word that sounded like love – glove? lug? nudge? – and still made sense.

Finally she said, 'What?'

'Do you?' Grinning, Caspar leaned across the counter towards her, his grey eyes searching her face. 'The thing is, you see, rumour has it you do. But I don't always trust rumours. I prefer to hear things from . . .'

'. . . the horse's mouth?' suggested Jake.

'Thank you.' Gravely Caspar nodded. 'I didn't quite have the nerve to say it myself. Anyway, where were we? Oh yes, the rumour. Is it true?'

'Ouch – no!' shouted Jake, clutching his naked face, but Poppy, fuelled by adrenalin, was too fast for him. She snapped his expensive spectacles in two, tore the arms off for good measure and hurled the bits into the bin.

'You snake! You complete lowlife,' she hissed at Jake. 'I can't believe you told him!'

He looked indignant. 'I didn't. I only told Claudia.'

'And Claudia told me,' Caspar said cheerfully. 'Come on, Poppy, I'm still waiting. Do you love me?'

Poppy's fists were bunched in anguish. She wanted to break a lot more than a pair of lousy glassess. And her face, her treacherous face, felt as if it was on *fire* . . .

'Dammit, what kind of a question is that?' she howled at Caspar. 'I'll tell you, it's the most stinking rotten bloody question I ever heard! You can't go around asking people things like that, for crying out loud! You're *married*.'

She was trying to make a bolt for it but Caspar had somehow managed to grab hold of both her hands.

Still smiling broadly he said, 'No I'm not.'

It seemed safest, as Caspar drove her back to Cornwallis Crescent, to say nothing. Poppy closed her eyes and didn't open them until they reached the house. The smell of Brasso in the car was overwhelming.

When they were inside she bent down automatically to pick up the morning's post. The folded-up piece of newspaper slid out of her shirt pocket. Caspar picked it up, glanced at it and crumpled it into a ball.

'You won't be needing that.'

'This is bizarre,' said Poppy finally. 'If you aren't married, why on earth did you say you were?'

He shrugged. 'Seemed like a good idea at the time. You said I needed to sort myself out, to stop pratting around and settle down. You told me I should get married,' Caspar reminded her. 'So I told you I had.'

'But *why*?'

'I realised I was crazy about you,' he said simply. 'I also knew that as far as you were concerned I was the worst news since Hiroshima. The last person you'd *ever* be interested in was someone like me, with my abysmal track record.'

'I still don't see—'

'So I thought I'd give it a whirl, see what being married

390

felt like. I wanted to find out if I could be happy with one person, turning down offers from other women instead of always thinking what the hell, go for it, why not?' Looking pleased with himself, Caspar added, 'And I discovered I could. I actually enjoyed it. I was pretty bloody amazed, I can tell you. But it was great.'

'If it's so great,' demanded Poppy, now experiencing a horrible mixture of confusion and jealousy, 'why don't you marry Babette for real?'

'I like her. A lot. But I don't love her.' Caspar half-smiled. 'And before you say anything else, she doesn't love me either. She went along with the idea, got herself and her beloved company a ton of publicity . . . where was the harm?'

Poppy shook her head in bemusement; her insides felt so scrunched up she could hardly breathe.

'So what happens now?'

'I told her last night. She wished me good luck.' His mouth began to twitch. 'Even though, personally, she'd far rather I got together with Claudia than you.'

Fat-fingered cow, thought Poppy. But what Caspar had been saying was beginning, finally, to sink in.

'Look, do you mean this?' She spoke with a touch of belligerence. 'Are you serious? Because I'm warning you, if this is some kind of joke—'

'What, you'll break my glasses too? Really, Poppy, violence isn't the answer.'

He certainly picks his moments to get witty, thought Poppy. Aloud she said, 'I'm not sure I even understand the question.'

'Sorry, I don't appear to be making a great job of this.' No longer grinning, Caspar pushed his sunbleached hair away from his face. 'I'm nervous too, okay? I've never told anyone I loved them before. This is scary stuff.'

'It's supposed to be nice stuff.' Poppy was beginning to feel decidedly weak-kneed.

'I know. But what if it doesn't work? We've been friends for almost a year.'

'Maybe you should try kissing me first. See what that's like.' As she said the words, Poppy began to tremble. 'Then, if it seems okay, we can carry on. If it's weird or awful . . . well, we'll just forget it.'

She was standing there waiting for him, but Caspar was making an unhappy discovery. He couldn't move. A lifetime of confidence had abruptly deserted him – now, when for the first time it really, truly mattered. It was ridiculous. Walking into the antiques market had been easy. Telling Poppy he wasn't married to Babette had been easy. But this . . . this . . .

This wasn't.

Watching Caspar, knowing him as well as she did, Poppy realised what was happening.

It's up to me, she thought, bracing herself against the fridge. If I don't do it we'll still be here at midnight.

The trouble was, her knees were feeling horribly unreliable.

'You'll have to come here,' she told Caspar. 'I can't walk.'

When he did, she slid her arms slowly around his waist. Holding her breath, feeling as if her lungs were about to burst, Poppy touched her mouth to his.

'Okay so far?' She murmured the words against his lips, amazed she could even speak, what with all the firework effects zapping through her body. 'If not, I can always stop—'

In reply, Caspar held her so tightly and kissed her for so long, neither of them heard the front door open and close.

'Well?' gasped Poppy, her heart hammering like a road drill when they finally paused for breath, 'how was it for you?'

She was grinning. Caspar, hopelessly aroused and wondering whether to carry her upstairs or just ravish her right here on the kitchen floor, bit her earlobe.

'I suppose you'll never let me forget this. For the next fifty years, at every party we go to, you won't be able to resist telling people about the time I lost my bottle.'

'You lost your bottle?' Poppy kissed him again, pressing her hips against him. Starting to laugh, she glanced down at the front of his trousers. 'There, I've found it again. Gosh, it's a magnum.'

Caspar began undoing the buttons of her white cotton shirt.

'I love you, even if you are a mickey-taking bitch.'

'I love you,' Poppy retaliated, 'even if you did sleep with Angie Slade-Welch.'

'I didn't.'

'Yes you did.'

'Bloody hell, I did *not*—'

'We'll argue about that later. We can make a list of things to argue about. Right now I'd far rather be doing something else.' Overwhelmed with lust, Poppy leaned back against the fridge and watched him unfasten the last couple of buttons. 'Um . . . shouldn't we find somewhere a bit more private?'

Caspar smiled.

'We have some serious catching up to do. I'm going to make love to you in every room in this house.'

As he began to kiss her again, Poppy glanced up at the clock on the wall.

'Look, Claudia could be home at any minute. We don't want her to see us . . .'

Behind them in the kitchen doorway, a clear voice rang out.

'I've already seen you,' Claudia announced, her eyes glittering with anger, 'and the pair of you disgust me. You, especially, should be ashamed of yourself.' She turned her disdainful attention to Poppy's flushed cheeks and unbuttoned shirt. 'How could you do this to poor Babette?'

Chapter 59

'They're completely sick-making,' Claudia grumbled, struggling to scrape caked-on mud from the soles of her Hunter wellies while Jake loaded the morning's bargains into the back of the van. Though she would rather die than admit it, Claudia was beginning to enjoy these Sunday car boot sales. Last week at a particularly upmarket one in Virginia Water she had come away with three Jean Muir dresses and a Moschino jacket. If the woman – who owned a Range Rover – wasn't embarrassed to be seen selling them, Claudia decided she wasn't ashamed to buy them. And the Range Rover had been an N reg.

'What?' Straightening up, Jake slammed the rear doors shut. Rust showered off. Never mind, he thought contentedly, by this time next week he would have his brand-new van.

'Poppy and Caspar. You have no idea what they're like.' She pulled a face. 'They can't keep their *hands* off each other. I mean, how much sex can one couple have? It's indecent. Embarrassing.' Claudia climbed into the passenger seat and wound down the squeaky window. 'I feel so . . . in the way.'

'Do they make you feel in the way?' Jake started up the engine, which spluttered with damp.

'They go out of their way not to.' Darkly, Claudia added, 'Which makes it worse.'

Jake watched his fingers tighten around the steering wheel. It wasn't the most romantic of situations but it was the opportunity he had been waiting for. He had to ask her; had to know.

For the second time in a fortnight he said, 'You could move in with me.'

When he had made the offer to Poppy she had turned him down.

Claudia went pink with pleasure.

'Really? I'd love to.'

'Okay. We'll do that.'

Oh, what a momentous occasion! Jake had asked her to live with him and she had said yes. This, she thought excitedly, is the next best thing to getting married.

Claudia longed to fling her arms around Jake and cover him in kisses, but he was driving and the lane was narrow. She dug in her coat pocket instead and found half a packet of Fruit Gums, selflessly offering him the red one although it was her favourite.

'Well,' she said, chewing happily, 'that's solved that problem.'

It wasn't the most romantic of acceptances either. Jake braked as a sleek black top-of-the-range Audi pulled out ahead of them.

'That's a nice car,' said Claudia.

'If you like that kind of thing.'

She glanced across at him.

'I don't know how anyone could not like that kind of thing.'

But Jake wasn't going to get into an argument. Saying nothing, he concentrated on the road. As they rounded a bend, a glorious old house came into view, an ivy-clad rectory with a Victorian-style conservatory built onto the side. A For Sale notice swung above the driveway.

'Imagine living in a place like that,' Claudia sighed.

'I'm happy where I am.'

She gazed with longing at the house as they rattled past. Then she saw Jake's expression, which was grimly uncompromising.

'If you won't move, you could at least have a conservatory

built,' she pointed out, her tone fretful. 'You've got room. Go on, go mad.' It was almost – *almost* – a taunt. 'You could at least splash out on one of those.'

'Where are we going?' asked Claudia twenty minutes later. It was lunchtime, she was hungry and Jake had driven past endless promising-looking country pubs. She wished she hadn't given him that fruit gum now.

Jake carried on driving. Claudia wondered if he even knew where he was headed; this certainly wasn't the way home.

'Why are we *here*?' she demanded when they reached the outskirts of Purley. Spotting a sign for another car boot sale, her voice rose. 'Oh God, I don't want to traipse round any more bloody playing fields.'

But Jake, still looking as if all he wanted to do was waste petrol, swung the van right instead of left.

'Okay, this'll do.'

'For what?' Claudia stared incredulously at the dilapidated row of shops, nearly all of them closed. Spotting a frightful-looking transport café, she said, 'If you think for one minute I'm eating my Sunday lunch in that greasy spoon—'

'We aren't going in there,' said Jake, opening the passenger door and practically dragging her out. 'We're going to go mad, like you wanted.' He pointed to the seedy-looking betting shop next to the café. 'We're going to live a little. Have a bit of fun. In there.'

Claudia winced as Jake held the door open for her. A thick sea of cigarette smoke made her eyes water. The shop was full of men, the floor awash with discarded betting slips and stamped-out fag ends. There were sheets of newspaper detailing the day's racing pinned up along every wall, and half a dozen TV sets tuned to the afternoon's racing.

'So this is your idea of a bit of fun.' Claudia, who had never stepped inside a betting shop before, felt her upper lip curl with distaste. 'Go on then, hurry up. Have your stupid bet and let's get out of here.' Ostentatiously she shuddered. 'My jacket's going to reek.'

Jake studied the list of runners and riders flickering on one of the screens above their heads.

'Flirty Fay, evens. The Goodbye Girl, seven to one. Tango, nine to two.' He paused. 'Fortune Hunter, eight to one.'

'Bored and Hungry,' intoned Claudia without looking up. 'Dead cert.'

'Come on.' Jake took her hand, pulling her over to the cashier sitting behind her till. The woman – the only other female in the shop – smiled through the security glass at them. Claudia couldn't be bothered to smile back.

'Yes, love?' The cashier turned her attention to Jake.

'Fortune Hunter, running in the two thirty,' said Jake. 'Um . . . do you accept cheques?'

'Yes love, we do.'

'Half a million all right? It won't bounce.'

'Half a million pounds.' Echoing the words, the woman looked dazed. 'On the nose, sir?'

Jake nodded firmly. 'That's right. To win.'

'Hang on a sec, I'll have to check this with the manager.'

Fed up, Claudia had been leaning against the glass watching an old man smoke two cigarettes at once. No wonder, she thought disgustedly, the floor was inches deep in ash.

The next moment, Jake's words belatedly filtered through to her brain. She jerked upright and did a cartoon double-take.

'*How* much?'

'Sshh,' said Jake. 'She's asking her boss if it's okay.'

'For God's sake, have you gone completely mad?' Sounding like McEnroe, Claudia hissed, 'Jake, you can't be serious!'

'No problem at all, sir,' the woman announced, re-emerging from the office. 'Just so long as you can show us some form of identification. Oh yes, a driving licence, that's fine.'

'Jake, stop it,' howled Claudia as he filled out the betting slip. 'You can't *do* this—'

'You want to marry a millionaire, don't you?' He shrugged off her desperate pawing hands, wrote the cheque and signed it. Before Claudia could stop him he had pushed both the slip and the cheque beneath the glass. 'Well, right now, I'm only half a millionaire. Not really enough, is it? This way, ten minutes from now I could be four million pounds richer.'

Gibbering with rage, Claudia yelled, 'But what if the horse doesn't win? Then you won't have anything!'

'Of course I won't. That's what makes it exciting. I thought you *wanted* a bit of excitement,' protested Jake. 'You keep telling me to live a little, to splash out.'

Claudia wanted to cry. She even wanted a cigarette. The one thing she definitely didn't want was this kind of excitement.

When she finally looked up, the middle-aged cashier said, 'Cheer up, love. Fingers crossed, eh?'

'If I win,' said Jake, 'you can have that big house you liked.'

There was a new air of recklessness about him, a wild kind of glitter in his dark eyes. Demented with worry, Claudia snapped back, 'And if you lose, you can just fuck off.'

She couldn't bear to watch the race, and she didn't need to.

'. . . and Fortune Hunter has fallen at the second furlong,' relayed the commentator, 'Fortune Hunter's taken a tumble, both horse and jockey appear to be unhurt . . . and Tango and Flirty Fay are neck and neck going up to the third . . .'

Jake crumpled his betting slip into an ashtray.

'Looks like Fortune Hunter's having a bit of an off-day.'

Claudia snapped. 'She isn't the only one.'

'That's that, then. It's all over.'

'You bloody, *bloody* fool.' Feeling sick at the thought of half a million pounds wasted, she shrugged off Jake's tentative hand on her shoulder. All around them, other punters were urging on their horses. Only the woman behind the till was watching Claudia rather than the race.

'Well,' said Jake slowly, 'is it all over?'

She wanted to cry. 'Of course it is.'

'I meant us. Are we all over too?' He stood in front of Claudia, forcing her to look at him. 'The money's gone. I'm pretty much where I started. Do you still want to move in with me, or not?'

Cheers and groans erupted around the smoke-filled room as Flirty Fay won by a length. A volley of balled-up betting slips hit the floor.

'What is this, some kind of test?' said Claudia.

'If you like.'

'You sick bastard.' Her eyes filled with tears of dismay. 'You thought I was only interested in your money?'

'Call me a pessimist,' said Jake steadily, 'but it had crossed my mind. You certainly seemed interested in helping me spend it.'

Claudia couldn't speak. Didn't Jake understand how unfair he was being? Of course she was interested in helping him spend his money. Money was wonderful, it was there to *be* spent. And now it was gone.

'Well?' he demanded, 'what's the verdict? If you don't want to see me any more, I'll understand. I never thought I was much of a catch anyway.' His fingers were shaking as he pulled the van's keys out of his jacket pocket. 'Don't worry, I'll still give you a lift home. No hard feelings. We'll just say goodbye.' Jake's voice began to falter but his mind was clearly made up. Since it was the polite thing to say, he added stiffly, 'I daresay we can stay friends.'

A terrible sinking feeling swept like a tidal wave through Claudia's gut. Desolation mingled with panic. She could bear the loss of the money – just – but she couldn't lose Jake too.

'I don't care,' she whispered, because some of the old men nearest to them had begun to eavesdrop. 'I don't care how

399

much money you haven't got. Of course I still want to move in with you.'

'What?' Jake had to raise his voice; another race was in progress.

'I love you.' The old men were nudging each other now, chuckling between themselves and ignoring the race being screened above their heads. 'Wasting that money was the stupidest thing you ever did, but I still love you. Anyway, my mother was the one who said I needed excitement,' said Claudia, 'not me.'

Overjoyed, Jake took her in his arms and kissed her and didn't let her go.

'Bugger me,' guffawed one of the men, 'better than a flamin' cabaret. Wait till I get home and tell my missus about this.'

'Mine gives me earache if I lose more'n a fiver,' marvelled another.

'I didn't think you'd still want me,' Jake murmured in Claudia's ear. 'Oh God, I was so afraid you wouldn't.'

'Maybe it'll be fun, being poor,' said Claudia bravely. As long as she had Jake, nothing else mattered. Feeling giddy with happiness she whispered, 'I'll learn to economise. No more Manolo Blahnik shoes, no more getting my hair done at Nicky Clarke's. No more eating out,' she went on, improvising wildly. *Coronation Street* was full of poor people, wasn't it? 'I'll . . . I'll learn to make Lancashire hot-pot . . .'

'My mother has a brilliant recipe for hot-pot.'

This was love, this was serious. No longer caring that they were the focus of attention, Claudia clung to him and kissed him again, extravagantly, on the mouth. 'I want to meet your mother.'

The next moment Jake was unwrapping her arms from around his neck and the cashier was no longer behind her till, but standing beside them.

'What's wrong?' said Claudia, wondering if they were about to be asked to leave, kicked out for indecent behaviour.

'You said you'd like to meet my mother,' Jake explained, 'so here you are. Wish granted.'

'Hello love, I've heard so much about you.' Jake's mother smiled. 'Not all of it good, I have to be honest, but never mind, you saw sense in the end.'

Claudia stared at them both.

'Are you serious?'

'Of course I'm serious.' Jake grinned. 'I just wanted to find out if you were.'

'Here, love.' Jake's mother produced the cheque from the pocket of her uniform. 'Tear it up quick and for God's sake don't tell the boss. He'll have my guts for garters if he ever gets to hear about this.'

'But . . . but . . .' Claudia spluttered helplessly. 'You can't do that, you'll get the sack.'

Entertained by the look on Claudia's face, Jake explained, 'She didn't place the bet. It didn't go through the machine.'

Chapter 60

'Come on, get up,' Caspar announced, throwing back the duvet. 'Things to do, places to go. You can't spend all morning in bed.'

Poppy winced and tried to curl herself into a ball. 'It's my day off.'

'And we're going out.'

'Somewhere nice?' Cautiously she opened an eye. Caspar had showered already, and left it running for her. She watched him throw on a crumpled white rugby shirt and jeans.

'Somewhere extremely nice.' Hauling Poppy out of bed, he pointed her in the direction of the bathroom. 'The electricity showrooms. We need a dishwasher.'

'Why?'

'Because Claudia doesn't live here any more.' He threw a pair of Poppy's leggings after her. 'Hurry up.'

Outside the sun blazed down from a cloudless sky. They made their way towards the shops on foot.

'I can't believe you're making me do this,' grumbled Poppy, glad of her sunglasses. 'Not on my day off. Talk about domesticated.'

They were passing a delicatessen. Caspar glanced at their reflections in the window. Poppy's still-damp hair was piled haphazardly on top of her head, tied with a red scarf that was already coming undone. She was wearing RayBans, a cropped red tee-shirt, white leggings and gold sandals.

'You don't look domesticated. Cheer up –' he gave her waist a squeeze – 'think of all the washing-up we won't have to do. You'll be able to spend more time in bed.'

'Only if you're there too.' Reluctantly, because she was still supposed to be cross with him, Poppy broke into a grin. Sex with Caspar had been a total revelation; she couldn't imagine ever tiring of it. He had made her life idyllic.

How long did it take to choose a silly dishwasher anyway? Poppy brightened at the prospect of enticing Caspar back into bed. They could be home in less than an hour.

Recognising the glint in her eye, Caspar said, 'You are disgraceful. A shameless hussy.'

'I'm a happy hussy.' Reaching up, she kissed him. 'You're not bad, you know. Even if your idea of a romantic day out is a trip to the electricity showrooms.'

'Actually, I thought we might visit B & Q afterwards.' Caspar sounded amused. 'Take a look at kitchen units.'

'That would be too much excitement for one day.'

'I know how to give a girl a good time.'

'Come home with me,' said Poppy, 'and I'll show you a better one.'

As they began to cross the road she spotted a familiar figure, a vision in billowing violet chiffon, hurrying up a broad flight of steps leading into an official-looking building.

'Look, it's Rita! Wearing a hat,' Poppy exclaimed. 'Isn't that the Register Office? She must be going to someone's wedding.'

'Must be.'

'But that's weird. I asked her if she wanted to meet me for lunch today and she said she was visiting a friend in Kent.'

As she gazed over the tops of cars, Poppy's bewilderment grew. Rita re-emerged from the building, hanging onto her flower-strewn, Queen-of-Ascot hat with one hand and lighting a cigarette with the other. Behind her, clutching a suitcase, was . . . of all people . . . Claudia.

'Hang on, what's happening?' Astonished, Poppy pulled off her sunglasses. Now Jake had joined the small group at the top of the steps. And, looking intensely glamorous in a dove-grey morning suit, Hugo Slade-Welch.

She turned to Caspar. 'Is something going on that I don't know about? Is . . . is Rita marrying Hugo?'

'No. You're marrying me.'

'I'm *what*?'

They were still halfway across the road. Caspar steered Poppy safely onto the pavement. Fishing in his shirt pocket, he pulled out the heavy, diamond-encrusted gypsy ring she had last seen on that eventful afternoon on Jake's stall. The one she had thought he was buying for Babette. The one Jake had later told her he'd sold to an Australian tourist.

'Well, I'd like you to.' Caspar waved the ring at her. 'It rather depends on you saying yes.'

Shakily Poppy said, 'Are you serious?'

'Never more so.'

'You mean, you – you *planned* all this?'

'It helps,' said Caspar, 'if you want the guests to turn up.'

'My God, I can't believe it. But – my hair!' she wailed, clutching her head. 'And my *clothes* . . . whatever made you do it like this? Why did it have to be a surprise?'

'Look.' Caspar turned her to face him. 'With your track record, I thought it was the only way. Every time someone wants to marry you, you do your party trick and run a mile. Sometimes a hundred miles,' he added drily. 'I didn't want you pulling that one on me.'

'But I wouldn't!' Poppy stared at him, amazed he could even think such a thing. 'It's different this time. I love you.'

'Yes, well. I wasn't prepared to risk it. This way, you don't have a chance to get cold feet. Everyone's here already, waiting for us. In half an hour it'll be done.' Caspar took her trembling hands in his. 'That is, if you want to.'

Poppy frowned. 'You haven't asked me yet.'

He half-smiled, inwardly far less confident than he appeared. He just wished she would put him out of his agony and say yes.

'Sorry. Will you marry me?'

'On one knee.'

'Come on, not here.'

'Yes here.'

Caspar looked appalled.

'In the street?'

'Not in the actual road,' Poppy said generously, 'in case you get run over by a bus. You can do it on the pavement.'

Passers-by were beginning to take notice. An ear-splitting, four-fingered whistle rang out from the top of the Register Office steps. Rita yelled, 'Blimey, you two, are you getting hitched or what?'

'Hurry *up*,' shouted Claudia, holding up the suitcase. 'I've got your clothes in here. You can change in the loo.'

Further up the road the traffic lights had turned red. Cars, cabs and a couple of double-deckers ground to a halt. Interested faces peered down at Caspar as he sank to one knee.

'Say you'll marry me,' he hissed. 'Quickly.'

Poppy thought her heart would explode with joy. She flung out her arms and kissed him. Between kisses she said breathlessly, 'Yes, yes, of course I'll marry you.' Car horns tooted all around them as Caspar stood up, hugely relieved that ordeal was out of the way. The passengers on the nearest bus applauded.

'You look great.'

Rita, crammed into the loo behind Poppy, was handing over eyeshadow, mascara and lipstick like an efficient nurse in an operating theatre. Except efficient nurses in operating theatres didn't pass sterile instruments with cigarettes dangling from the corners of their mouths.

Poppy finished her make-up with sixty seconds to spare. She fiddled with a few tendrils of hair and hastily checked her overall reflection in the mirror.

'I'm getting married. I'm actually getting married.' As she spoke, a horrible thought struck her. 'Oh help, where are we

405

going after this? The house is a complete tip—'

'Don't panic, that's all sorted. Everyone back to my place.'

Poppy was touched. 'Oh Rita, you are brilliant. What would I do without you?'

'Silly girl. D'you think Alex would have wanted your wedding reception held anywhere else?' Rita hugged her. 'Oh Lord, don't you dare cry . . .'

'I wish he was here.' Poppy grabbed a handful of loo roll and dabbed her brimming eyes.

'I know, love. So do I. Now come on, we've got a wedding to go to. Anyway,' Rita announced, to distract her, 'there's another little surprise for you when we get home.'

Poppy didn't know if she could cope with any more surprises.

'What?'

'I've got Kenda's Kitchen doing the food.' Rita's grin was mischievous. 'For old times' sake.'

If you enjoyed

PERFECT TIMING

look out for the new *Jill Mansell* novel

THREE AMAZING THINGS ABOUT YOU

Out in January 2015

You can order
THREE AMAZING THINGS ABOUT YOU
now

headline
review

www.headline.co.uk
www.jillmansell.co.uk

🐦 @JillMansell
f /OfficialJillMansell

Jill Mansell

THE UNPREDICTABLE CONSEQUENCES OF LOVE

In the idyllic seaside town of St Carys, Sophie is putting the past firmly behind her.

When Josh arrives in St Carys to run the family hotel, he can't understand why Sophie has zero interest in letting *any* man into her life. He also can't understand how he's been duped into employing Sophie's impulsive friend Tula, whose crush on him is decidedly unrequited.

St Carys has more than its fair share of characters, including the charming but utterly feckless surfer Riley Bryant, who has a massive crush on Tula. Riley's aunt is superstar author Marguerite Marshall. And Marguerite has designs on Josh's grandfather . . . who in turn still adores his glamorous ex-wife, Dot . . .

Just how many secrets can one seaside town keep?

Just *Heavenly*. Just *Jill*.

Acclaim for Jill Mansell's fabulous bestsellers:

'Bursting with humour, brimming with intrigue and full of characters you'll adore' ***** *Heat*

'You'll fall in love with the characters in this lovely tale' *Sun*

'A warm, witty and romantic read' *Daily Mail*

978 0 7553 5593 8

You can buy any of these other bestselling books by
Jill Mansell from your bookshop
or *direct from her publisher.*

FREE P&P AND UK DELIVERY
(Overseas and Ireland £3.50 per book)

TO ORDER SIMPLY CALL THIS NUMBER
01235 400 414

or visit our website: www.headline.co.uk

Prices and availability subject to change without notice.